HOWARD JAY SMITH

Beethoven *in* Love; Opus 139

Concerto Quasi Una Fantasia

SAY YES QUICKLY BOOKS

Also by Howard Jay Smith

Opening the Doors to Hollywood

John Gardner: An Interview

www.BeethovenInLoveOpus139.com

Designed by Hans Teensma, www.impressinc.com

Cover art by Zak Smith

ISBN: 978-0-9965592-0-1

Printed in the United States of America

Beethoven in Love; Opus 139
is dedicated to the memory of my parents
Reuven and Liliana,
Robert and Lillian Smith,
and all who came before
and all who will follow

THE MAJOR CHARACTERS

Ludwig van Beethoven (December 16, 1770–March 26, 1827); the composer and our protagonist; also referred to as "**Louis**" and "**B**"; born in Bonn and moved to Vienna at age 22; in addition to the over 600 musical compositions he wrote during his life, Beethoven also kept a *Tagebuch,* or diary, between 1812 and 1818

Ludwig van Beethoven (1712–1773); his grandfather for whom Beethoven was named; *Kapellmeister,* or Chief Musician, for the court in Bonn; he died when Beethoven was 3 years old

Johann van Beethoven (1739–December 18, 1792); Beethoven's father, who died when Beethoven was 22; singer and musician for the court in Bonn

Maria Magalena Keverich Beethoven (December 19, 1746–July 17, 1787); Beethoven's mother, who died when he was 16; lived in Bonn

Casper Carl van Beethoven (April 7, 1774–November 15, 1815); Beethoven's brother, four years his junior; a musician and clerk; born in Bonn and followed Beethoven to Vienna

Johanna Reiss van Beethoven (1784–1868); **Casper Carl's** wife and **Karl's** mother; referred to by Beethoven as "The Queen of the Night"; lived in Vienna

Karl van Beethoven (September 4, 1806–April 13, 1858); **Casper's** son and Beethoven's nephew; born and lived in Vienna

Nikolaus Johann van Beethoven (October 1, 1776–1848); Beethoven's youngest brother, six years his junior; a pharmacist who preferred to be known as **Johann von Beethoven**; born in Bonn and later followed his brothers to Vienna; eventually moved to the city of Linz

Therese Obermeyer van Beethoven (1787–1828); **Nikolaus's** wife, and mother of **Amalie Obermeyer van Beethoven**, **Nikolaus's** stepdaughter; from Vienna and moved to Linz with **Nikolaus Johann**

Maria Margaretha van Beethoven (May 4, 1786–November 25, 1787); Beethoven's little sister, whom he calls "mon petit papillon," my little butterfly; born and died in Bonn

Leonore von Breuning Wegeler (1772–1841); Beethoven's neighbor and girlfriend in Bonn; also known by her proper name **Eleonore** and the affectionate name **Lorchen**; daughter of **Helene von Breuning**; sister to **Steffen von Breuning** and wife of **Franz Wegeler**; all of whom were close friends of Beethoven since their childhood in Bonn; later moved to Koblenz with her husband

Steffen von Breuning (August 17, 1774–June 4, 1827); neighbor, lawyer and lifelong friend of Beethoven; one of **Eleonore's** younger brothers; married first to **Julie Vering** and then after her death to **Constance Ruschowitz**, his son **Gerhard**'s mother; born in Bonn and later moved to Vienna

Gerhard von Breuning (1813–1892); **Steffen's** son and later a doctor and an author of a book of reminiscences about Beethoven entitled *Memories of Beethoven*

Franz Wegeler (August 22, 1765–1848); lifelong close friend of Beethoven beginning in Bonn, a doctor who married **Leonore von Breuning**; moved with his wife to Koblenz to open his new medical practice; also an author with **Ferdinand Ries** of a book of reminiscences about Beethoven entitled *Beethoven Remembered, The Biographical Notes of Franz Wegeler and Ferdinand Ries*

Ferdinand Ries (1784–1838); composer and pianist; Beethoven's student and assistant for a time in Vienna; later a well-known conductor;

son of **Franz Ries** who taught the young Beethoven violin in Bonn; also an author with **Franz Wegeler** of a book of reminiscences about Beethoven entitled *Beethoven Remembered, The Biographical Notes of Franz Wegeler and Ferdinand Ries*

Christian Gottlieb Neefe (February 5, 1748–January 28, 1798); Beethoven's first music instructor and advocate who began working with the composer when he was around 12 years of age, until he left Bonn for Vienna ten years later

Count Ferdinand Ernst von Waldstein (1762–1823); an early patron of the young Beethoven in Bonn and dedicatee of the *"Waldstein"* sonata

Prince Carl Lichnowsky (1771–1813); Beethoven's patron and friend; soon after Beethoven first moved to Vienna he even lived with the Prince and his wife, **Princess Christiane**; **Lichnowsky** was also a patron and close friend of **Mozart**

Wolfgang Amadeus Mozart (1756–1791); most famous and renowned composer of the late 1700s, whom a teenage Beethoven met and briefly studied with in Vienna

Josephine von Brunsvik Deym von Stackelberg (1779–March 31, 1821); one of the major loves of Beethoven's life; also known as **"J"**; sister to **Therese von Brunsvik**, **Charlotte von Brunsvik**, and **Franz von Brunsvik**; married **Count Deym** and later **Count Stackelberg**; among her children, one named **Minona**, born in 1813, was rumored to have been Beethoven's daughter

Therese von Brunsvik (1775–1861); one of Beethoven's lifelong friends and sister to **Josephine**, **Charlotte**, and **Franz von Brunsvik**; a highly accomplished musician; **Therese** never married

Giulietta Guicciardi (1784–1856); cousin to the von **Brunsviks** and one of the loves of Beethoven's life to whom he dedicated the *Moonlight* Sonata; will marry to become the **Countess Gallenberg**

Antonie Birkenstock Brentano (May 28, 1780–May 12, 1869); also known as "**Toni**"; one of the major loves of Beethoven's life; married to **Franz Brentano** and mother of five children; her youngest, **Karl Josef**, born in 1813, was rumored to have been Beethoven's son; born in Vienna but compelled by marriage to move to the Brentano estate in Frankfort

Sophia Brentano (March 27, 1770–October 31, 1806) and **Bettina Brentano** (April 4, 1785–January 20, 1859); **Antonie Birkenstock's** sisters-in-law resulting from her marriage to Franz Brentano

Jeanette d'Honrath (August 10, 1770–November 25, 1823); Beethoven's piano student and lover when he was a young man in Bonn; friend of **Leonore von Breuning**

Babette Koch (June 28, 1771–November 25, 1807); another of Beethoven's piano students and a lover when he was a young man in Bonn; friend of **Leonore von Breuning**

Magdalena Willmann (1771–1801); renowned singer and one of Beethoven's lovers; originally from Bonn; traveled widely but died in Vienna

Napoleon Bonaparte (August 15, 1769–May 5, 1821); French General and Emperor of the Republic; also known as "**N**" and the "**Sultan El Kabir**"; married **Rose Beauharnais**, whom he insisted upon renaming **Josephine Beauharnais**; after divorcing her because she bore him no children, **Napoleon** later married **Princess Marie Louise**, daughter of the **Austrian Emperor, Franz II**; she gave birth to the Emperor's son, **Napoleon II**

Field Marshall General Jean Baptiste Bernadotte (1764–1844); French General and Ambassador of France to the Austrian Court in Vienna; rival of **Napoleon** and later became, through adoption, the King of Sweden; he married **Desiree Clary**, who had previously been **Napoleon's** fiancée

Archduke Rudolph (1788–1831); younger brother by 20 years of the **Austrian Emperor Franz II**; an excellent pianist and musician; friend and patron of Beethoven, later installed as the Archbishop of Olmutz; Beethoven dedicated more of his works to the **Archduke** than anyone else

Liliana Donishefski (December 3, 1785–May 30, 1876); violin prodigy from the Lithuanian village of Smorgonie who studies with Beethoven in Vienna as a teenager; marries **Reuven Silke**

Reuven Silke (February 16, 1770–November 3, 1812); luthier and violinmaker, also from Smorgonie; later husband to **Liliana**

Johann Gardner (July 21, 1765–September 14, 1847); American writer, teacher, and linguist living in Europe who serves as a translator for **Napoleon** during the invasion of Russia and later meets and befriends Beethoven

Fanny Giannatasio Del Rio (1790–1876); also known as the **Lady Abbess**, proprietress of the boarding school in Vienna where Beethoven placed his nephew **Karl**; **Fanny** kept a diary of her encounters with Beethoven, later published as *An Unrequited Love: An Episode in the Life of Beethoven, from the Diary of a Young Lady*

Amalie Sebald (1787–1846); singer from Berlin who met and became friends with Beethoven at the spa in Teplitz

Dorothea von Ertmann (1781–1849); one of the greatest pianists of her age from Vienna; she was a friend of Beethoven and frequently played his works in concert

Rahel Levin (May 19, 1771–March 7, 1833); renowned German-Jewish writer from Berlin; poet and friend of Beethoven

Fraulein Lokitzvarah; Gypsy masseuse in the service of **Prince Lichnowsky**; also seen by Beethoven as an avatar of the goddess **Avalokiteshvara**

Isis; Egyptian goddess representing the divine feminine; also identified with (correctly or incorrectly), in Beethoven's times, the Roman goddess **Venus**, the Greek **Aphrodite**;, the Chinese **Kwan Yin**, the Japanese **Kannon**, the Hindu and Tibetan **Avalokiteshvara**, and the Catholic **Madonna**, or **Mary**

Shiva; a Hindu God

Ssu Ma Hao Hwa; mythical Chinese warrior in a tale told by **Napoleon**

PROLOGUE

The Death of Beethoven

Vienna, 5:00 pm, March 26, 1827

OUTSIDE Beethoven's rooms at the *Schwarzspanierhaus,* a fresh measure of snow from a late season thunderstorm muffles the chimes of St. Stephen's Cathedral as they ring out the hours for the old city.

Eins, Zwei, Drei, Vier . . . Funf Uhr. Five o'clock.

Beethoven, three months past his 56th birthday, lies in a coma, as he has now for two nights, his body bound by the betrayal of an illness whose only virtue was that it proved incurable and would, thankfully, be his last. Though his chest muscles and his lungs wrestle like giants against the approaching blackness, his breathing is so labored that the death rattle can be heard over the grumblings of the heavens throughout his apartment.

Muss es sein? Must it be? *Ja, es muss sein.* Beethoven is dying. From on high, the gods vent their grief at his imminent passing and hurl a spear of lightening at Vienna.

Their jagged bolt of electricity explodes outside the frost covered windows of the *Schwarzspanierhaus* with a clap of thunder so violent it startles the composer to consciousness.

Beethoven's eyes open, glassy, unfocused. He looks upward—only the gods know what he sees, if anything. He raises his right hand, a hand that has graced a thousand sonatas, and clenches his fist for perhaps the last time. His arm trembles as if railing against the heavens. Tears flood his eyes.

His arm falls back to the bed . . . his eyelids close . . . and then he is gone . . .

CHAPTER I

Plaudite, Amici, Comoedia Finite Est

Applaud My Friends, the Comedy is Over

BY ALL ACCOUNTS, my funeral was a grand success.

Despite the snow and slush soaking through their shoes, all Vienna turns out. Twenty thousand mourners or more, accompanied by the Imperial Guards, guide the grieving to my grave. Streets crowded, impassable. My coffin, lined with silk, covered in flowers, rolls through the chaos on a horse-drawn bier. Paupers and princes; merchants and mendicants; menials and musicians; clerics and commoners; they all come for this, their Beethoven's final concerto.

As if they ever owned me or my music . . .

Plaudite, Amici, Comoedia Finite Est. Applaud my friends, the comedy is over. Inscribed herein rests my final opus.

Ja. Yes, they are all patrons and lovers . . . lovers of my music, the very music the gods have forbidden me to hear. How cruel. To suffer my last decade without sound—any sound except the incessant surge of blood pounding through my veins—an eternity inscribed on the calendar pages of my life.

And so it is, these celebrants, anxious for one last encore, crowd the alleys and streets of the Hapsburgs' capital in throngs not seen since the defeat of Napoleon Bonaparte and the French *Grande Armée* oh so many years ago.

The cortege rolls on past the taverns and cafés of this fair city where dark beer, schnitzel, and sausages reward the day. Ah, the saints and sinners of Vienna have always loved a good party, never mind the excuse.

Are they singing? *Alle Menschen werden Brüder.* All men will become brothers. They must be, yet I hear nothing.

I wonder if she is among them. My muse; my love; my passion; my sacred fire; will she be there to safeguard my voyage through Elysium?

Or is she too denied me, as were the sweet sighs of love and the embrace of family stolen by gods capricious and uncaring? Are they so vengeful? So embittered by spite? Like Prometheus, have I dared too close to revelations reserved for them alone?

The clouds grow ever darker, ominous.

Must I embrace death silently ere my last symphony suffuses the stage? Is this my end? To be cast out as by our Creator as history's cruel joke, a deaf musician? A composer unable to know the vibrancy of his own scores?

Tell me why your Beethoven, your servant whose hearing once surpassed all others in sensitivity and degree, must suffer such humiliation and torment?

Are the crowds laughing? *Ja oder nein?* Yes or no? I know not. Am I such a failure, such a disgrace to be shoved off the stage without your mercy or compassion?

As surely as the warmth of summer vanishes and the leaves of autumn crumble beneath the crush of winter, has all hope been stolen? Can I escape this fate? What path must I travel? What tasks of redemption are to be mine and mine alone?

Come death; am I to meet your shadow with courage? Must I depart in this winter of anguish before the renewal of spring?

Can I not find release from this cycle of sufferings like a saint or a Hindoo holy man following the dance of Shiva or a Bodhisattva, back bent upon the path of the great Buddha?

The last echoes of joy inside my heart are already fading. Will I never hear or feel those vibrations again? Never? *Nein.* Forever. Lost for eternity in the fog on the road to Elysium; that is too hard, too harsh.

But surely a loving father must dwell in the starry canopy above. Are you there, oh sweet Isis, my goddess of compassion? Help me, help guide me.

Please Providence grant me this, my final wish . . . grant but one day, just one day, one day of pure joy to your poor Beethoven.

Is this too much to ask before I embrace darkness forever? Oh, to be in her arms once again.

CHAPTER 2

Leonore

Koblenz, April 1827

IT WAS long after midnight and Leonore von Breuning Wegeler could not sleep. She sat up quietly so as not to awaken Franz who slept soundly in the bed beside her. Twenty-five years of marriage and she loved him as dearly now as when they were teenagers in Bonn. He was a good man of great intellect, infinitely kind and gentle, inquisitive and patient, all the skills needed for the husband, the friend, and the physician he was.

And all the more reason the letter she had received only that afternoon from her brother Steffen in Vienna kept her from sleeping. Not only had Steffen described Beethoven's final days and death—marked by that surprise spring thunderstorm that had shaken Beethoven from his coma one last time—he also gave a sketchy account of the funeral procession and the subsequent search through his apartment for Beethoven's important papers. Leonore had reread the letter several times, and even then she could not fathom how much of the truth Steffen had actually shared with her and how much he held in reserve. True to her brother's years as one of the Emperor's top legal practitioners—he was a master of the fine art of obfuscation.

Only one fact remained incontrovertible, Beethoven, or "Louis" as he was known to his friends, their beloved Beethoven—her beloved Beethoven—was dead.

In the beginning, she remembered, in the beginning it was the pianoforte that brought them all together. And Louis brought them music, the most glorious music: Bach, Mozart, and ultimately his own compositions. And now that he was gone, would their secrets, some bitter, some sweet, follow him to the grave, food for the worms? Or would they emerge from the earth like nettles and weeds to once again abuse her tranquility as he had so many years earlier? And Franz, what would he think had he known? Friendship was an odd horse and carriage that conveyed the clutter of their lives to God knows where. Their young lives had been messy. Far messier than she was ever comfortable with—and with Louis, "messy" was merely the starting point—a point of departure that filled her with a disturbing cascade of emotions that flowed as dangerous and intoxicating as the Rhine in flood season. Or a long ago November bath in the mineral hot springs hidden in the woods above Bonn.

Arising from the bed with stealth intended more to secure her secrets from Franz than to avoid waking him, she drew on her slippers and dressing gown. Yes, even the dressing gown—a red silk Japanese kimono—had been a tenth anniversary gift from Louis that he bought for her when the Oriental treasures from the estate of Toni Brentano's father Baron Johann von Birkenstock were auctioned off in 1811 or 1812. Memories of Beethoven were as inescapable as were her jealousies.

Though Leonore had never met this woman, she knew of her but couldn't recall if it was through her brother's occasional letters from Vienna or notes Louis himself had passed along to her husband, Franz. Reading between the lines, it had always seemed obvious to Leonore that Toni Brentano, a married mother of four—or was it five—had been one of Louis's more secretive dalliances in that city. Even Franz had once confided to her that when their Beethoven arrived in Vienna, he was always involved in a love affair and sometimes made conquests which would have been very difficult indeed, if not impossible, for many an Adonis.

Toni must have been special enough that when her father, a statesman who had travelled the continent on behalf of the Hapsburg rulers, passed away, the rumors were that Louis took uncommon interest in helping her sell off an estate so large and rich in paintings, sculptures, and Asian artifacts, that it could have filled half the Louvre. The cataloging, auctions, and estate sales, which included paintings from Rembrandt, Raphael, Durer, Holbein, and Van Dyck, took almost three years.

Louis had sent her this particular kimono as recompense for an angora jacket vest Leonore had knitted for him years earlier—part of a childhood pledge they had made to keep each other warm and held close within the confines of their respective hearts.

Lenore reached inside the pocket and confirmed that a small key with a purple ribbon tied to it was still there. Satisfied, she then stepped one foot at a time, as slowly as possible so as to prevent any of the floorboards from creaking, until she reached the fireplace. Nights in Koblenz were still cold. She poked the coals in the bedroom fireplace, knowing full well that Franz, who preferred a toasty room at night, would hopefully sleep well past dawn if their bed chamber stayed warm. She then headed out of the bedroom and secured the door behind her. In the dark, Leonore found her way to the stairs and made her way down two flights to a room that doubled not only as the family study and library but also as the music room.

Yes, it began with the pianoforte, this intertwining of the lives of the von Breuning clan with the Wegelers and the Beethovens. Yes, Leonore reflected back, way back to the 1780s when she was but a teenager and lived with her three younger brothers, Christoph, Steffen, and Lorenz, in Bonn. Leonore, whose name everyone close to her had either shortened from the more formal "Eleonore" or altered into its affectionate diminutive "Lorchen," was the eldest. Christoph, later a physician like Franz, followed her by two years. Steffen, now a great bear of a man, and a fixture in the War Department at the Emperor's Court, was then just a thin slip of a boy and was three years behind her.

Their father, a Court Councilor to the Elector of Bonn, had died in a fire just before Lenz, the youngest, was born, leaving the four of them in the sole care of their mother, Helene. As the eldest and without a father around, Leonore became the responsible one often tasked with watching over her brothers. Growing up in a court household in those times, it was *natürlich*—taken for granted—that all of them received a well-rounded education in Latin, all the basic sciences, French, the arts, and most especially music—and that meant the pianoforte. It pleased Leonore that her family also maintained a music room on the lower level of their house in Bonn and filled it with string instruments and a pianoforte. Typical for the times, their keyboard was small and certainly nothing as robust as Beethoven's by now famous Broadwood, which itself was now being dwarfed by ever greater, sturdier instruments with cast iron, instead of wooden, frames.

They all played, but to advance and gain the requisite skills necessitated a teacher. Franz Wegeler, who in those years was their neighbor and friend and but a teenager himself—yes, albeit a handsome one—told of a young composer he had befriended, who—though only 14 years old—played all the keyboard instruments as well as the violin and viola in the court orchestra. Quoting a notice that had appeared in the *Magazin der Musik,* Franz read how the young Beethoven, *"plays the clavier very skillfully and with power, and reads at sight very well,"* and how he *"would surely become a second Wolfgang Amadeus Mozart were he to continue as he has begun."*

Franz had described the boy's family as dirt poor. Louis's father, the court singer, Johann van Beethoven, was an unrepentant alcoholic who practically drank more florins worth of wine than his meager salary as a member of the choir could ever bring in. Louis had two younger brothers and a baby sister, all of whom he cared about deeply—especially Margaretha, the baby, the one he called *mon petit papillon*—my little butterfly. More mouths than an incompetent musician such as Johann van Beethoven could easily feed.

Suffice to say, the von Breunings needed a piano teacher and poor young Louis needed the work. None of them had ever seen Louis play, and Leonore, ever the practical and insightful one, asked Franz if they could audition this young musician before bringing him into their home.

An audition? Reflecting back, she could only shake her head at the audacity of her wanting to audition the boy who as a man destiny would proclaim as perhaps the greatest composer of all time. What had Steffen written in his letter about the funeral to her? *"Mozart was an angel sent from heaven to charm us on a Saturday night. But Beethoven . . . our beloved Beethoven was born of the black earth to entertain the gods for eternity."*

And bring him into their home? Oh yes, Leonore's mother, Helene, and her brothers would welcome Louis into their home as if he were one of their own. And she, well, that was another story, wasn't it? Oh, and Mozart and his *"Don Giovanni,"* what she could have told Steffen about this "angel's" devilish influence upon Louis—none of it good—at least not as far as she was concerned.

Franz, whose natural skills at friendship enabled him to succeed in getting along with people, especially difficult people, knew even back then that Louis hated having anyone watch him play in private. Eccentric? Neurotic? What new words would the men of the medical world create to describe Beethoven? He would have absolutely rebelled at the notion of an audition. Louis had his quirks, even as a child. It was one thing to perform as part of an orchestra or to steal the stage with his keyboard work in front of an audience of his own choosing but quite another to be watched and studied in private. It didn't necessarily make sense but a lot about Louis then and now never made sense to her. Franz had shared with Leonore how Louis as a child had routinely been forced by his father to practice on the pianoforte for endless stretches during the day, and again at all hours of the night, to entertain his father's friends while they engaged in some drunken sing along.

It had been the elder Beethoven's dream to parade Louis about as a prodigy much as the child Mozart had been run through all the capitals of Europe a generation earlier. Talented as Louis was though, he was no Amadeus. And yes, given a childhood marked by such blatant paternal abuse, it was more a wonder Louis had not come to hate music. Somehow, the inheritance of harmony and melody

Beethoven received from his *Grossvater* captured young Louis's soul as a child far more than his father's rough ways repelled him. And though Louis had suffered at his father's hands, in the end were we not all the better for it?

Leonore lit several candelabras and placed them on tables around the music room, including one upon her letter desk. She then stoked the fire and banked the coals. Returning to the desk, she sat before the mirror and lifted off her night cap. Unpinning her hair, it fell to her waist. Leonore studied her own reflection. She had aged, but well. A few wrinkles here and there, perhaps more than a few, but save for the streaks of gray, her auburn hair was still as dense and wavy as when she was a teenager. Leonore slid open a draw from which she lifted out a wooden box. With the key from her dressing gown, she unlocked it.

Inside the wooden box was a small stack of letters neatly tied up in more of the same purple ribbon. She started to untie the ribbon, but abruptly stopped. Was he really dead? Never to laugh again? Never to cry? Never to touch her soul? Tears that had welled up in her eyes rolled off her cheeks and fell onto the stack, staining the paper. She knew what was inside and had no need to open the faded and yellowed envelopes. She retied the bow, then set the stack aside. At the bottom of the box were pieces of equally ancient sheet music written in B's own hand. These she lifted out and carried to the piano.

In the beginning it was music that united them. She began to play—for him—in memory of him—in memory of her own remembered pain. It was one of Louis's earliest compositions, one he dedicated to her, variations on a theme from Mozart's *Figaro*. Damn that Mozart.

She could hear Louis's voice as if it hung in the ethers, *"The variations will prove a little difficult to play, particularly the trills in the coda, but do not let that frighten you. You need only concern yourself with the trills; omit the other notes as they are also in the violin part."*

She let her sadness, her grief, her love, her memories, flow through her fingers, which were long and unusually graceful, as she sought consolation at the departure of a man who had changed her life forever. "*I would never have written such a piece of this kind had I not often noticed here and there in Vienna a man who after I had improvised one evening, would write down some of my peculiarities and boast of them as his own the next day.*"

This was the man she didn't marry—kind, generous, brilliant but with a fire, an inner anger, a temper, "*Foreseeing that these things would be stolen and soon appear in print, I made up my mind to anticipate and embarrass these local pianoforte masters, many of whom I consider my mortal enemies. I wanted to have my revenge in this way, for I knew in advance that my variations would be put before them and that they would make poor exhibitions of themselves.*" Yes, this was the man she didn't marry. The man who had been her husband's lifelong friend. The man who had been . . .

She remembered what Franz had warned her about all those many years ago: There was no way Louis would have sat still for an audition, so if they wanted to see their potential tutor at work, Leonore had best come up with a better plan. She did. Leonore knew the buildings of the Elector of Bonn's court inside and out as if the chambers had been her playground—which they were in the day when her father was still alive and served the Elector. She proposed that the best way to observe this "Louis van Beethoven" was to sneak into one of the lofts above the main hall so that they could watch this young genius without him knowing. And if they liked what they saw, they would hire him as their teacher.

In those days, the keyboard for the pipe organ that Louis played was off in a separate room behind the main hall where the rest of the Elector's music ensemble would gather. Elector Max Franz, the ruler of the Germanic states along the Rhine and the younger brother of the Hapsburg Emperor Joseph II, loved music, played not a little himself, and cultivated one of Europe's best orchestras outside of Vienna. The string, horn, and woodwind players—all world class musicians themselves—would sit on chairs arranged in a semi-circle around any singer that might be performing for the Elector and his guests.

Over the years, Leonore and Franz had gotten to know them all, for among the musicians were many who would long play a role in Louis's career. Principal among them was Christian Neefe, who had joined the orchestra in 1779, and had not only introduced Louis to the works of Johann Sebastian Bach, which were little known outside Leipzig at that time, he had also tutored him in composition and would help publish B's first work. Then there was Franz Ries, Ferdinand Ries's father who was not only the orchestra's lead violinist, but also taught Louis the violin and viola. Years later in Vienna, Beethoven would return the favor as he was wont to do by taking Ferdinand in as his student. The court cellist was Joseph Reicha, who introduced Louis to that instrument and it was his son, Anton Reicha, who would later perform most of Beethoven's string quartets for him in Vienna. Even the chief horn player, Nikolaus Simrock, later turned publisher and produced many of Beethoven's works.

The organ room was situated in the back of the main hall to not only accommodate the many pipes needed to produce its sounds but to also avoid overwhelming the rest of the players with its power. Above the organ room was a loft which allowed one to observe the organ below and also gain access through a trap door to the tallest of the organ pipes so they could be cleaned and serviced when necessary.

Franz, whose father also had much business at the court, didn't think it wise for all five of them to go sneaking around and thus suggested that just he and Leonore—*"Meine Lorchen"*—go alone, a prospect that Leonore, who already had an eye on Franz, thoroughly appreciated. Even as a teenager, Franz Wegeler exuded a maturity and male strength that not only reminded Leonore of her own father's presence when he was still alive but also made her feel secure and confident whenever he was around her.

And he called her *"Meine Lorchen,"* a term of endearment which pleased her almost as much.

It was late on a Sunday afternoon when Franz and Leonore slipped into the court building and hid up in the lofts above the great hall where the court orchestra was to rehearse Mozart's opera, *Abduction from the Seraglio,* and several Bach chorales for a performance in front of the Elector later that week.

The *Kapellmeister* at the time was a Venetian named Andrea Lucchesi, more known for his pomposity and girth than his talent. Old school and rigid, Lucchesi had taken on the position not long after the death of Beethoven's grandfather and in so doing blocked young Louis's father from that title—not that the Elector would have ever placed such responsibility in the hands of Johann van Beethoven. Though Louis detested his father's behavior toward him, Johann was still his father and the boy felt some loyalty toward him and not a little antipathy toward Lucchesi—an attitude that that often resulted in Lucchesi becoming the butt of Louis's practical jokes.

Although she and Franz would be able to watch Louis from their hideaway in the loft and satisfy their initial purpose, Leonore found herself increasingly distracted by the sheer pleasure of being this close to Franz. Even when he had reached for her hand to pull her up into the loft, it seemed to awaken her in ways beyond her imagination. She only reluctantly let go of his hand as they wedged themselves into a corner of the loft. Here she was alone with a boy, tucked into their tight hiding space with her body pressed up against his and it felt good, very good. And why not, at this same age were not many of her girlfriends already engaged or married?

"A sword," mused Leonore to herself as she recalled that day. Those of us who knew Beethoven as the grand eminence of Viennese music, a man of powerful stature and imposing presence, would struggle to imagine him as a young teen. Like the other members of the court orchestra, Louis wore a military style uniform complete with a sea-green frock coat, matching green knee britches with buckles, stockings of white silk, shoes with black bowknots, an embroidered vest with pocket flaps—the vest bound with real gold cord—his hair curled and with a queue, a crush hat on his head, and a sword on his left side with a silver belt.

It was near impossible for Leonore to compare the Beethoven she knew—a man of immense majesty—with this image of a green-suited performing monkey. And even more amusing to think that Louis actually loved that suit, especially in the beginning. It gave him a stature he had not experienced elsewhere. It was one thing to be a boy genius, another to have it recognized.

And that day, when Louis dove into the Bach with all the verve of a Bohemian cliff diver, Leonore knew right off she was witnessing something revolutionary. Whereas most keyboardists back then sat up straight like a squirrel with paws perched on keys as if at prayer, Louis, after first quietly and serenely nodding his head in the direction of the sheet music, veritably threw himself into every gesture as if he was wrestling the very soul of the music out of the organ's pipes. None of the daintiness of a periwigged court fop for Louis. She had never seen anyone's hands fly across the keys with such frenzy. His entire body rocked and swayed with an intensity as rare as diamonds. His arms darted first left, then right, then back again. And in him, in his movements, she divined something special that she had observed nowhere before: passion, passion, and more passion. Louis not only played the music, he embraced it as one would a lover, a friend, or an enemy. Whatever it was—sad, soulful, poignant, blaring, or military—he married the notes to his soul. He was the chords and the chords flowed through him. Inseparable. It fascinated her.

As she watched him prowl the keyboard with the hunger of a wolverine, Leonore knew that not only must she have him as her teacher, she knew with unabashed certitude that she had fallen in love with this wild child. It wasn't that she didn't adore Franz. Louis and Franz were complete opposites. And one day—but only after Franz completed his medical training—she would marry him. Yes, Franz's maturity and strength attracted her, but it was Beethoven's razor's edge and sizzle that turned her inside out.

"He'll do," Leonore whispered to Franz as Louis seemingly transported the prelude towards its inevitable end.

"I knew you'd be pleased," said Franz, who perhaps would never know her secret of just how much Louis did please—and hurt her. Below them Lucchesi glanced at his score and puffed himself up, awaiting the queue for his opening lines.

But Louis didn't stop . . .

Instead of grounding the prelude to its conclusion and allowing Lucchesi to sing, Louis pumped up the organ pedals and effortlessly segued into an entirely new improvisational sequence of the Bach at full gallop.

Leonore watched as the thick-fingered Lucchesi flipped through his score in frustration, at first imagining he had simply missed his entrance. Once more the *Kapellmeister* braced himself to sing again. Leonore and Franz were both puzzled in that moment when they saw the band members—who knew better—chuckle and smirk. The joke was on Lucchesi. Louis was never going to let him sing. Each time Lucchesi inhaled and puffed up his bloated gut, Louis would whip off another improvisation.

Lucchesi screamed for Beethoven to stop, but our boy wonder kept it going, getting ever louder, ever faster, ever more frenzied. Louis's fingers dashed across the keyboard as he pivoted seamlessly from the prelude to Bach's *Toccata and Fugue*. While the organ pipes groaned with a pleasure that held the entire hall in its thrall, Lucchesi—red with fury—propelled his obese self back towards the organ room.

But the waddling *Kapellmeister* was no match for the speedy Louis, who reached across and locked the door to the organ room whilst not missing a beat. Louis, as if possessed by demons or drunk on the sheer power of sound, kept at it.

Years later, Louis would confess to Leonore that he gave up playing the organ because his nerves simply could not stand the power of this gigantic instrument, even as he sought throughout the rest of his life to replicate its depth and range on the pianoforte.

Lucchesi pounded on the door and hurled all manner of threats. Louis ignored him and like a wild beast in flight kept charging straight forward. Lucchesi cursed him one last time in Italian, then key locked the room from the outside and stormed off to fetch the Elector.

When at last Louis let the organ fall silent, the band applauded with laughter and cries of "Bravo!" Still, Louis's moment of triumph was short-lived, as it dawned on him that he was trapped and risked the wrath of the Elector himself.

Without thinking, Leonore made the call that changed her life forever. "Here, boy, this way." She flipped open the trap door surrounding the organ pipes and dropped down the rope ladder used by the Elector's servants when they cleaned or tuned the instrument. . . . As Louis scampered up the ladder, Franz and Leonore each reached out a hand to pull him up and in that moment of spontaneous inspiration a new future was born for all three friends.

Perhaps needless to say, when Lucchesi returned with the Elector, Louis was long gone.

And now he's dead. Leonore cleared the past from her mind and played the *Variations*—she played the trills without fear over and over again until the candles burnt themselves out. She played for Louis, she played for Beethoven, she played for her broken heart—and she cursed Wolfgang Amadeus Mozart one last time.

In the morning, Franz Wegeler found his wife asleep at the piano and—at first—all he could think was how beautiful she still looked even after all these years. And yet, when he saw the open wooden box and the stack of letters tied with a purple bow and stained with her tears, he could only wonder. . . . They were addressed from his best friend and sent to his wife . . . his wife. He could only wonder, what else, what else is there to know? And what would he learn now that Beethoven was dead?

CHAPTER 3

The Path to Elysium

LIKE A FUGUE or rondo composed by a madman, my final dream keeps repeating itself over and over again. First there's a flash of lightening across the sky. Then my eyes open, glassy and unfocused. I raise my right arm and clench my fist. The air is always thick. Sometimes it's cloudy, other times my view is obscured by fog and once even by snow. The bolt of light is followed immediately by the vibrations—*ja,* just the vibrations, not the rumble of thunder. Even in my dreams the gods have rendered me deaf. Such a fate. *Muss es immer sein?* They must be crazy. The gods won't even let me dream with sound.

Or are they just plain cruel?

As a small child in Bonn I loved thunderstorms. Great ribbons of lightening would explode out of the clouds whenever storms worked their way north up the father Rhine. Volleys as brusque and brutal as the French cannon fire when they took Vienna would echo off the cliffs of the *Siebengebirge* on the eastern shore and drown out the arguing that inevitably occurred between my parents whenever my father was drunk. And when wasn't he? They could have bottled the bastard's blood as fortified Burgundy.

I loved thunderstorms—that is until that night my grandfather—I was named Ludwig after him—until the night he died. I was only 3 years old. I loved him. And he loved me. Oh, how his bass voice, solid as a bull, would resonate throughout our house whether he was singing me to sleep in his arms with a lullaby or ordering my father about. I hung his portrait by Radoux, our Bonn court painter, on the wall by my desk so my esteemed *Grossvater* could watch me work and I could hear him sing all these many years. *Mein Grossvater der Kapellmeister* taught me to play the keyboard. He gave me music. He gave me my name. He gave me . . . me.

It was during the middle of one such storm—a blizzard, actually, the night before Christmas, but it sounded like a thunderstorm and that's how I remembered it with tree branches banging against the house. . . . Anyway, my father grabbed my hand and dragged me over to Grandfather's bed—I would have gone willingly, gladly—but he was always too drunk to know that. "Say goodbye to your grandfather, he's dying."

Dying, I didn't even know what the word meant. My grandfather stretched out his hand with the grace of a conductor and motioned for me. "Come, Louis" he said, pronouncing my name the way the Flemish and French did with emphasis on the final "e" sound. His skin was translucent as porcelain, his fingers little more than bone. As I stepped forward, my father pushed me hard against the side of the bed.

"Say goodbye!" He—my father—wreaked of what I would later learn too well was the stench of rotten gums, cheap wine, and bad digestion.

"Hurry up, he's dying. He's going off to heaven," as if heaven were just another stop on the stagecoach line between here and Cologne.

My grandfather put one arm around my shoulders and brushed the hair from my face with his other hand. His eyes, I still remember his eyes. We stared at each other. If ever there was a window to the soul . . . Radoux's portrait had kept them alive for me.

"May I visit you *auf dem Himmel*? If I go, will you play pianoforte with me?"

He pulled me closer and even though he spoke softly, so softly I could scarcely hear him over the sounds of rain pelting the window and trees creaking in the wind, the sweet vibrato of his bass voice still echoes inside my head, *"Not knowing life, Louis, why worry about death?"*

With that, my beloved grandfather went cold and stiff. Mother, a dear and always gentle woman in her sixth month of pregnancy with my brother, Casper, unwound grandfather's arm from my shoulder and crossed it on his chest. Then she closed his eyes and kissed his forehead—just as I would do for her thirteen years later when I was but 16 and the grave master, that calls us all in due time, invited her home.

And my father? They say a man is not a man until his own father dies. My father poured himself a glass of wine, and then another and another as if to toast his own liberation. But he would never be a man. No, the bastard was just a conduit from Grandfather to me, and a savage one at that.

And then . . . and then, my dream played a reprise: I was swimming in what I imaged was a natural pool, or the baths at a spa, but I was deep beneath the surface. At night. Or at least it was dark. The water was dense and murky with minerals. I could taste them. Bromine, a hint of sulfur. Lavender. Others familiar but unnamable.

Once more I saw the ripple of lightening and shadows flickering above me. Then a deep tremor followed. The gods were at work. *Aber nein*, but no, no sounds penetrated these ears, just vibrations. *Ja*, still deaf.

Not only was my hearing gone, I could barely focus my eyes. As if I needed another ailment. Were they tears? Even here in the depths?

Something or someone stirred the waves above me. Shadows moved. Legs kicking, bare skin, a thatch of pubic hair, curves, nipples—a woman most naked?

Was there a woman here in the baths with me? I shot my right hand up and grabbed onto what I imagined was her ankle. . . . *Nein*, its rough texture told me I had grabbed the crook of a tree branch that extended over the water. Ah, foolish Beethoven, always wishing for what was not to be had.

With an effort so great it made the muscles in my arm tremble, I tugged on the branch and lifted my head out of the water. The air rushing into my lungs was filled with a sweet, smoky scent reminiscent of a swaying incense censor at a requiem mass at Saint Stephens—or was it just her perfume? Devilishly pungent. Hunger. I felt hunger, a man's hunger for a woman. Even here. A prisoner of flesh to the very end.

At first I could see nothing but fog, a dense screen having settled over the baths. Was I even at the baths? This didn't look or feel like Baden, Karlsbad, or even Teplitz. Perhaps a natural spring hidden in the *Wienerwald*—the Vienna Woods—or the hills above the Rhine? Where could I be? Where should I be?

I certainly felt better than I had in months. The pain in my chest was gone. My stomach—once bloated with fluid and disease—was flat and youthful. The aches of age in my shoulders and hips had vanished as well. My skin, without pockmarks or scars, felt smooth to the touch. A young man's complexion. Even the scars from those bed bug bites that had tormented me nightly and made sleep inconceivable had vanished.

A mist from these waters that had seemingly healed me rose up and married itself to the fog. I paddled toward what appeared to be the edge of the pool, or at least rocks along a shoreline.

Once there, I rested a moment to gather my bearings while continuing to inhale the sweet air. As I did so, the fog seemed to draw in and out as if it too was a living, breathing animated creature. How strange. Turning round, I saw that the pool was at the mouth of a cave, the entrance of which was half shielded with strands of rust-red heather. Damn this flesh. Perhaps it was my state of mind, or the dulled focus of my eyes—but for the life of me, the soft pubic hair-like curls of heather around the portal gave the cave an appearance exactly like the moist, quivering lips of my Immortal Beloved opening up her essence for me. Those Viennese philosophers who argued about the meaning of our dreams in the cafes of the old city were right, weren't they? In the end it was all about sex—even here—where ever here was. And what would they say about my music a hundred years from now? Two hundred years? Would those damnable critics think it was all about sex?

Another flash of light shot like an arrow from the heavens down to the lips of the cave, illuminating as it did so, footprints—petite, delicate, and oddly glowing—surely a woman's—which led from the pool toward the cave.

A prisoner to my male nature—and having no better notion of what to do next—I followed the glow of the footprints past the strands of heather and slipped inside the cave. Why not? Somehow being inside felt familiar. And good. And warm. And consoling. Had I been here before? I was sure I had, but where or when? Was it with Her? *Ja,* Her. I was ever more certain. It had to be here, all those years ago. November, November in the hills above Bonn. All the scene lacked was butterflies. Rhineland butterflies. Beautiful Rhineland butterflies that made a man dream. And tears, my tears, my most painful tears.

Even inside the cave, the fog remained too dense to gain clarity, though I detected the soft glow of a light emanating from within the depths of the cavern. Barefoot, I stumbled over the rocky floor of the cave toward the light until I came to a bench. A bench, a marble bench where I found my clothes—fresh, clean, new, laid out for me. Beside them was the source of light—my bamboo walking stick which was glowing as if it had captured the lightning's essence. The cane was a gift from a lover who wanted me to always think of her and her curves every time I handled it. It felt silken yet firm to my touch, as I am sure she once did. Age diminishes us all, doesn't it?

What was her name? A lifetime of women, a lifetime of memories: Toni, whose eyes bespoke legions of love, devotion, and disappointment? Or Jeanette, whose blond locks once held me prisoner until she escaped? Or Giulietta, my bejeweled princess wrapped in silk hiding her true heart? Babette, enchantress of Bonn who could never understand or venture into the world beyond? Or Josephine, a queen of compassion whose heart was fully conflicted? Magdalena, whose songs while alluring as honey, held her trapped as if in amber? Leonore, brave Leonore, the long-legged beauty of my youth who could outfox fate itself? Or Fanny? *Ja*, Fanny—Giannatasio's daughter. Was it her? The Lady Abbess? The one who always went about with lovesick eyes? Would that she and her sister had showered as much attention on my boy, Karl, when he was at their school as they did me and perhaps he would not have turned out like some hothouse flower who couldn't survive the storms of the world as they swirl about us.

How odd that this bamboo shaft, stained and hardened with the sweat and toil of every Chinaman, Hindoo, and Turk that had cut, shaped, and transported it from the forest of Asia to the markets of Vienna, would be glowing. The only light in this endless fog. A cane. How odd. Was this Fanny's way of forever carrying a torch for me? Her Beethoven. . . . As sweet as she was, I just couldn't. And why was she, or at least her cane, in my dream? A gift from the one I let fly away?

I dried and dressed quickly, then slipped into a pair of equestrian boots with heels and toes tipped in silver that caressed my soles with Italian leather so supple that even my clumsy feet felt like dancing a jig or a landler. With boots like these I could have conquered the salons of Paris.

And suddenly I was dancing—uncontrollably so. Me? Beethoven? Partnered with my walking stick, I three-stepped about the cave to the string quartet in my head, *"Alla Danza Tedesca"* I danced better than ever—not that I ever could. Were these waters so healing they could cure clumsiness or transform God's great oaf into a swan? Such sweetness to savor. Simple pleasures are best, aren't they, even here.

Still I could not escape the thought, if the baths were so potent, why, oh why, was I still deaf? Damn. Lacking answers, alas, I let the question drop and simply allowed the melody of my own landler to fill my head with song. I danced until dizzy, or at least until the glowing light emanating from my cane dissipated. Thank you, Fanny Giannatasio Del Rio, for bringing light onto me.

Things came and went here without much warning or logic—or at least any logic I could understand. Perhaps someday all my mysteries will dissipate so gently as well.

What now? Surrounded by shrouds of fog so dense I could see nothing at all, I calculated the odds. After all they say, when the blind lead the blind, everyone runs the risk of falling into a ditch—or in this case, back into the baths.

Recalling a lesson from the *Gita,* I inhaled as deeply as Brahma, then out again. And when I did so several times over, the fog once again appeared to move in and out with me as my breath had reanimated the world about me—or at least the fog. Control. I had some control over this dream, didn't I?

After a time—how long I am incapable of knowing, a minute, an hour, a day, a week—the mists parted reminiscent of the opening of the curtains for *Fidelio* at the *Theater–an-der-Wien* the week Napoleon's *Grande Armée* marched into Vienna. Their tricolored uniforms matching their blue, white, and red battle flags, they filled most every seat. Enlisted men on the back benches; cavalry officers up front; generals and their aides up in the boxes. What a night, a bad night. I could remember no one applauding—no one—until a young corporal, an aide, from a horse regiment judging by his well-polished boots tipped with silver—much like mine—who sat in the center of the first row beside the stoic and stiff officer he most likely served, began to clap. And the rest followed. But without enthusiasm. Sadly, my *Fidelio* lacked a singer with dramatic flair to cast equal to the starring role of Leonore. Unlike the Italians who sing and act with a fluidity inherent in their language that permeates body and soul, we Germans are all too cold and unfeeling when it comes to opera. *Fidelio* closed two nights later. One more financial disaster in a life filled with such frustrations.

Would my heroine reveal herself here in the baths to save this composer anon? I begged for a vision. And clarity came at last as the mists rose enough to reveal the ruins of a Roman temple on the far side of the pool. Still, the fog was so dense I saw little more than a few yards in any direction. Circling around the pool with great care, I entered the ruins—really little more than a collection of rubble and pillars.

Wraiths of fog flittered in and amongst the remaining pillars like so many actors on a stage. In their midst, perched upon a sculptured half clamshell risen up on sea foam, stood—not a Leonore to rescue me—but a marble carving of the goddess, Isis. How perfect, the temptress herself!

There she was, my muse, my Venus, the woman of my dreams not more than a dozen yards off. Even frozen in stone cut from the quarries of Carrera and painted with life-like colors in the Roman style she was as beautiful and striking as ever imaged by this mere mortal. And why wouldn't she be? A goddess in all her perfection, her long dark curls piled up loosely on her head, a translucent complexion, a silken sheath wrapped loosely round those inspired curves and over the dark delta between her legs. A man's dream of womanly perfection, or at least this man's dream. And there she was . . .

They say in the course of life every woman manifests all the qualities of a goddess—beauty, sexuality, motherhood, compassion, wisdom, love—just not all at the same time. And it is the gods' blessing and curse upon all men that we live in a perpetual state of desire for the very sirens who bedevil us.

More footprints, those same petite, delicate footprints, trailed off in a half dozen different directions. I scratched at the ones closest to me with the tip of my cane while contemplating a next move. It was then I noticed Isis's feet were wet and stained with mud. What manner of statue was this Isis? Had my muse been swimming in the baths with me after all? I called out to Isis but deaf becomes her. My goddess remained stone silent.

What next?

Turning away from Isis, I sat down upon a rock, fixed my eyes on the baths and once again began to breathe as Brahma who created the world. In and out. In and out. I had a plan. In and out . . . over and over again until the fog thinned out. Mind you, it never went away, but it thinned out enough for me to see forests all around.

I turned back around for Isis but now, she was gone, vanished down a path. Which one? Good questions should never go unanswered, even in dreams. . . . And so, while I debated which path to follow I gazed deep into the fog, searching, searching, searching for some clue. And of course as always happens in the logic of dreams, I spied Isis far off in the distance running through the mist—playing hide and seek between the pillars—camouflaged only by so many webs of gossamer.

Ever the romantic—or classic fool as some would characterize me—and with my boots my only chariot—I followed as quickly as my feet could carry. But would that suffice? While I hurried much as humanly possible, the goddess drew upon celestial strengths. Isis quickly outpaced me. Once more my temptress vanished beyond the borders of vision. Only her footprints remained behind. But at least the goddess had left me a path to follow. And follow I would.

The path chosen seemed to climb gradually up slope. The luminescence that had once embraced my cane now lingered once again on each of her footprints as I approached. Their respective glow would dissipate and fade away after I'd moved forward. The air—formally sweet with incense—was now rife with the primal scent of nature: dark black topsoil enriched by a dense and decomposing mulch of leaves.

And so I went on in silence, step by step. My chest muscles and lungs wrestled like giants against the encroaching darkness. Though the fog shrank in at inhalation and expanded out at exhalation, my outward breath seemed to move it ever farther away until I began to be able to identify the actual scenery, landmarks, and topography of this new world.

The path or way—didn't Schiller, or was it Goethe or Kant, write somewhere that the Chinese have a funny little word for it, the *Tao*? No, it was Sir Walter Scott describing Napoleon's fascination with the *Analects of Confucius* and Lao Tzu's *Tao Te Ching,* where the concept of the "way" meant finding an organic balance, a harmony for treading the path of life. This *Tao,* this way, this path, was on a ridgeline. To the left and down slope were meadows and fields divided by irregular patches of woods. Little streams and rivulets began below the path and flowed towards what might be a river hidden from my sight by a copse of willows and foxtails along its probable shore. Farther off in the distance beyond the river were high mountain meadows covered in more of the same red heather that had triggered my most base hunger. Beyond that, the slopes climbed ever upwards towards a distant line of mountains graced by waterfalls. Can anyone love the countryside as much as I do? How happy I am to be able to wander among these bushes and herbs, under trees and over rocks. In them do we not find the divine in us all?

To my right, just yards below the path, stood a dark and dense forest reminiscent of the stagecoach road between Karlsbad and Teplitz. It was populated by the well expected oaks, elms, and scrub pines but oddly juxtaposed and mixed in as if I were viewing some Egyptian oasis with towering coconut palms, black bamboo, and wind-rattled banana trees.

It was then that the butterflies appeared . . . not your ordinary monarchs, not the ones I'd chase as a child along the Rhine . . . these that swarmed around me were giants, with wing spans like those of a great horned owl and bodies near as thick. Their silken wings were painted in bright iridescent blues, greens, and reds that sparkled even in the fog. Electric shades and tones I'd never seen before—and probably never would again. They swept around me, faster and faster until I could see nothing but a rainbow of colors crafted by the fluttering of their wings. Grasping me with their claws—do butterflies have claws—they lifted me off the ground.

Away we flew as far away as Syria where Jesus performed his miracles—did he really raise Lazarus from the dead—and then on farther to India to where the Buddha expounded his wisdom in the shade of the Bodhi tree and Shiva danced through a ring of fire to destroy the world thus allowing Brahma to recreate it. Then, turning around I crossed back through Arabia to the gardens of Mohammed, until finally I came indeed to Jerusalem, the Holy City, land of the Hebrew prophets.

Was I still dreaming? Or was I Beethoven dreaming I too was a butterfly, flying about here and there enjoying a life on wings just as I had as a child? Or was I a butterfly dreaming I was Beethoven? A deaf Beethoven chasing after his muse? *Déjà vu*, I had had this dream before. And probably would again. Such was the nature of my existence.

Leaving Jerusalem, we flew past the moon, beyond the sun and over Mount Olympus until at long last they returned me to my path through the fog. And just as abruptly as they had appeared, the butterflies vanished, leaving me to walk alone.

Strange companions indeed. But ever more unexpected were the diverse ruins I passed by as I continued my climb up and up the ridge trail. When the mists, with their gray pallor that obfuscated all sunlight, would lift enough to see the horizon, I would find scattered here and there among the shadows the crumpled down walls of a Crusader castle; an abandoned medieval village; Greek pillars sprouting like so many orchards of stone; a shepherd's fallen down hut; fragments of a Roman amphitheater; the remnants of an Egyptian monument to Isis; a half-built pyramid; stretches of a great Chinese fortress wall; a Hindoo temple honoring Shiva; and scattered everywhere, seemingly strewn at random, the statues of gods and goddesses from across the seven seas—all in some manner of disrepair.

Truly, the history of mankind's intoxication with the gods was at my feet. All in all it resembled nothing so much as walking in a colorless dream universe where only the past seemed to exist. I saw no people, no animals domestic or wild, no birds and nothing one would associate with the land of the living.

Just as Plutarch had taught me patience in the face of adversity, I soldiered on. Somewhere ahead was Isis. Where? I was on her path. The path to Elysium. The path to the gods' own heaven. The path to a blessed and eternally blissful life. The path to one day, one day of endless joy. I would find her!

I kept climbing. This surely wasn't the *Wienerwald* but I kept going. Truth be known I loved walking in nature. My execrable hearing never troubled me there, where trees and stones send back the echoes that all humans desire. How many of my compositions—paeans to the ecstasy of the woods—began here in the forest? Perhaps them all. If the divine lives in the natural world, what was my music but this poor man's effort to manifest the gods in song?

How long my mountain ascent lasted I don't recall. Was it a year spent in sacred pilgrimage? Or merely a momentary splash down in time?

As the *Tao,* the way, steepens I dig my cane deep into the black earth to pull myself ever upward, ever forward. The *Tao,* I like that word, embracing as it does a tonal harmony I thought to use in a next composition—if there was a next composition. A tenth symphony? Another concerto? Opus 139?

Placing my fingers on my jawbone just below my ear, I close my eyes and then pause to repeat the word as if chanting: *Tao . . . Tao . . . Tao . . .* I can feel the vibrations as powerfully as if I'm pinging a gong. The vibrations crescendo before fading. *Tao . . . Tao . . . Tao . . .*

And that does the trick. . . . Stepping out from between the twin curtains of fog and mist, there is Isis beckoning me forward like a prima diva bent on seduction.

She knows my hunger. And she moves and shimmies the way Toni had once upon a time enticed me into her bed. Or was it mine? The tease. Playing to my weakness. But even as I rush forward and push myself hard up the path toward her, my sweet muse, ever the trickster, steps behind the curtains of mist and vanishes once more behind the fog.

Faster, faster, faster I climb. Good boots work wonders. As my desperation to catch up to Isis grows, I can't help but be distracted by a single thought—an odd one at that: Will the gods let me keep these boots even after my dream ends? Would that they could carry me through Elysium forever, yes?

I dive into the depths of the fog with only Isis's glowing footprints to lead me through the darkness.

And when I emerge back into the light, I find myself in another valley—a desert valley—through which a river flows. And though it at first resembles the great father Rhine, it can't be. Instead of Bonn or the cathedral at Cologne, there is, incongruously enough, another set of ruins nestled within a riverbank oasis: this one clearly Egyptian. I recognize it from a drawing in the book *Description de l'Égypte,* assembled by those men of science who had accompanied Bonaparte's invasion force into Egypt back in 1798. It is the Temple of Isis, a place—I have read—of rebirth where the purified fire of the Goddess swallows up all of our troubles then causes us to arise anew like a phoenix.

Have I arrived? Am I about to witness my own rebirth here on the banks of the Nile in her arms? Oh Isis, goddess of compassion, show yourself.

I walk closer. I'll catch her now, I think. Joy, my moment of joy awaits.

But no. There, sitting on a stone, legs crossed like a Buddha, is not my muse, but a man, a military man in full winter garb; trench coat, cape, earmuffs, gloves, hat—the tricolor hat of an officer, and boots—those self-same cavalry boots tipped with silver which I recognize immediately. As this man turns and looks at me, he pulls off his earmuffs and stuffs them into a pocket of his coat.

Many are my mortal enemies.

There is no mistaking this living portrait of a man who has just escaped the icy grasp of Moscow, and now blocks my path to Elysium and Isis. It is the French General himself, Napoleon Bonaparte.

Trespassing in my dream . . . my mortal enemy.

CHAPTER 4

Trois Trios Pour le Piano Forte Violin et Violincello, Oeuvre Un

Three Trios for Pianoforte, Violin and Cello, Opus One

IN THE DAYS and weeks following Beethoven's death, his friends, admirers, and enemies marked his passing in their own distinct ways. Fellow pianist and composer Johann Hummel, a onetime rival and long-term friend, brought his 15-year-old student, Ferdinand Hiller, with him to pay their respects at the *Schwarzspanierhaus.* Young Hiller, who would go on to become one of Europe's leading conductors, clipped a lock of B's hair and after having it framed for posterity, he would eventually will it to his own son. During the funeral procession, Hummel would be among the torchbearers leading the cortege to the grave. At the cemetery he was joined by thousands of others, including Fanny Giannatasio Del Rio and her sister, Anna, who each shed their own fair amount of tears at seeing their beloved friend return to the earth from whence he had come. Among the first to throw a handful of dirt—and perhaps a stone or two—into that grave was Johanna Reiss van Beethoven, Louis's embittered sister-in-law, who could not be blamed for having mixed emotions upon seeing Beethoven finally exit out of her life.

It took more than a few days for the news to reach the farther corners of Europe. From a military base in Iglau, Moravia, a young army cadet—a relative of Beethoven—took leave from the Austrian 8th Infantry Regiment and hurried much as he could to reach Vienna before the funeral but failed. In Berlin the poet, Rahel Levin, quietly marked the occasion by cutting Narcissus flowers—which are always among the first to bloom each spring—from her garden. She would place them in a vase on her writing desk beside a *jahreszeit* candle and chant the words of the *Yizkor*, the Hebrew prayer for the dead. In Bonn, Ferdinand Ries would organize a memorial around a performance of the *Ninth Symphony* by the Philharmonic Society. In Vilnius, Liliana Donishefski, a young Jewish violin prodigy, who had studied with Beethoven when she was a teenager, arrived by wagon from her village of Smorgonie to stage an encore concert of the *Kreutzer Sonata* at the Grand Synagogue in the heart of the old ghetto.

But perhaps one of the more unusual and heartfelt tributes occurred in the west German city of Frankfurt, the adopted home of Antonie Birkenstock Brentano. Antonie and two of her servants had wheeled her youngest son, 14 year old Karl Josef, to their private booth at the opera house to listen to a performance of Beethoven's chamber works, including the *Opus One: Three Trios for Piano, Violin and Cello,* and a new *String Quartet in B-flat major, Opus 130,* a copy of which had just arrived by post days after the news of his death. Adding much to Toni's burdens on the day of the memorial concert was the immutable fact that Karl Josef, nearly a decade younger than her other now grown children, was not only partially crippled but also suffered from mental retardation and a host of emotional and behavioral problems. The dark-haired boy was constantly agitated and other than grunts, shrieks, and screams, speech of any sort was difficult for the boy. One of the few activities that calmed him was listening to music, particularly Beethoven's. To that end, Toni would often sing softly to him a song, *An die Geliebte*—To My Beloved—that Beethoven had composed and dedicated to her less than ten months before Karl Josef was born.

The tears of your silent eyes,
With their love-filled splendor,
Oh, that I might gather them from your cheek
Before the earth drinks them in.

As she sat in their booth at the opera house waiting for the concert to begin, she sang the lyrics softly, over and over again like a prayer for Karl Josef until he fell into a quiet, almost hypnotic state. And what could have been more appropriate, to sing of tears, her tears, and Beethoven's tears as she imagined his coffin being lowered. Yes, lowered, *before the earth drinks them in.*

A devout Catholic now in her 47th year and one of Frankfurt's most notable citizens, Toni had accepted her fate with a degree of equanimity that would have been impossible when she was younger and struggling. Now that Beethoven, or "B" as he was known to all of his friends in Vienna, had started on his own journey to the Fields of Elysium, Toni could imagine no better celebration of his life than to bring her son to this concert which she had played more than a small hand in organizing. Toni, who believed in the healing power of music, verily wanted to bathe Karl Josef in a waterfall of musical vibrations by Beethoven, her beloved friend whom she would never see again and who would never meet this child—a pity. That a copy of the *Opus 130 Quartet* had just arrived by post a few days earlier made the event that much more special. The sixth and final movement of the quartet was not only the very last composition Beethoven ever inscribed on paper, virtually no one had ever heard it played. And with the *Trios* being the first B ever published, Toni ensured that the performance would cover the full span of his musical endeavors.

There was a time in her life after the death of her father back in her hometown of Vienna when Toni was often ailing for weeks at a time, suffering to such an extent that she would withdraw to her room. Wracked by headaches, depression, and fatigue, there she would remain indisposed, unfit to see anybody. On such occasions Beethoven would nonetheless come almost daily to the forty-room

Birkenstock family mansion in the heart of the old city. Without any fanfare or discussion, B would seat himself at the piano in her antechamber and improvise, saying only, *"Now we will talk to each other in tones."* Whenever B spoke to her in this musical language, Toni felt as if she were listening to a choir of angels celebrating the entrance of her poor, deceased father into the world of light. She had not known that there was such power in music, until Beethoven guided her through it with compassion and grace.

She believed in her heart that a spiritual and emotional communion existed between certain people even before they were introduced or knew each other. And once they had met, they would understand each other in an instant. Reflections about events or other people would have brought them to similar convictions and conclusions which did not have to be verbalized. So it had been between her and Beethoven ever since those precious days they had spent together. Ordinary people did not enter into such relationships, even if one strove to bring them in. They could not grasp these affinities.

Beethoven became, for her, one of the dearest of friends and more . . . Toni understood B's nature to be simple, noble, and good-natured. How could anyone listen to his piano compositions such as the *Pathetique,* or the *Sonata in C-sharp minor* that was later to become more popularly known as the "*Moonlight Sonata,*" and not grasp the depth of emotions B held in his soul. His tenderheartedness was manifested through this spontaneous playing. It was if he had his own urgent need to alleviate her suffering, something which he was able to do for her with music so transcendent that she imagined it could even uplift the spirits of angels in paradise. After having received such solace and comfort from him, Toni would often begin to sob. Through this process her grief found both expression and relief. B would continue playing until her tears had exhausted themselves. When he was finished, B would wipe her cheeks dry, then press her hands in his. Most days he would leave as he had come, quietly and without taking notice of anybody else. Yes, on most days he would leave quietly, but not every day. . . . And those other days, the days he would take her, those were the ones Toni savored in her memories most of all.

During his life, Beethoven had composed over 600 works, many of which Toni adored, including two—the *Piano Sonata in C-minor, Opus 111* and the *Thirty-Three Variations on a Waltz by Diabelli, Opus 120*—that he had dedicated to her, and the *Piano Sonata in E-major, Opus 109,* whose dedicatee was her eldest daughter, Maximiliane. But the ones that held a special place in her heart were the *Opus One Piano Trios.* They were his first published compositions and more significantly, the first of his works she had ever heard way back when she was a lonely, awkward, and shy 15-year-old girl recently returned from the cloistered isolation of a convent school.

Despite the fact that the *Opus One Trios* had given joy to thousands of listeners, it thoroughly annoyed Beethoven that she thought so highly of them. When she asked him why, he would respond that he could produce much better works now. Like most artists, B always thought his latest compositions were his best because he could always see the flaws and limitations of his earlier ones. Nonetheless, Toni never let B's grumblings about his own works get in the way of her pleasures.

At the time of his death, Toni's father, Joseph von Birkenstock, was one of the richest men in Austria and famous for his extensive art collection. Birkenstock, who had been the honored and devoted Counselor to the late Emperor Joseph II, was a well-dressed, grave-looking man with prominent features who walked with a bamboo cane at a measured and stately gait. Her father could be very charming, knew a lot about everything, and visitors to their home always enjoyed his company. Birkenstock cared little for modern affectations and after he retired from active service, he was almost solely preoccupied with his collections and antiquities. Toni grew up in their Vienna mansion surrounded by the artistic visions of Rembrandt, Raphael, Durer, Van Dyke, and dozens of others Birkenstock had acquired.

But life changed for Toni when her mother died. She was only

8 years old, a frail redhead with china-white skin when, like an orphan, her father sent her away to the Ursuline Cloister in Pressburg. Intensely lonely and separated from everyone she loved, she would write him, *"Farewell, dear, dear, dearest Papa, please write me soon. It is my only happiness and consolation."* As an anodyne to her despair and isolation, Toni sought to please the convent sisters. Her education included English, Italian, and the classics as well as a thorough reading of the German and English romantic writers. Toni took voice lessons—she was particularly fond of Mozart's arias—and also excelled at playing the guitar, the cello, and the pianoforte. At all times she followed orders, behaved properly, and was the top student not so much for herself but rather to make her superiors happy. Nonetheless, Toni felt like a mouse—invisible, unseen, and certainly, never noticed.

Several times a year her father would visit the cloister and for weeks afterward she would dream that he would return to rescue her. But he didn't. As she grew older and ever more isolated, Toni imagined that if she deferred to others, behaved properly, and was simply perfect enough, Birkenstock would take her home. She would write in her diary, *"She who lives by the good name of the father is like a new fruit of the same tree. Happy is the daughter who does not live far from an old hearth in which the flame burns as if it had never been extinguished."*

Despite Toni's unhappiness and yearnings, Birkenstock would leave her cloistered for seven years, until such time as he considered her marriageable. He wrote to her with the news that he was bringing her home, *"Come to your father's arms, after so long a parting, sweet child."*

At 15 Toni was, if nothing else, an obedient daughter. Grateful to be free of the closed world of the convent, she was only too willing to comply with her father's every wish if it meant she could stay in Vienna. She added this prayer to her diary, *"Remain in your homeland. Remain even in your hometown. If possible, remain in your father's house. Blessed is the house where the industriousness and the virtues of the parents never depart."*

One of the first gatherings Birkenstock took her to after her return home was a musical soiree held at the Vienna palace of Princess Christiane Lichnowsky and her husband, Prince Carl Lichnowsky, who were known far and wide as the champions and patrons of Mozart. Although the program was to feature a touring singer originally from Bonn, Magdalena Willmann, performing a selection of arias by Mozart, Princess Christiane had informed Toni's father that they would also be among the first to hear several trios dedicated to her husband and performed by a young pianist the Lichnowsky's had taken into their household.

Toni felt as out of place at the Lichnowsky's as her crippled son, Karl Josef, would have been dancing a ballet on the stage of the Frankfurt Opera House. Lacking any maternal—or even feminine—guidance, as to what to wear or how to dress that day, she picked out her wardrobe so as to be as inconspicuous as possible, right down to bonnet she wore to not only hide her long red locks, but to shield her face as well. In other words, she had all the stylistic flair of a cloistered nun. Her only concession to beauty was a simple gold pendant necklace she wore that featured an oversized black and white pearl.

The musical events of the day had already begun when Toni and her father arrived more than fashionably late. Lichnowsky's servant led them down corridors and through rooms until they came to the grand salon adorned with silken draperies and fitted out with chandeliers lavishly supplied with candles. On the walls hung rich, splendidly colorful oil paintings by the great masters mounted in broad, glittering golden frames which bespoke the lofty artistic instincts as well as the wealth of the Lichnowsky family. Birkenstock was immediately drawn into a swirl of greetings and conversations in an antechamber and as had long been his habit, he left his daughter to fend for herself. The young Antonie fell into the only role the Ursulines had trained her for, that of a wallflower. More than simply shy and timid, she was terrified by the crowds. She hastily positioned herself as far from anyone as possible in a discreet nook surrounded by potted plants, where she hoped no one would notice her.

But another young woman did . . . only a few years older than Toni, the stylishly dressed blond who wore a high-waist Empire gown—the latest in Paris fashions—introduced herself as Sophia. She handed Toni a glass of champagne.

"And you must be Antonie," Sophia said, more a statement than a question. "Your father said to expect you here."

While Sophia proved to be both charming and helpful in identifying the many personages present at the soiree, she was also full of probing questions for which Toni had no answers, only nods and the occasional shake of her head. Though their conversation was decidedly one-sided, Toni did learn much, including the identity of the musicians currently playing a quintet chamber ensemble piece that neither she nor Sophia recognized.

On first violin was the esteemed master himself, Josef Haydn. Their host, Prince Lichnowsky, played second violin and at the keyboard was his wife, the Princess Christiane Lichnowsky. Their brother-in-law, Count Razumovsky, played viola. On cello was Prince Lobkowitz. Although the piece was executed with a fair amount of verve and expertise, its very substance Toni found stiff, mechanistic, and lacking heart. At the Ursuline cloisters, Toni had spent a fair number of years studying the Spanish and Italian guitar masters whose music had a vitality and genuineness which was absent in the staid music of the Viennese. She yearned to hear something with verve such as a Vivaldi concerto or with true heart such as the promised Mozart arias.

Although the champagne was delightful and the music pleasant, Antonie felt trapped by Sophia's incessant questions and chatter. Too timid to break off the conversation and leave, Toni instead feigned interest while letting her eyes wander. She hoped her father would reappear to rescue her but when that did not happen, she found herself staring into another antechamber at a stunningly beautiful woman with dark, almond-shaped eyes, thick black hair, and perfect rosy-cheeked skin. The woman, who wore an exquisite Empire gown of black silk embroidered with silver thread over a pair of matching high-heeled boots, was with two well-dressed men, one slightly balding and the other with thick and wild dark hair. They were laughing and obviously having a good time. They were too far away for her to hear their conversation, but the affectionate way in which the woman leaned into the dark-haired man sitting closest to her was readily apparent. There was something about this couple that bespoke great intimacy.

"That's Magdalena Willmann, today's singer," said Sophia, who was clearly keen enough to understand both what Toni was thinking and what she was doing. "From Bonn. On tour. Isn't she just gorgeous?"

Ever embarrassed that Sophia had read her mind, Toni could only nod and look away. Still, she wondered if the man at Willmann's side was indeed Mozart himself. That would please her enormously, to meet the great master composer himself.

Just then, the quintet ended. As the assembled guests thundered down with applause, the players left their seats. And that must have been the signal Magdalena was waiting for.

With the dark-haired man on her arm, the singer started out of the antechamber. The two were still chatting affectionately as they passed by Toni.

She overheard the dark-haired man offhandedly suggest to Willmann, "We should marry, yes? And run off to a villa in Sicily?" To which the singer replied, first with a kiss to his cheek and then a shake of her head, "Of course not. You're ugly . . . and half-crazy!"

The singer's rejection only made the dark-haired man and his friend laugh ever more so as they passed by Toni and headed toward the front of the grand salon.

The dark-haired man seated himself at the pianoforte while Magdalena Willmann took center stage and began to sing Dona Anna's aria from Mozart's *Don Giovanni*: *Or sai chi l'onore Rapire a me volse—Now you know who is the one trying to rob me of my honor.*

"Shadows of midnight all around me were gathered;
In my own quiet chamber
Sitting alone,
By misadventure and dreaming,
When all at once there came in, wrapped in a mantle,
A man, whom for the moment I had taken for thee.
But soon I had discovered
How great was my error!"

When Toni, in a whisper, asked Sophia if the pianist was Mozart, the other woman shook her head with astonishment.

"Mozart?" Sophia replied, "Where have you been, my dear girl? Mozart has been dead for four years."

Once more Toni was stunned and embarrassed by her ignorance, especially considering that at school she knew herself academically to be far ahead of the other girls. Mozart was four years gone and not a word of real news had ever come to her at the Ursuline Cloisters? The degree of isolation she had experienced while away staggered her. As much as she loved her father, she vowed she would never live in such ignorance again.

After taking a deep breath to summon up courage, Toni turned back to Sophia and asked her bluntly, "Who are you and what do you want with me?"

"Your father did not inform you?" Sophia asked.

"Clearly not." Toni snapped back, still feeling an inner rage.

"Oh, my dear, my apology. One would have thought Baron von Birkenstock would have—"

Toni cut her off. "I asked about you, not my father."

The other woman was taken aback. "I'm Sophia Brentano, sister to *Herr* Franz Brentano of Frankfurt. And to be blunt, with your father's blessings, I am here to meet you on behalf of my brother who is one of the leading merchants of that city."

"So I'm to be married off and sent to Frankfurt?" Toni was completely shaken by this news and began to hyperventilate.

"Negotiations are ongoing. And you did not know?"

"No," Toni said, struggling to control her breathing. She knew she knew nothing and if she had had the courage she would have fled the palace right then and there.

Sophia took her by the arm and led her away from the grand salon, "Come, my dear, I understand how you feel. All this must come as a shock. Let's walk."

In nearly total silence they strolled at random through room after room at the palace until at last they came to a solarium garden. Sophia had Toni sit on a bench while she fetched water from a nearby fountain. For her part, Toni closed her eyes and focused on breathing in and out as slowly and steadily as possible. All she wanted to do was to settle her nerves and push away the fog of confusion that obscured her own thoughts. As she began to calm, she became increasingly aware of the sounds of nature around her. First was the soft flow of water in the fountain; then the chirping of birds; then the hum and buzz of bees and insects flying by; and then, from not too far off, the plaintiff yet exquisite voice of Magdalena Willmann harmonizing with a pianoforte.

> *"Fear and doubting quite distract me,*
> *All my head is in confusion,*
> *It is a vision, a vile delusion!*
> *Be this masking, be this masking never forgot!"*

When at last Toni regained control of herself, Sophia handed her the water.

"Thank you," she said, as she realized their wander through the palace had taken them full circle. The solarium was immediately adjacent to the grand salon. The windows were open and although they could not see the performers, the tree-shaded solarium provided perhaps the most natural and beautiful environment Toni could have imagined to listen to her Mozart.

Though still digesting the shocks of the day, the beauty of the music itself allowed Toni to finally rest at peace.

After Willmann concluded her arias to the sounds of rapturous applause, Sophia broke the silence and asked Toni, "Do you want to go back in?"

Toni shook her head. "No. Go in if you must. I feel better listening from here."

"As you wish, my dear," said Sophia who obligingly departed.

Toni was soon rewarded when the first notes of the piano trio jumped out at her. Later she would learn this was Beethoven's *Opus One, Number One in E-flat major.*

The opening *allegro* was lovely and alive, everything Toni could have wanted. It felt familiar, like Mozart, but different, energized and produced on a grand scale. In length alone the *Trios* were three or four times longer than anything anyone else had composed. The *largo* that followed was full of warmth and deep, soulful bowing by the strings. And the *scherzo*—it was just brilliant. Rising up after a quiet opening, it was laden with wonderful textures and unexpected turns. These led to a rousing finale so inspired that even the birds in the garden joined in singing along.

Looking back at that day with three decades of hindsight, Toni could only laugh at the earlier self she saw and wondered what her life might have been had she been raised differently—not the shy, all too well-behaved and sheltered girl who stayed in the garden all day. No, she did not go back inside until Baron von Birkenstock finally arrived to take her home. And no, she did not meet Beethoven—at least not then. It would be another fifteen years before that happened and when it did, her father was dead and she was already the depressed and despairing wife of Franz Brentano, merchant of Frankfurt, and the mother of his four children.

And here she was now listening with equal joy to those same three *Trios* in her private box at the Frankfurt Opera House with her fifth child, the brown-eyed, brown-haired Karl Josef. Despite all his handicaps, her son was nothing if not a portrait of ecstasy listening to the music of Beethoven. Moments of tranquility with Karl Josef were rare enough. That he was calm and blissfully attentive to what seemed like every note; that he smiled and waved his index fingers in time to the music; that he was truly happy, all that was beyond belief and further testament to the healing power of B's music.

The *Second Trio in G major* was as charming, grand in scale and unique in that B gave equal voices to all three instruments. The violin and cello attained parity with the piano as the three played off of one another. This had not been done before, not by Mozart, not by Haydn. For B, a trio was no longer about the piano as performer supported by two amateur accompanists. Instead it became a conversation between three equals who spoke to one another in the language of tones and what they said had meaning and content. But it was not the literal language of the spoken or written word; it was a primal language, one derived from the infinite vibrations and natural tones that emerged out of the very fabric of creation. In his first publication B, who was still only 24 years old, had achieved something his two esteemed predecessors had never even conceptualized, and this revolutionary step, small and insignificant as it might have seemed at the time, would go on to characterize virtually all of his later work. Single-handedly, B had changed the rules. Music was no longer about pretty forms and structures. Instead, form and structure became vehicles subordinate to the expressive needs of a musical composition.

And perhaps Haydn unconsciously recognized this and found it discomforting—as did many of those Beethoven would go on to characterize as his enemies. Years later B would tell Toni how the older composer strongly suggested that Beethoven not publish the third of the three *Trios*, which carried the concept of parity and personal drama even further.

That last *Trio*, which was set in C minor, a key Beethoven would come to use often in his later works, including his *5th Symphony*, topped off the set with its wild and raucous four movements. The only moment of calm moderation came in its brief *Andante Cantabile*. Full of turbulence and emotional tension, the *Trio* was the one

B liked the most, particularly since it laid out the path he would follow in so many of his later, more famous compositions. That Haydn could not fully grasp what B was attempting—and successfully so here—did not surprise Toni at all. In hindsight, she understood that the seeds of the revolution that transformed music from the sedate confines of eighteenth-century Viennese classicism to the dramatic romanticism of the nineteenth century were planted that night in that third *Trio*. Whereas boring old Haydn remained a champion of form over emotions, her Beethoven understood that form had to be contextual and adaptable to the needs and sensibilities of each composition. It was, Toni imagined, as if Haydn and his contemporaries wrote for the cloistered realms she had just escaped while her Beethoven composed with a passion for life in all its emotional complexities. Music would never be the same. She loved it, then and now.

And so did Karl Josef. She had never seen her son happier than when he was listening to Beethoven, which led her to wonder if, in his sadly disordered mind, he could still have the ability to comprehend a musical reality that had even eluded her. Though B had never met the boy, she wondered if there was a spiritual and emotional communion between them. Did they meet and share perceptions in the ethereal realm of music? Did they understand each other in the instant of each note, of each chord? Toni wondered if she could grasp the affinities that might exist between the two of them, but then, realizing the impossibility of such a chore, she gave up. Better to sit back in her chair, watch Karl Josef smile blissfully, and enjoy the performance. Yes, her Beethoven was gone but there was no denying he had brought one day, one day of pure joy into the life of this child.

Both mother and son continued on listening in a state of happy abandon until the performers reached the fourth movement of the *Opus 130 String Quartet, Alle Danza Tedesca—A Dance in the German Style*. Upon hearing the sweet and gentle rhythms of this peasant dance, a Landler, Toni sat bolt upright. The melody was so familiar and it took her a moment to recall why. So many years before, when B had consoled her following the death of her father, the *Danza*

Tedesca was one of the improvisations he had played for her regularly on the pianoforte, so much so that she associated it with the sounds of paradise. Such a gift. Though it brought tears to her eyes, it leavened her heart with a deep, deep and abiding aura of contentment.

And it had a similar impact upon Karl Josef. Out of the corner of her eye, she caught the boy struggling to get up from his wheelchair with the use of his bamboo cane that had once belonged to his father. With the help of her servants, she quickly came to his assistance. Together they stood Karl Josef upright. With the pride of a gallant courtier, the young man with his wild brown hair and dark eyes reached out to his mother and put his arms around her. And while the string quartet serenaded them, together mother and son danced to the sounds of Elysium, *Alle Danza Tedesca.*

Oh, to gather the tears of our love,
Before the earth drinks them in.

Toni understood that Beethoven had left her once again, but this time, he left her at the gates of paradise. And what could be better than that?

CHAPTER 5

Bonaparte

As a younger man, naïve to the ways of demagogues and demons, I was, like many others of my generation including Kant, Schiller, and Goethe, so swept up in the radical fervor of "*Liberté, Égalité, Fraternite,*" that I confess to having bowed in admiration of Napoleon. I not only held him in the highest regard and thought him comparable to the most noble of ancient Roman Consuls, I even composed one of my most revolutionary symphonies, *Bonaparte,* in his honor.

Initially hadn't we all viewed this Napoleon as not only a hero but a liberator who dismantled the aristocracy in every territory his *Grande Armée* conquered? All Europe—save the kings and their kind who despised him for obvious reasons—had looked up to him. He was the epitome of our era of Enlightenment, *Das Zeitalter der Aufklarung, L'age d'Eclaircissement,* and like me, an entirely self-made man who rose to preeminence not by a fortunate birth but by dint of his own sweat. The press called him a "dealer of hope" who threw off the yoke of the royals. He convinced us all that the *Ancien Régimes* of the old Europe would forever be destroyed, and a new world, one where *Alle Menschen werden Brüder,* one where the rights of all citizens were respected, would replace it.

Though many in Vienna feared the Hapsburgs' secret police, all anyone whispered about over coffee and wine in the cafes of the old capital was how Napoleon not only ended feudalism and the abuses of the common man by the royals in France, he also swept away the *Ancien Régime* in the provinces of Italy, the German states, Poland,

and the Low Lands, and established free republics where we were all equal before the law. Equal, consider it—we were all equal to rise and fall by our own merits. It was his new code of justice, the Napoleonic Code, which became part of the fabric of laws that protected every citizen throughout the continent—excepting England, Russia, and our Hapsburgs' Austrian empire.

Bonaparte even broke the thousand year stranglehold of a corrupt church that choked independent thought by granting full religious freedom to all. *Mein Gott,* in every city his troops liberated, Napoleon even ordered the gates of the Jewish ghettos, which held Hebrews as if in slave quarters, ripped down. His command, repeated in town after town, gave rise to rumors that Napoleon's Ligurian ancestors were in fact originally Spanish *Conversos* who had fled the Inquisition of 1492. True or not, my friend Rahel was one of those who approved of his action. Most brain-owners were. Rahel once wrote me, "*What for a long period of my life has been the source of my greatest shame, my most bitter grief and misfortune—to be born a Jewess—I would not at any price now wish to miss.*"

There was much to love about Bonaparte and the Revolution itself but truth be known, after his great betrayal, I—like so many others—became furious with him. I had to calculate that among my enemies who were not few in number I must now also add this deceiver, this so-called "Emperor." When at last his armies were defeated at Vittoria in Spain at the hands of the English under Lord Wellington, had I not written the *Battle Symphony* to celebrate his demise, a celebration I shared with all the statesman and dignitaries who had assembled at the great Congress of Vienna?

And now he has the audacity to commandeer my dream. As I thought back to the premier of *Fidelio,* why hadn't I recognized Napoleon when he was disguised as that little corporal who sat center stage and applauded? Those silver tipped boots should have given him away.

Bonaparte's blue-grey eyes—those of a natural born commander—were indeed piercing and they sparkled with a look of recognition that said he'd been expecting me. And now I had to confront him, the one I once thought exiled and dead. . . . Ja, dead.

What omen does his apparition portend? Something ominous? Or something delicious to be savored? And how should I approach him? In fear and wonder as one might a ghost? Or in wariness and with courage as Lord Wellington's army had before engaging him in combat?

In the end I settled on approaching him with an attitude taught me as a teenager in Bonn by my first teacher, Herr Neefe. What he had said was simply this: "When confronting either a new or difficult composition or when facing an unruly or even hostile audience, bow or nod ever so slightly in the direction of the sheet music *mit unerschütterlicher Gelassenheit*—imperturbable nonchalance." The "nod" he went on to say was not for them but for me, a silent gesture which I was to use to draw mental focus away from all distractions, external or otherwise, and to shift my consciousness to the task at hand. "Embrace that moment," Neefe would say. "Bring the sole focus of your very being—your soul, your consciousness—into the task at hand. Sole for soul. If you learn nothing else from me, let it be that."

And so, thanking Herr Neefe, I walked steadily toward Napoleon, confident, firm, and nurtured by courage.

But the General, perhaps sensing my hostility, had other plans afoot. As I neared the rocks where he sat, Bonaparte waved his right hand around as if commanding the heavens and suddenly a great swirl of desert wind twisted itself out of the clouds. This monstrous dust devil spun like a cyclone. Sand flew everywhere, stinging my body, forcing me to close my eyes and shield my face.

The winds roared and howled about me but of course I could not hear them, I only felt the titanic force of a tornado spinning about me. I gripped my cane tightly and huddled in darkness and silence. Even so, as I clung tightly to the bamboo handle, a vision of Fanny's firm young hips flashed though my memories—oh, how lovely it was to stand with my arm around her waist. So trim, so dainty, so sweet. Why had I abandoned her? Could happiness have been mine then and with her? Or with any woman from my past?

When at last the storm subsided I turned my thoughts back to the present situation and opened my eyes. Even Herr Neefe could not have prepared me for this; my world was transformed again. It was as if Brahma's avatar Krishna from the Bhagavad Gita had taken a lithograph out of the pages of the Description de l'Égypte and used his breath to manifest it into life. Here we were in an Egyptian oasis surrounded by vast deserts. All it lacked was a young Gerhard—my good friend Steffen von Breuning's son—allowing me to read his lips while I lay in my deathbed as he narrated what would happen next. With the enthusiasm of a teenager, Gerhard would have described the coconut and date palms and the banana trees and grape vines growing tenaciously in their shade. He'd paint a portrait in words noting how oceans of sand were topped off by pyramids marking a distant horizon. Closer in to this tiny oasis, but still a little ways off and down a steep cliff, were the silt-laden waters of the Nile. Gerhard would surely have described with relish how the river was no doubt filled with man-eating crocodiles. He was a good boy, the son I wish I had had instead of the madness of a custody war over my brother's orphaned child . . . but that is a complaint for another day.

Gerhard had once read to me that Napoleon was born under the sign of Leo, and that his birth name meant "Lion of the Desert" in his native Corsican dialect. When Napoleon fought the Ottomans for control of Egypt and the Holy Land, the natives referred to him as the *Sultan El Kabir*—the "Sultan who is Commander-in-Chief." Before me this Napoleon—who took to the desert as some men take to the sea—had been transformed as well. The "Sultan" was garbed as if yet another historic lithograph had come to life: He sat cross-legged on his rock with a scimitar strapped round his waist and wore the flowing white robes, head scarf, and pantaloons he adapted while ruling Egypt.

Within arm's reach and to the right of the "Sultan" was the vertical slit entrance to the Temple of Isis. A vertical slit, how appropriate. And if I needed to force my way past him to enter Isis's Temple, would this beast of a man fight fiercely?

Bonaparte waived me forward. In his lap was a hefty tome of a book opened to a blank page. Though his wave appeared a calm gesture of friendship, the General was known for his uniquely unconventional feints and surprise attacks. Was this one such deception? It's a pity that I did not understand the art of war as well as I did that of music; I would have used my skills to conquer this *Sultan El Kabir* straight off.

I nodded as *Herr* Neefe advised and *mit unerschütterlicher Gelassenheit,* walked closer.

Behind Napoleon and wrought from a native stone that at first glance rendered them practically invisible against the desert sands were endless rows of bookcases filled with what must have been hundreds of thousands of leather-bound volumes seemingly encompassing all the world's knowledge. Was this the long-lost Library of Alexandria? Had the scientists of *El Kabir's* expeditionary force found that as well? Or perhaps the books were the General's own private collection. According to Sir Walter Scott's history, Napoleon was not only a well-read man, fond of quoting everyone from Julius Caesar to the *Analects of Confucius,* he even brought books along when heading out on military campaigns. Gerhard said Napoleon was also an author who had written several novels and stories of his own. I would have loved to spend much time perusing his collected works, particularly the texts of Confucius and Lao Tzu, imagining they would have much to offer on the subject of the *Tao* of which I had little knowledge, but there were clearly more pressing issues.

Beside Bonaparte was a teapot nestled on a brazier. In his hand was a length of straw of the type used by the ancient Israelis to build bricks for the Pharaohs' temples. Napoleon reached out with the straw toward the narrow vertical orifice that opened into Isis's sacred space and the tip immediately—almost violently—burst into flame. With it Napoleon nonchalantly set a flame burning under the teapot.

I shook my head in amazement—had I just witnessed the General use the sacred fire of Isis—the Goddess's fire of rebirth—to ignite the burner beneath the teapot? And that fire—would I be capable of passing through that self-same flame to enter her temple?

Perhaps in deference to my deafness, Napoleon said nothing, but motioned for me to sit on a stone across from him. I reached for a conversation book and pencil, but Bonaparte waived them off. Only after I sat down, did he at last speak.

Naturlich, I watched his lips and though I heard nothing as they moved, yet another most peculiar thing happened in this dream already filled with an endless cascade of other-worldly events. When his lips parted, butterflies, little ones—miniature versions of the giants that had carried me to India and beyond—flew out of his mouth. And then these rainbowed beauties swirled around and shaped themselves into letters. The letters framed words and the words sentences. I could read them clearly as they floated in space before ultimately disappearing.

Was this how we were going to communicate? Quaint, charming, pretty, but effective? Oh how I longed for the days of my youth when I could simply speak, hear, and be heard.

Nonetheless, this is how our conversation began and this is what he said through the medium of butterflies:

"Mon Dieu, Monsieur—my God, man—how extravagant you are, throwing away women like that. Someday they may be scarce."

"What?" I replied aloud. "Are you speaking of my muse, Isis?"

He answered with his army of butterflies spelling out the names of lovers lost to me over a lifetime, "Toni, Leonore, Magdalena, Josephine," *und so weiter,* and so on, until the last name lingered and hung in the air between us, "Isis."

"Where is Isis? What have you done with her?"

"Your muse? You must know Isis exists only in your imagination," the butterflies wrote, "So of course, if you are here, she's here."

"And where are we?" I demanded, not willing to yield an inch to Bonaparte. I may not have known the arts of war, but after fifty-six years of life, it was already in my nature to be as tough-minded, stubborn, and obstinate as he was, if not more so.

"We are here," the butterflies wrote.

"Here?

"We are here. Here is where you are," *El Kabir* indicated with another sweep of his arms and though we sat in daylight, above us a starry canopy sparkled in a spectacular night sky. Was there still a loving Father above to safeguard us?

"Why are you here in my dream?" I asked.

"This is not a dream. Come, B—may I call you B as your friends do? Come have a cup of tea."

"Not a dream? I don't believe you." I said.

"Then don't. Belief is optional."

"Are we in Elysium? The Gods' paradise?"

"You ask a lot of questions for one so arrogant," Napoleon said, "particularly someone who has made such a shamble of his life."

"Must you mock me too? Is there no release from this suffering? Don't I have any control over my own dream?"

"Consider what you are asking. Even Socrates said, *"To know yourself, is the most difficult task conceivable."* And joy? One day of joy? That's what you want?"

"Ja. That is all I want before I die. One day of joy."

"Don't you understand anything?" Napoleon set two cups before us, "Once you had the foresight to manifest a truth of life in *Fidelio* that women can be our rescuers. *Oui,* you are correct, I did see your opera performed in Vienna. How can it be then that you do not understand that in times of great crisis, it is the fate of men that women—the true daughters of Elysium—appear to soften our misfortunes. Did you compose that by accident? I think not. But you, *Gesu,* you've thrown them all away. Where's the joy in that?"

Much as I hated to admit Bonaparte was right, he was. Never did my own music produce such an effect upon me; even now when I recall *Fidelio,* it still costs me a tear. . . . And my history with women? A disaster of my own making. . . . I acknowledged as much as the General opened the lid and inspected the contents of the teapot.

The steaming amber liquid resembled no beverage I'd ever known before.

"Soma," he said as if knowing my thoughts, "Nectar of the Gods. You must grasp firmly and with absolute resolve that to acquire knowledge without wisdom is akin to tossing pearls into a dung heap. We cannot see the whole of what we look at from one little corner. Now that you are here and perhaps open to seeing, this will help."

I watched as Napoleon, or "N" as I decided I was going to address him if he was going to be familiar and call me "B," began to fill my cup with this Nectar of the Gods. It had a distinctly primal, earthy aroma. As I reached for my cup, N kept pouring. The steaming liquid flowed over the top of the cup, stinging my hand.

I jumped back. "What are you doing?"

Ever so calmly the butterflies floated out of his mouth and inscribed his response, "The teacup is like your mind. How can anyone add to it if it's already full?"

"Why are you doing this to me?"

"You ask questions, but you're not ready to hear the answers."

"Hear the answers? I am deaf, accursedly deaf, a victim of God's cruel joke and you want to play another on me?"

"*Mon ami*, my friend, your inability to hear is the least of your obstacles."

Was this some battle tactic? Insult me? Push me out of equilibrium? Better to take control and redirect our conversation. "I came here for the comfort of my muse, not you."

"Art thou blind as well, *Monsieur*? Doesn't one's muse always appear when needed? Or would you prefer this?"

N snapped his fingers and instantly disappeared from my sight, replaced by Isis garbed as if an Arabian woman replete with headscarf and veil.

"Ja!" I thought, she is here. How strange to realize though, that in all my imaginings of my muse, I'd never seen her with clothes on. Just a woman perfected in all her welcoming nakedness.

However, as I reached out to lift the veil off my muse, any hope I held of finding compassion in her arms vanished. Like N, she too instantly disappeared and in her stead was a ghoulish and ghostly young girl with scraggly wet hair flecked with dirt and mud. Had this creature just crawled out of a grave? An involuntary shudder swept through me. *Nein*, this was not my muse. The apparition before me, the one who seemingly had escaped from the land of the dead, was none other than my own little sister, Margaretha.

Her eyes embraced me with a look filled with unrelenting pain and anguish. She sang, and though I could not hear her words, they nonetheless entered my consciousness directly, like daggers without any need for intermediaries, butterflies or otherwise. How could I not know the melody—it was a coarse, plaintive, and bitter rendering of my *Ode to Joy*.

"*You could have saved me,*" she sang of tragedies of oh so many years ago. "*Why didn't you help me?*"

I was but a man-child then and she much younger than she appeared now, just a toddler.

"Darkness parts those whom sweet custom had united. You abandoned me," she screeched. The truth of her words buried itself in my heart like a knife ripping flesh. *"You were with HER, with HER. You who have failed thus, must steal away alone and in tears."*

Her recrimination set the guilt inside me boiling. I had, hadn't I? A November so long ago. It was too much to endure. Closing my eyes, burying my head in my hands, I sobbed uncontrollably until a consoling hand touched my shoulder.

Hoping once and for all for Margaretha's forgiveness, hoping for a return of her gentle affection, I sought out her eyes but instead only found Napoleon. The *Sultan El Kebir* was back. My sister was gone—along with any chance to extirpate my guilt. What cruelty I am continually forced to confront in my own dreams.

N raised his tea cup in a toast, *"Salut, mon ami*. The longest journey begins with the first step."

I followed in kind though I am still not sure why, *"Prosit."* I imbibed the warm drink. While the soma slid down my throat as smooth as a delicate liqueur, it tasted like fermented twigs and mushrooms. And almost immediately it set my head spinning. Had I been drugged?

N spoke again but with my head and scalp buzzing from the soma, I could hardly read the language of the butterflies. I struggled to understand everything he said.

"I know you wrote your *Third Symphony* about me, the "*Eroica*"—"*Bonaparte*"—you called it at first. But the one I love the best is the *Ninth*."

"The *Ninth*? But you were dead when I wrote that."

"I may be dead, but I am not deaf. One virtue of Elysium is that I can listen to any piece of music anytime I want."

Ouch. *"Dead, but not deaf."* Could he not twist the blade any harder? Indeed I composed the *Ninth, the Choral Symphony*, my "*Ode to Joy*," while totally deaf, such was God's cruel irony. The "*Ode*" was my most beloved work, one my muse inspired me to create as a paean to Margaretha. It was our secret, our dirty little secret that the melody was based upon *"eine kleine"* ditty Margaretha hummed the sing-song way toddlers do. Yet poor old, deaf Beethoven—I have never ever heard the "*Ode*" sung aloud. Why? Why have I been so cursed? Why has even the simplest joy of hearing that chorus been denied me?

N held up the book that had been in his lap. "That's not in here."

"What are you reading?"

"Your biography. Nowhere does it say that your "*Ode to Joy*" was inspired by Margaretha."

I had not said that aloud. Nor had I ever told this to anyone. Yet, this Napoleon, this creature was reading my mind. Was it the soma?

"I heard that," N acknowledged. "And yes, it is the soma. With its blessings and good fortune, you will now see many things, which is why it is called a gift of the gods. Your journey, *mon ami*, is just beginning."

Mein Gott, he was reading my mind.

I grabbed the book out of his hands and looked at the cover, *Biog-*

raphie von Ludwig van Beethoven, Verfasst von Anton Schindler, Munster, 1840. Written by Schindler in 1840? Thirteen years in the future. What was that all about?

"Es ist Scheisse," I thought, no longer having to speak words aloud. "Anton Schindler *ist Scheisse*. His book *ist Scheisse*. The man is a lying piece of shit who knows nothing about me or my life."

N heard me and now through the magic of the soma I grasped N's thoughts through direct communion. *"Merde!"* exclaimed the General. "Schindler claims to have been your private secretary for many years and that on your death bed you authorized him to write a biography."

"*Scheisse*. Whatever he's written, it's worthless excrement. The man is a liar and a thief. If we'd even spoken thrice, it would be an exaggeration." I wasn't going to ask how it got here or why Napoleon had a book from the future, though I thought I perceived N mumble something about having excellent foresight. Even in direct communion people still mumbled. Fascinating.

"Never mention his name again," I declared—glad to be forever free of any talk about this moron Schindler. I threw the book over my shoulder. It sailed through the air directly into the entryway of Isis's temple, where it burst into flames. The Goddess's fire consumed the text so completely that little was left except a small cloud of ash that fluttered down and away like so many brown moths.

Nein, not like moths. The ash became moths. The moths swarmed through the air of the oasis until they settled at last on the lip of the entryway of Isis's Temple and there they spelt out words. *Ja*, words, I should be getting used to this by now. And this is what they wrote:

"He Is Only And Solely Of Himself And To This Only One, All Things Owe Their Existence. I Am That Which Is. I Am All What Is. What Was What Will Be. No Mortal Man Has Ever Lifted My Veil."

I recognized the words. They were ones I had copied out onto a single sheet of paper one night during a particularly introspective time in my life and then placed under the glass of my writing desk beside the Broadwood pianoforte.

Seeing those quotes anew made me all the more anxious to be done with this Napoleon and continue my quest for Isis herself. She will rescue my soul with her boundless compassion, I know it.

"You want to enter her Temple, eh *Monsieur*?

"Certainly Isis can answer my questions better than you."

Napoleon stood up, effectively blocking my entrance to the cave. "So, are you ready for the first step of your journey, to brave Isis's cleansing fire no matter what form it takes?"

"*Ja*," I stood up but leaned heavily on my cane to mitigate the lightheadedness triggered by the soma which caused our every action to float by my eyes as if in slow motion.

"Answer this question and you will pass unmolested."

"And if I refuse or can't?"

"Oh give it a try, you stubborn old codger. What have you got to lose except your life?"

"If it gets me away from you, go ahead."

"Here it is: *What is the sound of a kiss in a time before Creation?*

"You're right. I'm too old and cranky for your riddles."

"*Mon ami*, he who wishes to be reborn must die first. Isn't that the message of your *Third Symphony* where the funeral march is but the second of four movements?"

"Movements? You want movements? I'll give you movements! Out of my way!"

Although our respective gestures feel as if we are stuck in a tub of molasses, I nonetheless startle N with a jab to his chest with the full force of my cane. *El Kabir* staggers backwards. He draws out his scimitar and approaches. Trusting the strength of Fannie's cane, I easily parry his every thrust.

Perhaps I understand more of the art of war than I had imagined. N retreats, then comes back at me again with the exaggerated movements of a sword-swinging mime stuck in slow motion. *Mit unerschütterlicher Gelassenheit,* I wallop his wrist with a lateral blow from the cane and knock the scimitar free. His blade clatters, then shatters on the rocks. Confident, I lunge—perhaps float would be a better description—I float towards N's gut with the tip of the cane, intent upon pushing him aside.

N however spins away just in time to dodge my attack. As I recoup and prepare to strike again, the General keeps spinning, round and round like a child's toy top. Slow at first, then faster and faster until all I can see is a blur of hallucinatory colors—reds, blues, whites, greens, purples. And when at last all motion stops, there is nothing left but a giant chrysalis suspended from, and effectively blocking, the entrance to Isis's Temple.

I poke at the cocoon which, being somewhat translucent, allows me to see an embryo rapidly expanding inside. Abruptly, vibrations, deep and rhythmic as a beating heart shake the air. This thing is alive. I watch as legs, a head, and a torso grow. And arms—four of them. The shaking, now as ponderous as the thunderstorm that initiated this dream, grows in strength. The walls of the temple shake. I struggle to stay upright as the very ground I stand upon trembles with the surging force of an ever intensifying earthquake.

The body growing inside the chrysalis continues to expand in size so quickly that at last the membrane bursts asunder with a volcanic shower of sparks, which ignites fires throughout the oasis. Out from the burning remnants of the cocoon steps Shiva, the Hindoo God of Destruction.

In one of his fours arms Shiva holds a drum—no doubt the source of my dream's earthquakes—with which he beats out the rhythmic vibrations of our little universe. The shaking knocks me to the ground. I look up at Shiva and see in another hand that he holds a ball of fire that glows powerfully as the sun. Shiva looks at me with his piercing blue-grey eyes, the same eyes as Napoleon. He does not speak but his words rumble inside my consciousness with a voice as old as the universe, *"I am the taste of pure water and the brilliance of the sun and moon. I am the sweet fragrance of the earth and the radiance of fire. I am the life in every creature and the hunger of all that is human.*

I am the courage and fear in their souls and the striving of every seeker. I am their sacred words and all vibrations of music in the air. I am time, the greatest destroyer of all. "

I nod knowingly.

"Look not upon me nor away from me, for I am death, the one who devours the world."

Without warning, Shiva hurls the ball of fire in my direction.

I spin aside. His fiery orb crashes into a palm tree, which explodes into flames and ash. Though still drugged by the soma, I nonetheless scramble backwards in retreat. Shiva throws another and the banana trees around me ignite. Smoke fills the oasis. He throws another and the ground before me goes up in flames. With the entire oasis now burning, I flee from the onslaught into a thicket of grapevines on the cliff above the Nile.

With the river my only escape, I prepare to jump. Below, an equal danger waits. A man-eating Nile River crocodile poses with jaws stretched wide-open.

I pray for Isis to come to my rescue. Will my beloved muse appear and rescue me when I most need her? But cruel fate—as it so often did in my life—betrays me. Shiva's drumming shakes the ground so much so that I lose my footing and slip backwards over the edge of the cliff. Only my luck in grabbing onto a grapevine saves me from tumbling into the maw of that croc.

Suspended only by the strength of my arms, I face the certainty of annihilation above and annihilation below.

It is then that I see a reflection of Isis on the iridescent skin of a grape only inches from my lips.

How sweet, she comes for me. . . . Letting go the vine, I reach for my muse . . . gravity does the rest.

Talk about falling for a woman . . .

CHAPTER 6

Eine Kleine Nachtmusik

The Vienna Apartment of Wolfgang Amadeus Mozart, April 1787

"I PREFER my grapes fermented," said Prince Lichnowsky to *Fraulein* Lokitzvarah, as he sipped a sparkling wine from a crystal goblet. "And my women just as effervescent." In his glass he could see a reflection of the young Gypsy woman who straddled his hips and massaged his back. The *Fraulein,* who wore nothing save a lotus flower in her hair, had dense black curls that reached to her narrow waist, half hiding a pair of perfectly pear-shaped breasts that had pleased and comforted him on many a prior night. The long-limbed and lean *Fraulein* Lokitzvarah, whose dark complexion easily revealed her Gypsy heritage with roots that stretched back in time to Persia or India, had the musculature and achingly strong fingers of a well-trained masseuse. She was his favorite, so much so that upon discovering her at the spa in Teplitz he had hired her into his service the year after. All this made the Prince a very happy, a very contented man.

Although they were comfortably ensconced in the drawing room of Mozart's apartment, the scene before Lichnowsky more resembled a bordello—which also pleased him to no end. The Prince, much like his close friends and peers, Counts Razumovsky, Waldstein, and Lobkowitz, knew he was a rascal devoted to enjoying the riches of a life few mere mortals would ever know. And why not? With power, wealth, and taste, was nothing forbidden?

Though it was nigh onto noon, thick drapes blocked any chance of sunlight penetrating the room and the intoxicatingly sweet aroma of perfume still hung in the air. Cushions, blankets, pillows, and the discarded skirts, blouses, and petticoats of seven young women from the girls' choir at St. Stephens covered the floors and couches. Sleeping soundly on and around these piles about the salon were these delightfully uninhibited girls that Mozart had inveigled over to assist in his *Forschung*—research—for his latest opera under construction. The singers' current lack of modesty and attire made *Fraulein* Lokitzvarah with her lotus blossom appear overdressed. While some thought *Don Giovanni*—about a Venetian lothario bent on amorous excess—was inspired by Casanova, the Prince knew better. It could have been him or any one of his compatriots—such was the life they led. Yes, the girls with their red coral lips, nimble tongues, and white, creamy skin had played their parts well. Most were still wrapped innocently enough in one another's arms after a night of dreamy excess with him, with Mozart and with that young Rhinelander—a piano-playing 16-year-old who had turned up somewhat unexpectedly the evening before, bearing an introduction from the Prince's distant cousin, the Elector of Bonn.

It was a good life. Moments earlier *Fraulein* Lokitzvarah and Lichnowsky's livery servants had tiptoed into the apartment right on schedule with trays of steaming hot coffee, meats, bread, cheese, fruits, and the aforementioned sparkling wine. Lichnowsky and Mozart had been fast friends now for a half-dozen years during which time the Prince had used his considerable wealth to serve as Mozart's essential patron and in turn to have Mozart act as his teacher. And though the Prince was proud of the dissolute life he led, Lichnowsky was no mere musical dilatant. He played an excellent violin, composed a bit, and handled the keyboard with finesse as well. He and Mozart were the same age, thirty-one, and shared much the same loves: music, women, wine, and elegant clothes. As a child, Mozart had been the most famous musical prodigy in history. During his grand tours, the young Mozart—the quintessential perfect *wunderkind*—had been received, honored, and showered with gifts by most of the royal families in Europe, including the Hapsburg Empress, Maria Theresa; her daughter and the Queen of France, Marie Antoinette; her son the Emperor Joseph II; and even the Pope himself, Clement XIV.

And these nights of *"Forschung"* which began years earlier when Mozart was composing *The Abduction from the Seraglio* never failed to please the Prince—particularly when the composer's wife, Constanze, was away at the baths in Baden seeking a cure for whatever may have ailed her that week. *Ja, es war ein gutes Leben,* which *Fraulein* Lokitzvarah's fingers made even better as they raked jasmine scented oils over the muscles in his back.

With a mug of coffee before him, Mozart, dressed only in a plush nightshirt, was already standing at an upright writing desk on the far side of the room, oblivious to everyone else around him. Mozart hummed softly as he copied out the ideas that had no doubt floated through his consciousness during the night.

In one of two bird cages off to the side of that desk was Mozart's pet canary. The second cage held a tamed starling. Both were particularly amicable creatures known to sing along—accurately at that—whenever the composer played the piano.

The Prince watched with bemusement as the young Rhinelander stirred and slowly awoke on a sofa, only to realize he was wedged in between Daphne and Wanda, two most naked and *zaftig* choir girls who still slept soundly. The wide-eyed expression on the boy's face told all as he probably no doubt realized where he was and perhaps remembered what had happened during the night. Lichnowsky was certain the boy was a virgin, or at least had been when the pouring of the fruit of the vine and the real *Eine Kleine Nachtmusik*—a little night music—commenced hours earlier.

The Rhinelander's appearance the evening before had not been totally unexpected. Letters from the Court at Bonn had arrived some weeks earlier asking Prince Lichnowsky to look after him in Vienna while the young man began his studies with Mozart. One affidavit from *Herr* Neefe, the Bonn court organist, even went so far as to suggest that with the right training, the young *Herr* Louis would one day rival Mozart himself.

High praise indeed, but neither Mozart nor the Prince gave any of it much in the way of serious thought. There were hundreds of keyboardists in Vienna in those days, many of whom often sought to challenge the supremacy of Mozart but these egoists always came up short. There was only one Amadeus and in truth, everyone—not only in Vienna, but throughout Europe—knew it.

Still, even Lichnowsky had to admit, this boy had talent enough. When he knocked on the door the previous night, the choir girls had already arrived and were deep into the champagne. Coats were off, shoes shed, and blouses untied. Mozart, who was as equally anxious to listen to the girls sing parts of the opera as he was to play the role of the lover, Don Giovanni, himself, was a bit put off by Louis's intrusion. *"A kick in the arse and he'll be out of here,"* Mozart had said to Lichnowsky. Nonetheless, he took the young Rhinelander directly to the pianoforte, imagining that in a matter of minutes he would be done with the boy and they could get back to the more delectable tasks at hand.

Herr Ludwig—or Louis—as he asked the Prince to call him, was a wild-haired, rough, young man dressed informally in the fashion—no fashion was too strong a word—in the less-than-casual getup of a country rube. Was there ever a greater contrast than that between the plush satin embroidered suits of the fastidiously coiffed Mozart and this coarse youth?

At Mozart's instructions, the young man set some sheet music he had composed on the pianoforte. Louis nodded politely, then began to play. His style, like his manner of dress, was most unorthodox, a bit crude, and anything but subtle. Instead of sitting up straight so as to approach the keys with a gentle touch, Louis drove his entire body into each gesture as if to squeeze every nuance possible out of the keyboard. His body rocked, his shoulders swayed, and his hands darted this way and that with a drive so forceful that the strings of the pianoforte snapped left and right.

Though Louis's entire manner was completely unorthodox and idiosyncratic, he played surprising well, a fact not lost even on the beauties of St. Stephens. The young women, who were initially put off by the boy's peasant manners and had remained aloof until he started to play, were so impressed with his craftsmanship at the keyboard that they set aside their wine glasses and crowded around to hear him.

Still, this was Mozart's home and it was he and he alone who would pass judgment upon the Rhinelander and so when he spoke derisively, no one, not even the Prince, was surprised.

"Bravo, *Herr* Louis. No need for my housekeeper to polish the keys. My dear boy, you've done it for us. Yes, you've hammered away with some imaginative writing, but you must remember that even in the most terrifying moments music must never offend the ear or the audience will kick you in the ass. You must develop it more—like this." Mozart verily pushed the young man off his stool and proceeded to play a half-dozen variations upon the boy's theme. The sheer elegance of Mozart's improvisations charmed the assembled choir with a heretofore unheard and delicate magnificence. Louis cringed.

But to his credit this boy was not so easily daunted. The young Rhinelander said nothing, but his actions spoke volumes. He grabbed at random a piece of sheet music from the *Don Giovanni* score that Mozart had been copying out, then flipped it upside down and set it in front of himself. He sat himself back down, nodded politely in the direction of the piano, and plunged into the piece at hand with such breakneck speed, fervor, and emotion that even Mozart's pet starling and canary began to sing along wildly. Louis attacked the keyboard with the same verve a young Leonore von Breuning had witnessed several years earlier. With astonishingly deft control and rapid-fire execution, Louis improvised variations of Mozart's work that, in the end, led Mozart to laughter. When at last Louis concluded, Mozart turned and said to Lichnowsky, "Keep your eyes on this Rhinelander. One day he'll give the world something to talk about."

Turning back to the young man, Mozart added, "Excellent! Finally they send me someone with good hands and a hard cock. You play well but a little rough still. Your first lesson begins tonight. I'm copying out an opera with the help of these young ladies. You're welcome to stay and observe."

"Is it true, what they say," Louis asked of Mozart, "that you 'see' the notes, even entire scores, in your head before you copy them out?"

"Why do you ask?

"I like to compose when I walk," said Louis. "I see the notes float like birds or butterflies onto the bars of the staff. That's when I write them down. And sometimes the notes come in colors—you know, reds for passion. . . ."

Mozart stopped the boy before he could finish. "I am always inspired by the possibility of greatness in every creation. That being said, if a blind peacock shit on my score, I'd play it if it worked. We each have our own path, our own way, provided you find the right balance, the right harmony between high and low, dark and light. And, yes, it's sometimes true, that a piece—even a long one—does stand almost complete in my head, where I can survey it like a fine painting or a beautiful woman undressing for bed. Yes, I do see it such before I commit it to paper. It may be done quickly enough after that, but it is always work. Nothing is ever sucked out of the ethers. To compose is to sweat even if what I write on paper rarely differs from what it was in my imagination."

"*Danke,*" said Louis. Thank you.

"Look, it matters not what I see or do. It's of no importance. You, my young friend, must cultivate your own path. Seek perfection, accept failure."

"Accept failure? I don't understand."

"Listen carefully then. Although the province of humans is to strive in our every action and deed for a perfection only the gods can truly achieve, we, as mortal flesh and bone whose needs cause us suffering, will always fall short. The trick is to not care. Just do your best, accept fate, and let your talent carry you as far as it will. And you have promise, great promise, perhaps more so than any of my other students, but only if you work hard and keep at it."

"You'll take me on as a student then?"

Mozart affirmed it with a nod.

"Then it's settled," said Prince Lichnowsky. "*Sehr gut,* Louis,"—very good—"we'll see about finding lodgings for you tomorrow. Oh, and there's a letter here for you somewhere in this mess that came from Bonn just this morning. From a Johann van Beethoven. Your father?"

"Ja, mein Vater," replied Louis, his voice a mix of disdain spiced with just the slightest pinch of anxiety. "May I see it?"

Lichnowsky fumbled through a stack of papers on Mozart's writing desk but, unable to find it, he seized an open bottle of wine instead and refilled his glass and one for Louis. "Don't worry, it will turn up."

Without further hesitation Mozart turned to Daphne, the tallest of the choir girls, with a deep chalky voice that could pass for a male tenor's, and handed her some sheet music, "The Prince will sing the Don Juan part first while I watch and you will voice his manservant, Leparello. And Wanda," he said to the youngest of the entourage, a delicate blond with ample breasts and a milk-white complexion, "you will be Donna Anna, daughter of *Il Commendatore,* who sings the aria *Or sai chi l'onore Rapire a me volse."—Now you know who is the one trying to rob me of my honor*—"Look the part!"

Wanda twisted around toward Lichnowsky and lifted the hem of her skirt, flashing the delicacy between her thighs.

Mozart scowled, "For now, sing! You can play with the Prince's magic flute later." Then, turning back to Louis, he added, "I prefer open vice to ambiguous virtue. At least I know where I stand."

"Es war ein gutes Leben." The Prince wet his lips as he watched the girls primp. In his mind's eye he was already doing his best impersonation of "Don Giovanni," calculating how many of these sweet buds he would devour by night's end. Whatever the number, the Prince was certain: They were as hungry as he was. Later in life Lichnowsky would boast—correctly—that he had slept with at least 3,000 different women. Tonight, these seven sweetmeats

would be welcomed appetizers on his life's menu.

And as for the young Rhinelander, yes, the boy's first lesson began that night.

By the time the Lichnowsky's livery servants arrive the next morning, the opera has been rehearsed, the Prince satiated, and the girls amply rewarded.

"*Guten Tag, Herr Louis,*" the Prince half whispers. "Did you sleep well?"

Mozart, after realizing that the young Rhinelander is now awake, grabs an envelope out of a stack of papers on his work table.

A groggy-eyed Louis sits up naked on the couch.

"Finished with sword play?" continues Mozart, "Sheath your blade and get dressed. Have some coffee and we'll talk." He tosses the envelope at the boy.

It flutters through the air and lands soft as a butterfly on Daphne's breast. Louis deftly picks it up so as not to disturb her but as he does so his eyes most definitely linger on the graciousness of her female form. Yes, let it be said his life lessons in love began that night.

The first break in this mood of lovely excess comes when the young Rhinelander finally opens his letter. The joy of receiving news from home quickly evaporates upon seeing the contents. Louis wails so loudly that it wakes the girls from the choir. His face goes numb with shock.

"What is it," the Prince asks.

Fraulein Lokitzvarah finishes with Lichnowsky's massage, slides off his back, and throws on her robe. Daphne and Wanda immediately stand up and though they don't exactly know what is happening, they have sense enough to move away.

"My father says my mother fell ill. Consumption," says Louis, crumpling to his knees. "She's dying."

It is, the Prince notes, the first and only real emotion this Louis has shown.

"My father wants me to return to Bonn immediately."

"You must, then," says the Prince.

Louis is stunned. "How can I . . ."

Mozart cuts him off. "You must go. It is your mother."

Even if the Prince knows he a licentious cad—and he is—when it comes to women, Lichnowsky is anything but insensitive to the plight of this young Rhinelander, whom in one short evening he has come to like and admire. He motions for the choir girls to gather up their clothing and leave, which they do. And upon the Prince's signal, *Fraulein* Lokitzvarah goes over to the grieving teen and wraps her arms around him. Though the Fraulein appears not much older than Louis, she strokes and soothes him as compassionately as a Madonna would a child. Comforted and secured in her embrace, Louis's tears flow without end.

Mozart comes over with a cup of coffee for the boy. When our poor Louis finally stops crying, Mozart sits him down at a table and speaks, "Listen to me. When I toured Paris, not much older than you are now, my mother traveled with me. It was just the two of us. She endured many hardships on that trip. It was a cold, brutal winter. Money was scarce and she saved every *franc* and *pfennig* she could, even if it meant skimping on firewood to warm our apartment, meager as it was. The constant cold worked its way into her bones and when she turned ill, she refused to spend anything on medicine. And even when I sought after a doctor, she refused to see any until it was too late."

"Understand she was the omega to my father's alpha and by that I mean, she was my closest friend. My father—he told us where we were to go—where we would play, what we would play, who we would associate with, and so forth—but it was my mother who honored me with her support and unconditioned love. Without her I was nothing.

"When at last a doctor did visit, the first thing he said in private to me after his examination was quite unexpected. *'I fear she will not last out the night, you had better see that she makes her confession.'* I was alone and at wit's end. Unable to reveal to my mother that she was going to die, I told her instead that a German priest who was eager to hear me play would visit us the next day. When the priest did arrive, she made confession and partook of the Sacrament and received Extreme Unction. For the next three days my mother lingered, constantly going in and out of delirium, until on the last day she lost all sensation and consciousness. I pressed her hand and spoke to her but she did not see me, she did not hear me. All feeling was gone. She lay thus until her life flickered out like a candle. . . .

"I had never seen anyone die. And although I had once wished to witness death out of what you might think morbid curiosity, how cruel was it that my first experience was to be that of my own mother? I dreaded it most of all and prayed earnestly to God for strength. At the moment of her death I too wanted to die. Indeed, I wished to depart with her. . . .

"When I was strong enough to finally send a letter and break the news to my father and sister who lived back in Salzburg, I wrote with my tears, *'Weep, weep your fill but take comfort at last. Remember that Almighty God wills it thus and how can we rebel against Him?'* I took consolation in the thought that she is not lost to us forever—that we shall see her again—that we shall live together far more happily and blissfully than ever in this world. You can easily conceive what I have had to bear that day and since—what courage and fortitude I have needed to endure calmly as things grew steadily worse. I have indeed suffered and wept enough, but to what avail?

"From time to time I have fits of melancholy, but I find the best way to get rid of them is to compose or perform, both of which invariably cheer me up again. But, believe me, since that day I often wonder whether life is worth living. There is always a cause for these sad feelings. Frequently I am numb, neither hot nor cold, and don't find much pleasure in anything. After such trauma, it is a victory just to return to being normal, to being average. If you love your mother, you must go. You must be with her."

"Don't worry," says the Prince. "You will come back soon. Vienna will always be here. We will all work together yet again, my young friend. You have my word as a Prince, a gentleman, and a knight of the empire."

"Yes," agrees Mozart. "When you return, be it a few weeks or months, we'll recommence."

Fraulein Lokitzvarah, who had been so silent since arriving at the apartment that one might have imaged her as a mute, kisses Louis on the forehead. She slides one hand inside Louis's shirt. Placing it over his heart, she whispers in his ear so that no one else can hear, *"The wisdom of life lies here in your heart. You do not know it now, but if you listen . . . listen carefully and your path, your road, your way, will unfold. The wings of a goddess will embrace you. And when that happens, I will be there. I will be there to lift you up."*

CHAPTER 7

The Immortal Beloved

Vienna, March 1827

IN THE DAYS following Beethoven's funeral Steffen von Breuning, Beethoven's executor, returned frequently to the apartment at the *Schwarzspanierhaus* with his 14-year-old son, Gerhard. Of four old friends from a childhood west of the Rhine in Bonn, Steffen was the only one who, like Beethoven, had relocated himself to Vienna. A musician by love, a lawyer by training, Steffen worked as the Hapsburg Emperor's Court Councilor in the War Department. Ferdinand Ries was back in Bonn writing and conducting. And Franz Wegeler, who long since had traded his cello strings for a scalpel, had married Steffen's older sister, Leonore, almost twenty-five years ago, and now practiced medicine in Koblenz. Consequently, the trustee's task of settling the estate rested with Steffen, little as he physically felt up to the work at hand.

Though much needed to be done, from marking up the library and furniture for sale to sorting through a lifetime of papers, Steffen could not shake the *"te-dum"* of our Beethoven's *Marcia funebre* from the *Eroica Symphony's* second movement that rang in his ears. The brass band that accompanied the cortege all the way to the little cemetery at Wharing had played it over and over again along with other sentimental favorites such as Mozart's *Requiem*, much to the delight of mourners who had pressed hard against the torchbearers lighting the way.

Even as the pallbearers lowered Beethoven into his grave, Steffen wondered how long before his own ailments would invite him to join his friend for eternal rest in Wharing where his first wife, Julie, was also buried. Little wonder he couldn't shake the death march from his ears. It's an invitation no one is at liberty to refuse. Thankfully he had Gerhard with him, whose youthful energy and adoration of Beethoven made the task of organizing every last item for sale or auction tolerable. Even the Graf and the Broadwood pianofortes would go. Yes, even the Broadwood.

Documents were stacked everywhere, the logic of their organization known only to the deceased composer who no longer answered Steffen's queries. B never threw anything away. The apartment was sheer chaos.

Stacked haphazardly on a nightstand by the bed were B's favorite bamboo walking stick, an alabaster clock presented to him by the Prince Lichnowsky's wife, Christiane, several volumes of Handel's collected scores, a copy of Sir Walter Scott's recently published *Life of Napoleon*—an excoriation of General Bonaparte that had fascinated B much in his waning days—and a "conversation book."

Although B's ability to hear anything except the lowest tones was almost non-existent at this point in his life, his more than two-decade-long decline into deafness had been so gradual and progressive that he had developed an uncanny ability to read lips. In the last years of his life however, B never went anywhere without a conversation book, little notebooks where his friends would write down their comments or questions. B would read them and then reply verbally. It was just easier that way.

Gerhard, who had visited Beethoven most every day since New Year's, often read aloud to him, consciously allowing the bedridden composer to follow his lips. Other times Gerhard would watch from across the room as B perused the Handel scores, waiving his index finger in time to harmonies only he could hear in silence. Little had Gerhard understood how much B suffered those last few months until after the night of the thunderstorm. Only when the breath had left Beethoven's body and the surgeon came for the autopsy did they realize the extent to which B's back and legs were covered with bed bug bites and bloody sores. Was death a blessing? A release from pain, Gerhard wondered?

The other books Gerhard would read aloud to B from the composer's own—and vast—library were an eclectic lot that included Shakespeare's *Complete Works;* the poems of Goethe and Schiller; the Greek classics, such as Plutarch and Homer; and perhaps surprising even to those closest to him, translations by Johann Kleuker and Georg Forster of the *Bhagavad-Gita* and other Oriental classics. A map of B's intellectual fascinations would have encompassed the globe. All these too would soon become the property of the highest bidder. An entire life on the auction blocks.

Yes, as Gerhard discovered in those final few months, our Beethoven—baptized Catholic, a man who had composed the *Missa Solemnis* for his friend and student, Archduke Rudolph, when he was enthroned as the Archbishop of Olmutz—found much solace in the Hindoo *Gita.* B once described himself to Gerhard during one of their daily sickbed chats as a Pantheist, a man who found his gods everywhere and had no need for any man's *Kirche.* He even described for Gerhard how the Hindoos—who seemingly worshiped an endless stream of deities and icons as well as a *"Trimurti,"* or trinity, of gods—Brahma the Creator; Vishnu the Preserver, and Shiva the Destroyer—actually saw the many gods as merely different aspects of the "One." His *Tagebuch,* a diary B kept during the meanest and most contentious years of the custody war over his nephew Karl, was embellished with innumerable quotes from the *Gita* and other Asian sources, including several Gerhard re-copied into his own notebook. *"Free from all passion and desire, that is the Mighty One. He alone. No one is greater than He, Brahman."* And, *"God is immaterial and for this reason transcends every conception. Since He is invisible, He can have no form. But from what we observe in His work we may conclude that He is eternal, omnipotent, omniscient, and omnipresent."*

But B's spiritual wanderings were the least of their surprises for, even in death, the revelations concerning his life only grew in depth and complexity.

Aside from the burial, the task Steffen knew to be most critical as executor was locating all of B's financial documents, including the purported seven shares of bank stock, whose sale would be necessary to support his remaining heirs. Beethoven, who had never been a wealthy man and understood little about finance, long feared becoming as destitute in old age as had some of his former patrons. Great nobles and friends such as Count Waldstein, who had recognized B's genius back in Bonn and opened the doors of Vienna's nobility for him; Prince Razumovsky, who commissioned the revolutionary *Opus* 57 string quartets; and Prince Lichnowsky, a musician and string player who had been B's most ardent patron in Vienna, had all seen their own lives ground into poverty before death welcomed them.

The bank investments, valued at some seven thousand florins, represented the bulk of Beethoven's estate and the very end of his feeble attempts at saving money for old age. And though Steffen and Gerhard had exhausted each corner, crevice, and crack of the apartment in their search, the shares were nowhere. Had B's nephew, Karl, made off with them along with the pistols he had used to shoot himself in the head?

And what a disaster the whole custody battle over Karl had been. Medical inquests, police reports, public scandal, and press scrutiny; things one would want to avoid even in the best of times but ever more so under the regime of Prince Klemens Metternich, Emperor Franz's Prime Minister, who valued order and obedience above all else. Steffen was certain the incident had led to B's decline and death, not to mention the damage it had clearly inflicted upon his nephew. If the *Ninth Symphony* had been Beethoven's greatest triumph, then the war with Karl's mother, his sister-in-law Johanna, over the boy had to be judged as his greatest failure as a man. Such ugliness masquerading as love.

It wasn't until *Herr* Holtz, B's former assistant these last few years, responded to Steffen's request and came by that afternoon, that the mystery of the missing bank shares would be resolved—but in so doing, it opened the portal to even greater intrigues, ones that would perplex Steffen until he found relief in the cool earth of his own grave.

Holtz led Steffen and Gerhard to the oak cabinet with beveled glass panes adjacent to B's writing desk. There he triggered a hidden lever and a heretofore secret compartment dropped open. Inside were not only the missing bank shares but a miniature portrait of a young woman, an oval shaped ring set with emerald chips, and a dusky pearl, and lastly, a letter on much-yellowed velum.

Steffen lifted out the bank shares. "Thank goodness. At least they survived Karl." He pulled out his reading glasses to examine them in detail.

Gerhard held up the miniature to Holtz, "Who is this? She's beautiful."

Holtz shook his head, he didn't know. "Why B kept them locked away with the bank shares, I don't know. He never explained. . . . And it wasn't the sort of thing I would have ever felt comfortable asking him. You know how prickly he could be about that sort of thing."

"Yes," agreed Steffen, who probably knew B better than anyone. How many times had Beethoven lashed out at a friend—or even total strangers—for some perceived fault or misunderstanding? And how much worse had it become as his hearing loss progressed over the last decade. Even they had had a falling out that lasted too many years. Was it over the libretto for *Leonore*—or did B end up re-titling it *Fidelio*? B had always complained to Steffen that, "*We Germans could never write a sound libretto. Only the more lyrical French or the Italians could.*" Not that it made any difference now. Turning his attention to the portrait, Steffen's face grew pale, as if he couldn't make sense of what he saw. "I don't believe in ghosts but B, he's still here. I feel his presence. Best read the letter," he said to his son. "Maybe it will explain this."

Gerhard unfolded the sheets of velum with deliberate care so as not to tear them and began: *"Teplitz, July 6, in the morning."*

"Does it say what year?" Steffen asked.

"No," said Gerhard.

"Go on."

Gerhard continued, *"July 6, in the morning . . . My angel, my all, my very self . . . Only a few words today and at that with a pencil, yours I think. Not till tomorrow will my lodgings definitely be settled upon. What a useless waste of time.*

"Why this deep sorrow when necessity speaks? Can our love endure except through sacrifices? Can we do anything to alter the fact that you are not wholly mine, and I am not wholly yours? Oh God, look at the beauties of nature and comfort your heart with that which must be. Love demands everything and rightly so. Thus it is for me with you, and for you with me. But you forget so easily that I must live for me and for you. If we were wholly united you would feel the pain of it as little as I do."

Gerhard looked up at his father. "Who is he writing about?"

"Just go on," said Steffen, still perplexed by what he was hearing. And when was Beethoven at the Bohemian spa town of Teplitz? Steffen couldn't remember. Perhaps it was in the years they weren't speaking with each other. That *Leonore-Fidelio* thing again.

"My journey was a fearful one; I did not reach here until four o'clock yesterday morning. Lacking more horses, the post coach chose another route, but what an awful one. At the last stage, I was warned not to travel at night. Already terrified of the forest, those words only made me all the more anxious. Was I wrong? Surely the coach was bound to break down on this dreadful wretched road, a bottomless mud pit. Without such stallions as I had with me I should have remained stuck on the road. Even Prince Esterhazy, traveling the usual route here, had the same fate with eight horses that I had with four. Yet in the end I did get some pleasure out of it, as I often do when I overcome difficulties. . . .

"Now a quick change to matters internal from things external. We shall surely see each other soon. But today I cannot share with you the thoughts I have had during these last few days touching my own life. If our hearts were always close together, I would scarcely have made such observations. My heart is full of so many things to share with you . . . Ah, there are moments when I feel that words amount to nothing. Have courage,

remain my true, my only treasure, my all, as I am yours. The gods must send us the rest, what for us must and shall be ordained. . . .

"Your faithful, Ludwig . . ."

"Is that it?" asked Steffen. "And you are sure there's no date, no year?"

"No, there's no year written anywhere, but there's more, another page" said Gerhard, shuffling the papers.

"Evening, Monday, July 6 . . . You are suffering, my dearest creature. Only now have I learned that letters must be posted very early in the morning on Mondays and Thursdays, the only days on which the mail coach goes from here to Karlsbad. . . .

"You are suffering. Oh, wherever I am, you are with me. I would arrange it so that we can live together. What a life! Thus! But without you—pursued by the goodness of mankind here and there—which as little I deserve or want to. The humility of man towards man pains me. And when I consider myself in relation to the universe, what am I? And what is he whom we call the greatest? Within us lies the divinity of all.

"I weep when I reflect that you will probably not receive the first news from me until Saturday. Much as you love me, I love you more. But do not ever hide your thoughts from me. Good night! As I am here for the baths, I must go to bed. Oh God, so near, yet so far! Is not our love truly heavenly and as firm as heaven's vault?"

"I can't imagine who he wrote this to—or why he treasured this letter to the exclusion of all others," said Holtz. "The Beethoven I knew these last few years had given up on love. . . . Except for . . ." He stopped himself and looked over at Steffen. "You understand, yes?"

Steffen nodded, our B had more than once found solace in the streets, particularly after an affair gone awry. "But you didn't know our B when he was young or in his prime. There was never a time when our good friend was not in love." Steffen had seen them all, or at least most of them. Beethoven had a hunger in his day. Unquenchable. The daughters of princes, the wives of noblemen, the delectable elite of the empire. And they, with a royal abandon, would open themselves up for him. Discreetly of course, but Steffen knew. Oh, some would beg for lessons, others for a dedication; they'd flock about him like so many Christmas geese savoring the piercing blade of the spit and a night of roasting over a fire. And would B oblige? *Naturlich.* Next to music and his daily walks in the woods, were women his greatest passion? Perhaps.

Turning back to his son, he said, "Go on."

Gerhard, ever more intrigued, continued, *"Good morning, on July 7 . . . . Though still in bed, my thoughts go out to you, my Immortal Beloved, now joyfully, and then sadly, waiting to learn whether fate will hear us. I can live with you totally or not at all. Yes, I am resolved to wander so far away from you until that moment when I can throw myself into your arms and say that I am really at home with you. And I can send my soul wrapped in your presence to the land of spirits. Yes, unhappily there is no other way. You will not give in, since you know my fidelity to you. No one else can ever possess my heart, never, never. . . .*

"Oh God, why must I be parted from the one I so love. And yet my life in Vienna is now a wretched one. Your love makes me at once both the happiest and the unhappiest of men.

"At my age I need a steady, quiet life. Is that possible in our situation?

"My angel, I have just been told that the mail coach goes every day, therefore I must close at once so that you may receive the letter without delay. Be calm, for only by a calm consideration of our existence can we achieve our goal of living together. Be calm. Love me today, yesterday . . . . What tearful longings for you, you, you. My life, my all. Farewell. Never cease to love me. Never misjudge this most faithful heart of your beloved.

"Ever yours . . . Ever mine . . . Ever ours. . . ."

Steffen turned to Holtz as he reexamined the miniature. "Why was this portrait locked up with the bank shares? And hidden away with this letter? Do you know if he ever sent this? Or is this just a copy?"

"I don't have any answers," said Holtz, "but the look in your eye tells me you recognize the woman in the painting."

"I do," said Steffen, recalling how he and B had struggled on and off for years on the libretto for B's only opera, *Fidelio,* and its heroine, Leonore. “I do. It’s my sister.”

“Aunt Leonore?” stammered Gerhard. He struggled to grasp the implications of his father’s words. It was as if this revelation could render everything he knew about his own family—about his father, about his aunt and his Uncle Franz, and about Beethoven himself—into obsolescence.

“Yes, it’s our *Lorchen.* Painted before . . . well, a long time ago.”

“And this ring?” asked Holtz, “was this your sister’s as well?”

Steffen examined the dusky pearl set amongst the jewels of the ring. “No, I can’t recall ever having seen that before.”

CHAPTER 8

A Knight in Victory at the Garden of Venus

The Countryside outside Bonn, November 25, 1787

"OH, *beautiful spark of the gods,"* a 16-year-old Leonore intoned softly after the flame-red monarch butterfly landed on her arm. *"Oh Daughter of Elysium, may we enter your heavenly sanctuary? Let thy magic reunite those whom stern custom has parted."*

Thankfully, it was for November an unusually hot day. Dense clouds of vapors rising off the natural hot springs created a thick but warm and comforting fog which enveloped the entire canyon the way steam fills a Turkish bath. Though it had been with some difficulty, Leonore had calculated carefully to ensure that she and Louis would be able to secret away from Bonn and picnic here. The small limestone glen, which was tucked away in the hills outside town, was her most favorite—and perhaps most secret place. For Leonore, her girlfriends and generations of aristocratic women before them, it was simply known as the Garden of Venus. The thick blanket of fog gave it an ethereal, almost mystical appearance, one that very much appealed to the romantic in Leonore.

She blew a kiss toward the butterfly. *"Under thy gentle wing, all the world's creatures draw joy from nature's breast while following your rose-strewn path. Give us kisses and wine and a friend loyal unto death."*

In response, the brightly colored monarch flexed its wings and lowered its head as if to reciprocate with a kiss of its own. Leonore watched as the butterfly then lifted itself into the air and fluttered off into the mist. It circled around the glen and past the rust-red heather lined opening to a cave before landing on the bare breast of an ancient statue of a goddess. Carved from Carrera marble, the statue, which still stood intact inside a small circle of ruins—remnants of the Roman occupation of Germania fifteen centuries earlier—celebrated the birth of Venus. The goddess had once been painted with life-like colors in the classical style but these had long been weathered out. Only her feet retained a darker pigment, creating the illusion that Venus had been tramping barefoot through the mud.

"What was that you were reciting?" Louis called out to Leonore. He was neck deep in the nearly milk white waters of the hot springs that percolated up through the limestone, while she stood still fully dressed at the lip of a cave at one end of the springs.

"Bits of a poem by Schiller, Friedrich Schiller, called the "*An die Freude"—the "Ode to Joy,'"* she replied. Though Louis excelled in all things musical, she was well aware that he had not much in the way of formal schooling, that having ended when he was 10 or 11 years old and she was happy—actually more than happy—to share with him books, poems, histories, and philosophies, and other intellectual ideas of the times that he had never before been exposed to as it brought them closer together.

"And Elysium? I've heard the word but what exactly is it?" Louis for his part was like a sponge, his ravenous intellect verily soaking up everything with a delight and satisfaction of his own.

"The gods' paradise. In Greek and Roman mythology it's that part of heaven reserved for them and them alone. Now turn around and don't look," she said, both hoping and imagining that Louis would peek as she stepped out of her dress and stripped off her undergarments.

"The Hindus and Buddhists call it Nirvana," she added. "And for Shakespeare, the 'Fields of Elysium' was that corner of paradise for those mere mortals among us who were brave, glorious, noble, saintly, or simply revered."

"As I do you?"

Leonore blushed. "Perhaps, yes. Perhaps one day we shall all be welcomed guests in this paradise of the gods." She was confident her false modesty would enhance the seduction she had carefully planned. Once fully undressed, Leonore moved leisurely. Was he watching? She took great care to meticulously fold her own clothes, giving him every opportunity to spy on her nakedness. What was it she had read in *Don Quixote*? *"Hunger is the best sauce."* And her every movement was designed to enhance his appetite.

She set her dress and shoes on a marble bench just inside the cave where moments earlier she had secreted a gift from her family—a new suit of clothes and boots for Louis. The von Breunings knew their poor pianoforte instructor—and by now good friend—would never be able to afford anything proper to replace his usual rags. Leonore was intent upon using the occasion of their trip to the glen as the means to make a swap. Would Louis even notice?

With careful calculation she turned back around toward the hot springs as slowly as possible so as to not catch Louis glancing at her bare breasts and exposed privates. Welcome to paradise. Let him enjoy the view, she thought. As Leonore slid into the oh-so warm and comforting waters, she was certain he would welcome and treasure her next gift to him—that of herself.

Though Bonn was home to the Elector's Court, it wasn't much more than a small burg where everybody knew everybody. And given the possibilities presented her by a tryst she conceived in an arbor so secluded few outside of her small circle of girlfriends even knew of its existence, it was just that sort of gossip she was determined to avoid. Even at 16 years old, Leonore had already learned that in a town this tiny, if you didn't know what you were doing, everyone else did.

With secrecy high among her concerns, Leonore had lent Louis one of her family's horses the night before and arranged to meet him at noon at the crossroads several leagues out of Bonn—which he most dutifully did. In her saddle bags she had packed their picnic, a little wine, and her softest, most comforting blanket—one she planned for them to initiate in the shadow of Venus after the baths.

She had told no one of her plans and instructed Louis to do the same.

Louis had almost cancelled their tryst a few days earlier as his little sister, Margaretha, had been ill with a fever. Since the death of his mother in July, Louis had taken charge of the Beethoven household. His father was all too regularly a stumble-down drunk who could be counted on for little more than sleeping it off in the constable's jail. Fortunately, Margaretha had recovered enough for Louis to feel comfortable leaving his *"petit papillon"* in the care of the Beethovens' housekeeper and his younger brother, the 13-year-old Casper, who was the only one Louis had told that he was going to meet Leonore *"somewhere in the countryside."*

Louis's escape from town would have been perfect had he not encountered at the city gates Leonore's two girlfriends, Jeanette d'Honrath and Babette Koch, both of whom were also among Louis's aristocratic pianoforte students. Between the three girls—who often picnicked and bathed together at the garden, no secret was safe—and Louis, poor Louis was often the topic of their conversations. They'd all break into giggles talking about how nimble, gentle, and soft his piano-playing fingers were while wondering what it would be like to be caressed by those hands and pondering who might bed him first.

Easily recognizing the von Breunings' horse and tack upon which Louis rode toward the gate, and speculating that he and Leonore had a plan afoot, Babette called out to him in her best imitation of a less-than-coy Shakespearean wench, "Hurry, Louis, methinks our sweet Venus doth await a manly entrance to her garden."

Jeanette, a vivacious blonde with sweet blue eyes and a seductive voice, joined in. She couldn't help but tease him by singing the lyrics to a popular song, *"Oh Louis, parting from you this very day and unable to prevent it is too painful for my heart!"*

Bemused, Louis reined the horse to a halt and dismounted. Approaching Jeanette, he leaned in close and whispered seductively as he ever so assuredly ran his fingers first through her golden locks and then down, dancingly, over her dress. Jeanette froze in shock and surprise, her neck and arms covered in goose bumps as Louis's hands passed over her breasts and then down below her waist.

"If it amuses you to speak about me thus, please go on for I find no greater joy than to wander among these hills and forests. No one loves exploring the country as much as I do."

As Jeanette blushed red as fire, Louis turned to Babette who was equally taken aback when he tapped her breast with his index finger. Her body shuddered involuntarily.

"And if I should ever wake our muse, it is only so that she can send back to me the echoes of nature that all men, all men, desire."

Louis left the two girls speechless as he remounted his horse, nodded politely, and rode off through the city gate.

Lenore had seen Louis change much since returning from Vienna. No longer a boy, he had stepped up forcefully and with enthusiasm at being the man of the family. His father's progressive slide into a perpetual alcoholic stupor made the old man essentially useless around the house particularly when it came to tending to his ill wife, Louis's mother, Maria Magalena Beethoven.

With great pride, Louis took on responsibility for providing for his family. His work for the Elector's orchestra, along with providing pianoforte lessons for the daughters of the rich, yielded enough money to support his brothers, Casper Carl and Nikolaus Johann, the latter of whom was eleven; and the baby, Margaretha, a musically precocious, red-haired toddler with black eyes whom everyone, especially Louis, just adored. At home, they were inseparable. Louis often sat her on his lap when he played the pianoforte. She would pounce on the keys with such enthusiasm and not a small amount of inborn talent that even Louis thought that if anyone could have been another Mozart, it would have been her.

The months prior to his mother's death in July had not been easy on Louis, who had considered her his best friend. Ill with consumption, she died about seven weeks after he had returned from Vienna. Still, he bore both the tragedy of her dying and his new responsibilities with great strength and without complaints. Leonore, who had done her own share of growing up quickly after her father's death a decade earlier, was more than a little astonished at how quickly Louis matured into his new role. His brothers looked up to him and Margaretha positively clung to him with a delight and affection only toddlers can manifest. Now that Louis was compelled by circumstances to take on much the same sort of responsibilities as Leonore, the common bonds between them had grown even stronger.

Before the Vienna trip, Louis had been remarkably reserved around Leonore. Though he never spoke about his brief encounter with Mozart, she was certain something rare and defining had happened there that changed him. She wanted to know what had occurred but he refused to speak about his experience. Nonetheless, after his return, he was remarkably different. He had not only revealed a mature side, he had become more easy-going, warm, and light-hearted—traits that Leonore knew only survived if there was an inner confidence sustaining them. Though Louis was no less quirky and outspoken, he was full of humor, much of it often self-deprecating. During their still frequent piano lessons, Leonore often made mistakes just so he would be forced to take her hands in his own and shape her fingers to frame a proper chord. His hands were beautiful and his fingers had a touch so sensitive and so unlike anything she had ever experienced that it verily excited her to be so close. If they inadvertently touched or bumped each other during those lessons, they'd both let the moment linger with an unspoken sweetness. Was he that way with his other students? It wasn't that she didn't trust Jeanette and Babette and the others. . . . Well, no, she didn't trust them—nor they, her.

Leonore noticed that Louis's affection for her had become more readily apparent in the weeks following Franz Wegeler's September departure from Bonn for Vienna to continue his medical training. Whenever Louis would come by the house, he no longer averted his eyes when greeting her. They would both gaze deeply for just a moment, a lingering moment—provided no one else was around, especially her brothers with whom he had also developed close friendships. The inner confidence he manifested in her presence felt good to Leonore, very good indeed.

As she rode alone to the crossroads that morning to meet up with Louis, Leonore's thoughts flashed back to Franz. What was there to think? After all, Franz—who shied away from making any commitment to Leonore before heading off to Vienna—was gone now two months with no plans to return until whenever his schooling was complete. That might be in two or even three years, an eternity to a 16-year-old. She could wait, as Babette and Jeanette had suggested, but wait for what? Franz to change his mind and leave Louis to the other girls? She scarcely knew her own mind and Franz had not even given her any cause for encouragement one way or another. But Louis, Louis was here; back now some six months since his mother's consumption forced him to return to home. And he was going to stay as long as his family needed him. Still, the last thing she wanted was to engage with one and have the other find out.

No, she had never taken Franz to the glen and, yes, it had taken a fair amount of effort to make it possible for Louis to join her at the Garden of Venus. Now that they were joined at the crossroads, she regretted not an ounce of it. Fortunately, Margaretha was on the mend and in the good hands of their housekeeper.

The path to the garden crossed into rugged hills on lands owned by the Elector. Though trespass by commoners was forbidden—thus adding to the glen's inherent secrecy—Leonore von Breuning and her friends were of the aristocratic class where such strictures did not exist. She and the girls came and went as they pleased, particularly since the mineral-rich waters were considered to have mystical healing powers for female ailments.

About a mile past the crossroads, the trail to the garden followed a ridgeline. On either side and downslope were meadows and fields divided by irregular patches of woods. Little streams and rivulets began below the path and flowed towards tributaries of the great Father Rhine itself, which was hidden from sight by a copse of willows and foxtails. Farther off in the distance beyond the river were high mountain meadows covered in more of the same red heather that lined the mouth of the limestone cave at the hot springs. Babette, who had flaming red hair herself, once remarked when the three girls were sunning themselves naked in the glen that the opening slit of the cave resembled her own *Muschi*. Though Leonore restrained herself from looking at Babette's genitalia, the comparison seemed apt enough to make them all roar with laughter.

As they rode on, the slopes climbed ever upwards towards a distant line of mountains graced by waterfalls. After some prodding by Leonore, Louis shared some of what Mozart had told him about the death of his own mother; of how Mozart said he chafed under the thumb of his autocratic father in Salzburg and of how he didn't find his own way musically until he went out on his own in Vienna. Leonore envied Louis. He had a dream to pursue and even if part of it was now delayed by the unfortunate circumstances of his mother's death—a delay Louis had come to peace with because of his love of family—she could feel his determination and confidence grow stronger every day. She understood how much it meant to him knowing that one day he would push past his own father and return to Vienna to work with the great master, Wolfgang Amadeus Mozart. What musician wouldn't have wanted that?

Scattered here and there among the meadows they rode past were the crumpled down ruins of ancient farms and even an abandoned medieval village. If there was one thing Leonore had learned in her short life, nothing was predictable and tragedy struck us all. And though suffering spared no one, the solution was to embrace the good, and find blessings whenever they occurred. Her greatest moments of peace came when she wandered among through the forest over stones and under a canopy of trees. The wilderness was her true church and it made her more than happy to be able to share with Louis the divinity of nature.

As they neared the gardens, the trail turned steeply downward into a narrow canyon that cut through the white walls of karst and limestone. Leonore led the way. The glen, as noted earlier, was draped in dense mists which rose and drifted by like webs of gossamer. Water from a stream flowed somewhere off to their right. The steamy air was rife with the scent of lavender and other late blooming wild flowers mingling with hints of bromine and sulfur. Wild fruit trees—apples, pears, plums, and peaches—lined much of the trail, as did a bramble of vines filled with ripe blackberries, strawberries, and grapes. Louis was surprised by their presence and the sheer bounty of fruit so late in the season, until Leonore explained how warm air rising up from the hot springs created its own climate zone in the canyon.

"But how did they get here?" he asked about the trees and berries.

"Women are more like birds than you imagine," she said, plucking an apple off a tree as she rode by. "They have been coming here for centuries, eating their fill and leaving the seeds behind." She took a bite, before tossing the apple back to Louis.

"Ah," he said, "and fertilizing the Garden of Eden as they did so. *Wunderbar.*"

When they finally arrived at a stream whose waters were milk-white, Louis was doubly surprised, first by the color of the water and secondarily to find the stream not on their right, but on their left. Leonore pointed out that they had crossed over a natural bridge and then she showed him how the stream flowed through an ancient karst formation already pocketed with hot springs bubbling up from deep inside the earth. Over the centuries the rapidly flowing hot waters ate away at the limestone. This not only turned the water white as breast milk, it shaped a quarter-mile-long tunnel under the glen which opened through a narrow aperture fringed with an inverted triangle of red heather between two white walls of stone. As Leonore and her girlfriends had joked, the resemblance to a woman's vagina was readily apparent, even to Louis, whose eyes sparkled all too knowingly when she pointed this out to him.

Tethering the horses, Leonore pointed to the statue of Venus inside the small circle of ruined pillars. "I don't know whether the women who came here in Roman times named the garden after her or whether she was named after the garden, not that it matters anymore."

"She's perfect, every drummer boy's dream," said Louis, as he walked over to the statue and then used his fingers to not only caress it with the same tenderness he would one day use while playing the *adagio cantabile* of the *Pathetique Sonata* but also to draw out from the stone the very essence of it creation. "Who wouldn't fall in love with her?"

When Louis, admitting he knew little of Greek or Roman mythology, asked if she would share her knowledge of Venus with him, Leonore did so happily. It was one thing to study the pianofòrte with a musical wizard, another to be able to repay the debt by sharing her wisdom with him in turn.

"The ancients all over the world," began Leonore, "revered and celebrated their belief that every woman in the course of her life manifested all the qualities of a goddess—beauty, sexuality, motherhood, compassion, wisdom, and love."

"Tis a pity to be a musician instead of the sculptor of such a goddess," said Louis. "We create beauty that one only hears here and here." He tapped his head and heart. "But the artisan who crafted this, he knew the true feel of such wonders in his hands, in his fingers. I envy him"

"Every civilization, Louis," she continued, "even our most ancient ancestors, created images that honored the feminine. The Greeks called her *Aphrodite*; the Romans, *Venus*. The Chinese knew her as *Kwan Yin*; the Japanese, *Kannon*. The Hindus and Tibetans revered their *Avalokiteshvara,* and the Egyptians worshipped her as *Isis*. We Catholics portray her as the *Madonna*—our mother, Mary."

Louis kissed its marble lips. "Isis, *Ich liebe dich*—I love you."

Feigning jealousy, Leonore issued a rebuff, "I'm the one who brought you here, not her."

"Perhaps a trio?" Louis propositioned with a whisper, "a piano trio?"

Leonore caught the little wicked glimmer in his eyes. Yes, her Louis had changed.

"If you want to dance on these keys," she said, "duets only."

For the first time ever, Louis put his arms around Leonore as one would a lover. With his lips, he caressed her neck with a mix of desire and tranquility that had her tingling. Leonore could sense his hunger, a man's hunger.

"They say every artist needs a muse for inspiration," he whispered in her ear. "Now I have mine. *Danke, danke schoen, meine Lorchen."*

However, just at the moment Louis leaned in to kiss her lips, the butterfly returned. Leonore pulled back and let it land on her hand again.

"Sometimes I dream I'm a butterfly," she said. "Could you imagine that? Floating from flower to flower, living on nothing but nectar. How sweet. Such a life."

With her free arm she pushed Louis back toward the cave. "Why don't you put your clothes there on the bench and then take in the baths. I'll join you as soon as I lay out our picnic."

While he dutifully followed Leonore's instructions, she busied herself laying out her blanket as well as the wine and food. After discreetly watching Louis strip down and make his way into the water, she went into the cave and surreptitiously replaced his rags with the new suit of clothes and a pair of black leather boots. She looked deep into the cave and tried to see if she could see all the way through to the other side where the stream entered, but the shadows were too deep. Perhaps later, when the winter sun slipped farther down on the horizon. At those moments sunbeams often shot through the far opening, casting odd shadows and reflections on the walls of the cave.

Leonore finally slid into the steamy pool and floated over to where Louis was resting on the far side. He started to move towards Leonore but she kept him at arms-length, determined to tease his appetite for as long as she dared.

"What happened in Vienna? With Mozart? What did he say? What did you learn?"

There was something in the way he looked back at Leonore—his dark eyes burning with an intensity she's never noticed before—

that unnerved her and made her wonder if she had completely miscalculated.

"There's nothing to speak of."

"*Nichts?* You're lying," she said, trying to tease it out of him. "Ludwig van Beethoven, I know you well enough to tell when you are hiding something from me."

"*Ja,* I played for Mozart. He made a few comments and agreed to take me on as a student. Then I saw the letter from my father urging me to return home at once."

"That's all? What did he say about your music? Your playing?"

"I'll tell you this only because you are my dearest friend," he said firmly and with an inner surety that made Leonore question her girlish expectations for the day, "but you must not repeat it to any one—not ever. Agreed? No one?"

"What happened?"

"You must not think me wicked or full of malice when I tell you this." He described for Leonore in explicit detail of how he played variations from *Don Giovanni*—upside-down no less—as Prince Lichnowsky and the women of St. Stephen's choir listened. "When I was done, Mozart laughed—not at me, mind you, but with incredulity at what I had just done. And in that moment I knew, I knew in my heart and with complete certainty—not arrogance, not the arrogance or crimes of a youth, but with the complete certainty of a man—that I was to be his equal. This was the truth that came to me, one I could never deny even before the throne of God. I would be his equal. Mozart's equal."

Louis raised both hands out of the water, tapped his head and heart, and then flexed his ten fingers. "Right here I have everything I need."

"Will you go back? Return to Vienna to study with him?"

"It would be my greatest wish, but how can I? There's Margaretha and my brothers to take care of."

In her mind's eye, Leonore saw Louis transform from a boy she wanted to seduce to a man whose thrall she had fallen under.

Deciding it was finally time to surrender to God and nature, she verily glided onto his lap and awaited their first kiss. What would it taste like?

As Leonore and Louis wrapped themselves in each other's arms, miles away, back in Bonn, another Beethoven and another von Breuning do the same. Only this time it is fear—not passion—that drove a panicked 13-year-old Casper to find refuge in the arms of Leonore's mother, Helene von Breuning.

Casper, who along with the housekeeper had been left to watch over both his younger brother, Nikolaus Johann, and sister, Margaretha, only knew he was to tell no one that his big brother has gone off to the countryside with Leonore. When Margaretha's fever abruptly spiked only hours after Louis had left, Casper hesitated, not knowing what to do. Where was Louis? Medicine, a doctor, they're expensive and out of the question. And he had no money. The housekeeper—not much more than a child herself—suggested a cold bath, which Casper reluctantly tried out of desperation. It worked, but for only a little while, only until Margaretha started having fits and seizures, at which point Casper knew he had no other choice, he had to find Louis. But where and how?

Leaving Margaretha with Nikolaus Johann, Casper ran to the von Breunings and pounded on the front door. When Helene opened the door, he broke down in tears and collapsed into her arms.

Ever resourceful, Helene knew well how to handle a crisis. Though filled with grave doubts about her Leonore's judgment when she grasped that her daughter had rendezvoused with Louis, she submerged her concerns and instantly took charge. She dispatched her son Steffen to find *Herr Doktor* Gross. "Have him meet us at the Beethoven house." And son Christoph, she ordered him to track down Jeanette or Babette. "They'll know where Leonore and Louis are hiding. Find them, bring them back, now!"

The kiss Leonore so fervently expects never comes. Instead there are only the shouts of a rider racing down the trail toward the glen.

It's Babette, her flaming red locks flying, emerging out of the fog, her horse lathered in sweat. Breathless, her words catch in her throat as she calls out to Louis, urging him to return quickly. Margaretha is in trouble.

Babette waits and watches as Leonore and Louis scramble out of the water. Babette's eyes pass from noticing Louis's hands and his powerfully-built chest and arms to his still-hardened manhood. *Why not her instead of Leonore?* she thinks, as the couple darts into the cave. The rays of the low winter sun, which now shoot through the tunnel and reflect off the white walls, half blinds them all.

As Louis throws on his shirt and pants with a keen determination to return to his sister's side as quickly as possible, Leonore wonders if he even realizes his clothes are different or new. So much for her 'gifts' on this day gone astray. What was it her mother had once said to her? *"If you want the Gods to laugh, tell them your plans."*

Fragments of Schiller's poem weave themselves in and out of Leonore's thoughts as they remount for the sprint home.

Joyously, as the sun speeds through Heaven's glorious order, hasten, brothers, on your way, exulting as a knight in victory.

At a gallop, Louis leads the race back to the city. Leonore follows. No joy, no exultation, only haste, she thinks, where's the victory in that?

Babette trails behind, suddenly conscious not only of the powerful muscles of the stallion that arc and flex below her but of damp secretions spreading between her legs. Oh, what hunger is this?

As soon as they reach the Beethoven house, Louis takes Margaretha in his arms. *"Mon petit papillon."* She is cold and shivering. He kisses her forehead.

CHAPTER 9

The Creatures of Prometheus

ILLUSIONS . . .

Everything is an illusion. I wake up from the hallucination inside my dream—which N keeps insisting is not a dream but even he has no other word for it—and find myself lying on the ground kissing the teapot.

"A kiss for all the world!" N's words reverberate inside my consciousness with what feels like a dose of laughter. He tugs on my ear. "*Gesu, mon frère,* do you still imagine that a loving sister dwells above our starry canopy?"

There is no Shiva, no fire, no croc, no grapes, no soma; just my dream, my endless dream, and now my lips planted around a tea pot.

Napoleon, who resumes his cross-legged posture on his stone seat, takes the teapot from me and sets it back upon the brazier. He's garbed as when I first saw him, in his winter uniform. Moscow must have been cold, very cold indeed for that image to keep returning.

"Russia cold?" He's reading my thoughts again. "*Oui,* if you really care, I will tell you about it in due time." Lifting the lid, N sprinkles some fresh jasmine leaves into the pot "*to sweeten the soma,*" he says. It is then that I notice a familiar image on the side of the tin from which he has taken the tea—a dancing Shiva surrounded by a ring of flames. Below that is the stamped logo of the British East India Company.

Had it all been an illusion, a mirage, a hallucination, my voyage through the desert sands of an imaginary oasis? And all that inside a dream?

"What happened?" I ask.

"The longest journey . . ."

". . . always starts with the first step. I'm beginning to get that. But why you?" I ask, "Why are you my . . . my what . . . my guide?"

"Why Napoleon Bonaparte, you ask? Well, *mon ami,* there are at least three, or perhaps four, good reasons. None of these may make sense to you at first, but allow me to explain. I'll begin with curlicues."

"Curlicues?"

"I can't stand them. Curlicues drive me mad."

"I'm lost. What is so incendiary about curlicues, especially if you're already dead?"

"Indulge me, B. I know curlicues are not a musical term. . . ."

"Most certainly not."

"If I understood music as well as I do war, perhaps I would express this differently, so please bear with me." N pauses to refill our cups. The scent of jasmine permeates the air. "Most concert music, that which I hear around the court, especially in France, or before an opera. . . ."

"By that you mean the overture?"

"Yes, the overture. I know I am ignorant of the proper terminology, but could you sight and load a field cannon with grapeshot to stop a stampeding mob?"

"Nein." I find myself inexplicably drawn back to the soma though I have neither thirst nor hunger.

"When I say curlicues I simply mean music which has an excessive obedience to form and a seeming mandate that everything performed must be restrained yet pretty. Have you ever watched the hands of a concert master conducting a chamber ensemble? They dance around in curlicues."

I watch N's hands flail about as if to mimic his words. He's no conductor.

N continues, "It's as if these musicians are so afraid to go outside the boundaries of what some sycophant defines as "good taste," that they're condemned to mince around and subject us, their audience, for eternity with nothing other than syrupy-sweet minuets. Granted, they may do what they do with brilliance and verve like Haydn, but I cannot abide it. These silly fops remind me most of the Austrian generals I would face off against in my early military campaigns on the Italian peninsula. Had my foes half as much concern about the strength and vitality of the men who fought for them as they did the ermine linings of their coats and the gold braid on their uniforms, victory would not have come so easily to me. Once, when I was growing ever more weary of this sing-song musical pabulum, I cornered our *Kapellmeister* at his piano and asked him for someone who played and wrote like a man, someone whose compositions revealed substance, emotion, heart, honesty, truth, passion. Our *Kapellmeister* returned only one name to me, 'Beethoven,' as he played your '*Moonlight Sonata*.'"

"*Moonlight*? What's *Moonlight*? I've never composed anything called '*Moonlight*.'"

"You did. It's the nickname for your *Piano Sonata No. 14 in C-sharp minor*. Your friend, the poet Ludwig Rellstab, came up with the name some years back because the opening *Adagio sustenuto* reminded him of moonlight shining upon Lake Lucerne and that's how the whole world refers to it."

"*Moonlight*? Rellstab said that? Such madness. The sonata has nothing at all to do with *moonlight*."

"But everything to do with the perfect transformation away from Haydn's banal compositions to the profound—and the title helps. Your "*Moonlight Sonata*" is perhaps the most famous and popular piano sonata ever composed. It sells copies nothing short of a miracle. Why, there's an American composer, B.B. Koenig, who upon hearing it once said, '*The Moonlight, it's like the Blues, and the Blues ain't nothing but a good man feeling bad.*' The "*Moonlight*" is the epitome of the Blues with its bittersweet balance between sadness and beauty. Such a great work."

"And you sought me out because my "*Moonlight*" lacks curlicues?"

I am incredulous with the arcane nonsense this apparition throws my way. Talking music theory with an unschooled ghost.

"Précisément!" N's face is full of animation.

I could fill N's library with what he did not know about music composition, but was educating a dead man even worth the effort? Was it not sufficient to suffer teaching the daughters of the aristocracy—at least they came adorned with perfume sweet as sandalwood, a soft touch and curves that nourished a man's desires—but N? N, the cogwheel of this endless dream was already a ghost. And the 'blues,' what was that all about? "All right," I bark at him, my voice filled with annoyance and anger, "you've offered up one reason I'm stuck with you. What are the others?"

"My second point, well, *mon ami*, you've just proved."

"How so?" Once more the soma slides down my throat, but oh how I longed for the jolt of a good shot of Turkish coffee—black as all evil—to clear my head and escape this hallucination.

"You must understand my true nature is to always remain calm, even in the most hostile situations. An even temperament has often been the key to my victories."

"Is this where you are going to tell me that at night, when the cannons were raging all around you, you had no problem sleeping?"

"Indeed."

I tell N how this was one of the few compliments Sir Walter Scott paid him in his exhaustive biography. "But what has this to do with me?"

"Haven't you, my dear Beethoven, been known to roar like an artillery brigade when matters do not go your way?"

"*Vielleicht.* Perhaps."

"Perhaps?" N is incredulous. "Shall I rattle off a dozen instances?"

"*Nein.*" Among those Viennese all too fond of their *Sachertorte und cappuccino* I am often condescended to as an unlicked bear from the wrong side of the Rhine. *Fick das*—fuck that.

"Who better to be your concert master, than a general who could sleep through the sound of carnage?"

Ever weary of N's logic, I reluctantly ask him for the third reason.

"You and me, B, we're much alike," he informs me. "Born a year apart, both self-made men—outsiders rising up the ranks on the strength of our own wits and talents. Both fond of espresso. And you, a Rhinelander conquering Vienna; me, a Corsican among the French. . . ."

"Who also conquered Vienna," I add.

"*Oui.* And when the stories of these times are written, two names will tower above all others, Napoleon and Beethoven."

"You can stop right there," I say. "I've read your biography. It's neither flattering nor is it filled with towering compliments. . . ."

"Nor is yours," he rebuts. "History, my dear B, is a set of lies agreed upon and retold by the victors. For now our genius lies fallow, but in the future—*Gesu*, B—you and I, we're but stepping stones to a future more glorious than you can imagine even in your wildest dreams. . . ."

"Wilder than this?"

"*Oui.* One day our truth, our aspiration, the dreams of our hearts shall be known—and celebrated. But for now, you are my charge, my responsibility, not the other way around."

"Give me one reason to trust you," I snap. As Emperor, Bonaparte undermined the very democratic policies he had sworn to defend.

"Do you believe in 'Original Sin'?" N asks me. "Do you believe that people are inherently evil or inherently good?"

Never one to become entangled in the dogma of any particular faith, I reflect for a moment on what years of observation on the nature of humans has revealed to me. "We all know there are good people and there are bad people."

"*Précisément!* Not knowing me in life, B, do not judge me in death. At least not yet. What I accomplished in my allotted time on this earth was immense. Two thousand years ago Confucius laid it all out in his *Analects* when he said it is the obligation of a ruler to renew himself in order to inspire the people by his example. Haven't I done just that? Are we not all entitled by birthright to a share of the earth's produce sufficient to fill the needs of our existence?"

I have no patience for N's prevarications. By crowning himself "Emperor" back in 1804, Napoleon betrayed the aspirations of an entire continent and destroyed my faith in him as well. I recalled vividly the day the news arrived. My friend and student, Ferdinand Ries, who probably wasn't more than 20 at the time and had been helping me out as my assistant, was the one who brought us the news. I had just finished the full score of my *Third Symphony*, the one originally entitled "*Bonaparte.*" Steffen von Breuning and a few other friends were over at my apartment in Vienna. As was often the case when we gathered, the conversation, which should have been on a draft of *Fidelio* that Steffen and I were re-working at the time, had drifted to women and, ultimately, three in particular who were students of the pianoforte. The Brunsvik sisters, Josephine and Therese, were the fair-haired and charming daughters of a Hungarian aristocrat. Josephine, the one who most caught my eye, had already by age 26 been married and widowed, courtesy of the late Count Joseph von Deym.

We were all debating the virtues of each sister when a highly agitated Ries burst into the house. He brought with him the news that the French Assembly and Senate had issued proclamations which elevated Napoleon from the elected post of First Consul of the Republic to the position of Emperor and that he would have himself crowned as such in front of the Pope, no less.

I flew into a rage upon hearing this news and shouted aloud, *"Is he nothing more than an ordinary human being? Now he too will trample on all the rights of man and indulge only his ambition. He will exalt himself above all others and become a tyrant!"* I went over to my table where I had left the score and with my pen scratched out the title, "*Bonaparte.*" Later I changed the title to the *Eroica*, which is how everyone knows it.

"I am no Royalist!" N declares, his words permeating my consciousness like a hammer. "Certainly no more so than you, my dear Beethoven. You lived on the largesse of the nobility. Would there even be a Beethoven if there had been no Count Waldstein, no Prince

Lichnowsky, no Archduke Rudolph?"

"Nonsense," I shout back at N.

"No, *mon frère*. You are the hypocrite. Admit it. With you that day besides Breuning and Ries were your patrons, Prince Lichnowsky, his younger brother, Moritz, and Prince Lobkowitz."

"How do you know all this?" I ask.

"Omniscience B, omniscience. It's a great skill to have. There is nothing I do not know. Yet one more reason I am your, as you put it, your 'guide' on the path to Elysium. And if I recall correctly—actually being omniscient, I always recall correctly—Lichnowsky, your patron, was concerned that your infatuation with the widowed Countess Josephine Deym was a distraction to your work, the work he was supporting with a rather serious stipend."

"So I took their money to write music, what of it?"

"I've never been moved by the patronage of a prince or the tears of a countess," N declares. "My commands came from the aspirations of our people and it is their sufferings that touched me. What I had decided to do was revolutionary, and what I had projected for the future was still more so. Understand me, B, I envisioned a new European order to replace the old. There would be but one people in all Europe, served by one common Code of Laws applicable to all. For this I was hated by the aristocracy throughout the continent but most especially by the Austrians and the British. And don't get me started on the Brits. More than any other nation they make a pretense of being civilized and enlightened while perpetrating the worst atrocities on their colonies throughout the world—and long after you and I are gone they will retain the monarchy and a supportive aristocracy based on the absurd notion of "Divine Right." The English press calls me the Corsican tyrant—a tiger let loose to devour mankind. They write that I am an abomination, a half-African, half-European mulatto. I am not a gentleman who plays by their rules and I am one, therefore, who cannot be trusted."

"To which I still agree. I don't trust you," but N ignores my snickers and continues.

"You must understand that your endless dream is also Napoleon's dream. Napoleon Bonaparte is your guide because we share the same vision of a world where all men are brothers and only by joining together can we make that happen. By bringing order and justice to France, I rendered the Revolution attractive to people outside its borders. If I had been able to maintain a blanket of peace over the continent for a few more years where might our vision of *Liberté, Égalité, Fraternité,* not travel? Oh, how the British feared us, not our armies but our ideas. Even their Prime Minster, Edmund Burke, once declared on the floor of the House of Commons, *'It is not the enmity but the friendship of France that is truly terrible. Her intercourse with nations furthers by her example, the spread of her doctrines; these are the most dreadful of her arms.'* Consider this B, a Europe united in peace; their empires and their colonies freed from the yoke of imperialist fortunes. The world needed me to cross that bridge too far in order to destroy the old and usher in a new age. Not only did we need to behead the tyrants of Europe in order to preserve *L'âge d'Éclaircissement,* I personally had to forever eviscerate feudalism even if it required the strength of Prometheus."

"Spare me justifications." I insist. "When your cannonades blasted into the heart of Vienna, I was there huddled in my brother's basement, pillows over my head to protect what was left of my hearing. The suffering you caused. Hunger, disease, death. Twenty years of wars—five million dead? What songs of mourning shall we sing for those corpses left rotting on the battlefield?"

"I grieve too. While it's true that in life I had no trouble sleeping while opposing armies sat in heated opposition, I never rest in Elysium. Each and every time I close my eyes in search of sleep all I hear is the screams of every soldier, every civilian, every child that died during those battles."

"I may not be dead, but thankfully I'm deaf." One can gloat, even in dreams. Sweet. But of course the General one ups me with his next retort.

"Your death will come before the bells of St. Stephen's crackle over dinner. How you fare on the road to Elysium remains undecided. And right now, your prospects are not as bright as you might desire. Unless . . . unless, no I've said too much already."

"You have foresight, omniscience. So what? I can take care of myself. What I really want to know is this: Why did you betray the revolution?"

"Did I betray the revolution? No, I did not. Every battle from the streets of Paris to the mud of Waterloo was in defense of the Republic. Four wars we fought. In none were we, the French, the aggressor. Even my *Grande Armée's* march to Moscow was in retribution for attacks along peaceful borders. Did you know why Czar Nicholas was so terrified when I freed the serfs and tore down the ghetto walls in neighboring Poland?"

I must have poked N just right and exposed a raw nerve. I watch and wait. Regardless of justifications, N's vibrations can no longer conceal his own guilt and sense of failure.

"The Czar feared that our beloved concepts of freedom, equality, and liberty would infiltrate the border faster than his Cossacks could quash them. He broke the truce and we responded. But why do we do anything? That's the real question. Why did you turn away from your 'Immortal Beloved'? Why did you destroy your nephew? And why are you so angry? Anger and joy are incompatible."

N is shaking, shivering as he speaks. Is he remembering the chill of a Russian winter gone astray? Or the 500,000 French soldiers who never returned home, their bodies food for the wolves?

"Perhaps you need me more than I need you?" I say. "Perhaps I am here for your confession, not the other way around?"

"It's the Emperor's crown and the throne that still troubles you, isn't it? One is two bits of gold, the other wood cushioned by velvet. *Gesu*, B, they're just props in a grand theatrical production whose sole objective was to preserve the Republic."

"That gamble worked out well, didn't it," I smirk. "You lost your bet. We die, while Metternich and the emperors of Russia, Austria, and England remain. You not only brought down France, but democracy as well."

"I lost because after two decades of fighting my enemies had time enough to study, understand, and imitate the very tactics I had used so often to defeat them previously. Do you know why I became an emperor?"

In my mind's eye the warmth of the soma allows me to see only one word writ large by those giant butterflies: *Megalomania.*

"Hardly," he rebuts. "I knew my coronation was going to be a source of disillusionment. Perhaps I did reach too far, but from the moment the Assembly elected me a leader of France, the plots against me, the plots against the Republic became a constant threat. I feared assassination not for the cost of my life but for the price the people of France would pay were I were struck down. The British, who as you well know, have savaged me in their histories, sought to murder me and destroy the revolution I embodied. If they could not defeat our armies on the battle field, they would try to eliminate me singly and foist Louis XVIII onto the throne."

I remain ever the skeptic, so N insists upon sharing one example.

"My beloved Josephine, Josephine Beauharnais, and I were to go by coach to the theater. On stage an orchestra of the new France Republic was to perform Haydn's *Creation.* A festive occasion, yes? Josephine and I dressed for the gala but as so often happens with women, she was late in her preparations. The crowds gathered in a square by the theater. Just as our coach travelled into a narrow lane, a bomb planted in a horse cart by English agents collaborating with a group of Royalists goes off. The explosion kills dozens—most are children."

"You survived owing to the vanity of women?"

"*Oui, mon frère. Oui,* the vanity of a woman saved our lives, but beauty fades and is no long-term defense. This attempt on my life was but the first of many."

"This is true?" I ask, never having heard or read of these events.

"*Metternich,*" he replies with the name of the Austrian Prime Minister, a man known wide for his spies and suppression. "Nor would you ever read the truth without a free press uncensored by the very foxes that oppose liberty. Believe me, I feared not for my own life but for the Republic. In the minds of most Frenchmen, the Revolution, the foundation of the Republic was embodied in my own personage. Had I been killed, could our cause survive? No, *mon ami*, under royalist pressure it would collapse and the Bourbon heirs would reclaim the throne."

Though politics is not my forte, I am still perplexed about the wisdom of N's argument. While feudalism certainly had the potential to return along with the *Ancien Régime*, was not the cause already lost when he crowned himself Emperor?

"I swore," N continues, "to find a way to ensure that our freedoms would not be lost nor would democracy vanish. Our ruling assembly and my closest advisors debated by what means we could make the survival of the Republic less dependent on me. And we hit upon a process that our enemies would easily understand: a hereditary throne. By making my position one that could be inherited certainly made it less personal. The idea was finally proposed to name me Emperor but with a difference befitting the Republic. We would establish a monarchy not by divine right but one granted by the will of the people. If Napoleon Bonaparte was assassinated, then my heirs would rule. The continuity of leadership would be preserved and along with it the Republic."

"Don't you see the inconsistency of this logic? How can you preserve *Liberté, Égalité,* and *Fraternité* with a hereditary throne? Where go justice and the rights of man? Up in smoke?"

"I understand your concerns B. Even my Josephine thought as you do now. She was opposed to the idea as she claimed—perhaps rightly in hindsight—that no one would understand the necessity or logic behind our decisions. After hearing and weighing her concerns, I decided I would only agree with the plan if I was voted in by the people of France. We held a plebiscite. Three million Frenchmen voted '*Oui.*' Only a thousand voted 'No.'"

Napoleon Bonaparte's coronation—which resembled a spectacle

more befitting the Roman coliseum—was universally attributed to unbridled ambition and pride—which in fact is how history records it. Freedom-loving people here and elsewhere still disparage his actions. It is my turn to offer a rebuke. "Why is it you failed to heed your Josephine? *Mein Gott,* is it not you who said that in times of crisis, it is the fate of men that women appear to soften our misfortune? But you, you threw Josephine away. You divorced her and married the Hapsburg's daughter—the very royalty you fought to overthrow—to produce an heir. You buried the revolution with the efficacy of a piano trio; first Moscow, then Vittoria, then Waterloo. And for these misbegotten blessings, for these, you are consecrated as my guide?"

"I am here only because you have chosen me to reveal the future—but to do that you must also understand the past, your past, our past, and the first Revolution."

When I query N about this "First Revolution," he brings up the name Prometheus and the conquest of fire. "Consider this," he offers. "Can you name any other species on the face of the earth that has been able to conquer—that is, *control,* fire?"

Though I cannot fathom why he's taking our discussion off in this direction, I agree, it is we humans alone who have made fire a utility to our lives.

"The ancients," N continues, "understood this on a primal level. Fire is not just a utility, *mon ami,* it is what made us human; it is what separated us from other animals. Through the control of fire, our species became the first and only one on this planet to gain some measure of control over our environment. Fire was our earliest ancestors' first weapon against the natural world. It gave us heat. It became our defender. It altered the balance of power between us and other predators. It enabled us to cook and to preserve food. The art of chemistry was born in the kitchen. Scholars postulate that fire enabled us to move out of the trees and forest—where most primates still live for protection—and on into the grasslands. Our lives became mobile and the world opened up to us. That we could now visualize another dimension, that of the transformation of matter into energy, became the boundary line between what science and religion now define as human versus non-human consciousness. The conquest of fire was the first building block of civilization. With it came imagination, awareness, manipulation of our environment, and the ultimate birth of all that we consider civilized: language, culture, religion, art, politics, and, for you, music. The myth of Prometheus, the Titan who fought against Zeus in order to give fire to mankind, is how our ancestors retold this story to their children and their children's children. I would even go so far as to say that even in Genesis that which Eve gave to Adam in the Garden of Eden was not just the wisdom to understand good and evil, but the control of fire. Our First Revolution was that of knowledge, the knowledge that made us human. And just as priests swear that *Gesu* died for our sins, from our ashes a new Jerusalem, an earthly paradise bathed in the glow of freedom and human dignity, will one day arise—that is the next revolution. Our dreams are merely the path."

When I ask him how this will come to pass, N rhapsodizes once more about his foresight and the glories of the world ahead. "Wait until you see what Europe looks like in a hundred or even two hundred years. But as for you, *mon ami*, never forget, your strength is your weakness. Your weakness is your strength."

Somehow inside my head I hear Mozart's *Requiem* and a faint echo of the composer's voice urging me to *always be inspired by the possibility of greatness in every creation.* "What's next then?" I ask N.

He points to the soma and urges me to drink. "*Gesu* died for somebody's sins but . . . "

With a thirst suddenly unbearable, I gulp down the soma until even the dregs of jasmine are gone. The butterflies reappear and spell out N's final words just as the world before my eyes goes black, *"There is no resurrection without death."*

CHAPTER 10

King Lux Aeterna

NO, I WAS NOT DEAD . . . at least not yet, though the darkness before me was profound enough to be befitting a final resting place. I had opened my eyes at Napoleon's nudging insistence but saw nothing except a blackness so overwhelming I could have been sitting inside an inkwell. And time, I'd lost all sense of that as well. It was just when I began to wonder if I was already in my grave that a flash of light illuminated the chamber around us.

Little in life prepared me for what I saw. We were inside a cave, a real cave. Napoleon had aimed a beam of light generated by some sort of strange lantern onto the stone wall before me. There were the painted figures of two horses facing away from each other. Both had thick black manes and bodies covered in spots like a leopard. Surrounding the horses were the outlines of handprints, small, delicate handprints.

"Where are we?" I asked Napoleon.

"*Pech Merle,*" he answered, "a cave in southwest France near the *Dordogne*. We're about a dozen leagues northwest of the village of *St. Circq La Popie* in the *Lot* River Valley. Upstream from *Cahors.*" None of the names registered with me nor could I ever recall having ever been in France proper, though I had once upon a time considered leaving Vienna for Paris.

As N panned the light around the walls other painted figures came into our view: large bison pawing the earth and herds of antelopes with enormous racks of antlers. Nearby were several elephants covered in thick hair. "*Mammoths,*" Napoleon called them.

"Why are we here?" I asked.

"The road to Elysium takes many turns. There is much you need to understand before your journey ends."

"But why a cave in France? And why these paintings?"

"They're 25,000 years old," N declared as he refocused the light back upon the horses. "And painted by a woman, who might very well be the grandmother of us all. Look at the hand prints. Those, for lack of a better word to reflect our limited understanding of what these people were doing here, are her signature."

I was both perplexed and fascinated by his explanation. Twenty-five thousand years old. "How do you know this? Foresight? Omniscience?"

"*Oui*. You're catching on, B. This is the cave of our ancestors, one of many scattered through the region."

I had never known or ever heard anything about these places and said so.

"It will be another century before they're rediscovered and opened for study by scholars and for viewing by our people. And in due time the scientists of a future generation will be able to analyze those hand prints and extract something they call "DNA 3.0," or "Shadow DNA." It's nothing you need understand—just know that all living creatures are composed of this chemical compound—and by studying the attributes they can tell much about a person. Our DNA is passed along generation to generation to us in roughly equal amounts by both our mother and our father. Though we share most of this chemical in common, its expression is unique to each individual. And within the unique threads each of us carries, are fragments of the traits of our ancestors. Using new tools of calculation that you and I cannot even imagine, scholars will map out these threads and link us both backwards to our parents, grandparents, great-grandparents and forward to our children, grandchildren and great-grandchildren and, most importantly, sideways to our sisters, brothers, and cousins. And one day, what they will be able to announce with definitive certainty is that you and I and most everyone born in Europe is a descendent or relative of the woman who painted these horses. And this mother's great-great-great-great-great-grandmother, who came out of Africa thousands of years earlier, is related to everyone everywhere on the face of this sweet earth."

As I absorbed the impact of these ideas, N shone the light onto a footprint frozen in what looked like mud but was in fact hardened stone.

"The same woman who painted those horses left behind that as well. Judging by its size, she was probably a teenager no more than five feet tall."

As I knelt down and placed my fingers in the grooves created by her toes, I at last understood why Napoleon had brought me here. They felt alive and in my mind's eye, I could see Isis before me. "If she is our mother, then truly *Alle Menschen werden Brüder—all men are brothers.*"

"Précisément! And if all mankind shares the same ancestors, any claim the aristocracy have to their title as coming from the divine right of God simply disintegrates in the face of such evidence. Through this shadow DNA we are left with is biological proof for *"Liberté, Égalité, Fraternité,"* as the natural state of all peoples. And that, *mon ami*, is why your *Ninth Symphony* will continue to resonate throughout the world for eternity."

"And you are certain about all this?"

"But of course . . . Why these same scientists have even determined that every person on the face of this planet who has blue eyes is also related. By calculating the changes that occur each generation in this DNA compound, they have been able to determine that blue eyes came from a single mutation some 6,000–10,000 years ago. And if all blue-eyed people are descendent from the same ancestors, then it stands to reason that all brown-eyed people are related as well."

"And you know this how?" I was still puzzled by much of what N had said, though it did seem to add up logically. "Have you seen the future?"

Napoleon held up his lantern. "You are seeing it right now. This is *Une torche électrique, eine Taschenlampe:* a flashlight. It captures electricity—the same force you keep seeing over and over as lightening in your dream—and stores it in a device known as a battery." N demonstrated how easily it was to turn his *Taschenlampe* on and off pushing what he called a "switch." On and off, on and off he went, each time plunging us back into total darkness.

"It's like magic," I said.

"No, it's science, 20th-century science. In the future mankind will harness this electricity for all manner of wonders."

"And you've seen this yourself?" I asked, not being able to fathom how they captured lightening in a bottle.

"Of course. And perhaps one day you will experience this as well . . . but for now it is the past—your past—that you need to understand."

N shut the light off one last time and began to count, *Un, deux, trois, quatre, cinq heures.* Five o'clock. A jagged bolt of lightning exploded around us, followed immediately by the vibrations—*ja,* just the vibrations, not the rumble—of thunder.

But this time, unlike earlier adventures in this endless dream, after the flash of lightening, we emerged from the blackness of an ink pot into a well-lit sky. No, we were no longer inside the cave of *Pech Merle,* but rather, right back at the oasis beside the Temple of Isis. Travel should always be this easy. Beats a kidney-jarring stagecoach ride on dirt roads any day.

We sat cross-legged like two Buddhas on our respective stone seats, cups of soma firmly in our hands and a small fire in the brazier at our feet.

"If everything you say is true, then each time I've slept with a woman, in fact, I'm sleeping with my sister? Or mother? Or daughter?"

"In a manner of speaking, yes. There's a Viennese doctor not yet born who will make the claim, to sleep with one woman is to sleep with all women—metaphorically speaking of course. But you, how is it you—for all your affairs—you never slept with the first love of your life, Leonore von Breuning, before you left Bonn for Vienna the second time in 1792?"

"By your logic I have—innumerable times."

"You couldn't sleep with her or you wouldn't sleep with her? You were in Bonn for another four years before moving to Vienna, yes?"

Truth be known, Leonore and I would have had—did have—many opportunities to lie together but neither one of us could. The specter of Margaretha and that November day always came between us. If I went to kiss Leonore, all I saw was my sister's anguish and I had to withdraw. And whenever Leonore sought to approach me, a wave of guilt would often sweep across her face and leave her in tears. We spoke openly of this but nothing could get us past these sad feelings. Much as I loved Leonore and much as she loved me, neither one of us could shake the shadows of that day. In my mind's eye I would struggle to replace images of poor Margaretha with that of my Lorchen undressing beside the hot springs as we each played at that game of pretending to not look and yet look. More than any woman I had ever known, Leonore naked moved with such *unerschütterlicher Gelassenheit,* that I forever remained in awe of her poise, grace, and womanly beauty. Fortunately, all was not lost. Instead of letting those pains part us from each other, we turned that love into friendship. I grew closer to her than I was to Steffen or Wegeler. There was almost nothing we could not share with each other—except intimate contact.

Over time, the pain of that November faded from our consciousness, but it never entirely went away. And although we each moved on with our lives, somehow we both presumed we would end up together despite all that transpired around us at that naïve age.

Even Steffen and Wegeler—who had returned from medical school in Vienna—thought this. I continued writing, composing, and playing with the orchestra in Bonn. I gave lessons, took care of my brothers, and saw to it that they both had the schooling I did not. Circumstances made me both mother and father to my brothers, who relied on me for everything—a condition that would persist for the entirety of our lives. Casper, who loved music and also gave lessons but did not have a flair for composing, took up business; and Nikolaus Johann, who had no musical aptitude, trained as an apprentice to a pharmacist.

It was the lessons, those damnable piano lessons, however that kept getting me into trouble. Jeanette d'Honrath and Babette Koch, among other young and entrancing friends of Leonore, were my students.

"Ah, the suggestive power of the feminine," offered up Napoleon. "You were no doubt engaged with each of them in some sort of amorous entanglement?"

Ja, it's true. Seduction came easily at that age, particularly when detached from love. Imagine if you will what it was like to be regularly posed in close proximity to such desserts. My appetite grew with each pianoforte lesson and I imagine for them as well. Alone for hours, bodies pressed close upon each other—wisps of hair framing a gracefully tilted but otherwise exposed bare neck, hands and fingers often entwined above the keyboard, the aura of jasmine perfume masking natural female scents, and breasts, so artfully curved, sighing with each breath—what a life.

Babette fell first and Jeanette not long after, though in each case I kept imagining it was Leonore whom I was with. I say fell, but our tumbles into bed were mutual. They were each as much in love with the notion of making love disconnected from real love as I was at that age. With Babette it was of little surprise. Though I had perhaps shocked her on the day I rode off to the garden with Leonore, she was mightily inspired to return the favor.

We were alone at the piano in the music room of her family's estate. I had just demonstrated the proper fingering to use on a particularly difficult fugue, when, saying she had a different approach in mind, Babette took one of my hands in her own. She slid it beneath her blouse and placed it firmly round her breast. What a jewel.

The pianoforte fell silent as she whispered in my ear, "And if I wake your muse, it is only to enjoy the echoes of your desire." She put her other hand between my legs. I grew stiff immediately.

We completed the balance of her lessons on the couch, her sighs and moans providing all the choral effects necessary for this most primal harmony—one we would repeat every now and again right through her engagement and up until the day she married a minor court official. I even played the organ at their wedding. And though there was never a serious moment between the two of us, I confess to being transfixed by her red hair, particularly the flaming delta between her thighs that so much so resembled the entrance to the cave at the Garden of Venus. Our last night together, I even let the candles burn bright—the better to scan and forever memorialize in my consciousness, the fiery beauty of Babette's Temple of Isis.

Long-legged and lean, Babette verily melted whenever I played a sonata. She loved how I touched the keys of her piano. I quickly came to understand how women who craved sensitivity and passion found little of it at the hands of most men. But we musicians—we creative musicians—we were a different breed all together. That which the female of our species craved verily flowed through our fingers most naturally. We understood without thought the power of a delicate touch. Whenever I played, women would always come on to me. Babette was no exception. Her pulse would race, her face would go flush with desire, and often at such times when we were alone she'd lift her skirts and bury my head between her thighs. My tongue would probe the little knob between those lips until she came, her scent, her juices as intoxicating as the soma.

"Do you know what that's like?" I asked Napoleon, "To dine upon a woman and feel her tremble with delight until she finally explodes in one final mad burst of unrestrained passion?"

"*Oui,* my Josephine Beauharnais was as much a tiger. Pity I had to divorce her in favor of Marie Louise. The Hapsburgs were never known much as lovers. Scholars have told me that music is the aural expression of love, affection, of all our emotions. It is the "love calls" of our species and the most direct way to communicate a knowledge of reality. The perfect work of art excites the aesthetic emotion to its maximum. The nearest analogy to this state would seem to be provided by the sexual orgasm. Yet, your passion for Babette Koch seems to have left impressions that were little deep as were those made upon the beauty that caused them. And Miss d'Honrath, I imagine you had your way with her as well?"

"A far more complicated story, one that also involves the singer, Magdalena Willmann," I told N as he refilled our teacups, "and one that caused no end of difficulties between Leonore and me."

In the autumn of 1791—a year before I left for Vienna again—there was to be a meeting of the Teutonic Order at Mergentheim, several hundred miles southeast of Bonn. The Grand Master of the Order was our own Elector, Maximilian Franz, and given that the visit was to extend for a full month, ample provision was made for theatrical and musical amusements. Twenty-five members of the Elector's orchestra—myself included—as well as a choral ensemble were to travel up the Rhine and Main rivers in two large river yachts, the *Lorelei* and the *Drachen*. Each boat had a mast and sail, a flat deck with a railing, comfortable cabins with windows, and a full galley for cooking, as the journey would take many days in either direction. In these river boats our company made the slow if not downright tedious journey against the current of the Rhine.

It was the most pleasant season of the year for such a journey, as the coolness of the river tempered the lingering heat of summer. The deep gorges of the Rhine were strikingly exotic.

The hills, covered with vegetation, were at their best and brightest. The romantic views of the old towns and villages along the river had not yet suffered the degradations of the continental wars soon to break upon them. This little voyage, which was the source of the most enjoyable visions and escapades, still lives bright and beautiful in my memory.

And the most beautiful of those visions was Magdalena Willman. Trained initially in Bonn, the city of her birth, Magdalena possessed a superlative voice that had been cultivated in tours around the capitals of Europe. To hear her sing was to be seduced. Magdalena was preparing to head off on yet another tour, first to Munich and then Venice, Rome, and Naples. The Elector, who wanted her to be both his principal female singer and the lead voice in the choir, insisted she join the excursion at least as far as Mergentheim, and she agreed.

Before we left Bonn, the company of musicians assembled and elected the bass singer, *Herr* Edward Lux, "King" of the expedition. Though I had discreetly petitioned our King Lux to place me on board the same yacht, the *Drachen*, as Magdalena, Count Waldstein intervened at the very last moment and insisted I travel with him on the *Lorelei*. As the ranking Teutonic Knight on the journey, the Count had accepted King Lux's designation as Overseer of the Kitchen. I was assigned, along with Waldstein's personal servants, to join the scullery crew.

My disappointment at not having the chance to get close to Magdalena was offset by the Count's far more serious offer of remuneration for helping him with the score of an orchestral composition he was working on. My family endured constant poverty and I was always pressed to acquire ever greater compensation for my talents. Waldstein imagined the long trip through pleasant surroundings would provide us with that opportunity when not otherwise occupied with the tasks necessary for our journey. In that regard he was a true and honest friend, sharing not just our common love of music, but his wisdom, wealth, and humanity as well.

After dinner was long past on the first evening away from Bonn, the Count and I sat alone drinking wine in the kitchen. He repeated a refrain he had said many times over the past year, which was that I must return to Vienna if I was to continue to grow as an artist. In that way he was one of my greatest supporters in those early years. As a musician himself and as a nobleman who had travelled widely—and constantly, Waldstein knew better than me how I compared to other composers and performers. He reminded me that my brothers were now old enough to manage by themselves as each had completed or nearly completed his own training. But even as he praised me for the selfless work I had done in raising them, he insisted it was time to stop considering their needs first and take care of my own. *"Be selfish,"* he would say. *"Consider your own career."* He saw Bonn as a backwater, a second-tier orchestra where I was already, at 20 years of age, the best and most advanced player. Much as he admired Neefe, Franz Ries, and the others, there was nothing more for me to gain by staying. And as for money—of which there was never enough—he insisted I not worry. He would use his influence first with the Elector to ensure I was paid an adequate stipend to study in Vienna with Mozart or Haydn and he assured me he would also write many letters of recommendation to his friends there, the crème de la crème of the aristocracy, whose potential commissions and connections would also prove invaluable.

When I told the Count that I could not thank him enough for his support and encouragement, he insisted I repay him by assisting him with his concerto, to which I heartily agreed. Waldstein handed me the key to one of the several cabins assigned him—which were the most luxurious on the *Lorelei*—and said he left the score on his bed. Would I retrieve it?

I agreed. With an oil lantern in hand, I left the ship's galley and traversed the yacht below deck until I found Waldstein's cabin. The key fit smoothly. I turned it and entered, not at all prepared for what awaited me. Lying in bed dressed only in a thin, silken nightgown that hid nothing was the beautiful, blue-eyed, and blond Jeanette d'Honrath. Due to her particularly sweet singing voice, Jeanette had been asked to join the choir for this journey as a temporary replacement for another singer who was taken ill. She had agreed for this occasion only.

"Lock the door," were the first and, if I recall correctly, the only coherent words Jeanette said to me that evening.

We spent the entire night together, but it was nothing like my escapades with Babette. Jeanette was virginal, timid, inexperienced, shy, and lacking the hunger that comes with passion. It mattered naught what I did or how I did it. Try as I might, she remained willing, but taut; hungry, yet devoid of energy; wanting, but passive; desirous of romantic passion, but absent any herself. In the end it was rather sad, not that either one of us were at fault, or that any blame was leveled. We were just not suited to each other's temperament or needs—or so I thought.

In the morning I slipped out to work the breakfast kitchen and it was there I again encountered Count Waldstein reading a recent translation of the *Bhagavad-Gita*. Always a paragon of discretion, he asked me, "Did you find the score satisfactory?"

I nodded, "The notes were all there, all in the right places, but the Coda . . ." I said, reflecting back to the lack of a noticeable climax, "the Coda needs work."

"It's a pity," he said and then, after a pause for reflection, he added, "Vienna. Forget the Coda. Go to Vienna. All else will unfold. Let me tell you how." He waived his copy of the *Bhagavad-Gita*. "Did you know that the Hindoos believe that by performing one's own work, one worships the Creator who dwells in every creature? Such worship brings that person to fulfillment. It is better to perform one's own duties imperfectly than to attempt to master the duties of another. By fulfilling the obligations one is born with a person never comes to grief. If you seek perfection, you will find harmony in every action of life, provided you have the inner wisdom and self-compassion to accept your limitations—your failures—with grace. Remember, we humans are the definition of imperfection. And you, my friend, you need to go to Vienna."

During the rest of the boat ride up the Rhine I worked on Waldstein's score with him. This suited Jeanette perfectly well. She ignored my existence by day but at night when there were no prying eyes around, it was a different story—a sad and secretive short story to which I fell into collaboration with, and one I soon regretted.

Our cruise upriver proceeded in this manner until there was a stopover at Aschaffenburg, where the Elector of Mainz had his summer palace. Living there was the Abbé Sterkel, a man of some 40 years who had been a musician from childhood. Sterkel was considered one of the finest pianists in all the German states and without rival. His style both as composer and pianist had been refined and cultivated to the utmost, both in Germania and Italy, and his playing was in the highest degree light, graceful, pleasing, and, as the elder Ries once described, "*somewhat ladylike.*" Ries took several of us younger musicians to pay our respects to this master, who, complying with our request, sat himself down to play. Up to this time, I knew nothing of the finer nuances in the handling of the pianoforte. My style of treating this instrument, which derived from the organ, was so different from that usually adopted, that my playing was still judged rude and hard by those—like Sterkel—who had trained on the harpsichord. Sterkel lacked emotion and power in his execution, favoring instead precision, grace, and delicacy. After the Abbé finished, they invited me to take his place at the instrument but I hesitated to exhibit myself after such a display. I hesitated until I saw that joining those of us who had assembled there were several singers, including Magdalena Willmann.

The Abbé, perhaps thinking he was shrewd and could goad me on, continued to question my ability. A year or two before, the composer, Righini, a colleague of Sterkel's, had published *Dodeci Ariette.* I in turn had composed five widely circulated vocal variations for one of them, *Venni Amore.* Some of these melodies were exceedingly difficult, and Sterkel now expressed his doubts whether I could play them. Sensing the eyes of the woman I very much wanted to impress were upon me, I finally agreed to a turn on the pianoforte.

Taking these melodies as my theme, I played not only the variations so far as I could remember them, but went on with a number of others no less difficult, in a precise imitation of Sterkel's playing style. And to the great surprise of the listeners, Magdalena Willmann spontaneously joined me by singing the vocal portions of the variations to perfection.

After mimicking Sterkel, I went on to play other compositions, including portions of one of my own cantatas. Here, too, Magdalena was only too happy to improvise and accompany me.

The combination of her seductive voice and my impassioned playing stunned and overwhelmed those who had gathered around us. Everyone assembled there that day, excepting the Abbé—whom I would later be forced to reckon with as one of my enemies—came to understand that I had attained the height of excellence whereupon I now stood by a path of my own discovery, a path I was determined to follow.

When it came time to re-board our river yachts, Magdalena insisted I join her cabin on the *Drachen,* a request I was only too happy to accommodate, especially since it meant ending my nocturnal trysts with Jeanette.

Never before—and perhaps since—had I been so equally matched with a woman who was so much my opposite.

"She was the *Yin* to your *Yang*?"

"My what to my what?" I asked N.

"The *Yin* to your *Yang*. It's a Chinese concept, one Confucius or Lao Tzu would use to describe the two complimentary and interlocking halves of the *Tao*." N sketched the symbol in the sand with his finger. It looked like a circle bisected equally by an "S" from north to south. "Light—dark; good—evil; high—low; sun—moon; night—day; male—female."

Magdalena was that and more. In the week before she would leave Mergentheim to start her journey south we shared every moment possible together, day and night. Perhaps it was our youth, perhaps it was the knowledge that we knew not when—or if—we would see each other again, perhaps it was just good fortune, but we each found in the other the desire to wrestle and devour each other into exhaustion like two dragons, not just in bed, but around the keyboard as well. She was more than a singer who echoed lyrics. She was an inspired artist who found the soul of a song by reading between the lines to discover the depths of its creation. She even presented me with a copy of Schiller's "*Ode to Joy,*" and suggested that I use my talents to set it to music. The poem was one of her favorites.

Truly I had met a woman who echoed all my dreams as a creative artist and when she left for Munich, we each wondered if we would ever meet again. The future, a future I had imagined, a future which I held in my hands as if it were a fledgling, spread its wings. Sadly, Magdalena was that migratory bird and off she flew. I must confess that after our parting I fell into a deep funk that must have been all too obvious to the others in our little orchestra.

At dinner one night in Mergentheim some of the other young men from our company paid one of the serving girls to ply off her charms upon me. She had shapely hips and ample breasts barely contained within her peasant's skirt and blouse. No sooner had the girl startled me by sliding onto my lap and caressing my neck with her lips and tongue, than I saw Jeanette walk into the dining hall. Jeanette, who immediately noticed me thus engaged, turned away ever more quickly. I tried to repel the advances of the serving girl, but was too late. Jeanette disappeared. Encouraged by the others, the girl persevered until I lost all patience and put an end to her importunities by a sharp whack to the back of her head.

The next morning I learned that Jeanette had abandoned the company immediately after dinner and returned to Bonn by coach, alone. It would be another three weeks before the rest of the company—myself included—returned home by the river yachts as we had come, during which time I foreswore relations with any other women and continued working with Count Waldstein on his score.

No doubt Jeanette had informed Leonore as to all that had transpired, for when I first encountered my Lorchen at the von Breuning's home, the fire in her eyes told all. It was weeks before Leonore would even deign to speak with me. Something had changed between us, and that sense of inevitability, the sense that we would—despite the wanderings of youth—eventually end up together, fell into question, an open yet unanswered question.

And after weighing Count Waldstein's advice, over the next few months I began to give serious consideration to leaving Bonn for Vienna. *Herr* Neefe, who had been my principal teacher for almost ten years, agreed with the Count. There was nothing anyone in Bonn could teach me. If I wanted to grow, I had to go. Casper agreed, reminding me that he and Nikolaus were old enough to stand on their own. When I went to the cemetery and sat beside the graves of my mother and sister, I could hear their voices urging me to move forward as well.

My plans, however, were temporarily retarded when Waldstein, who had just returned from yet another journey to cities back east, brought the news to my brother Casper and me that Mozart had died unexpectedly just before Christmas. Still, he urged me to go forth nonetheless, writing that, *"The Genius of Mozart is mourning and weeping over the death of her pupil. She found a refuge but no occupation with the inexhaustible Haydn; through him she wishes to form a union with another. With the help of assiduous labor you shall receive Mozart's spirit from Haydn's hands."*

The Count then described a memorial service for Mozart in Prague with mourners in such numbers that the crowd overflowed into the square outside the church. Mozart's *Requiem*—the very piece his untimely death at age 36 left incomplete—was performed by an orchestra and a chorus of 120 under the direction of a woman, Josepha Duschek, who had been one of the composer's many lovers. Waldstein said, *"It was performed with such nobility that Mozart's spirit in Elysium must have rejoiced."*

I turned to Napoleon and asked him bluntly, "How is it Mozart was able to rejoice in Elysium at the sound of his own music, and I, and I remain God's joke—a deaf composer?"

N turned introspective, "One of our tasks in this realm is to learn patience and humility, traits that do not come naturally to either one of us. Our friends, the Buddhists and Hindoos, believe that the last thoughts one holds dear at the moment of death determine the character of our next life, our next incarnation. For those who gain entry, Elysium has such infinite attractions, so much so that one may sincerely ask the dead if they regretted clinging to life when they arrived at this next stage. How will it be for you B, how will it be for you?"

"Not knowing life," I said to Napoleon, recalling my grandfather's death bed advice, "why worry about death?"

"You will, man," he mumbled.

"I will what? Know life? Or worry about death?"

"You, Willmann," he repeated, "You will know death. Now turn the page."

CHAPTER II

Trois Trios Pour le Piano Forte Violin et Violincello, Oeuvre Un, Redux

Three Trios for Pianoforte, Violin and Cello, Opus One, Redo

Vienna, the Palace of Prince Lichnowsky, 1795

WHEN THE QUINTET that Haydn had been leading mercifully ended, the assembled guests, as expected, all applauded, though most had no concept as to how droll the performance had actually been. The players, including our hosts—the Lichnowsky's, Prince Lobkowitz, and Count Razumovsky—rose from their seats and bowed to acknowledge their joyful reception. With that as our signal, Magdalena Willmann took me by the arm and we started out of the antechamber.

Wegeler followed us out and went to join my brother, Casper, who was already sitting in the Grand Salon. Magdalena continued on about the eccentricities of her fiancé, Count Galvani, a wealthy businessman she had nicknamed, "*the Merchant of Venice.*" Fortunately for me, the "*Merchant,*" who was known more for his facility with coins and cash than kisses and carnal knowledge, had not joined her for this trip. Knowing Magdalena and her appetites as I did in the biblical sense, I offhandedly suggested, "We should marry, yes? And run off to a villa in Sicily?"

Magdalena kissed me on the cheek but let her lips linger longer than one would have expected. When she finally pulled back, she shook her head. "No, of course not. You're ugly . . . and half-crazy! And as poor as a parish priest."

"But you'll still meet me tonight?"

"Absolutely," she said, as we both broke into laughter.

I seated myself at the pianoforte while Magdalena Willmann took center stage. We locked eyes and smiled at each other as she commenced her portion of the concert with—appropriately enough—Dona Anna's seduction aria from Mozart's *Don Giovanni*.

"Shadows of midnight all around me were gathered;
In my own quiet chamber
Sitting alone,
By misadventure and dreaming,
When all at once there came in, wrapped in a mantle,
A man, whom for the moment I had taken for thee.
But soon I had discovered
How great was my error!"

Four calendar years—ones I could best describe as transformational—had passed since I had last seen Magdalena in Mergentheim. Her surprise appearance at the premier of the *Opus One Trios* was a "gift" from Prince Lichnowsky, who appreciated the physical attraction she and I had for each other. When it came to matters of a carnal nature, who better to arrange an assignation than the Prince? It's been said about Lichnowsky that he was so fond of prostitutes that even his wife, Christiane, would sneak into his favorite brothel dressed as a whore whenever it was time to produce another royal heir.

And the songs of seduction from *Don Giovanni*? That was my Magdalena's doing. She had selected them with an eye I suspect to teasing me ever more—not that I ever minded waiting for my justly rewarded desserts to be served on the silken platter that was her bed.

During those four years of separation from Magdalena, my life had been totally altered. I moved from being a functionary in the Bonn Orchestra to living in the home of a prince in Vienna and now, here I was, premiering my first major compositions, the *Three Trios of Opus One*. I could not have been more delighted to have been reunited with this lovely siren—engaged or not—particularly coming as it did on the occasion of our soiree at the Lichnowsky's.

As a small measure of recompense, I dedicated the *Trios* to Prince Lichnowsky, who had taken me into his home and welcomed me as if family. Thanks to his support and friendship, I would go on to earn as much for these *Trios* as I would have in two or three years of salaried employment back in Bonn. Add in what coins I gathered from teaching, and I was doing all right. Attending the premier was—as he and Waldstein had described them—the crème de la crème of the Viennese aristocracy. In addition to an endless parade of bejeweled beauties whom I had to pretend not to notice with Magdalena on my arm, the crowd of patrons, sponsors, and court sycophants included Count von Browne-Camus, Baron von Birkenstock, Count Deym, the Countess Thun, Prince Esterhazy, Count von Fries, Prince Lobkowitz, Count Razumovsky, Baron van Swieten, and Count Keglevich, as well as Joseph Haydn, who at 63 years of age was acknowledged as the greatest living composer in the Empire. Personally I found "Papa's" music—while of the highest technical caliber—essentially silly and boring, the stuff of old ladies, doilies, and, as Napoleon would say, all too full of curlicues.

Through Waldstein's letters of introduction and Prince Lichnowsky's influence, I had indeed not only come into acquaintance with the highest realms of society, but so impressed them that many of these wealthy aristocrats would become my patrons over the next decades. Initially, though, these royals came to know me more as a keyboard player and not as a composer. With Mozart dead and gone in the year before my arrival, there was a hunger for a great keyboardist to replace him in their salons. By dint of my talents and connections, I fell into and filled this void. Often I was pitted against other players deemed of the top rank. We competed like bears and bulls thrown together in the ring for the amusement of our partisans. In short order I defeated all comers, including Joseph Wolff, Johann Baptist Cramer, Muzio Clementi, Abbe Sterkel, Abbe Joseph Gelinek, Daniel Steibelt, and Hummel. After this, I truly had no other rivals for the attention of the aristocracy. My fame within this circle grew so much so that I was no longer known by my given name. To all I was simply "Beethoven." In the words of Napoleon, I had become *Une étoile de roche; ein Felsen-Stern; a Rock Star;* a term of endearment N claimed was commonly used in the future.

Remember, I was only twenty-four. And in demand everywhere I went. And composing music as no one had even imagined possible. Still, writing for fame and honor was never my dream. None of that mattered—except as it allowed me the freedom to conceive and compose whatever I wanted. In truth I only wrote that which weighed on my heart and needed expression. If the aristocracy paid me well for my efforts, who was I to turn their kreutzers away?

That endeavor began in earnest with the *Opus One Trios*. And I could not have been more delighted and encouraged at the premier than when Magdalena Willman arrived quite unexpected at Lichnowsky's soiree. Magdalena, who was a year younger than me, came wearing her black silk stage gown looking even more beautiful than I remembered—and we would reunite again later that night. That she was recently engaged to her *Merchant of Venice*—a marriage of financial convenience—mattered not a whit to either one of us.

As exciting—and satisfying—as it was to see her again, those four years had not gone by without some degree of difficulty. First, my exodus from Bonn was challenging enough. I had had no money. Certainly not anywhere near enough that which would have been required to move to a foreign city, support myself, and pay for instruction. Additionally there would be the financial burden of ensuring for the care of my brothers back home while they finished their respective apprenticeships. Beyond the money issues, there were other concerns as well. I had to ensure that Casper and Nikolaus were shielded from our alcoholic father, and I desperately needed to sort out the wreckage of my relationship with Leonore.

First I had needed a plan, which *Herr* Neefe and Count Waldstein not only conceived on my behalf but assisted in the execution as well. It began in the summer of 1792 when Papa Haydn was returning to Austria from a successful two-year residence in London. His route home took him through Bonn. While Haydn was there, Neefe and Waldstein introduced me to him and they showed him my earliest compositions. They then arranged for the Elector, Max Franz, to pay for me to travel back to Vienna that coming autumn to study with Haydn while still receiving my full orchestra pay along with an additional stipend for expenses. Further, Max Franz had half of my father's pension designated directly for the care of my brothers.

I thanked *Herr* Neefe profusely for all he had done for me. He had been my essential teacher for over ten years. Whatever greatness I might experience in my career, none of it would have happened were it not for him.

As these arrangements fell into place, it was agreed I would leave Bonn in November of 1792 for Vienna. In the weeks before my departure Waldstein sat down with me and Casper. He told my brother that he had arranged for Franz Ries to handle money issues and for Helene von Breuning to continue to offer support around the house. He then cautioned us about the Viennese and their attitudes, warning that unlike Bonn, where aristocrats and commoners mingled freely, no such commerce occurred in the capital. If I was to succeed, I must be audacious, even go so far as to let them believe that the Dutch "van" in front of our name meant the same as the German "von" before theirs—which it most certainly did not. *"Never lie,"* the Count said, *"but be bold enough to let them draw their own assumption that you are of the nobility even if that assumption is entirely incorrect. Many of the aristocrats you will encounter in Vienna are like spoiled children. Most have too much money and know nothing about anything—and this terrifies them. Consequently, they are always relying on subtle clues from one another to acclaim rightly or wrongly what is the 'best.' It's a bit of the blind leading the blind into a fool's paradise. Hence the best way to gain an advantage over their arrogance is to be ever more so. The more you engage them thusly, the more successful you will become."*

Still my greatest failing before leaving Bonn was with Leonore. I should have, but could not bring myself to state aloud to her the most simply of truths: that I loved her and could not imagine life without her. In hindsight, it all seems so simple, but at the time I was too caught up in myself to understand any of this at all. I had no real knowledge of what a relationship entailed nor any appreciation of the inner needs of another. This flaw is a disease N claims is commonplace among those deemed *une étoile de rocher,* and one for which there is no known cure.

Leonore was perhaps more gracious and understanding than me when she wrote in my farewell autograph album, *"Friendship, with that which is good, grows like the evening shadow till the setting sun of life. Your true friend, Leonore von Breuning."*

Whether it was preoccupation, guilt, or stupidity over the affairs I had engaged in that kept me from responding immediately, I don't know. It was a year later, a year after my move to Vienna before I finally summoned the courage to write to her:

"November 2, 1793 to Admirable Leonore, My dearest Friend,

"Only now that I have spent almost a whole year in the capital do you hear from me, and yet I have preserved you in my memory both vividly and constantly. Very often I conversed with you and with your dear family, only often without the inner calm for which I would have wished. It was then that I remembered the fatal quarrel, during which my behavior appeared so despicable. But it could not be undone. Oh, what would I not give to be able to root this whole episode out of my life, this past conduct of mine, so dishonoring to myself, so much opposed to my true character. Certainly, there were several circumstances that always kept us apart and I imagine it was mostly the whispered speeches of one against the other that prevented an understanding. Each one of us believed that he was speaking with true conviction, and yet it was only anger kindled by others, and we were both deceived. It is true, my dear friend, that your noble character assures me of your forgiveness; but it is said that the most sincere

repentance is that in which one admits his own faults; this was my intention. Now let us draw the curtain on this whole episode and only stop to point to the moral: that when friends become involved in differences, it is always better not to employ any middlemen in such matters, but turn to one's friend in person.

"Herewith you will receive a dedication from me to you and I only wish that the work were greater and more worthy of you. They are variations on a theme from Mozart's "Figaro." Here I am plagued with requests to publish this little work, and I avail myself of this opportunity, my admirable Leonore, to give you some token of my esteem and friendship for you and of my everlasting memories of your home. Accept this trifle and bear in mind that it comes to you from a very admiring friend. Oh, if it gives you a little amusement, then all my wishes will have been granted. It should serve to recall the time when I spent so many delightful hours in your house; perhaps it will help to preserve your memory of me until my return, which certainly will not take place in the near future. Oh, how we shall rejoice then, my dear friend! You will see a happier man in your friend for time and better fortune have smoothed out the furrows left by his repellent past. . . .

"You would give me great pleasure by doing the favor of writing to me soon. Should my letters give you pleasure, I promise you with all certainty that, as far as is possible for me, I shall oblige you in this, for I welcome all things whereby I can prove to you how entirely I am 'Your True and admiring friend, LVB.'"

Our exchange of letters continued apace in this manner, a sign I hoped that Leonore had forgiven me for my indiscretions—my multiple indiscretions. I even asked Wegeler—the only one I would trust with such matters and who, owing to his growing medical practice, travelled frequently between Bonn and Vienna—to look after Leonore whenever he was home. Wegeler considered it an honor to do so. Occasionally Leonore would send me gifts, and I her, though I must confess that being separated by hundreds of miles made new distraction of the feminine variety all too easy. And I was easily distracted.

As for my brothers, they managed well with the extra stipend that came when our father left this world for the better not long after my move to Vienna. Casper joined me in Vienna two years later. It was 1794 when he arrived and by using my already voluminous connections with the aristocracy I was able to secure him work as a pianoforte tutor. Casper also helped me enormously as an assistant and on occasion as a business agent. I hated dealing with publishers and Casper was seemingly the only one I could trust who kept my best interests at the fore until the day he died.

My youngest brother, Nikolaus, arrived in Vienna not long after the premier of the *Trios*. I arranged with my patrons that he would be taken on as a pharmacist's assistant, his chosen profession and one he would grow most successfully.

I also wrote to Babette Koch but never heard back from her. It appears that she finally found herself a genuine aristocrat to bed. Her mother, Anna Maria Koch, ran a tavern and an adjoining bookstore which was a favorite meeting place for intellectuals in Bonn. Before leaving for Vienna, I stopped there one night hoping to say my farewells and ended up sharing drinks instead with a writer and teacher, Johann Gardner, from the Americas who was touring the continent while doing research for a novel on Niccolo Machiavelli and his impact on politics and statecraft. Gardner, though born on a farm in New York State, was of Welsh extraction and a naturally gifted storyteller. After entertaining us most of the evening with tales of his adventures traveling the world, he shared with me two bits of instructional doggerel that he tried to impart to all of his students. The first went like this: *"When you are writing a story, what you are doing is creating a vivid and continuous dream in the reader's mind that is so powerful and so all-encompassing that the next thing that reader knows is that someone is calling him to dinner. Whatever you do that breaks that dream—no matter how brilliant or wonderful it might appear to be—is no good. Throw it out."*

Johann's second premise I found to be of equal import. He would remind his students that regardless of what they wrote and whether they were conscious of it or not, their stories expressed an attitude, a moral, a philosophy of life. Whatever they wrote on that last page—and he used that term metaphorically—whatever they wrote and however the story turned out, was in fact the expression of that life philosophy. He insisted that writers be aware of what they were saying and that the entirety of their composition be structured properly so as to make the expression of that theme consistent throughout. Gardner's advice struck me not only as wise counsel for the written word but for music as well. And they may have been the most important lessons I ever learned about composition, bar none. Wasn't that what I was after in each score, the expression of a substantive concept through a vivid and continuous dream?

I never did get to see Babette Koch again. It didn't surprise me though when I heard that she had married a count after first having been the governess to his young children. Sure he had to divorce his now ex-wife first, but what man could resist those curves and her ever so long and stately legs? And in that way Babette was able to give meaning and purpose to her own dreams as the Countess Belderbush.

Once in Vienna, my growing stature among the aristocrats as *ein Felsen-Stern* did not come too quickly or too easily. First there was the matter of Haydn. The excuse for me to go to Vienna at the expense of the Elector was ostensibly to study with the old master. In truth I knew there was little Papa could teach me that I had not already gleaned from reading his scores. Though it strained my finances, I lived as cheaply as possibly in those first months by renting out a tiny attic room. I then hired another musician to do the exercises I would turn into Haydn while pursuing my own modes of instruction separately. That charade fell apart after a year, but by that time the world had changed. The Elector in Bonn had no sooner called for my return home than the first of the continental wars broke out. Max Franz himself fled the Rhineland for safety along with his court far away from the French border—and in the ensuing political upheaval I was able to remain—and find work—in Vienna.

The revolution which had begun at the Bastille in Paris in 1789 and the subsequent beheading of King Louis XVI and his Queen, Marie Antoinette, during the reign of terror had its own impact upon the Habsburg Empire. Antoinette was the sister to Max Franz and Emperor Joseph II himself. Perhaps knowing their world of privilege and wealth existed on borrowed time, the aristocracy took great steps both physically and emotionally to isolate themselves from change. By the time the French took Bonn and the Rhineland in 1794, the secret police in Vienna were actively taking steps to smother any rebellious streaks inside Vienna itself. As I wrote to Simrock, the horn player turned music publisher in Bonn, *"People say the gates of Vienna leading to the suburbs are to be closed at 10:00 pm. The soldiers have loaded their muskets with ball. You dare not raise your voice here or the police will take you into custody."*

The Lichnowsky's soon brought me into their home—their palace—as a long-term guest and treated me almost as if I was one of their own sons—the one not conceived in a brothel. For income, I once again took up giving lessons to the daughters, wives, and mistresses of the aristocracy. And they, with typical royal abandon, would all too often open themselves up for me. Discreetly of course. As I once shared with Steffen, some would beg for lessons, others for a dedication; they'd flock about me like so many Christmas geese savoring the piercing blade of the spit and a night of roasting over a fire. And would I oblige? *Naturlich.* Next to music and my daily walks, were women my greatest passion? *Ja*, and why not? Imagine, if you will, being delivered to the finest bakery in Vienna only to be offered up one crème-filled sweet upon another. I was only 22, 23, 24 years old, and at such an age what young man would not welcome such gifts? And though through the years I was known famously for my walks around the city or countryside, who suspected indeed their real purpose was to further those delicious assignations?

Pleasure however did not come without its expectations and pains. I could not accept ever being treated as a servant as Haydn had with Prince Esterhazy's family for almost 30 years—yet that was often the attitude of the aristocracy regarding any musician.

My aversion to playing on demand for an audience not of my own choosing became so strong over time that whenever I was urged to perform my good humor would disappear and I would fly into a rage.

This condescension common among the aristocracy towards all musicians was something I truly hated. Once, when derided by some officious count that I was neither a Haydn nor a Mozart, Prince Lobkowitz tried to soothe my anger by noting that since I was still young, it was no insult as most people refuse to believe that one of their younger contemporaries will ever achieve as much as the older or dead ones who have already won their reputations. I replied to the Prince, *"Unfortunately that's true, your Grace, but I will not and cannot have any commerce with persons who will not believe in me simply because I haven't yet established my reputation."*

On another occasion, the Countess Thun, mother-in-law to both Prince Lichnowsky and Count Razumovsky, got down on her knees and begged me to play when I was chatting up a young woman. Even her I refused. Grabbing my hat, I left, immune from pleas and demands to stay. At times like that I would hike over to my brother Casper's place, or Wegeler's apartment, gloomy and out of sorts, complaining that they had wanted me to play, even though my fingers ached and the blood under my nails burned. Wegeler—who knew better than anyone how to handle my moods—would tell a joke and try to amuse me. Eventually he'd find ways to calm me down until a conversation would develop between us.

After some time had passed Wegeler would intentionally let the conversation drop and seat himself at his writing table. If I wanted to continue talking I had to take the only other seat available, the one in front of the pianoforte. Soon enough I would aimlessly strike a few chords, and from these I would gradually develop some new improvisations. It was awhile before I caught on to my friend's tricks, but truth be known I greatly appreciated them—and his lifelong friendship.

And that brings me back to Haydn and the premier of the *Trios.* After we completed the performance to much acclaim and had taken the appropriate bows, I was just about to leave with Magdalena for her hotel, the Black Swan, when Papa stopped me.

"It would be my considered advice, Louis," he said rather stiffly, "that you not publish the last *Trio*. I do not believe it will be quickly or easily understood, nor will it be favorably received by the public."

His remarks astonished me and ruined the otherwise celebratory nature of the evening—especially since at the time I considered the third the best of the *Trios*. Although it troubles me now when people praise any of my early works to the detriment of later ones, it is true that the *Third Trio* is the one which has had the most profound impact and provided my audiences the greatest pleasure. For Haydn, trios were a trifle, a toy for amateurs. He simply could not conceive of, nor understand creating them as I had done on grand scale, one that equaled his greatest symphonies. I could only imagine that Papa was envious and jealous, and perhaps ill-disposed toward me for achieving in a matter of years the recognition it had taken him a lifetime to garner. He was now one more musician in Vienna that I must count on my list of enemies.

I sincerely tried to reclaim the good cheer of the evening by fleeing the Lichnowsky palace arm in arm with Magdalena for the Black Swan but sadly I encountered an even worse fate soon thereafter.

We were entwined in amour at the very height of pleasure when abruptly there was a buzzing in my ear that would not go away. . . .

CHAPTER 12

Giulietta et Romeo au clair de lune

Giulietta and Romeo in the Moonlight

Baden bei Wien—Baden by Vienna, May 1801

ALTHOUGH it was Casper van Beethoven's first trip to Baden, he had no trouble at all finding the villa that the Lichnowsky's had secured for the fast approaching summer season. Befittingly, it was of course the grandest and most impressive estate in the village. Even though the sun had set an hour earlier, the residence stood out clearly atop a hill in the light of the full moon. The prince and princess were not due at the villa themselves for another week. Except for the servants, the Beethoven brothers would have use of the villa all to themselves.

The Lichnowskys' kindnesses towards Casper's brother were endlessly remarkable. A year earlier the Prince enabled Louis to be financially stable, if not quite independent, by issuing him an annual annuity of six hundred florins. What made the payment unique was that it was tied to neither a particular composition nor to any form of servitude. It was simply an annual cash stipend that allowed our Beethoven to write and work on whatever he saw fit without obligation. Lichnowsky and his wife, Christiane, had also gifted Beethoven with an alabaster clock, several marble busts including one of the Prince himself, and, most significantly, four instruments: two violins, a cello, and a viola crafted in Cremona a century earlier by Joseph Guarneri, Nicholas Amati, and Vincenzo Ruger. These Italian-made instruments were each among the finest of their class. Beethoven used them regularly when he composed his first six string quartets, whose publication as *Opus 18* Casper had just negotiated. Their success established Louis, not yet 30 years old, as a compositional equal to both Haydn and Mozart. Not only had Beethoven demonstrated that he could mimic the style of both of those masters, his compositional innovations proved that he could go beyond their limitations, expand the genre and make it his own. Casper was rightly proud of his brother as well as the small but critical role he had played in that success.

Although the four-hour coach ride to the spa town southwest of Vienna had shaken his equilibrium, Casper could hardly contain his excitement over the new bidding war he had created over several of his brother's older compositions, including a pair of Bonn-era *sonatinas*. He walked slowly, using the few blocks between the town square and the Lichnowsky villa to stretch the muscles of his thick frame and shake off the fatigue caused by the bone-jarring coach ride. Thankfully the weather had been perfect—neither too hot nor too cold—and the air was filled with the natural springtime aroma of the flowering gardens and orchards that surrounded the spa town.

Casper had been actively engaged in representing Louis to music publishers almost since the day he arrived in Vienna seven years earlier. Together they had put more than thirty Beethoven compositions into print through publishers in Vienna, Leipzig, Bonn, London, and Zurich. These included a dozen piano sonatas, a first symphony, the *Trios*, several cello sonatas, the six string quartets of *Opus 18*, a dazzling collection of violin sonatas, and a variety of other no less minor works.

After the public premiers of his *First Symphony* and his first two *Piano Concertos*, Beethoven's stature grew ever more. No longer was his rising star limited to the aristocracy. The music-crazed Viennese public embraced him as well. Although his works, revolutionary as they were, continued to baffle the critics, sales from his publications could not have been more impressive.

Louis had been more than delighted with the success Casper had engendered on his behalf, noting in a letter to their younger brother, Nikolaus Johann, *"My art is winning me friends and renown and what more do I want? And this time I shall make a good deal of money."* With the demand for new Beethoven works so great, Casper felt as if the potential sale of these older and previously unpublished works from the Bonn years would be one of his greatest coups, something Louis would certainly take great pride and joy in.

Beethoven had asked him to arrive at the Lichnowsky villa when the town clock struck eight o'clock neither sooner nor later. Casper was used to his brother's odd requests and as always, he followed those instructions to the letter. Their fraternal collaboration these several years had been particularly fruitful for both of the Beethoven brothers in more ways than just music. Yes, Casper knew how fortunate he was to share his brother's name and to be a young man in Vienna surrounded by the priceless jewels of an empire.

Casper clearly recognized his brother's genius and had no issues being the junior and subservient partner in this relationship. After all, it was Louis who had in truth raised him and their youngest brother, Nikolaus Johann, and protected them from their now deceased father. Why, even at Margaretha's funeral, when Johann van Beethoven—drunk as usual—took the occasion to at first berate, and then beat Casper, blaming him for her death, Louis forcefully stepped in. He shoved their father up against one of the oaks shading Margaretha's grave and threatened him: *"You are no longer our father. If you ever raise another hand against any of us, Max Franz has assured me that he'll have you exiled or locked up. The choice is yours."* Confronted thusly by his now matured son, Johann visibly shriveled and then slunk away. Johann never so much as raised his voice nor threatened his boys again, something Casper was extremely grateful for.

When Casper first followed his brother to the capital, it was Louis who helped him secure work as a music teacher and piano instructor. The name "Beethoven" proved magical in aristocratic circles and for every young beauty that Louis deigned to teach, there were always one or two others who fell to Casper. Yes, indeed it was a beneficial collaboration, even if Louis did get the crème de la crème and Casper got the froth. Yes, even the froth still tasted sweet.

In return for this good fortune, Casper assisted his brother with all manner of needs, from running errands and proofing printers' drafts to handling correspondence and negotiating contracts with publishers. Louis had even helped Casper secure a full-time position as a clerk in the Hapsburgs' Office of Finance just the previous year. Though the salary was slight, the responsibilities were as well. He still had time to handle the negotiations with publishers for Louis, who now passed some of the more tedious issues, such as proofing drafts, to Ferdinand Ries.

Young Ries, the son of a Bonn court violinist, Franz Ries, had moved to Vienna to study with Louis just as Casper began work for the Finance Office. Ferdinand, who was only a child of 8 when Beethoven left Bonn, presented a letter of introduction from his father, Franz Ries, when he first arrived. Beethoven never bothered to read or respond to the letter. He simply welcomed the young man as if he were family and without hesitation took him on as a composition student. After all, the Beethovens were grateful for the immeasurable assistance Ferdinand's father, Franz, had shown their family, especially after the death of their mother. In exchange for his lessons on composing, Ries equally welcomed the opportunity to serve as an assistant to the "Great Beethoven."

At first Casper had been grateful to pass a lot of the menial tasks related to helping his brother onto Ries, but Ferdinand did have this habit of questioning everything. *"Why do you do it this way? Or that way?"* the young man would always be asking Casper, a distraction he always found to be both annoying and naïve. "Because," Casper would answer, "my brother wants it that way." And regardless of how many times he said that to Ries, the young composer would start all over with the questions each time he was assigned a task, however simple. There was a lot of tension between the two of them.

Louis had been somewhat secretive and mysterious about the motives behind this latest request that Casper join him in Baden. The clock in the Baden town square struck a quarter to eight as he hiked toward the villa. Casper slowed his pace even more, not wanting to arrive too early. He suspected his brother's request had something to do with a woman—it almost always did. Though Casper guessed that Louis's latest paramour was either the Princess Odescalchi, Giulietta Guicciardi, or some other discreet baroness he had not yet met, he clearly could not keep up with nor track his brother's multitudinous flirtations.

Why, only two years ago Louis entertained the notion of dating either one of the two older Brunsvik sisters that might accept his advances. Therese and Josephine had come with their mother, the Countess Brunsvik, to Vienna on a brief, three-week exploratory visit for the express purpose of determining whether or not Beethoven would take the daughters on as pianoforte students later that year. Casper remembered the day when the Countess Brunsvik brought the sisters to his brother's apartment. These aristocratic ladies climbed up three steep flights of stairs in their long cloaks and dresses, hoping to engage Louis's services. Beethoven, who was friendly and polite as he could be upon meeting these lovelies, listened as the daughters auditioned. Therese, easily the most musically gifted, sang the violin and cello parts of Beethoven's *Third Opus One Trios* while simultaneously playing the pianoforte part. Josephine was not quite as agile on the keyboard but still demonstrated great promise and acumen. Impressed by their skills as well as beauty—and seeming availability—Beethoven agreed to take on teaching the sisters.

For the next sixteen straight days until the von Brunsviks left for home, Louis would go to their hotel suite at the Golden Griffin. Though the lessons were supposed to last only an hour, Beethoven would linger and let them run on all afternoon. At this age, Louis never grew weary of teaching students of the feminine gender—particularly as it was often the first step along a path to seduction. Whereas most keyboardists has been taught to hold their hands high and straight, Louis's method called for them to be held lower and with fingers bent. Louis delighted in taking hold of their hands to *"break bad habits."* Often he would stand directly behind them and take both hands in his own to demonstrate the desired placement. His touch was so sensitive that most young women would become flustered and blush upon contact. The Brunsviks were no exception. It was while there that Beethoven met their young cousin, Giulietta Guicciardi, who was just 16 at the time.

Among the three, Louis initially focused on Josephine. There was a gentle yet sweet vulnerability that she possessed which appealed to him. Even her voice was soft and alluring in a most innocent fashion. The attraction was decidedly reciprocal, but it remained unexplored. Any hope of an affair progressing further ended abruptly when the Countess Brunsvik hastily arranged Josephine's engagement to the Count Deym. The Count, also a friend of B's, was some 30 years her senior. He ran a museum in Vienna which at the time and unbeknownst to anyone else was horribly in debt, debts that would plague the Deyms' marriage.

Therese, sleek and handsome, and perhaps the most talented and literate of the clan, would have been up next on Beethoven's agenda. Both Casper and Louis, however, sensed that Therese, who had once declared that she was dedicating her life *"most solemnly as a Priestess of Truth who abhorred the notion of becoming someone else's property through marriage,"* was ultimately more interested in other women than men, thus ending any notions of a romantic nature. Our Beethoven nonetheless thoroughly enjoyed Therese's company along with that of the youngest sister, Charlotte, and their only brother, Franz von Brunsvik. They all stayed friends for life, with B often visiting them in Vienna or at their Hungarian estate, Martonvasar.

After the Brunsvik sisters, Casper watched as his brother then fell into a brief and seemingly one-sided infatuation with another student, Barbara Keglevich. That too ended quickly when she married and became the Princess Odescalchi. Or did it? When, wondered Casper, had marriage ever been a barrier for his brother? While publicly B often railed against infidelity, privately it seemed not to matter a whit.

And try as he might, Casper never quite understood what it was with his brother and women. Although Beethoven was always engaged in some romance, most of which lasted little more than a few weeks or months, Louis complained continually to Casper that he couldn't find the right woman to marry and share a life with.

This past January, Beethoven even briefly rekindled his affair with Magdalena Willman—now the Countess Galvani. She had returned to Vienna from Italy to participate in a benefit concert, one that Louis also performed at. Unfortunately, Magdalena contracted a fever soon thereafter and died abruptly. Louis was heartsick, sullen, and depressed for weeks afterward.

Beethoven was working on the second of the two piano sonatas of *Opus 27*—aka, the *"Moonlight Sonata"*—during those months. Although Casper knew better than anyone not to ascribe specific autobiographical content to any particular composition, he was certain the melancholy and sadness Louis felt over Magdalena's unexpected death, and the contrasting joy he had experienced with her while alive, had to have influenced the sonata.

Back in Bonn all of their acquaintances had always imagined that Beethoven would end up marrying Leonore von Breuning and although their exchanges of letters continued irregularly for many years, Casper had his doubts about that as an eventuality. Steffen von Breuning, Leonore's brother who had also recently moved to Vienna to take up a post as a lawyer in the War Department, had confided in Casper that their "Lorchen" was spending ever more time with Wegeler in Beethoven's extended absence from Bonn, an absence that had now grown to nine years and had no hint of ending.

When the town clock struck eight, Casper knocked on the door to the villa as directed and was immediately met by a liveried servant who led him to the main salon. The servant left Casper alone in the two-story high room roofed with glass panels through which the rich light of the full moon poured through and illuminated a pianoforte in its midst. On one side of the room glass doors opened out to an Oriental style reflecting pond filled with lily pads, lotus flowers, and goldfish. The languid waters also snared the lush rays of the moon and bounced them back upwards. On the other side of the salon was a stairway that led to a second floor balcony off of which were a series of what Casper presumed were bedrooms. All the doors were closed save one from which he thought he heard the low murmur of voices and the ruffling of clothes.

On the pianoforte keyboard was a note in Louis's hand. It read simply, *"Dear Brother, Play until the clock strikes ten."*

Beside the piano was an easel holding both an initial sketch and a large painter's canvas of a moonlight balcony scene straight out of Shakespeare's *Romeo and Juliet*—only here, the lovesick Romeo was Beethoven and Giulietta Guicciardi was the fair maiden on her balcony peeking out from behind a curtain. The painting was so freshly wrought that Casper could smell the rich scents of the oil paints. Though far from a masterpiece, the canvas revealed a fair degree of skill. Casper wondered if Giulietta Guicciardi—if that's who Louis was in fact courting upstairs—could be the one for his brother. She was a sweet, but coy young woman whom everyone considered musically talented, attractive, and charming. As had her cousins, she became one of Louis's favored students. For her part Giulietta seemed to delight in her sway over Beethoven, whom she thought of as a love-struck boy to be trifled with. Casper feared she was too young and flighty to even consider marriage—if that was what his brother was truly after.

Though nowhere near as talented as his brother, Casper was nonetheless an accomplished keyboardist who not only delighted in entertaining but was also in high demand on many a special occasion—occasions for which Louis would have absolutely refused to submit himself.

And now Casper was at Prince Lichnowsky's Baden villa playing love songs for his brother's assignation. He began slowly, focusing on the adagios of a few of his own compositions. When Casper exhausted those, he segued to bits and pieces of various Mozart scores he knew his brother admired—and women swooned over.

Unlike his older brother, Casper had no illusions about trying to be an artist. He was content to be an entertainer, performing simply to make people happy. He was adept at improvising on any piece for any occasion. If the mood was jovial, he could do that; if it called for romantic, Casper could do that as well, culling his memory for a store of sweet adagios. When Count Deym did marry Josephine von Brunsvik, Casper played at the ceremonial ball afterwards in Deym's hundred-room Vienna mansion. And when Toni, the redheaded daughter of Baron Johann von Birkenstock, married *Herr* Brentano, a wealthy merchant from Frankfurt, Casper was engaged as the organist for that occasion at St. Stephens Cathedral.

And once, he was almost trampled in a riot when the French ambassador, Jean Baptiste Bernadotte, who was entertaining Prince Lichnowsky and the Beethovens, hung a Tricolor flag outside his embassy residence and ordered Casper to play *La Marseillaise.*

Bernadotte was such a music lover himself that he even brought in his retinue the violinist Rodolphe Kreutzer with him from Paris. The ambassador was frequently in the company of Lichnowsky, Lobkowitz, and the Beethoven brothers while in Vienna. The ambassador, a close confidant of Bonaparte, shared much about the First Counsel with them. This included little known details such as the fact that a young Napoleon, after his first taste of combat, had written a tragic romantic novella, *Clisson et Eugénie,* about a soldier and his lover. The muse and inspiration for the story was none other than Bernadotte's own wife, Desiree Clary. Before marrying Bernadotte, Desiree had been Napoleon's first serious affair in the days when he still fancied a future career as a writer. Casper knew his brother was a great admirer of Napoleon and often wondered if it was Bernadotte's visit to Vienna that inspired Louis to begin work on notes for yet another new symphony, one that would become his third and was to be themed around heroism. *Vive la revolution!*

Casper played from memory—eyes closed—without any sheet music; all the better to visualize the chords in his mind's eye. He thought about his own romances. He too had had many an affair, the good, the bad, the melancholy, the bittersweet. Much like his brother, Casper longed for the perfect wife and companion. Unlike his brother though, Casper had no illusions about marrying into the aristocracy. Even the crème de la crème melts and sours when left out in the light of day. He wanted a real woman for his wife—one to cook, clean, and raise his children—not a princess-bride glittering in satin, silk, jewels, and debt. Casper yearned for a simple life.

Every fifteen minutes the town clock chimed and in this way Casper tracked the hours as he played. Whenever he did open his eyes, he would note the progress of the reflected moon as its glow played not just upon the pond outside the open glass doors but over and across the painting of Romeo and Giulietta. The subtle movements of moonbeams upon the still damp canvas made the painting seem alive. As he worked in some Hummel and a little Cherubini on the keyboard, embellishing and improvising freely, he imagined he could actually hear the two lovers reciting the lines Shakespeare had gifted them.

> *Arise, fair sun, and kill the envious moon. . . .*
>
> *What's in a name? That which we call a rose, By any other name would smell as sweet. . . .*
>
> *Oh, swear not by the moon, the inconstant moon, That monthly changes in her circled orb, Lest that thy love prove likewise variable.*

As it neared the ten o'clock hour, Casper's mood shifted. He thought to play something of his brother's to conclude the evening though he had never done that before.

> *Oh gentle Romeo, If thou dost love, pronounce it faithfully:*
> *Or if thou think I am too quickly won, I'll frown, and be perverse, and say thee nay. . . .*

All that could come to mind though was the new score for that piano sonata—the one in *C-sharp minor, Quasi una fantasia,*—he had read over on his brother's desk not long ago: the "*Moonlight.*" He began the *Adagio sostenuto* slowly, gently, almost mournfully while reflecting on his own loves lost. A few minutes later he moved through the light-hearted *Allegretto* until he arrived at last at the explosive *Presto agitato.* His own emotions poured out as he pounded the pianoforte with such rapid-fire motion that he failed to notice just how loud he was playing—until he was startled by a shout from the balcony.

"Stop!" Louis screamed.

Beethoven came raging down the stairs, yelling in a controlled and constrained manner, "Stop! Stop! Stop!" Wearing only a long dressing gown, Louis ran over to the pianoforte and even though Casper had already ceased playing, he grabbed his brother's hands away from the keyboard.

Casper cringed. Though annoyed at his brother for yanking him thusly, he knew his brother well enough to hold his emotions in check—for now.

"She's sleeping and I don't want her to hear this—not yet anyway," said Louis, regaining his own calm."

"Who? Giulietta?"

"I'm dedicating the *C-sharp minor* to her. She must not know of its existence until then."

Casper offered up an apology, "Forgive me then. Did I wake her?"

B shook his head and patted his brother affectionately on the back. Their fraternal bonds were strong enough to override any momentary ripples. "No, not yet anyway, though I must needs awake her soon and you will escort her to back to her hotel before . . ."

Casper nodded, needing no further explanation. The brothers had been through this more than once before.

"Then let me share with you," Casper started, "the good news from Zurich and Leipzig."

"Ja?"

"I have at least three publishers, maybe four, battling up the sale price on those two *sonatinas* and . . ."

Casper never had a chance to finish his sentence. Beethoven was furious.

"I don't want those published! Not now, not ever! They're trifles, embarrassments!"

"But you agreed," insisted Casper, "we can get as much for them as you did for the *Trios* five years ago. And I'm committed to the highest bidder."

"The hell you are!" Beethoven slammed his hands against Casper's shoulders. "It's an insult to have my name on those pieces. They're house music, trifles. And I never gave you permission."

Casper shoved his brother right back. "You did! I asked you specifically about them last month."

"Did not!" Beethoven shoved Casper. They were like two children fighting tit for tat.

"Did so!" Casper pushed back.

"Did not!" Beethoven screamed.

"I did so. I asked you not once, but twice as we were walking out of the *Theater-an-der-Wien* if you wanted the collection sold and you kept nodding your head up and down, up and down."

"I did not! I never heard you! I never heard you."

Beethoven slammed into Casper one more time, knocking him backwards. Casper crashed into the *Romeo and Giulietta* painting, taking it to the ground with him. That did it for Casper. All restraint vanished. In a flash he jumped up and dove into his brother. Within moments they were wrestling each other all across the floor of the salon, inadvertently tearing and mangling the portrait in the process. Fists flew right and left.

Louis broke away, but Casper went at him again. This time they tumbled out the doorway and directly into the reflecting pond. Fish and lily pods were thrown every which way. Their watery immersion did little to cool the brothers' passion for fighting.

The battle continued until a fierce feminine voice froze them cold as marble statues. They looked up.

In the moonlight stood a half-dressed Giulietta, looking for all the world like Satan's avenging angel. The torn and tattered *Romeo and Giulietta* canvas hung from her hands. Rage fired out of her eyes. "A plague on both your houses!"

CHAPTER 13

La Malinconia—Questo pezzo si deve trattare colla più gran delicatezza

The Melancholy—This piece is to be played with the greatest delicacy

Once again a fog settled in on the oasis with a density so thick that all I could see was N sitting Buddha-like across from me strumming a guitar—*ja*, a guitar. Gone from sight were the pyramids, the River Nile, Napoleon's library. Even Isis's Temple had vanished in the mist. Gone from our sight, everything. For all intents and purposes, we were alone, two ghosts staring each other down.

N sang, *"Il y a une maison dans la Nouvelle-Orléans ils appellent le Soleil levant, Et cela a été la ruine de beaucoup de garçons pauvres et Dieu que je sais que je suis celui."*

Though I could not hear his words, they still drove themselves into my brain as, *"There is a house in New Orleans they call the Rising Sun, and it's been the ruin of many a poor boy and God I know I'm one."*

"What are you singing," I asked, "and why?"

N stopped. "The Blues . . . The Blues were born in New Orleans, which I had to sell to the Americans in order to pay for the wars against the Brits and the Hapsburgs. Disgusting . . . So, you didn't hear your brother Casper tell you he wanted to sell the *sonatinas*. And that wasn't the first time, was it? You'd been pretending to hear perfectly for some time, bobbing your head up and down like a drunken peacock, *oui?*"

Even confessing to myself that I had been pretending to hear clearly for years was embarrassing. My hearing loss, which had begun with that damnable buzzing I felt when I was with Magdalena, had progressively worsened. "Imagine," I told N, "that for these last few years, I had to avoid almost all social gatherings because it was impossible for me to shout aloud to people, *'I am deaf.'* If I had belonged to any other profession—a butcher, a baker, a candlestick-maker—it would have been easier, but for me, a musician, a composer, a performer, it was a terrifying state."

"And your enemies, what did they say?"

"In the beginning I was fortunate that in conversation there were many people who did not notice my condition at all. Since I had generally been considered absent-minded and eccentric, most accounted for it in that way."

"Including Casper?"

"My poor brother knew nothing and was the easiest to fool. He was only trying to help."

"And rather than confide in him, you just nodded your head and pretended. No wonder you fought."

"Even now it saddens me to think how I abused him. The truth was that all too often I could scarcely hear anyone if they spoke softly. I would catch the raw sounds, but not their words—not with clarity. When I went to the theatre I had to get very close to the stage to understand the actors. If I was even a little distant I could not hear the high tones of the instruments or the singers. And should anyone raise their voice or shout, the pain in my ears was intolerable."

"Still you wrote this . . ." Napoleon's fingers moved at white hot speed across the guitar as he somehow simultaneous played all the parts of the fourth movement of my string quartet, *Opus 18, Number Six*. How he recreated the sounds of four bows arcing simultaneously across strings with his fingers alone, I'll never understand.

And somehow he pumped up the volume to an intolerable level, forcing me to cover my ears until I could take no more and screamed for him to, "Stop!"

"La Malinconia, oui," N laughed.

"It was meant to be played with the greatest delicacy," I said. At this point in my endless dream nothing N did surprised me, not even playing the guitar and singing what he kept calling "The Blues," so rather than comment on his actions, I decided instead to move on. I felt a compulsion to share with him the degree to which the first stages of my hearing loss were indeed intolerable. "Some days I was fine," I said, "other days brief moments of incomprehensible silence overwhelmed me and I was at a loss as to what to do."

N switched back to that song he'd been singing earlier, "*Oh mother tell your children, Not to do what I have done, Spend your lives in sheer misery, In the House of the Rising Sun.*"

Misery, my misery is all I could think about. Meanwhile N finished with such a riotous flourish I could not begin to fathom how he derived such sounds from a mere guitar.

N looked up at me and laughed again. "Electric," was all he said.

"Electric? Like the *Taschenlampe?"*

"Oui, mon ami, just like the *Taschenlampe,"* noted N, who was in a better and more upbeat and cheerful mood than ever before. "There's a lot of that electric stuff in the future. Do you know that the Blues could have become the quintessential French music genre if I hadn't been compelled to sell Louisiana? Think of it, Mississippi Delta Blues, Memphis Blues, St. Louis Blues, New Orleans Blues, even Chicago Blues, they all could have been French. Instead we get Edith Piaf, Techno-pop, and Electronic Euro-dreck while those damnable Brits and those upstart Americans get the Blues instead. And that led to rock and roll and the Rolling Stones. *Mon Dieu!* You would have loved the Rolling Stones. . . ."

"Rolling Stones? What's that?"

"A 20th-century guitar quintet, but I digress. You were just about to tell me about that invitation that came from Wegeler."

"I was?" I asked. "Sometimes I wondered what N was talking about, and why it was he kept bringing up the future, a future I had no understanding of, and yet at the same time insisting I converse about matters from my past when, as he claimed, he already knew everything.

"Because you don't know anything," was his instant response. "The future will unveil itself when you are ready. Now, go on about Wegeler."

I did. Wegeler, who was now back in Bonn, had written inquiring after me. Would I be receptive to a trip home to the Rhineland come spring of the following year?

"That would be March of 1802," intoned N.

Wegeler had planned a celebration with the von Breunings—something about setting up a new life. I missed my friends and wrote back immediately:

"How greatly I thank you for thinking of me. I have so little deserved it or any kindness from you. Writing, as you know, was never my forte. It's sad to realize that even my best friends have not seen a letter from me in years. Yet you are so good and refuse to be offended by anything, not even by my unpardonable negligence, and remain always my true faithful and honorable friend. . . .

"You want to know something about my situation, it is not so bad. I often work on three or four pieces at once. I live only in my music and one score is scarcely done before another is begun. My compositions bring in a fair sum, and I have more commissions than it is possible for me to fill. Besides, I have six or seven publishers chasing after each piece and might have more if I chose. People no longer bargain with me. I ask and they pay. . . .

"Young Ries and Steffen are both here now and we are together almost daily. It does me so much good to revive the old emotions. Concerning Ries, I think he would have better luck in Paris than Vienna. Vienna is overcrowded with aspiring composers and even the most able find it extremely difficult to maintain themselves. In the autumn or winter I shall see what I can do for him. Steffen, meanwhile, has really become a

good, splendid young fellow, who knows a thing or two, and like all of us, more or less has his heart in the right place. . . .

"However, that evil demon, my bad health, has put a spoke in my wheel. Know that my noblest faculty—namely my hearing—has grown steadily worse during the last three years. When you were still with me I felt the symptoms but kept silent; now it is continually growing worse and whether or not a cure is possible has become the question. My ears sing and buzz continually, day and night. You can scarcely believe how lonely and sad my life has become. My bad hearing haunts me everywhere like ghosts and I flee from mankind. I appear as a misanthrope, and yet I am far from being one. I can truly say your Beethoven is living a wretched life, quarreling with nature, and cursing our Creator for my miserable existence. Heaven knows what will happen to me. If possible I will bid defiance to my fate, although there are moments in my life when I am the unhappiest of God's creatures."

"*Oui, mon ami*, you most decidedly have the Blues," imparted N. "But remember what Mr. B.B. Koenig said, '*the Blues ain't nothing but a good man feeling bad.*' Now go on."

I did. In the faint hope that the good doctor might have some insight to my condition, I detailed for Wegeler all the medical experts I had visited and all the treatments I had undertaken:

"I also sought help from an endless queue of Viennese physicians, the first being Herr Doktor Peter Frank. He wanted to strengthen up my body through tonic medicines and restore my health with almond oil but sadly, nothing happened. My hearing grew worse and worse. I had a frightful attack and fell back into despair. Then came a medical ass who advised me to take cold baths for my health. No good. Later a more sensible physician advised warm Danube baths. They worked wonders for the rest of my body but sadly my deafness remained and in fact became even worse. . . .

"Until I can find a cure, I beg you in confidence to say nothing of my condition to anybody, especially my good Lorchen. Give warmest greetings to all, including Madame Helene von Breuning, and let her know that I still do experience divine inspiration whenever I have a 'raptus.' I shall look upon the time when I see you again and greet our Father

Rhine as one of the happiest moments in my life. When this shall be I cannot tell you, but when you do see me again I will account for myself as a better man."

Before hearing back from Wegeler, and calculating that my condition might demand a surgeon, I did visit *Herr Doktor* Vering, whom I had great confidence in. Vering prescribed a kind of herb for my ear, stating there might be some improvement but not a complete cure.

Then, over the next few months, Vering had vesicatories made from a particular tree bark placed on both my shoulders. This was a very unpleasant remedy inasmuch as I was robbed of the free use of my arms for a few days until the bark had its effect, to say nothing of the pain one had to endure. While it was true that that the buzzing and singing in my ears was somewhat diminished, especially in the left ear where my deafness began, my hearing did not improve in the least. In fact, it may have grown rather weaker by the time Wegeler's response arrived, a response that offered little medical advice:

"Our fatherland, the beautiful country in which you first saw the light of day, is still as tranquil and welcoming before our eyes as when you left. If your condition continues thusly you must return to Bonn next spring. We shall hire a house for you in some pretty place in the country nearby us and for half a year you shall become a peasant and rest while we care for you."

Rest in misery in my own *House of the Rising Sun*? No, I could not. For the second time I wrote back and thanked Wegeler for his concern on my behalf, but declined, reminding him my life was in Vienna. I asked him not to speak of "rest," for I knew of none outside sleep. In truth I feared seeing pity on the faces of my old friends at every moment and knew that would only make me more miserable. Even Wegeler's kind solicitude would have pained me. I drafted a reply and sent it out by post that day:

"A quite life? No, I feel I am no longer made for that. Plutarch has taught me resignation, which has become my only refuge, a wretched one at that, yet the only one remaining open to me. As I am compelled by circumstance to hustle about most actively to support myself, such a jour-

ney home is impossible, much as I would love to revel in the beauty of our native land. Were it not for my deafness I should have traveled half the continent by now. Oh, if I were rid of this affliction I would embrace the world for there is still no greater delight for me than to practice and show my art. That would have been my joyous fate by now but for this misfortune. . . .

"What is there that would make me happier? Well, I am forced by these conditions to take fate by the throat, so it shall not wholly overcome me. As a result of my fortitude and despite my misfortune, there have still been a few blessed moments within these past months to share with you, my dearest of friends. Really, I feel my youth is just beginning. My physical strength has for some time past been steadily gaining and also my mental powers. Each day I move towards the goal which I sense but cannot describe—only in this way can your B exist. I strive to live a more pleasant existence now and try to mingle more with people. And for the first time I feel that marriage might bring me happiness. This change has been wrought by a dear, fascinating girl who loves me and whom I love. Oh it would be so beautiful to live life a thousand fold."

"That would be Giulietta Guicciardi, *oui*?" N confirmed.

"*Ja*, Giulietta."

"Not much of a future there?" N fired back.

"I'll leave omniscience to you," I said. "But my Giulietta would make a fine young bride if she ever takes my entreaties seriously."

"Women," began N, "in the future we don't understand them any better than we did in the past. Fortune is round like a ball and therefore does not always fall on the noblest or favor the best. Though perhaps if I share my history with you it might help a little bit."

In a sprint N went on to describe his struggles as a young man—a junior officer with limited resources and pay in a time of turmoil following the storming of the Bastille and the early days of the Revolution. Disappointed with his chances of moving up the army ranks and replacing the dunderheaded aristocrats who paraded about as generals and field marshalls, he for a time saw his only future as a writer. He would be the next Voltaire, the next Rousseau. All my ghostly companion wanted back then was a good quill pen, sheaves of parchment paper, and a muse of great beauty to inspire him.

And a muse he did find! Into his heart he took a willful young woman of aristocratic birth, Désirée Clary of Marseille. And write he did: political treatises, stories, and that novella. Not only did he publish, N confided in me that the merry-go-round nature of his romances became the stuff of literary legend. Napoleon went so far as to claim that a play, *La Ronde,* scripted by *Herr* Arthur Schnitzler—another future name I did not recognize, and one which would one day scandalize Vienna—was inspired by his amorous adventures. Was it true? Who knew?

N described the affairs and women in his life as if they were in naught but a game of musical chairs—or beds: He sought the hand of Désirée, but she was attracted to his older brother, Joseph Bonaparte. Though Joseph was ahead of Napoleon in calendar year, he lacked the verve to be the forceful leader our N was already becoming. N persuaded Joseph to switch his attentions away from Désirée to her older sister, Julie. Joseph happily married Julie—and claimed her dowry—thus leaving Désirée vulnerable to N's entreaties.

Though Napoleon proposed to and became engaged with Désirée, our N soon discovered that he could not reshape her into the type of woman he wanted. She lacked the intellectual, literary, and social graces he sought.

So, when N, my new *bon ami,* was reassigned to a post in Paris, Désirée remained in Marseille. N soon discovered that while in the French capital he was not only as easily distracted by the allure of the feminine gender as I was, he in fact did spot a widow, Rose de Beauharnais, who indeed manifested the charms he sought. But she was sleeping with his immediate superior, a Director of the Republic, Paul Barras—and before Barras she had been married to a Royalist husband who had only recently lost his head on the guillotine. Fortunately for Napoleon, Barras was tired of Rose and he graciously allowed her to slide into N's arms.

Although at first Rose was less than impressed with Bonaparte as a lover, she was savvy and a survivor. In such dangerous times, with heads rolling left and right, security for her children and herself was a first priority—and who better to shield her from the vicissitudes of the reign of terror than a rising star in the Republican Army?

Though Napoleon was still betrothed to Clary, he prodded Bernadotte, then one of his senior-most aides, to step in and take Désirée off his hands, thus allowing him to end their engagement. Now formally a free man, N took up with Rose de Beauharnais, whom he insisted upon renaming Joséphine. He married her on March 9th, 1796. Two days later Napoleon joined his regiment to begin war on the Italian peninsula against the Austrians and their allies. Three days later Joséphine began her own battle campaign inside her Paris salon, fighting for the advancement of carnal pleasures with a cavalry lieutenant, Hippolyte Charles.

Though initially unawares of Joséphine's ongoing infidelity, Bonaparte told me how he sent her daily love letters while on his battle campaigns, first from Italy and later from Egypt. He loved her with such infatuation that he even insisted on formally adopting her son Eugène, and then he married off her daughter Hortense to one of his own younger brothers, Louis Bonaparte. And when Napoleon eventually learned about the full extent of Joséphine's affair with Charles while he was playing at *El Kabir* in Egypt, he reacted by taking on Pauline Bellisle Foures, the wife of a junior officer, as his mistress. Poor Pauline became known as Cleopatra after the ancient Egyptian queen.

When Napoleon wrote from Egypt to his brother Joseph—the one who had originally been in love with Désirée Clary—regarding this *Opéra comique,* his correspondence was intercepted by a British naval patrol. Much to N's embarrassment, the letter was reprinted in the London *News Press,* where he was once again mocked as a degenerate Corsican:

"Since I left you, I have been constantly depressed. My happiness is to be near you. Incessantly, I live over in my memory your caresses, your tears, your affectionate solicitude. The charms of the incomparable Joséphine

kindle continually a burning and glowing flame in my heart. When, free from all solicitude, all harassing care, shall I be able to pass all my time with you, having only to love you, and to think only of the happiness of so saying, and of proving it to you?"

His battle plans stymied in Egypt, N abandoned Cleopatra to her rightful husband and he returned to Paris to square matters with Joséphine—and the Republic, which once again was at war with its continental enemies. In the end, N would crown Joséphine Empress of France, only to divorce her a few years later when she failed to produce an heir. After invading Austria twice and seizing Vienna, N would eventually marry Marie Louise, daughter of the very Austrian Emperor he had tried to overthrow.

Precisely why he told me all of this, I wasn't quite sure. . . .

"I tell you this," N insisted, "so that you will be prepared for the next round of news to enter your life."

"What? That our lives and loves are as unpredictable as a penny novel? Or that marriage is full of difficulties? I saw that with my own poor mother who once said, *"Women, if they wanted a happy life, should never marry."* Or as I watched when Josephine Brunsvik was hustled off to Count Deym only to find that poverty would soon became their only companion. "

"No," intoned Napoleon, "I tell you all this because you are about to receive a letter from the only woman you had ever truly loved, Leonore von Breuning. . . . And it will break your heart."

Abruptly the fog closed in around me, carrying as it did the weight of my soul as it plunged into despair. Even Napoleon and his guitar began to disappear from my sight as well.

His last words were once again something mumbled: "You must learn humility to gain humanity."

And suddenly he was gone. Alone, I was totally alone. The mists made it virtually impossible to see and my deafness made hearing equally so. And it was cold; a damp bone-chilling cold was all pervasive.

What else would the gods take from me? My Leonore, my

Lorchen? I read her letter when it arrived, then tore it up and threw the scraps into my fire stove. With joy, my Leonore announced she was to marry my best friend, Franz Wegeler. That is why they wanted me to return to Bonn. . . . A wedding . . . their wedding . . . truly, my life had been cursed.

I could not have felt any lower or more depressed. Why was I made so different? God's joke . . . a deaf musician . . . Without love, without life. I had failed on such a grand scale that if the clock of my life had shattered right then and there, it would have been a blessed relief. . . .

I would end it all now if I could.

But then the oddest thing happened—well, perhaps not the oddest in this endless dream turned nightmare. In German the word for dream is *Traum,* unusual in that it shared a linguistic root with the English word implying just the opposite: trauma. And that is all I could feel: trauma, shock, despair.

Like sand settling to the bottom of a bottle of water, I watched as the fog began to settle all around me. No longer was I in the oasis surrounding Isis's temple. Instead transported by the power of grief and this trauma, I stood atop Mount Olympus. Below me and in all surrounding directions was a carpet of clouds. Behind me and at a very low angle to the east was the rising sun.

The rays of sunlight turned that blanket of clouds into a bright, orange-red quilt. Its beauty rivaled anything I had ever seen anytime, anywhere. I raised my arms up above my head as if readying to conduct an orchestra. Abruptly, a short and narrow sword appeared in my hand. It was the very saber the Elector of Bonn, Max Franz, had presented to me when I was officially enrolled in his court orchestra when I was but 11 years old. My shadow followed moments later, presenting as it did a staggeringly huge black aura that filled the horizon before me. I'd never seen such a spectacle in all my life—or death. . . .

And then I heard it; for the first time in my endless *Traum* I heard sounds, music, notes, and singing. This chorus of clouds was indeed singing variations of Christoph Tiedge's *Urania*, while an orchestra warmed up and pulled itself into tune.

And if I look up to consider my Fate,
When my days are departing,
these last rays of light,
grant me a vision upon the borders of this earthly dream;
The light of the clouds arise
from the nearby sun!

Impossible, I thought. Music. Was I dead? Finally dead? Was death the price I must pay to hear again? Was this the death of Beethoven?

The players and the tools of their craft were all made of clouds. In those wisps I could see the shapes of heaven's instruments—the bows of violins perched and hungry to play, the percussionists with their sticks raised, the horns at the ready. . . . At my signal, the orchestra became alive.

In *tutti* we began with a *coup d'archet*, but it was god awful—a cacophony of chaos with the strings going every which way. Raising my sword as one would a baton, I immediately tapped on a music stand, also made of mist, and signaled the orchestra to a halt.

We would start again. I pulled my fog-bound musical warriors back into ready mode. And then with a mighty slash, I set them loose and out came quite clearly the opening *tutti Allegro con brio* of my *Third Piano Concerto*. The sound reverberated throughout the entirety of the heavens with a lushness that overwhelmed me, brought tears to my eyes, and filled my soul with one moment, one brief effervescent moment of immeasurable satisfaction.

I listened in awe as my orchestra made of clouds performed ever more perfectly, ever more precisely, than I could have ever imagined, even inside my head. Bows made of mist danced across strings made of gossamer. If this was death, if this was my entry to Elysium, I would do it my way, but as fate would have it, my surprising good fortune abruptly turned against me like the tides at midnight.

Just at the moment the pianoforte was to enter my concerto, the instrument appeared before me like a giant wave of fog. The fog lifted itself up higher and higher until the pianoforte transformed itself into a massive hand at the end of a long arm. How odd. And when I pointed with the sword at that hand to enter and play, everything went silent. Total silence. Nothing. I pointed a second time. Was I deaf again?

Just then I heard my dead father's voice echo inside my head. It was the same drunken voice that screamed at me the day I joined the Bonn orchestra.

"How dare you embarrass me like that!" That hand turned into a fist, my father's fist but not one of fog and mist, but of flesh and bone: hard, crunching bone smashing into my face. He walloped me with such force that it sent me summersaulting off of Mount Olympus and into a free fall through the fog.

"Death take me," I said aloud as I continued to tumble wildly head over heels, wondering if in fact this was how it was all going to end.

Then, abruptly, the spinning stopped. I hung suspended midair in the fog, unable to tell up from down and the memories, that were so long blocked, flooded back.

I was 11 years old when *Herr* Neefe invited me to formally join the Elector's orchestra. There was to be a brief but highly ritualized welcoming ceremony at the court. With pride, I donned my green band uniform for the first time. I remember buttoning the jacket and marveling at what it was like to have tailored clothes that actually fit. Soon thereafter Elector Max Franz himself welcomed me to his circle of musicians by presenting me with my sword and sash. Franz Ries, our concert master, did the honor of belting it around my waist. Then, one by one, each member of the orchestra came up and, after bowing to me, shook my hand and gave me a welcoming hug.

After that there was a reception with music, cake, and wine. My father, there as a member of the Elector's choir, wrapped his hands around a bottle of Riesling and never let go. During the reception I was to play a short Bach prelude on the violin but my shoulder hurt so much from the beating my father had given me the night before that I fumbled through the piece and was near to tears from the pain by the time I finished. I swore I would never let my father do that to me again.

My father, drunk and pickled like sauerkraut, soon stumbled off his stool and knocked down a vase. Franz Ries suggested I take him home before he got worse and offended the Elector. I did as asked but nonetheless my drunken brute of a father cursed me all the way home for insulting him with my poor bowmanship. And I seethed under my breathe, blaspheming the bastard. When we arrived at our house and walked through the front doorway, my mother welcomed me with a congratulatory embrace and a kiss on each check. But the moment she let go and turned toward our father, out came his fist. He smashed me across the face and knocked me to the ground.

"Take that, you little runt, humiliating me in front of the entire court."

Tasting my own blood, the rage inside me grew. Looking up I saw my grandfather staring back down at me from his portrait on the wall. I reached deep into the very corners of my soul for every ounce of strength I could gather. Heedless of the consequences, I knew I had to fight back even if it was suicidal. Never again, never again, I thought. And then, rather than endure one more moment of abuse, I went ballistic.

Focused like a cannon ball, I launched myself into my father's chest. He stumbled backwards more in disbelief than anything else. He cursed me, then got up again. He swung wildly the way drunks often do. A few of his punches landed solid, but I didn't care. I charged into him again, hard as I could. As I smashed into him, I could hear his ribs crack. Howling in pain, the bastard collapsed on the floor in front of my grandfather's portrait. . . .

The glare on his face said there would be hell to pay. But I didn't care. For once, victory tasted sweet, even if it was my own blood.

CHAPTER 14

The Tempest

MY HEAD over heels tumbling through the fog of Elysium continued until I landed in yet another sea of memories, this time the tiny spa town of Heiligenstadt. It was October of 1802, some six months after the Bonn wedding of Leonore and Wegeler—which I had assiduously avoided. How could I embrace their joy while bearing witness to the pity that would have filled their eyes?

Instead of returning to my home town, I hid out alone those many weeks in an isolated cottage an hour and a half northwest of Vienna where, as my physicians advised, I could live in silence and rest my hearing. And while I worked diligently on my *Second Symphony* and a few other minor compositions, I avoided human contact much as possible and, even when in the presence of others such as at the baths, I scaled all conversations down to their bare necessity. So severe was my prescription for rest that, much as I would have been cheered by my sweet Giulietta's soft comforts, I encouraged her to spend that same summer with her cousins, Josephine and Therese von Brunsviks, at their family's castle in Martonvásár, near Budapest and far away from me. Other than a few visits by young Ries to proof drafts or run errands, my only companions were the hawks and eagles soaring over the River Danube and the Carpathian Mountains beyond.

And even when Ries was there, I refused to let him play even a single note on the piano lest it pain me. His presence only served to remind me of how my damnable hearing had failed to improve.

Months earlier, I had told Ries that not only would I allow him to perform my *Third Piano Concerto in C-minor* at a public concert one day, I would even turn pages for him if he could write a *cadenza* equal to the task. He struggled all that summer, wanting very much to impress me with how far he had progressed writing that piece—two pieces actually—a "safe," easy one and a second whose complexity would challenge the finest of pianists. Occasionally, after reviewing his drafts, I would sanction him joining me for walk in the countryside. Often we would eat something in one of the surrounding villages and not return home until three or four in the afternoon. On one such outing, Ries asked me if I heard a whippoorwill singing off in the distance. I could not hear anything at all and I became extremely quiet and gloomy. Another time when we were out walking he called my attention to a shepherd up on a pasture hillside, who was apparently playing most pleasantly on a flute cut from lilac wood. At first Ries repeatedly assured me that he did not hear anything either—which, no matter how he tried to pretend, I knew was not the case. What a humiliation for me when I had to admit I heard nothing. Such incidents drove me to despair.

Having sought redemption and a cure for my hearing loss when none were to be found, I vowed to end my life. . . .

Just past my cottage was a rugged trail which climbed along the cliffs overlooking the south side of the river. Below a stretch of rapids there was a ridge of rock shaped like a bowl where the waters swirled most fiercely—that locals had nicknamed the "Tempest." If, when I came to the Tempest, my melancholy still prevailed, I would leap from the cliffs, and let the river swallow up all memory of my 30-odd years of existence on this planet earth. And if not, I would take it as a sign to return home to Vienna.

Prior to setting out, I roughed out yet another draft of a last will and testament intended for . . . *"You, my brothers, as soon as I am dead, ask Dr. Schmidt to describe my malady, and attach this written documentation to his account of my illness so that so far as it possible at least the world may become reconciled to me after my death. . . .*

"At the same time, I declare you two to be the heirs to my small fortune, if it can be called such. Divide it fairly; bear with and help each other. What injury you have done me you know was long ago forgiven. To you, Casper, I give special thanks for the attachment you have shown me of late. It is my wish that you may have a better and freer life than I have had. . . .

"You who think or say that I am malevolent, stubborn, or misanthropic, how greatly do you wrong me. You know not the secret cause which makes me seem that way to you. From childhood on my heart and soul have been full of the tender feeling of goodwill, and I was ever inclined to accomplish great things. But, think that for six years now I have been hopelessly afflicted, made worse by senseless physicians, from year to year deceived with hopes of improvement, finally compelled to face the prospect of a lasting malady whose cure will be impossible. . . .

"Though born with a fiery temperament and ever susceptible to the diversions of society, know I was soon compelled to withdraw myself, to live life alone. If at times I tried to forget all this, oh how harshly was I flung back by the deeply sad experience of my bad hearing. Yet it was impossible for me to say to people, 'Speak louder, shout, for I am deaf.' Ah, how could I possibly admit to an infirmity in the one sense which ought to be more perfect in me than others, a sense which I once possessed in the highest perfection, a perfection such as few in my profession enjoy or ever have enjoyed. Oh, I cannot do it; therefore, forgive me for those moments when you saw me draw back. I would have gladly mingled with you. . . .

"My misfortune is doubly painful because I am bound to be misunderstood. For me there can be no relaxation with my fellow men, no refined conversations, no mutual exchange of ideas. I have lived almost alone, like one who has been banished; I have mixed with society only as much as true necessity demanded. If I approached near to people, a hot terror seized upon me, and I feared being exposed to the danger that my condition might be noticed. Thus it has been during the last six months which I have spent in the country. By ordering me to spare my hearing as much as possible, my intelligent doctor almost fell in with my own present frame of mind, though sometimes I ran

counter to it by yielding to my desire for companionship. . . .

"Oh, Divine One who sees into my innermost soul, you know that therein dwells a love of mankind and the desire to do good. My fellow men, when at some point you read this, consider then that you have done me an injustice. Despite all the limitations of nature I have nevertheless done everything within my powers to become accepted among worthy artists and men. . . .

"Farewell and love each other. Thank all my friends, particularly Prince Lichnowsky and Professor Schmidt. I would like the instruments from Prince L. to be preserved by you, but not to be a cause of strife. As soon as they can serve a better purpose, sell them. How happy I shall be if I can still be helpful to you from my grave. Farewell and do not wholly forget me when I am dead; I deserve this from you, for during my lifetime I was thinking of you often and of ways to make you happy. . . .

"Thus, then, I take leave of you, and with sadness too. The fond hope I brought with me here, of being to a certain degree cured, now utterly forsakes me. As autumn leaves fall and wither, so are my hopes blighted. Almost as I came, I depart. Even the lofty courage that so often animated me in the lovely days of summer is gone forever. . . .

"With joy I hasten to embrace death, come whenever it will. I shall meet it bravely and free myself from a state of endless suffering."

Having at last reached the cliff above the rapids, I placed the letter in an envelope addressed to my brothers and slid it into the pocket of my jacket. I took off my shoes, coat, and shirt and neatly folded them in a pile beside the trail where a passerby would certainly notice them and hopefully deliver my last will and testament to my brothers.

As I stared down at the river and wondered how quickly the Tempest would consume me, I heard coming from the opposite direction the melodic chords of a pianoforte that at once sounded both familiar yet new and strange. Turning round I saw another forest trail—one I had never noticed before—that headed back into the hills. Lining the bark and branches of the trees on the path were thousands of nesting monarch butterflies. "*Patience,*" they wrote; that is what I must now choose for a guide before reckoning an end to my life. "*Patience fur-*

thers one to cross the great waters." It seemed to me impossible to leave this world until I had extinguished all curiosity within me. Thus, I decided to endure my wretched existence a little longer. I would follow this newly beckoning path in search of that music.

Those chords led me to a small cottage, the front of which was also covered in nesting monarchs. "*Welcome.*" The door was wide open and so I entered. There, seated at a massive pianoforte the likes and size of which I had never seen before was none other than *Fraulein* Lokitzvarah, she of the lotus flower. And although some fifteen years had passed since our first meeting at Mozart's apartment, she appeared to have not aged a single day.

Her keyboard work and the effects she drew from this fortepiano were astonishing . . . superior in every degree to anyone I had ever witnessed before, Mozart and myself included. Listening and watching her, I was humbled, profoundly humbled. And the music itself, *mein Gott,* where did it come from? Every chord, every refrain was fresh, vibrant, full of emotion; woven with complex textures that somehow felt familiar as if they had been drawn out of the very fibers of my own being.

And the instrument she played upon produced sounds more powerful and vibrant than any I had even imagined possible. Before me was the fortepiano of my dreams, one with sounds as robust and bold as a church pipe organ, yet subtle and crisp enough to enliven the most tender *adagios.* Printed above the keyboard was the maker's name, model and date: a *Bosendorfer Imperial, 1902.* It had to be at least nine feet long, triple strung, instead of double, and, astonishingly enough, it was constructed with an iron frame instead of a wooded one. And with ninety-seven keys, it covered a full eight octaves. It made the typical Viennese fortepiano appear as if a mere toy made of balsa and string.

Fraulein Lokitzvarah waved me over to her and then, placing her hand on my chest, she repeated what she had said to me all those many years ago, "*The wisdom of life lies here in your heart. You do not know it now, but if you listen . . . Listen carefully and your path, your road, your way, will unfold. The wings of a goddess will embrace you. And when that happens, I will be there. I will be there to lift you up."*

Napoleon was right, I understood nothing, not then, not now. At a momentary loss for words, I stood there, dumb as a statue, until at last I summoned the courage to ask her what it was she had been playing.

But *Fraulein* Lokitzvarah would not answer me. Instead she stood and had me replace her at the keyboard of this wondrous *Bosendorfer.*

"Play," she said.

"What?" I foolishly asked.

"The future." *Fraulein* Lokitzvarah came around behind me and pressed her chest, soft and warm as it was, tight against my back the way I would when teaching my young lovelies. Using her arms as if they were the wings of a goddess, she reached around me and took my hands in hers. "Play the future," she repeated in my ear. Her body seemed to meld into mine and we became but one creature. "Turn off your mind, relax, and flow downstream. This is not dying." I felt my fingers begin to dance across the keyboard and before I knew it, she had me playing those harmonies that had lured me into her cottage.

"It is the very nature of existence that causes all humans pain and suffering. No one escapes, no one, not you, not Prince Lichnowsky, not Mozart. The secret to life, B, is learning how to manage that pain. This is your music, the music you might write, compose, or perform if you avoid extinction today at the feet of the Tempest."

And indeed it was. Somehow *Fraulein* Lokitzvarah had gotten inside my soul and was revealing to me every composition I could potentially write—if I choose to live beyond my thirty-second year—from my next symphony to my last string quartet and beyond. That is what she had been playing, the future, my possible future. Together we played for what seemed like a week on that exquisite keyboard.

The portrait of my grandfather, Ludwig, which as if by the magic of dreams, had appeared on the wall directly before me, spoke up. I could see his lips smiling, his eyes winking, his head nodding.

"Bravo! Rise up! Free yourself!" I heard him say. *"The greater your challenge, the greater your triumph. And never, ever say die, for that hour will arrive soon enough of its own accord."*

How long had I been estranged from happiness? Having heard a possible future I realized that if death comes before I develop all my artistic capacities, it will indeed arrive too soon. Perhaps I shall get better, perhaps not. What is, is. Though plagued by a body that could easily be thrown off from the best to the very worst of conditions by any sudden change, my determination to thrive grew firm. I resolved to endure all until it pleased the gods to break my life's thread.

"Even if you chose life," *Fraulein* Lokitzvarah abruptly warned, "there are no guarantees any of these compositions shall come to pass. We all abide in the realm of the great unknown. And as long as you allow yourself to be ruled by your weaknesses instead of guided by your strengths, you will fail. You will fail." She could not have been more emphatic.

I thought about Mozart who died at 36 and wondered if all that music that he "copied down" from those visions which originated inside of him had come to an end. Did he finish his life and write everything inside that he was supposed to? He never finished his *Requiem*. Can it be said he nonetheless completed his purposes?

And what about my little sister, Margaretha, *"mon petit papillon,"* who learned to walk the day our mother died? We were alone, my brothers having taken our father to the market while I watched over my poor mother who was suffering terribly. When not hacking and coughing, her body was wracked by fever and her face contorted in pain. I did my best to comfort her as she had once done for my grandfather. My little butterfly, who had just turned 1 year old two months before, surprised me when I set her down to attend to our mother.

No sooner had her feet hit the floorboards then she took her first stutter-steps across the room to our pianoforte. Once there, she grabbed a hold of the bench and giggled uncontrollably as she turned back around and looked at me. I knew from her expression that she wanted me to lift her up so she could play. I obliged. Once in my lap Margaretha banged out with clear intent the first few notes of her little ditty, *"a, a, b-flat, c, c, b-flat, a,"* a sequence that would one day become my "*Ode to Joy.*" She did this thrice over, each time stopping and clapping with glee at what she had accomplished.

Hearing the music from across the room, my mother, finding peace within, gathered the last of her strength and blew Margaretha a kiss. That was her last breath. She coughed, fell back, and was gone. Six months later, *"mon petit papillon"* followed her to her grave.

Was that the "right" end to each of their lives? Mozart? Margaretha? My mother? Or was that simply an irrelevant question, one we would never answer?

"Do you know?" I asked *Fraulein* Lokitzvarah. Resting on the index finger of her right hand was a sole, solitary monarch butterfly testing its wings.

"To die but not to perish is to be eternally present," she said. *"Aber Ich bin nicht Fraulein* Lokitzvarah—But I am not *Fraulein* Lokitzvarah; *Ich bin Ava, Avalokiteshvara;* I am Ava, Avalokiteshvara."

"Avalokiteshvara," I said aloud as I gazed back at this siren and, in her piercing blue-grey eyes, I saw Shiva, I saw my muse, I saw Isis. Avalokiteshvara, the mother goddess, just as Leonore had once taught me: "*The valley spirit never dies; it is the woman, our primal mother. Her gateway is the root of heaven and earth. It is like a veil barely seen. Use it—it will never fail.*" Kwan Yin, Kannon, Venus. *A rose by any other name.* The goddess of beauty and compassion. *Ja,* it was the wings of a goddess—and the inspiration of my own art—that held me back from the Tempest.

"*Surrender yourself humbly; then you can be trusted to care for all things. Love the world as your own self; then you can truly care for all things.*" These were her last words.

Thanks to Avalokiteshvara and Kwan Yin and Kannon and Venus and Isis I did not end my life in the river. Instead I found myself chanting her names all the way back to Vienna . . . .

"Avalokiteshvara, Aphrodite, Venus, Kwan Yin, Kannon, Mary, Isis;
Avalokiteshvara, Aphrodite, Venus, Kwan Yin, Kannon, Mary;
Isis, Avalokiteshvara, Aphrodite, Venus, Kwan Yin;
Kannon, Mary, Isis, Avalokiteshvara;
Aphrodite, Venus, Kwan Yin;
Kannon, Mary,
Isis."

As I passed under and through the Vienna city gates I wondered if I would find my strengths by virtue of her divine intervention, or would I still fall victim to those weaknesses that had blinded me to life and love?

CHAPTER 15

The New Path

Vienna, Mid-Winter, 1802–1803

NO SOONER had Beethoven returned to Vienna from Heiligenstadt than he and young Ries resumed their composition lessons. For Ries this meant arriving by five in the morning at Beethoven's apartment for a breakfast of strong coffee, macaroni with shaved cheese, and some hard sausage; and then working through drafts of his two *cadenzas*, one of which he was by necessity going to play at his debut concert. Ries could not decide which one to use—the first being too easy and the second far too risky. To make matters worse, B refused to involve himself in the selection. After each early morning lesson, Ries would accompany Beethoven as he walked and talked their way haphazardly around the city—which was B's way of providing a lesson in counterpoint. Every day B would insist that they take a different path. If yesterday they turned right at a particular corner, the next morning they would turn left. Each excursion would flow by as if a random improvisation, yet somehow they would arrive precisely where B intended. Today their first steps took them toward St. Stephens Cathedral.

"So, if I understand you, sir," Ries began, "In this dream you had in Heiligenstadt, you saw the goddess Isis dressed as this woman, *Fraulein* Ava Lokitzvarah, whom you knew through Mozart?"

"Dressed?" mused Beethoven. "Ries, she wore a lotus flower in her hair. When I dream, I dream of the best, the most exquisite, the most desirable of God's creations. It is the same with music.

If your desire is to become a truly great composer, you will learn to do that as well. Seek perfection. . . ."

"Yes, sir. A lotus flower, perfection. I'll remember that."

B's almost excessive euphoria and the strange story that was unfolding about butterflies and goddesses as they trod the streets of Vienna had Ries concerned about B's sanity. Was this a "raptus?" One of those odd moments of inspiration his teacher was known to have experienced? B seemed so elated upon his return from Heiligenstadt that poor Ries was frankly afraid to interrupt B's revere over his latest *Traum* with disturbing bits of news about his brothers and Giulietta. Before retreating to Heiligenstadt, Beethoven had promised three of his latest sonatas to Nageli in Zurich, but while he was still away, Casper negotiated the sale of those same compositions to a publisher in Leipzig with help from their pharmacist brother, Nikolaus Johann—who was now running about Vienna calling himself "Johann von Beethoven"—much to B's annoyance. Ries firmly believed that the brothers' continuous and most unnecessary meddling in B's business arrangements were detrimental to his teacher. Ries and Casper had almost come to blows over one incident. And as if that was not disturbing enough, just last night at the ballet Ries thought he had witnessed B's Giulietta—in a distinctive cobalt-blue gown—accompanied by one Count Gallenberg, alone in a private box and seemingly behaving all too familiar. And what about Ries's own *Cadenza*? B had read and edited both scores but refused to actually hear Ries practice—and the concert in the salon of Count Deym's mansion was today.

They were passing just north of St. Stephens Cathedral when B nudged Ries with his elbow and pointed across the street to a smartly gowned young woman carrying a cello who was heading in the opposite direction. She wore high-heeled boots. Her to-the-waist, tightly curled blond hair was tied in a pony tail that, along with her long skirt, freely danced in pace with her steps.

"Look at those hips rock and roll, Ries," chided B. "Now there's a woman who'd make an excellent mother to your children."

"Who is she, sir?" Ries asked, admiring the natural beauty of this *zaftig* young cellist who could not have been more than 17 years old.

"Am I to know every *Sachertorte* in Vienna? You might better inquire of someone more knowledgeable such as Prince Lichnowsky."

"Yes, sir, I will. She appears to be heading towards the Count Deym's house. Should we follow her?"

"Ries, Ries, Ries, haven't I told you over and over again there are times in a musician's life for love, and there are times for music. On occasion those events are inseparable but at other moments they are incompatible. And when the opportunity to discern the difference occurs, only you must choose. What shall it be on today's path? Your lessons or that vixen? Art demands that we not stand still. I can walk in either direction."

"Let it be music, sir." Maybe, Ries thought, maybe he was wrong, wrong about everything. Maybe it wasn't Giulietta he saw after all. And maybe . . . and maybe B had approved the Leipzig contract. Ries finally concluded it was best to say nothing. Putting those thoughts aside, Ries turned his focus back to B's dream.

"And on this fortepiano, this one you called a *Bosendorfer Imperial* 1902, the one the two of you played, it had an iron frame and was triple strung?"

"And don't forget the ninety-seven keys!"

"I've never heard of any such thing."

"It's the future, Ries, the damn future, I was dreaming of the damn future. The sounds of this *Bosendorfer* 1902 are identical to what I hear in my mind's eye when I compose, not these tinny little creations that would be better consigned to a furnace for kindling."

"And in this dream you heard all of your future compositions?"

"There's the rub," said B. "We didn't play my future compositions; we played all of my 'potential' future compositions. There were eight piano concertos, twenty-two symphonies, thirty-three string quartets, an army of piano sonatas, oratorios, several masses, and five operas. The list seemed endless. And *Mein Gott,* was I tired. I slept for two straight days afterwards."

"I don't understand the differences, sir. God, I have so many questions. What did they sound like?"

"What did they sound like? They sounded like me, like Beethoven, or at least the music I might write one day."

"I'm confused."

"Of course you are, so let's approach this from a different direction. In my apartment I have a violin gifted to me by Prince Lichnowsky that was made by *Maestro* Guarneri over a hundred years ago. Every tune, every melody, every sonata that violin has and will ever produce until the day of its destruction is already inherent in its very being. In order to draw out those vibrations I need to add my two hands. Think of my left hand as the totality of all my skills and genius, and my right hand which holds the bow as the summation of all my life experiences up until this exact moment of our existence. Together this violin and my two hands combine to create music. What *Fraulein* Ava Lokitzvarah did was to show me my soul, my musical soul, as if it were that violin. She literally revealed to me the music inherent in my body, in my very flesh and organs. To that she added my genius and a glimpse of my future life experiences as seasonings. What I heard was the expression of my essential self."

"But if you heard them, sir, why can't you just write them down, 'copy' them out like Mozart did?"

"To write a dream, 'copy' it down? Oh, Ries, even for me, and I am what people call a conscious dreamer, it is impossible to be in two places at once. I can either be in the dream or I can observe the dream. The moment I try to write down auditory visions, that's the moment the sounds vanish. One might as well try and catch the wind."

"I am still not sure I grasp what you mean, sir. Either you heard your future music or not, yes?"

"I heard my 'potential' futures, Ries, not the 'certainty' of the future. And the question I am left with is to decide how I will live and thusly experience whatever is to come before me. You, my young friend, just spurned infatuation and chose music. Depending on which path I take, my music of the future will evolve this way or that. Or I might fail altogether."

"So what did you hear? What did you see? Can you at least share that, sir?"

"Well, of course. First, *Fraulein* Ava Lokitzvarah took me right around the corner of the calendar where I could hear a *Third Symphony* about heroism symbolized by the First Consul of France. . . ."

"Napoleon Bonaparte?" Ries interrupted. "You would write a symphony about one man, Bonaparte? I know you hold Napoleon in the highest regard, but, sir, I thought you despised program music?"

B wacked Ries on the back of his head, "How many times have I told you, Ries, to never, ever let old forms or musical rules get in the way of expression."

"Yes, sir," replied a sheepish Ries.

"My Bonaparte is not a literal story—music never is. It's a metaphor expressed through moods of music of heroism, tragedy, and the ultimate triumph of the human spirit."

"Yes, sir."

"Then," continued Beethoven, "as if knowing I'm considering relocation away from Vienna to Paris—you would do better in Paris as well my young friend—*Fraulein* Ava Lokitzvarah revealed a new and brilliantly vibrant sonata I am to dedicate to a French violinist, Rodolphe Kreutzer, whose craft pleases me very much. After that there was a truly rollicking piano sonata, that I'm inclined to use to honor Count Waldstein, and, oh yes, even an opera."

"An opera, sir? Really?"

"I have it in mind to compose an opera where it is the heroine who saves the hero."

"The heroine saves the hero? Not the other way around? No damsel in distress?"

"*Nein*, Ries. How can it have been then that you do not understand that in times of great crisis, it is the fate of men such as ourselves that women like my Giulietta—the true daughters of Elysium—appear to soften our misfortunes. When we're done today I want you to go to the libraries and booksellers or even publishers if you have to. There is a French *libretto*, entitled *Leonora, ou l'Amour conjugal*. I want you to find it for me."

"*Leonora, ou l'Amour conjugal?* Is that about the wedding of Steffen's sister Leonore to Wegeler?"

Beethoven again wacked Ries on the back of his head—this time much harder, "Of course not, you fool! The name *'Leonore'* is just a coincidence. Don't ever do that again. Just find me the *libretto* so I can set it to music."

"Yes, sir."

"When you grow up, Ries, perhaps you will learn a thing or two about women. They complete us and we, them. To achieve that harmony is to reveal the natural, organic balance in the universe—light-dark, positive-negative, male-female. In time we each move away from the trivial relationships of our youth, those of infatuation, lust, and carnality, into those of maturity, partnership, and equality. Within such a marriage as I plan with Giulietta lie the seeds of that true harmony, of family, of children, of compassion, of everlasting love. As *Fraulein* Ava Lokitzvarah reminded me before I left her cottage, *"On life's path it does not serve to yield to weakness when even a little effort toward spiritual awareness will protect you from your greatest fears. Arise with a brave heart and don't ever look back."*

Once more Ries debated inside his own head whether or not he should say anything to B about what he had seen at the ballet, but considering the last whack on his head, he again decided to chance nothing. They had reached the towpath canal that ran parallel to the Danube. Best to change the subject and return to B's raptus. "And this sonata for Waldstein, what's that like?"

"You will know it when I actually write it, but in all honesty I owe everything to the Count. If not for him and *Herr* Neefe—rest his soul—I would be nowhere. I must honor Waldstein lest I consider myself ungrateful."

"And will you write something for *Herr* Neefe?"

"Waldstein lives. Neefe is dead. Best to honor the living first.

Though among the many symphonies *Fraulein* Ava Lokitzvarah shared with me, the *Tenth* was the one that would honor the memory of Neefe, the faith he had in me and the music of Bach that he alone introduced me to as a child. It shall be one of my most glorious, that *Tenth Symphony*. And the *Eleventh*, that's for Margaretha."

"Who's that, sir? It's a name I've never heard you mention before."

"Margaretha is my little sister, the Mozart of the Beethoven family. You were but an infant when she died. Oh, how I loved her. Just as I was leaving *Fraulein* Ava Lokitzvarah's cottage, the butterfly that had landed on the goddess's hand transformed itself into *mon petit papillon*. I watched Margaretha at the keyboard, sitting in the goddess's lap, singing and playing her little song, "*a, a, b-flat, c, c, b-flat, a, g, f, f, g, a, a, g, g. . . .*"

"What a gift *Fraulein* Ava Lokitzvarah gave you, sir. To hear the future."

"It's not a gift, Ries. It's a curse. No matter what I do nor how I live, I shall reproduce only a portion of what this goddess shared with me. The rest will vanish into time and space without memory or logic."

Beethoven sighed deeply, so deeply that it took Ries by surprise, "*Ja*, even the aura of *Fraulein* Ava Lokitzvarah's lotus flower will fade away like the last reverberations of a sonata, never to seduce us again."

Beethoven picked up a small stone and tossed it into the calm waters of the canal. Circular ripples spread out from the point of impact.

"Do you see that, Ries?"

"What, sir?"

"Those ripples on the water."

"Yes, sir, I do."

"Good, because it is time for your next lesson in composition."

"I don't understand, sir. What has water to do with music?"

"Everything, Ries, everything. As you already well know and understand, music at its most fundamental is about vibrations. The strings of my violin, the brass of a horn, the skin of a drum, they all vibrate at certain pitches. By controlling those pitches the same way as a writer, such as Johann Gardner, manipulates the letters of the alphabet, we build, measure by measure, our compositions, our '*vivid and continuous dream.*' But what is often forgotten by most musicians caught up in the logic of forms and structures is the impact of those pitches upon the listener. Without a receiver to gather those vibrations and transport those signals to our brain, is there music?"

"Is this a riddle, sir? Like the one about the oak falling in the forest?"

"*Ja*, if no one is there to hear the tree fall, did it make a sound?"

"Unless there was an observer there, how would we know, sir?"

"Exactly, Ries. We wouldn't unless there was an observer. But what if the observer was deaf and didn't hear the tree fall, was sound produced?"

"I think so, but . . .," Ries started, but he quickly realized he was stumped and wasn't sure how to answer. He finally confessed. "I don't know."

"Come, follow me," said Beethoven as they turned away from the tow path and took a trail leading back towards town. "The scientists that accompanied Napoleon to Egypt did some exacting measurements on the nature of living bodies after studying the mummies they uncovered in burial grounds. What they discovered was that we, as humans, have bodies that are something like ninety percent water, blood, and other fluids. Drain us dry in an arid desert and we're as light as dust in the wind. When I threw that stone into the canal, what did you notice? Two phenomena, can you name them?"

"Well, sir, yes. First there was the 'plunk' as the stone hit the water and then there were the ripples in the canal."

"Précisément, Ries! That's exactly right. First the sound, then the ripples. That is the fundamental vibrational nature of music. Our instruments vibrate and we receive those vibrations, those pitches, not merely with our ears, but with our entire being. Just as the waters in the canal rippled from the impact of the stone, so too does the entirety of our bodies—ninety percent water—perceive music. The goal of a composer is to use his talents and genius to string together vibrations that convey a message, a message that communicates some concept or logic or emotion or feeling to the listener—not just through the ears but to the entirety of our bodies—whether we are conscious of it or not."

"Are you saying that even the deaf can hear?"

"It doesn't matter what I say, Ries, it only matters what you receive, comprehend, and then retransmit. The deaf be damned."

"And Mozart, sir, did you actually hear him play or was that a part of your '*Traum?*'"

Beethoven once again tapped Ries on the back of his head, though much lighter this time, "Ries, those who question do not know, those who know do not question."

Just as their walk took them back into the heart of the old city, Ries heard someone playing Beethoven's *Opus 22 Piano Sonata in B-flat* with a skill, vitality, and authority he had known only from the master himself. The music was coming from the music store of *Herr* Haslinger and Beethoven insisted they step inside and listen. Seated at the piano was a young woman, perhaps 22 or 23 years old, whom Ries would later learn was the Baroness Dorothea von Ertmann. She had a lofty and noble bearing and a beautiful face full of deep emotion and concentration. From the tip of each finger her soul poured forth. Through her hands she exerted dominion over the pianoforte. Every nuance of that great and beautiful sonata was turned into a song with such ease and expression. Ries had never witnessed such power and innermost tenderness combined even in the greatest virtuosi. Was this what his teacher had heard and experienced in his dream of the goddess? Was this young woman Beethoven's *Fraulein* Ava Lokitzvarah in the flesh?

Her focus and concentration was so great that the young woman did not even notice that Ries and B were standing, marveling at her work. When at last she finished the *Rondo Allegretto* with a flourish, Beethoven simply said aloud, "There it is, Ries."

This startled the pianist who turned around and saw Beethoven and Ries standing there.

Beethoven bowed before her, "Thank you, my dear. I am Beethoven. And that is how one should play my sonatas—like a goddess. "

Dorothea, who was by Ries's account simultaneously embarrassed and honored by the attention, quickly stood up and introduced herself as a great admirer of his teacher.

"Then you should become my student, though I fear there may be little more I can teach you."

"*Au contraire, Herr* Beethoven, it would be a most welcome and unexpected privilege," she said, her voice sweet as fresh honey while her eyes sparkled with warmth and delight.

"Then come around this week. For now Ries and I must be off."

Beethoven and Ries left the Baroness, still absorbing what had just transpired, and continued their sojourn through Vienna until they reached the museum and mansion belonging to Count Deym.

The Deym residence was set back from the street. From there a winding, tree-shaded pathway led to the front door, which was open. Standing just inside were four people whom Ries recognized. Foremost were Count Deym and his wife Josephine von Brunsvik Deym, who held a three-month-old baby on her hip. Beside them was Count Wenzel Gallenberg, a tall, handsome young man Ries's own age whose bearing was akin to that of a dashing cavalry officer though in fact he was actually a wealthy, if not quite established, ballet composer. Family money. Behind Gallenberg, Ries thought he espied Giulietta uncharacteristically wearing the same cobalt blue gown he had seen her in the previous night. Was she coming in or going out, he wondered.

It appeared to Ries that the Deym's—who had not yet seen him or Beethoven at the street—were bidding Gallenberg a warm "goodbye," for the young count soon turned away from his hosts and headed in their direction. The door closed behind him.

Halfway down the walk, Gallenberg glanced upward and noticed Ries and Beethoven.

"Ah, Beethoven," said Gallenberg, extending his hand forward in friendship, "Your ballet, *Creatures of Prometheus*. . . . Why is it that every time I audit a performance, it brings tears to my eyes? When will we hear something new to awaken those grumblers up in the upper tiers?"

Gallenberg's very bearing, thought Ries, exuded arrogance and, even though he knew little about the man, he took an immediate dislike to the count.

"I do not write for the galleries!" snapped B in response while ignoring Gallenberg's outstretched hand. "Do you think I give a damn about what people think when I compose?"

"Perhaps you ought to," said Gallenberg, more bemused than anything by the snub, "a few more coins in your pocket couldn't help but advance your wardrobe. And don't think you can compete dressed thusly."

As Gallenberg continued on past them, Ries turned to Beethoven, "There's something about that cretin . . . I don't know what it is, he sets me off the wrong way."

"Vienna is full of *poseurs*. A fool like that will have to compose for a very long time before he realizes he has no talent at all."

"Perhaps his skills lie elsewhere," suggested Ries.

"As do yours, Ries. Now come inside and make me proud of you."

The grand salon of the Deym's residence was filled with all the usual concert attendees, including the Lichnowsky's, Prince Lobkowitz, Count von Browne-Camus, Baron von Birkenstock, the Countess Thun, Prince Esterhazy, Count von Fries, Count Razumovsky, Baron van Swieten, the Brunsvik sisters Charlotte and Therese and their younger brother, Franz Brunsvik, Prince Kinsky, Count Keglevich, Steffen von Breuning, as well as Archduke Rudolph, the Emperor's younger brother whom Beethoven had just recently accepted as a composition student. Despite whatever financial difficulties Count Deym may have been experiencing in private, he still managed to hide it all by putting on a fine showing with food, drink, and entertainment in ample abundance.

Of course the Deym's—along with a gaggle of young children who always seemed to cling to Beethoven as if he were their playful rogue of an uncle—were there to welcome them. That children seemed to naturally gravitate toward Beethoven and he to them never failed to astonish Ries. Just one of the many particulars of life he knew he did not understand, yet there was his teacher on his hands and knees, teasing and chasing these little ones until they squealed with laugher and delight. Ries scanned the room discreetly as the Count embraced him warmly, but nowhere did he see Beethoven's Giulietta. Ries wasn't sure if that was a good omen or a bad one.

On the far side of the salon, the members of the orchestra who would back Ries during his concerto performance were tuning and preparing their instruments. Front and center to the orchestra was a fortepiano, a *Brodmann* model that was all the vogue in Vienna that year. Hovering over the strings and testing the tuning was the builder himself, Josef Brodmann. Assisting him was a young boy, no more than 8 or 9 years old. Beethoven greeted Brodmann warmly and Ries followed suit.

"Josef! Who is your assistant today?" Beethoven asked Brodmann.

Brodmann called the boy over, "Come say hello to *Herr* Beethoven and *Herr* Ries."

The boy stuck his hand out and Beethoven, with exaggerated movements, extended his as well, "So, you're fond of fortepianos, eh?"

"Yes, sir," said the boy.

"Then you are the master young Ries here must thank for tuning it?" asked Beethoven as he tickled a few of the keys.

"With a little help, sir."

"So tell us your name so *Herr* Ries can properly express his gratitude for the work you've done."

"Ignaz, sir, Ignaz Bosendorfer."

"Bosendorfer?" Beethoven roared with laughter. "Ignaz Bosendorfer. A good Austrian name to carry forward. What we have here, Ries, is the future of music. You ought to thank Ignaz, for surely, as the sun returns each day, I believe before long this young man will take us all on a path of new creations, one I hope we all live long enough to witness."

"Amen," said Ries, as he struggled to make sense of this intermingling of truth and dreams that seemed to weave their way in and out of Beethoven's narrative. He thanked both Brodmann and young Ignaz as he took a seat in front of the keyboard. Ries then set the score of the *C-minor Concerto* and the two *cadenzas* on the piano.

"Well, Ries," inquired B, "tell Ignaz which *cadenza* you are going to perform; the one a child could noodle through while sleeping or the one you are still unable to play?"

"That's her!" Ries suddenly exclaimed. "The cellist, the one we saw at St. Stephens." The piano was aligned such with the orchestra that Ries's line of sight just above the score was directly towards the blonde musician. She had a soft, curvaceous figure, a gentle, angular face with high cheekbones, and the blue-green eyes of a fox. When she realized Ries was staring at her, she smiled back—a gesture that melted young Ries's heart.

"That's Liliana Donishefski, a Jewess" said Brodman. "Prince Razumovsky invited her here from Vilnius to study with Schuppanzigh and his quartet. Positively brilliant! And that cello, it's a *Silke*."

"*Silke*? What's that?" asked Ries.

"Not 'what,' Ries," said Beethoven, "It's 'who.' Reuven Silke, from Vilna, is the finest *luthier,* violinmaker, this side of Cremona."

"Silke comes from a family of cabinet makers," said Brodmann, "and I'm told he uses a rare but densely grained hardwood from the Russian steppes that gives his instruments a particularly warm and rich tone. Liliana also has a *Silke* violin. Extraordinary—both her and Silke."

Beethoven leaned in close to Ries and whispered into his ear, "Look at how your bride-to-be clasps that cello between her legs. Play that *cadenza* flawlessly and it's you she'll be holding there tightly tonight." B's comment left Ries blushing.

After a brief warm-up, the concert began. And as promised

Beethoven did double duty. Not only did he conduct the orchestra, he would also turn the pages of his *Piano Concerto in C-minor* score for his student, Ries.

While waiting for the orchestra to reach the point where the pianoforte entered, Ries was terrified and his fingers trembled. He found himself continually distracted by the sight of Liliana. Unable to shake the image of her caressing him between her knees as if he were the cello upon which she played, Ries finally closed his eyes. Letting the music of the orchestra embrace him, Ries made his entrance perfectly and struck the keys as Beethoven had taught him—*mit unerschütterlicher Gelassenheit.*

When it came time for his *cadenza,* Ries opened his eyes and saw that Beethoven had placed the "easy" version in front of him. Ries looked up at B and then out at Liliana. Though he had practiced the more difficult draft diligently, he had never gained absolute confidence in his ability. Nonetheless, Ries knew what he had to do. Closing his eyes again he plunged headlong into the more challenging solo version without ever looking at the sheet music.

It may well be that no concerto Ries played was ever accomplished more beautifully. His solo came off flawlessly. When it was over Beethoven was so pleased that he cried "Bravo!" aloud. This exclamation electrified the audience who joined in with thunderous applause and cries of their own. Even the members of the orchestra stood and cheered thus immediately assuring Ries's standing among the artists of Vienna—and in the eyes of Liliana.

Beethoven leaned in and whispered to Ries, who was breathing heavily with relief and gratitude, "So when were you going to tell me you saw Giulietta at the ballet last night with Gallenberg?"

Ries was dumbfounded, "You knew, sir?"

"Of course. You think me blind as well as deaf?"

"No, sir."

"Well, good, there it is, Ries. Well done. But you are stubborn all the same! Just know that if you had muffed that passage I would never have given you another lesson."

Beethoven started away but then quickly turned back around to Ries, "Oh, and if it's ever a choice between you and my brothers, you do know who I'd choose, don't you?"

"Yes, sir."

"Although some decidedly wicked people have spread rumors that Casper does not treat me honorably, none of that is true. There's occasionally something uncouth in his behavior. That may be what put people against him, but he has always looked after my interest with sincere integrity. Now go meet your prospective bride and I'll do the same."

Leaving Ries to meet the cellist of his dreams, Beethoven found his way to the Deyms. His conversation with the couple immediately turned to Giulietta.

"She's upstairs, sleeping," said Count Deym.

"I gather she's rather fond of ballet lately," said Beethoven, "or at least ballets late at night."

"Please, Louis, speak kindly," said Josephine Deym as she put her arm through B's and, with the blessing of the count, pulled him aside.

Josephine's affection for her piano instructor appeared at least sisterly, if not more so. Even before she had been introduced to B three years earlier, his music, so full of verve and passion, had made her all the more enthusiastic to meet and know him. After their first lessons, the simple goodness of Louis's character—his gentle touch and the kind affection he displayed towards her and her sister Therese—only served to nourish her desires. These attributes, along with her deep belief in his inner worth, made her adore Louis, but the path to any deeper union had been abruptly turned aside by her mother's sudden insistence on her engagement to the Count under the assumption, soon proved false, that Deym's wealth would assure her comforts for life.

She had shared a bed but three times in three years with the count, a man 30 years her senior. Each conjugal union produced yet another child. Now a mother thrice over, Josephine thusly buried her feelings for Beethoven deep in her soul, knowing she should never allow any such kernels of love to sprout. Still, Louis had shown such continual affection and kindness to Josephine and her children—as well as her sisters and her brother—that she could never totally forget those stirrings inside her. She knew and accepted this, imagining that so long as she lived, she would constantly take interest in his destiny, and contribute what she could to his success—but no more than that.

"I adore you, Louis," she said most tenderly, "but you must proceed with caution. Please try to understand, Giulietta is young and confused. And her father, my uncle, is being anything but helpful. To him you are just a 'music-maker.' He's dead-set against any such marriage."

"I can hear him shouting, I am '*not one of her class!*' But what has that to do with love?"

"Love? What does Giulietta know about that? She's still a child, barely 17. How can she know you, the depth of who you are, when she doesn't even know herself from moment to moment? And this Gallenberg, he's young, charming. . . ."

"And a pompous ass."

"Yes, but one she admires for treating her as one would a queen. While you were away in Heiligenstadt, Gallenberg visited us regularly at Martonvásár. He and Giulietta spent much time together, chaperoned of course, but there were moments I fear, stolen moments. Please, Louis, she's just a girl."

"Are you saying it's impossible for us to marry?"

Averting her eyes from B's, Josephine looked down and slowly nodded her head, "Impossible? Yes."

"Josephine, my dear, dear Josephine, when I was in Heiligenstadt, I stared into the eyes of death itself. What have I to fear from Gallenberg or anyone else for that matter? I know my path in life and have found the courage to follow it anew."

"*Oh, swear not by the moon,* Louis. You may have set your compass, but Giulietta? *The inconstant moon, that monthly changes in her circled orb, lest that thy love prove likewise variable.*"

"She's upstairs? Please, guide me to her room." B motioned toward the stairs.

"Why waste your love on a child who doesn't value it?" Josephine answered bluntly, but she nonetheless acceded to his request and moved with him toward the stairwell.

"I may be fortune's fool, dear Josephine, but how can I go forward when my heart is here?" As they mounted the stairs in unison, Louis concluded, "On this issue I must confront Giulietta myself."

CHAPTER 16

Rumors of War

Bonn, Early Spring, 1804

THOUGH Leonore von Breuning Wegeler was indeed joyful to have married Franz, none of that distracted from loving her Beethoven. She had long ago come to accept him for the eccentric creature that he was and in her own mind had forgiven his faults, including the very last one of not returning for the wedding. She knew long before Louis ever would—if he ever would—that there could never have been a successful union between him and her. But this void—this undefined, unspoken distance between them—was unbearable. Was it wrong to love two people equally but differently? All the teachings of her church told her so, but her heart informed her of just the opposite. Regardless of what new or different paths their lives were to travel, Leonore knew that her affection for Louis would always live inside her heart, no matter what. No matter what. . . . She would continually honor that love, even if it was the one secret in her life impossible to share with Franz.

If not for the unexpected knocking—pounding actually—on her front door, Leonore would have allowed herself to stay by the fire in a quiet reverie on this rarest of nights—one where the newly full moon shone in all its glory upon the fresh jacket of spring snow covering the streets, fields, and alley ways of her home town.

And though all her world sparkled from this layer of white that lay before Leonore, the scent of war permeated everyone's thoughts. She knew "scent" was the wrong word, yes, but she couldn't imagine another word that quite captured the vague, unstable moodiness that pervaded the Rhineland. It wasn't that combat was all around them. No, the battle lines had been quiet of late, but just as she watched each individual snowflake tumble and float towards earth with inevitability, so too the gathering strife between rival empires felt predestined. It was almost ten years now that the French had taken control of the west bank of the Rhine, including Bonn. The Elector had long ago fled to safer regions in the heart of Germania, but for those left behind, including the Wegelers, their new identity meant being French, supporting Bonaparte, and watching their neighbors, their sons, and their brothers suffer the draft into the *Grande Armée* of the Republic.

Leonore could feel it in the marrow of her bones, this tension, this aura, this invisible amorphous scent that clung to every conversation, every thought, every action. Inevitable, yes, war was inevitable. And if daily routines, those regular affairs that preoccupied the citizens of the Rhineland, had little changed on the surface, Leonore knew beneath those illusions, life had definitely and permanently been altered.

Even her private sanctuaries were no longer safe. In her mind's eye she pictured the Garden of Venus, where snow would have buried the goddess. A thin layer of ice would cover all but the hottest corners of the baths, abandoned now by the ladies of Bonn for almost a decade after several young women bathing in the steamy waters were attacked and raped by renegade soldiers.

And news from the west, particularly Vienna, had become ever more scarce. She accepted that Louis had stopped writing letters in the two years after the announcement of her wedding to Franz, but even those from her brother, Steffen, had become rare now that tensions along the border had increased. All of this pained her. . . . And left her without resolution. How is that that she and Louis—her closest friend—had ceased communication? She could not, would not let the best years of her life pass by without engaging him once again to re-establish those bonds.

She had written Steffen months ago hoping to learn how it was with Beethoven since their rupture but had lived without response and this left her wounded as if an abscess infected her soul. It hurt.

Franz Wegeler was a good man, one she deeply loved, and marriage to him made her happy. It was a good life, but she also knew that she and Louis would . . . Would what? She wondered as she was met in the hallway by one of her servants, who announced that a French officer had come to the door, insisting he speak with her and her alone.

How odd, Leonore had thought. She had heard the snow-muffled hoof beats of the military patrol minutes before the pounding on her door. What was this about? Franz had been called away yesterday to attend to some injured soldiers at their bivouac some miles to the south, leaving her, save the servants, alone at their Bonn residence. Concerned but undaunted, she would see what the commotion was all about.

Standing just inside the foyer, his boots and cloak still covered with snow, was a high-ranking officer of the French *Armée* with enough gold braid on his uniform to ease the debt of a small city-state. She hadn't expected this. . . . A routine patrol perhaps, or a squad delivering Franz home, but this . . . no.

The officer bowed politely, "Forgive me, *Madame* for disturbing you. I am Field Marshall General Jean Baptiste Bernadotte."

A name she recognized. Everyone had heard of Bernadotte, a leader of the Republic. Leonore hid her surprise that such a high ranking officer, one known to be in direct service of Napoleon himself, would attend to her. Masking her concerns, she calmed her voice as she asked his business at such a late hour.

"We are alone?" asked Bernadotte, a question that instinctively made her snug her dressing robe that much more securely.

"My husband is asleep upstairs."

"Madame, please, I know that to be false for at this very moment your husband, *Monsieur le docteur* Wegeler—on my specific orders—is attending to my troops and will not be delivered here for another day."

"Since you have already framed and controlled this encounter, General, it appears I am at your mercy. What is it then that you are wanting?"

"Forgive me, *Madame,* for it is not what I want but rather what I have for you." Reaching into his coat Bernadotte pulled out a letter. "This comes for you via a diplomatic pouch from your brother, *Conseiller* Steffen von Breuning. I have been asked by certain friends in Vienna—who shall remain nameless in these perilous times—to ensure that this packet is placed directly into your hands and no others."

Leonore accepted the letter from his hands, "You are most kind. Do you know my brother? Is he well?"

"*Madame,* I have not had that honor, though we share compatriots in common and perhaps when this . . . this war business is at an end, I shall have that opportunity. For now, I must be off."

"Truly, General, I appreciate your kindness, but I cannot believe that one of the highest ranking officers in the French Republic has been transformed this very evening into a postal clerk."

"The truth, *Madame*?"

"Yes, good sir, out with it."

"Were there anything treasonous in that packet I handed over to you, I would have executed you on the spot myself—without hesitation."

"To live and breathe. You read my letter?"

"Indeed, *Madame,* I did." said Bernadotte, resting his hand on the door knob. "May I ask you one further question?"

"Please do. Am I not now alive by your good graces?"

"Would you be the same 'Eleonore von Breuning' I have heard *Monsieur* Beethoven speak of?"

"Should I admit to that identity without knowing of what matters *Monsieur* Beethoven has discussed," said Leonore, though she could not remember in the entirety of her life ever calling Louis '*Monsieur*' Beethoven. Louis would have laughed at that.

"The honor to share that knowledge with you is certainly mine, for he described you only in the most resolute of terms."

"*Répétez-vous s'il vous plait.* Out with it," she insisted.

"First and foremost, *Madame,* he described you as 'fearless.'"

"Fearless?"

"*Oui,* fearless, as well as wise, worldly, compassionate, and with a beauty that rivals only the goddess Venus herself—facts to which I can now attest to myself."

"You flatter me, good sir."

"No indeed not, *Madame,* for those words came from *Monsieur* Beethoven himself, along with this: He declared that you were his best, his closest, and the most honorable friend in his life."

That said, Field Marshall General Jean Baptiste Bernadotte bowed crisply before Leonore and then disappeared into the night of the full moon, leaving her alone with the letter from her brother Steffen.

Leonore returned to sit by the fire in the sitting room and opened the packet.

"Dearest Lorchen, first I must offer up my apologies for not responding to your request for news of our beloved brother, Beethoven, sooner, but rumors of war abound and given my office here I have been endlessly engaged each day with the sad minutia of military preparations. We, that is the Austrians, have little confidence in our own defenses after the last coalition failed to halt the French forces on the Italian peninsula, but in that regard I am at liberty to say no more than what has already been published in the press. . . .

"Know that I am indeed personally in good health and even have my eyes on a young woman. If all progresses well in heaven's vision, perhaps one day we too shall also join you in marriage. But let us speak of our dear friend, Beethoven. . . .

"Through the intersession of some great and powerful friends I am assured that this letter will be delivered directly and only into your hands. Much as Wegeler is my family too, what I have written herein is for your eyes alone as it concerns matters of intimacy. Do know and feel not any shame that even from a young age I was well aware of the friendship between our Beethoven and you. The truth be revealed, I am deeply

worried about Louis, for even though the nations of this Europe stand upon a rupture that will inevitably lead to further hostilities, our Beethoven himself lives in a world of perpetual conflict that I fear will not end well. . . .

"Where shall I begin? He has been at war with everyone, including me. Your wedding came exactly during the months when he realized his loss of hearing was both progressive and incurable. Though still unnoticed by most people in casual conversation, the decline of this aptitude had been extraordinarily painful for him. You cannot imagine how difficult this has been for Louis—and for those of us who surround him with our love. He is frequently angry, suspicious, and ill-tempered as if all the world and the gods were plotting against him. War rules the streets of Vienna. Louis has fought with everyone, from his brothers Casper Carl and Nikolaus Johann to young Ries; his publishers; his patrons; his fellow musicians and even most recently, the producers of an opera he is working on—but more on that later. And by fighting I mean not just with words but with fists. . . .

"These behaviors, so contrary to his good nature, act to depress his spirits and mood even more when they occur. Yet at the same time he has been writing, composing, and publishing at an extraordinary pace. His fame across the Empire, rising as it does from the outstanding and exceptional quality of his works, now rivals only that of Haydn and Mozart. . . .

"We dine together most every night at a local pub with Ries frequently joining us along with other friends, of which there are many. For those of us refugee from the Rhineland, we are as true family as when we were growing up. And as much as I find Louis's brothers troublesome and annoying, they mostly mean well, though their collective ineptitude is perpetually frustrating and in many cases provoking of unnecessary further conflict and embarrassment in regards music publishers. . . .

"As what might best be described as an armed insurrection against Louis last year, his brother Nikolaus, the chemist, has taken to calling himself Johann von Beethoven after their father but with the additional pretense of feigning nobility by using 'von' instead of 'van.' You cannot imagine the pain this use of the name 'Johann' has caused Louis. Nikolaus, I fear, was too young to understand the abuse their father laid upon the brothers and how Louis was compelled to fight back against that

drunk to protect the family. Or maybe Nikolaus does understand and his changing of names not only inflates his stature but also intends to gnaw and aggravate Louis for being too much of the big brother. Truth be, none of us find Nikolaus a pleasure to associate with. For good measure he too makes himself scarce in our lives much as possible. He looks to buy a pharmacy of his own. Perhaps here, perhaps in Linz and if he does move off, it may be the best outcome so far as Louis is concerned. . . .

"Casper means well and does his utmost to support Louis when he's not out chasing women. He handles a great portion of Louis's business correspondence, but his competence in these matters is questionable. His initiatives are often damaging to Beethoven's reputation and hinder his transactions with publishers. More than once I have been witness to fisticuffs between them. Still they love each other and, after the tempest has subsided, Louis and Casper will embrace and beg each other's forgiveness for their mutually outlandish behavior. No one other than Louis can preach a more beautiful sermon in a kind-hearted way than he does with Casper. Louis first shows Casper the true, despicable nature of his conduct, then forgives him completely. . . .

"Young Ries is perhaps Beethoven's greatest support though often unappreciated and, in some degrees, often abused on the battlefield of friendship and family. Ries frequently repairs the damage wrought by Casper with regards to publishers, particularly with Simrock back in Bonn. You must, I recommend, obtain copies of anything they publish of Louis's. His new works are, to my simple judgment, brilliant and fresh, representing as they do an entirely new course of action in regards to form, structure, rhythm, and drive. For all the frustrations that weigh upon Louis, his music grows incomparably well. . . .

"I am witness to much of his new work through the usual sort of misadventures which has led our Beethoven to join me in my apartments here in the 'Rothes Haus' as a roommate. For how much longer, I cannot say. On more than one instance he has flared up over some perceived slight that no one else would have even noticed. The greater cause of these behaviors appears to be in part his ever increasing hearing loss of which you must say nothing. His disability not only causes him to frequently miss words

in conversation and render the meaning and sense of a dialogue between compatriots into something altogether different, it makes him continually irritable and suspicious. His moods swing back and forth from rage to the most gentle kindness. He flares up and then grows remorseful and apologetic. Much as we love him, it is difficult to endure such vacillations. . . .

"Previously he and Casper were residing in an apartment attached to the Theater-an-der-Wien where he began preliminary sketches on an opera, the name of which—believe it or not—is thine own, 'Leonore.' Of course Louis vehemently denies that his choice of this story in which a loving wife in the costumed disguise of a young man rescues her husband from the prison of a despot was at all inspired by you, dear Lorchen. The name, he insists, is just coincidence, but I know that simply to not be the truth. The prison, I believe is but a metaphor for his own heart, one that is deeply troubled.

"Much as he avoids your correspondence, he still holds you dear in his thoughts. How do I know this? On those days when he crafts music for this Leonore or her male persona-in-disguise, Fidelio, he will, without being particularly aware, mention your name as we dine. We might be eating trout and he will note how you and he had shared such a dish on one of your last nights together. Or if he spies a pretty woman, his standard of comparison is the beauty of you, my lovely sister. This opera project, however, he has mostly put aside for now, as the owners of the theater have had a dispute of their own which resulted in Louis and Casper being turned out of residence. Casper took his own flat where he uses the allure of the 'Beethoven' name to seduce women—and who knows what trouble that will lead to. Louis has joined me here. Though Louis remains rigid about not letting anyone hear him play outside of public performances, he routinely forgets that I am around. This allows me to bear witness to the development of many of his recent compositions, which I will again say are brilliant and capturing the affection of the city—if not the critics and pundits—as swiftly as Napoleon conquered Italy and Egypt. . . .

"Prince Lobkowitz has purchased subscription rights to Louis's Third Symphony, which is entitled 'Bonaparte.' Though I have yet to hear it played in full score, merely the keyboard version, it's magnificent. The sec-

ond movement is a funeral march, which I swear that I could hear Louis humming to himself when the two of us joined the cortege delivering the remains of our dear friend, Count Deym, to the cemetery. Deym passed away this winter from pneumonia, leaving his grief-stricken wife, Josephine, penniless, with three children and a fourth on the way. Very sad. But can you imagine this? Right there in the midst of procession, Louis begins to hum this funeral march aloud. I am walking beside him, and we're right behind the family. The widow, who shed tears over the coffin, is eight months pregnant. She remains unawares of the distraction, but her sisters Charlotte and Therese, and the brother, Franz von Brunsvik, all glare at Beethoven with the evil eye as he—oblivious to them all—pulls out one of his little notebooks and begins to jot down notes to revise the score. Unbelievable! And these are the friends he's most fond of. Months later Louis would even help organize several benefit concerts on Josephine's behalf, but that day, that funeral, everyone was livid. . . .

"Much of Louis's pain and frustration inform his compositions and that may be the one blessing that has occurred. I have also heard of late a piano sonata Louis dedicated to Count Waldstein, and a violin sonata best described as heroic that has all the energy of two dueling swordsman crashing blade to blade. There's also the aforementioned opera—an oratorio about Christ on the Mount of Olives—as well as a pair of violin pieces that he calls romances, I think for Ries's benefit. Ries, though terribly shy when it comes to women, has been head over heels in love this past year—from a distance—with a charming and talented young string player from Smorgonie, near Vilnius. When our Beethoven, good hearted as he is known to be, realized the depth of Ries's infatuation, he arranged himself as a matchmaker by having Ries and this Liliana over to our apartments to play different parts of these romances together. Though complete in and of themselves, the two violin romances are perhaps studies for a violin concerto that he is just now contemplating writing for a mulatto violin virtuoso, George Bridgetower. Sadly, just as Ries summoned the courage to approach this Liliana on a more personal level, Bridgetower engaged her first—and aggressively so—when he encountered her with Louis at a pub. Our Beethoven, ever Schiller's 'Knight in Victory' to this damsel in

distress, fought with Bridgetower—and I do mean fought. Even platters of food went flying. The poor waiter, who got caught in the middle of this, had gravy from a roast running down his face. Beyond demonstrations of honor, all was for naught though. Liliana was shortly thereafter compelled for reasons unknown to return to her native land. That which was meant to be, never was. . . .

"The oratorio was written in great haste, two weeks or less I recall. At the time it seemed a natural fit for Louis with his damning hearing loss to identify with a beleaguered Christ. Why hast thou forsaken me? He is often in great emotional pain and wrestles with physical ailments as well, though the impetus for the oratorio stems from a much more banal incident. Your wedding, which at first propelled him to the brink of suicide, he later thought to replicate with a marriage proposal to a young woman, Giulietta Guicciardi, with whom he'd been seriously attached heretofore. When confronted with the reality of a conjugal life with our beloved friend, this Giulietta—first cousin to the widow Josephine—tossed him off like so much confetti and married an insufferable young count named Gallenberg. Louis raged for weeks afterwards. Luckily these newlyweds left Vienna for Italy immediately and have not darkened the mood of the city—or Louis—since.

"For respite, I encouraged Louis to join me at the spas at Baden. We were on the road to those baths last year and stopped at our favorite pub, the Three Ravens. There was a village band performing behind a female singer whose raspy voice reverberated as primeval as mother earth on the occasion of God creating the heavens. Her unique, earthy sound made her unforgettable. Her name, Patrizia von Schmidt. The very first lines of her song—a bold if not blasphemous statement of churchly rejection which still echoes in my mind thusly: 'Jesus died for somebody's sins, but not mine.' Beethoven heard that, pulled out his notebook and began sketching. He worked at a feverish pace—a raptus as mother used to describe his moods—in that little pub for over three hours, completely oblivious to my presence. That he is able to accomplish such undertakings whilst in the midst of swirling turmoil never ceases to both astonish and concern me. One critic watching the performance of the Oratorio when it finally

reached the stage noted: 'It confirms my long-held opinion that Beethoven in time can affect a revolution in music like Mozart's. He is hastening toward that goal with great strides.' Will he ever achieve that revolution? Not, I fear, if his life continues apace. . . .

"Why has he not returned any of your letters? You may as well ask why the moon is not as bright as the sun. He is who he is and in the two years since your wedding, he has more resembled a wild animal. His frustration with his hearing, the absence of a good woman in his life, and the annoying behavior of his brothers have combined to keep him constantly on edge. His only defense is to write, perform, and then write more. He is at his best when chained to his piano or desk. He is at his worst in all other matters and progressively so. Though I do love him as a brother, it is only a matter of time I am sure before he turns on me as well. . . .

"That he adores both you and Wegeler is a core truth with him. By marrying, you two— his best friends—forever ended that fantasy he held for so many years that he would return to Bonn and find you waiting. He knew returning was a pretense, but it was one he held fast to and that gave him a stable ground upon which to walk and reside here in Vienna. Yes, it makes no sense, but sometimes untruths are just as real as that which we know to be fact. Where he takes all this now, I do not know. He is painfully lonely without a woman in his life even though he is surrounded by a circle of good and close friends. Will he ever forgive you? Of course. He forgave you both immediately, but the pain still resides within him. That this Giulietta drew forth his affections before running off and marrying another has only added to his depression. I have not seen him with anyone of late—and you know Louis—what is he without a charming young woman on his arm? Still, I can only predict a miserable future for him if he does not radically change his life and behavior."

CHAPTER 17

Dangerous Liaisons

Vienna, early November 1805

INDEED, the stench of war was everywhere. . . .

Though Beethoven was due at Josephine von Brunsvik Deym's mansion within the hour, the widowed countess had still not made up her mind. Would she join the exodus and flee eastward to the family estate in Martonvasar in Hungary with her children as her sister, as Therese was insisting, or would she stay behind in Vienna to nurture the embers of a burgeoning *affaire avec Louis*?

Could she even call it that, this friendship, *une affaire*? She felt so unready. Why now? For so many reasons she hated the war, and the confusion it added to her life made her resent it ever more so. Couldn't the world wait? Hadn't she suffered through enough turmoil already?

The Austrians had joined England and Russia in a Third Coalition against the French less than a year after Bonaparte crowned himself Emperor. By the end of October, the Hapsburg's troops were once again out-maneuvered, crushed, and humiliated by Napoleon at the battle of Ulm. Was anyone surprised?

On All Saints Day, the 30th of October, Field Marshall General Bernadotte's troop secured Salzburg and Napoleon's Imperial Guards were marching along the Danube towards Vienna. The city was defenseless. The imperial court, along with most of the nobility and the great bankers and merchants, prepared to leave for the relative safety of the countryside farther to the east.

Not two years had passed since Count Deym's funeral and Josephine wondered how was it she had gone from being a carefree young woman of 20 to a destitute mother in a mere six years?

She rued the hasty marriage her mother, the Countess Anna Elizabeth, had arranged for her with Deym less than a month after their first arrival in Vienna back in 1799. Her mother, unsuspecting and perhaps naïve, had visited Deym's art museum and the mansion with over one hundred rooms and assumed the Count was fabulously wealthy. All that was just as much an illusion as the exhibits on display. She never looked at his account books or ledgers. A "mirage," her brother Franz had called them when, after the funeral, the general despair of their accounts became known.

In those first few months following Deym's funeral—and before the full extent of her financial crisis was exposed—the anguish of Josephine's mourning was muted only by those close to her—her family, a few friends, and Beethoven.

On the heels of her husband's death and the birth of her fourth child, Josephine wrestled with the unexpected chaos of her life. She had not even a notion of where to turn for help. Franz, who as the oldest son both inherited and controlled the family's properties in Hungary, had hardships of his own during these war years, and cash flow was almost non-existent. Charlotte's dowry to her fiancé had drained her resources and Therese, who foreswore relations with any man, remained unmarried and without property as well. Josephine even appealed to Emperor Franz II and though he promised her assistance, he quickly forgot his pledge when the gathering of a storm cloud entitled "the Emperor Bonaparte" came to preoccupy his court.

It was difficult enough to manage with four children under the age of five, but to be thrown into financial distress by the Count's death, that was completely unexpected. Deym's debts far exceeded the income and value of his museum and its collection of artifacts and statues. Josephine had been forced to manage the museum herself and rent out much of the remainder of her own mansion just to cover her expenses, two tasks for which she was untrained and ill-suited. Josephine felt as if she had been swept into the currents of the Danube by the flood of events and would drown unless . . . unless what? She couldn't even fathom what was necessary to save herself.

By June the tumult had exhausted Josephine. Her sister Therese put aside her own life to come and stay with Josephine. Together they and the children spent the summer in a country village outside Vienna. Even so, the verdant fields and sweet woodlands failed to ease her burdens, which continued to weigh heavily upon her.

Thank goodness for Beethoven who was staying nearby that season. Though he was intently at work on several sonatas and a new symphony, he nonetheless made the effort to come by to see her. He never failed to stop by at least once a week to engage Josephine's piano lessons and inquire after her health. Their friendship remained proper and platonic through those summer months as both found comfort and joy in their shared love of music and the distraction it provided from the agony of their separate lives. B was still seething over Cousin Giulietta's rejection and Josephine, for her part, remained the grieving widow. She loved to play the pianoforte—especially the challenge of engaging all of her abilities on the many new compositions Beethoven would pass along to her. Such an act of kindness on his part she thought—and a most welcome gift—brief as each visit was. Music felt like the only respite from drowning.

Still every day was a challenge. She dreaded opening letters from creditors in expectation of more bad news. Anxiety became her only constant companion and those tides of fear were pulling her down. She trembled insecure in the knowledge that each new knock at her door brought only more trouble. Her head was spinning. Everything was colored by her own distress: conversations with her sisters, dinners with her children, pleadings with her bankers. As the depth of Josephine's indebtedness increased, she found ever less relief in pleasant distractions, musical or otherwise. Some mornings she could barely manage to lift herself out of bed.

By late August she was a helpless wreck. She felt out of control, with alternating moods of laughter and tears. Therese insisted they return to Vienna and seek out a physician. During those first few weeks back at the mansion she saw no one, nor was she even capable. Some days were better than others, but all too many were worse. She had not the strength to play with her own children or nurse her baby, much less entertain visitors. Josephine's doctors identified her state as a nervous breakdown. Save tea or watered-down broth with bits of bread crumbs, Josephine ate and drank little. She lost precious weight. Her face went gaunt. Nights were the worst. She took to bed but was unable to sleep. Hiding under her quilts in the darkness, she dreaded closing her eyes for fear she would drown in the sea of her own troubles. And if she did fall asleep, she would often awake in the dark drenched in a cold sweat. The hardest realization was that she simply was not as strong or as much a survivor as she had once imagined. Without Therese tending to her and managing the children as well as the household staff, Josephine would have simply shriveled up and perished.

Only when the leaves of autumn began to turn and the air grew crisp did Josephine feel as if she could lift her head above the tumult that swirled around her. On a day when Therese was out with the children, Beethoven came by, his first visit since she had returned to Vienna. Though still frail and fragile, Josephine dragged herself out from her bedroom to receive B and veritably lit up when she saw him. And for Beethoven? It was all he could do to not react with shock upon witnessing her descent into illness.

Josephine spoke first in an animated, yet barely controlled explosion of joy and dread, "Dear kind Beethoven! Forgive me, please," she said, words spilling out of her mouth, "I've been unwell. How are you? What are you doing? Questions about you occupy me often, very often. I hope you received the books back that you loaned us—Therese did return them, yes? And for which I thank you very much—also the songs, both of which . . . Thank you, thank you." By the time she finished speaking, her body was quivering and trembling uncontrollably.

B said nothing. Instead, sensing Josephine's anguish, he took her into his arms and enveloped her in silence until the shaking stopped. Though B had not planned to stay more than a moment to deliver some piano scores, when he grasped the despair Josephine had fallen into, he changed plans and spent the entire afternoon at her side. Through his simple act of tenderness, Josephine felt as if he had just rescued her from the banks of the River Styx, the river of death. B's kind words and gentle manner pulled her back from the entrance to the underworld. They talked, sipped tea, and then he sat at her pianoforte and sang a joyful but poignant song:

I think of you when the sunlight shimmers,
beaming from the sea;
I think of you when the moon's gleam
paints the streams.
I see you when, on distant roads,
the dust rises up;
in deep night, when on the narrow bridge
a traveler quivers.
I hear you when there, with a muffled roar,
the waves rise.
In the still grove I go often to listen,
when everything is silent.
I am with you, even if you are so far away.
You are near me!
The sun sinks, and soon the stars will shine for me.
Oh, if only you were here!

That first visitation led to more. B insisted on stopping by several times a week to look in on her. Therese noticed how Josephine gradually began to pull herself together on those occasions, combing out her hair, applying make-up, finding the right dress—even playing with her children again. On one visit B arrived in bold spirits and succeeded in convincing her to go out with him for a walk. Their stroll didn't last long—she felt terribly weak and anxious—but the warmth of his companionship and the brisk chill in the air did her good. It revived her spirits and along with it her appetite soon began to return. She no longer felt as if she were drowning. And Josephine began to look forward with anticipation to his visits which began to reoccur with regularity.

Therese cautioned her that Beethoven—still recoiling from his split with Cousin Giulietta—might be falling in love with her. Josephine kept secret from her sister that Beethoven had long had her heart. Could he, however, be trusted to not wound it further?

After several such outings, B even had her join him for a coach ride into the countryside. The driver took them as far as Heiligenstadt. From there B helped her walk with him along the trail to the Tempest, whose roiling rapids she recognized from her own nightmares. Together they sat upon a boulder above the river as butterflies flitted to and fro. "Now that we are together again with no one to disturb us," he began, "let me share with you my real sorrows and the struggle I have had with myself for some time." Though at this stage, it was scarcely noticed by others, for B the trauma he had been experiencing over the deterioration of his hearing was profoundly frustrating. "My grief over this has robbed me of my usual energy, leaving me less diligent about writing than I ought to be."

He described how he had come here to the Tempest, intending to end his life only two summers before. What saved him? The *"wings of a goddess."* He talked about his *"Traum,"* and how the spirit of Isis had lifted him up out of his depression. . . . B recalled for her how he imagined the goddess playing the music of his future, music that would be life-affirming, music Josephine knew revealed an entire world of emotions. Even in her own weakened state, Josephine understood that this phase of B's music, so heroic, so bold, so vibrant, epitomized the struggle of each individual to reach for the positive and enriching aspects of their existence and, in so doing, overcome the endless travails of their lives. She wondered if she could somehow find the inner resources to do the same. It was then Beethoven made a confession of his own that at once uplifted her spirits and terrified her.

"And as my affection for you, my dear Josephine, has grown, this torment has strengthened ever more."

On his next visit B played for her a song from his opera-in-progress, *Fidelio,* imagining she might find further consolation in a piece he described as the "*Prisoners' Chorus*"—one that put into words the liberation his heart felt in her presence.

Oh what joy, in the open air
freely to breathe again!
Up here alone is life!
The dungeon is a grave.
We shall with all our faith
Trust in the help of God!
Hope whispers softly in my ears!
We shall be free, we shall find peace.
Oh Heaven! Salvation! Happiness!
Oh Freedom! Will you be given us?
Speak softly! Be on your guard!
We are watched with eye and ear.
Speak softly! Be on your guard!
We are watched with eye and ear.
Oh what joy, in the open air
freely to breathe again!
Up here alone is life.
Speak softly! Be on your guard!
We are watched with eye and ear.

As Josephine listened to the lyrics she envisioned herself reaching upwards for daylight, using B's strength to lift herself out of the terror that threatened her existence. It was as if the wisdom of his words had implanted themselves in her womb, awaiting a re-birth through his music. She would survive, she would recover, and with luck, she might even thrive and be reborn.

Nonetheless Josephine feared her own inability to share with B the raw emotions that churned inside her heart. As much as Josephine desired B's sincerest affections and found comfort in them, she dreaded that in her current state she could not possibly be receptive to nor capable of other, more physical forms of love. His notes to her were challenging enough, arriving as they did from time to time with salutations such as: *"All good wishes, dear kind Countess—in haste your Beethoven who worships you; or, My beloved J; or, Angel of my heart, angel of my life."* Could B understand or be capable of a platonic covenant without furthering the risks to her own most fragile soul. Would he demand greater proofs of her love and esteem in return? And if she were to yield possession of her very self to him, would he be satisfied? Or would the purity of her heart be despoiled anon?

The first time he reached out to caress and kiss her with affection, she gently pushed him away. "Please, Louis," she whispered tenderly, "do not try to persuade me further. *We are watched with eye and ear.*" Indeed they were and that also terrified Josephine. While her sister Therese adored Beethoven and judged him a friend, Therese did not hesitate to share her feelings. She insisted that Josephine have the strength to say no. *"It is a sad duty if not the saddest of all! Often one errs and is misunderstood in love. May the grace of God aid you so that you are not tormented and your health may improve."* Therese considered it dangerous for Josephine that, in her frail state, B would come by every second or third day to give her lessons or join the family for dinner.

Therese was aghast at the thought of Josephine engaging in an affair with Beethoven; and more so at the thought that Josephine might consider marrying a man not of their class after the financial and emotional disasters she experienced with Deym. Beethoven, though, was not deterred. Thanks to his continued kindness, Josephine's personal renaissance gathered momentum as the weather changed yet again. After the New Year came in, Josephine felt strong enough with B's assistance to host a series of musical soirees at the mansion as Deym had done before his death. At first the gatherings were small: Beethoven, Therese, her brother Franz, and a few other friends. But over the next few months, the gatherings grew in size parallel with Josephine's newly restored strength. Others in their circle began to attend. While the issue of her debts did not go away, Beethoven, with the occasional assistance of friends such as the pianist Baroness Dorothea von Ertmann, the young Archduke Rudolph, who played the cello and clarinet, and the violinist Schuppanzigh and his quartet, turned some of those evenings into small fundraisers which eased Josephine's financial burdens somewhat.

And then there was the night of the Spring Equinox when everyone else left and Beethoven stayed behind. While professing his love for her, B insisted that he was finished with the flighty little affairs of his youth. He desired that Josephine be his woman, his companion, his partner, and, perhaps someday, his wife. Though she still felt unready, her deeper desires let her succumb to his advances. B didn't leave her bedside until the first sparks of dawn lit the sky. He was a kind and gentle lover, slowly arousing in her a passion and release she had never experienced before, not just once but repeatedly. A mistake, she wondered, when she woke in the morning and found a love note from Beethoven on her pillow?

"Oh, beloved J, it is no mere desire for the other sex that draws me to you. No, it is just you, your whole self, with all your individual qualities—this has compelled my regard—this has bound all my feelings, all my emotional power to you. When I first came to you it was with the firm resolve not to let a single spark of love be kindled in me. But you have conquered me. The question is, whether you wanted to do so? Or whether you did not want to do so. No doubt, J, you could answer that question for me sometime. Dear God, there are so many more things I should love to tell you—how much I think of you, what I feel for you—but how weak and poor those words—at any rate my words—truly are. All good wishes, angel of my heart."

How should she answer him when they next met? Though she had broken down and given him possession of her most noble self, and the greatest proof of her affection, she knew she had gone too far. While her soul was enthusiastic to receive him and gathered nourishment from his affection, she was completely conflicted. His expression of love and the ongoing pleasure of his acquaintance should have been the finest jewel of her life if he could have only loved her less sensually. Would he be satisfied if she withdrew even a little? Or would he tear her heart apart? And if news of this affair became public, what then? She had no answers.

Therese insisted Josephine break off the affair for her own good. *"If all you have is love at the table, then you will be hungry afterwards and many a new sorrow will set in. Unless there is gold to live on, you will never be happy. Zero plus zero remains zero."* Therese added a warning that Prince Lichnowsky suspected something was going on between Josephine and Beethoven. Apparently he had seen the score for a song about hope, *An die Hoffnung*, lying about B's apartment with a dedication to Josephine and made the obvious conclusion.

All of this discourse and reflection only confused Josephine ever more. Unable to come to any resolution within herself, she procrastinated for weeks and did all she could to avoid encountering Beethoven. And now Napoleon's *Grande Armée* was sweeping down the valley of the Danube toward Vienna. It was only a matter of days before they arrived and Josephine knew she would have to decide.

She was pacing back and forth in the salon when Therese pulled her aside, "Before B arrives, let's chat."

"Must we?" replied Josephine.

"Don't be obstinate! Please, hear what I say and thereafter I'll leave you in peace."

"You'll never do that, so out with it. What have you got to say?"

"I believe Beethoven wants you for his wife, you do understand?"

"That is quite clear."

"And if you did consent . . ."

"We'd be married," she sighed. "His love, how glad it makes me . . . how sad it makes me."

"He'll want an answer soon, won't he?"

"Would you give us your blessing if we married?"

"Not if he embitters your life as Deym did. Once and forever, no, I cannot."

"Dear Therese, sometimes your heart is as hard as a stone. Must I be so cruel with him? Not give him a glimmer of hope? Is there nothing that would change your mind? Tell me!"

"And have us stay here with the French? You should not and I will not."

"I'm sorry for you, sis, but ever since B came back into my life everything around me and within me has changed. Do I wish to call him husband? I don't know. All I want is to wake each morning in peace in the arms of a man who loves me. That is my desire, and how happy would I be then?"

"You do know the dangers? With a musician like Beethoven your sufferings may never end."

"Isn't the union of two like-minded hearts the font of true happiness?"

"You would marry a composer who confessed to you that he is going deaf? His career cannot last much longer, and then what? Poverty?"

Before Josephine has a chance to respond, there's a knock at the front door. Therese leaves Josephine to receive the visitor. It is of course, Beethoven. Therese greets him warmly, then whispers in his ear. "Please let her go. Do not hurt her."

B waits until Therese is out of earshot before addressing Josephine, "Much as I adore your family, I will invoke all that is evil on the heads of your relations for all the confusion they have strewn. Oh, Josephine, will you stay? I mean to build our happiness by means of your affection. If only you would find some value in this."

Josephine freezes with indecision and says nothing. Tears fill her eyes.

Beethoven easily reads her mood. "I fear I love you as dearly as you do not love me."

"Must you abuse my feelings? Perhaps I've trusted you to read deeper into my soul than our acquaintance should have properly allowed?"

"Am I really unable to influence you?"

"Do know that I care for you, that I set value upon your friendship. But if you are not as noble as I believe you to be, what worth will I hold in your eyes?"

"My dear, dear Josephine, you are precious to me beyond all else."

"Still, in this circumstance, it is I who suffers much more—much more than you do—much more," she said.

"This tendency of yours to fall into sadness—please do not surrender. It hurts me to see you thus and the more so when I do not know how or in what way I can help."

"If my life is so precious to you, then treat me with more consideration, and above all, do not doubt me. I cannot express how deeply hurtful it is. To have sacrificed virtue and duty, and yet be compared to lowly creatures, if only in your thoughts and quiet suspicion—it is too much."

"My Josephine, only your love can make us wholly free. Do you really have such trouble making up your mind?"

"Sometimes *yes*, sometimes *no*."

"If I could say in words what I can with music, I would beg you to take these chains off my heart and stay with me in Vienna."

"I adore you, Louis, and value the depth of your character. You have shown so much kindness and affection to me and my children; I shall never forget that so long as I live. You must not take me amiss, however, if I . . ." Josephine stops mid-sentence before starting again in utter despair, "Play for me, sing for me, do anything to chase these blue feelings away."

Returning to a seat at the pianoforte, Beethoven complies with *An die Hoffnung*:

> *Is there a God? Will he someday fulfill,*
> *The promises for which our longing cries out?*

Will, before the court of the world,
This puzzle ever reveal itself?
One must hope. One cannot ask!
You, who so gladly celebrates on sacred nights
And gently and softly veils the grief that torments this tender soul,
Oh hope! Raised through you,
Let this sufferer feel that there above,
An angel counts our tears!
When, long hushed, beloved voices are silenced,
When, underneath dead branches, our memory sits desolate,
Then come closer to where your forsaken one mourns
And, looking around at midnight,
Supports himself against sunken tombs.
And if I look up to accuse Fate,
When, departing my allotted days, the last rays set:
Then permit me to see, at the rim of this earthly dream,
The light of the cloud's hem from the near-by sun!
Is there a Goddess? Will she someday fulfill,
The promises for which my longing cries out?
Will, before the court of the world,
This puzzle ever reveal itself?
I can only hope for that which I fear to ask!

CHAPTER 18

L'Amour Conjugal or Bonaparte Takes Vienna

"WOULD YOU like some more tea?" said N as he extended a cup and saucer in my direction. "The soma will clear your mind of all this 'Josephine' confusion."

Both the mental and physical fog that draped my *Traum* in yet further bewilderment had returned and along with it, my newly minted friend, Napoleon. Ever the conquering hero, he was dressed in full military regalia, with his Egyptian scimitar tucked into his belt sash. Once more we sat cross-legged opposite each other, though this time round we were in some sort of circular vessel about eight to ten feet across that resembled an oversized yet tightly woven basket. It felt as if we were floating on the Rhine in the *Drachen* or the *Lorelei*, except the sensation was lighter, gentler.

"I'd give anything for a cup of Turkish coffee. . . ."

"*Oui*, black as all hell and so thick the spoon stands up by itself," N added, finishing off my thoughts. "You can't always get what you want, B, but if you try sometimes, you just might find," he added as he swept his free hand over the tea cup, *"vous obtenez de quoi vous avez besoin,* you get what you need."

Like a magician, N's wave of his hand had transformed that tea cup into a demi-tasse of Turkish coffee whose scent alone had me salivating. N's wizardry never ceased to astonish—and I confess—please me. How he did these tricks, I did not know or care, assigning in my mind's judgment their success to the power of dreams—particularly since the coffee was perfection personified.

"Josephine," rued N, "Such women . . . yours and mine . . . my beloved Josephine Beauharnais, Empress of France, can't conceive a male heir and yours, B, your Josephine Deym gets pregnant almost every time she flops on her back. Best be careful if and when you spend the night together again."

"You're the omniscient one. Will I? Will we?" I asked.

"That outcome is already foretold." N then mumbled a further response, of which the last word—a name—was all I clearly understood: *Minona*. Before I could ask for a clarification, N immediately changed the subject to one that surprised me given his oft stated deep and passionate love for his wife, the Empress:

"No sooner did I have my Josephine crowned then I began to consider the necessity of a divorce. I needed a male heir to secure the throne."

"Spoken like a true Royalist," I said.

"A true pragmatist," he countered. "The only way to prevent another war from engulfing Europe was to build alliances. In order to do that, I needed a new wife drawn from my enemy's camp who could produce a son. Politics required me to inseminate a Russian or Austrian princess endowed with a fertile womb and milk-rich breasts."

"And you believed your foes would sacrifice a virgin on the altar of your empire?"

"Don't believe me? Look down," he indicated, but when I glanced at the floor of this basket, he added, "not there, over the rim."

I did as he suggested, turning to look over the lip of this basket within which we sat. "I see nothing but the fog of Elysium."

"Oh, excuse me," N apologized. "I forgot, you still see with the eyes of a mortal." With another wave of his hand, the clouds scurried away, like so many insolent children.

I looked out again and realized that we were floating, most stationary, hundreds of meters above a walled city while a stiff wind swirled around us. "Astonishing," I said, for the very majesty of the view of that city and the surrounding countryside was truly incomprehensible to someone such as me who had led life entirely earthbound. I confess I was beginning to enjoy N's succession of magic tricks. Would I be so fortunate to have them at my disposal after being admitted to Elysium? And if Napoleon had been appointed my guide, who in turn would I be assigned?

"Zimmerman, Robert." N again read and answered my thoughts.

"Who's that?"

"A poet, a singer, an American Jew hooked on Isis, and you're the only I artist I know with an intelligence surpassing his," stated N, after which he began to sing;

Isis, oh, Isis, you mystical child,
What drives me to you is what drives me insane
I still can remember the way you smiled
At me in the drizzling rain.

"But why spoil the fun," he added. "The times, they are a changing."

"The times, they are a changing?" What did he mean? Why was it I could never fully comprehend most of N's quips? "So tell me then," I asked, "where are we and what time is it?"

"Ah, Vienna, the evening of November 20th, 1805," was his response.

November 20th was the night my opera *Fidelio* premiered. Below us on the streets of the old city, I could pick out individual people who looked insignificant as dots. Moving about the square beside St. Stephens Cathedral were many who wore the uniforms of Napoleon's *Grande Armée,* which had peacefully taken control of Vienna a week earlier. Peering around farther and examining our situation now that N had chased the fog away, I realized we were in what I have heard scientists describe as the gondola of a brightly colored *Montgolfière,* a hot air balloon. There was some sort of burner above us, and above that was the balloon itself. Made of French, tricolored silk, it was brightly decorated with N's favorite Imperial designs, including his signature bumble bee motif.

"Would you feel any pity if one of those dots stopped moving forever?" N asked me.

"Would you? The majority are your French soldiers."

"Throw enough of them into combat and one of my enemies will offer up a royal daughter anxious to spread her legs and welcome Napoleon home. Mark my words."

With more careful observation I noticed many of those dots were heading towards the *Theater-an-der-Wien* to see my opera. Outside the theater itself, a multitude of coaches and wagons came and went. Some delivered more of those well-dressed dots; others carried new furnishing, couches, props, and other sundry supplies.

"Did your army transport this *Montgolfière* from Paris?"

"No," offered Napoleon, "I brought it from the future. These new ones are so much more efficient than the model 1806."

"Ah, the future; with all your tricks and gimmicks you make it seem most intriguing."

"Hardly. The more times change, the more human behavior remains the same. Haven't your readings of Plutarch and Shakespeare taught you that by now?"

"And this wind? How is it we are unaffected by it?"

His blue-grey eyes stared back at me and in one of them I witnessed an image of Isis and in the other Shiva burning bright and forcefully as the sun. With a resonance worthy of those gods N's words vibrated directly into my consciousness, "*I am the wind . . . I am the wind and all it touches. I am all that is and all that will be.*"

"*Ja,*" I nodded. The solemnity of his voice aside, sometimes I never quite understood how N's bag of tricks aligned with his intentions.

"How is it that you, my dear Beethoven, you who have not married, you who have not a wife, you who has not known *L'Amour Conjugal,* would have the audacity to write an opera celebrating the bonds of love between wife and husband? Ironic, isn't it?"

"Mein Gott!" I exploded back at him. "Who created these rules? Am I now no longer able to dream? Haven't you already seen that my life in Vienna has been a wretched one? And this issue of love—which makes me at once both the happiest and the unhappiest of men—can I not aspire to marriage? Or joy? Or perfection in the arms of a woman? Is that not possible in my situation? Why must I be kept from the ones I so love?"

"Come on, B, you wrote a 'rescue' opera, only as you told poor young Ries, you flipped it all around so that the wife, Leonore, is the heroic one who lifts her beloved husband Florestan back into the light of freedom. '*Oh what joy, in the open air; freely to breathe again!*' I may not be a literary scholar, but it doesn't take a genius to imagine *Fidelio* is really all about you waiting to be saved. A bit passive, wouldn't you say?"

"Me? Passive?"

"'*Hope whispers softly in my ears. . . . Oh Freedom! Will you be given us?*' Now get over it and look at the facts. You're a musician going deaf. . . . Josephine, your Countess, abandoned Vienna for Hungary. You're alone . . . unloved . . . no woman, no family. Really, nothing to look forward to, and you write an opera that cries out for psychological analysis of the composer," said N, using yet another term from the future, 'psychological,' that I did not understand.

"Psychology," he declared. "It's the science of the mind. Medical science. Mental illness, crazy people, anxious people—like your widow Josephine unable to make up her mind. Vienna becomes the birthplace and ultimately the hotbed for medical practitioners who specialize in this art—psychiatrists, they're called. Some are brilliant; others are over-educated morons who will assert that Beethoven and Napoleon both suffered from personality disorders."

"What is that?

"Personality disorders? It means we're highly sensitive, emotional, maybe even volatile and irascible. To which I say, 'Of course!' Isn't genius always hyper-sensitive? Hyper-alert? Hyper-aware? That is the definition of genius. These brain scientists crack me up. For example, there are the Sterbas, an American husband and wife couple—both psychiatrists—who claim to have insight into the sexual neuroses of long-dead historical figures."

"The Sterbas? Should I know them?"

"Hopefully you will never encounter them or be exposed to what they've written about you. Pure clap-trap. Worse than Schindler."

"Worse than Schindler, really? The world has never lacked for charlatans—and I should add, conquering armies. Can you imagine how frustrating it was to premier my opera—after all those years of work—in front of a hostile audience?"

"Truly, B, what did you expect? You run out a performance—in that coarse German dialect, no less—about liberation from tyranny in front of my troops a week after we occupy Vienna. It matters not that our men represent the forces of liberty and equality; we were still the invaders."

"What was I to do? Change the libretto on the spot? Your occupation drove my patrons and friends into exile, including the one chance I had for love and marriage. You chased my Josephine away, damn you!"

"That little bird? She would invent any excuse to fly off."

"I had her, right in my hand . . . and then your troops arrived. Damn."

"Perhaps we did land you in a perilous spot. Of all the theaters, in all the towns, in all the world, yes, we waltzed into yours. In truth that *Fidelio* text did need some editing but I admired what you had to say. There will always be those like your villain, Pizarro, who believe that the universe is theirs to control and dominate. They're crafty as a fox and have no scruples except that their desired end justifies their means. That includes propagandizing the masses with a set of collective delusions and then stifling anyone—such as your heroine Leonore and her husband, Florestan—who challenges that orthodoxy."

"I hated you French more than ever after that night. Everything I worked for, ruined."

"Lighten up, B. You should be grateful to have escaped from a life of insecurity with Josephine. But getting back to the import of the opera, the real problem with preserving liberty is not the overthrowing of tyrants, but the pudding-like attitudes of the common folk that support them; the ones whose nature is to never question the way things are. They just go on with their lives and gum up the works for the rest of us. These people complain a lot but never take action. Consider this, after food, air, water, and shelter, what is the most important need humans have?"

Having not the least of a clue, I shook my head.

"Story," declared N. "Story. People live and die for story. Call it fairy tales, opera, novels, mythology, gossip, the gospels, theater, religion, poetry, conversation, or what passes for news. If food, air, and water are the physical substances necessary to sustain life, then story is the psychic element equally needed to keep us alive. We all live and bathe within our own mythologies. For the masses the Church, the state, the King, the Emperor offer up stories to believe in. *My god is better than your god.* The unthinking hoard are delivered answers and set on a path that they do not question. Anyone who accepts such a scenario in which all the major problems of life are solved—even if those answers are detrimental to their existence—is likely to go through life with all the quivering calm of a lamb on its way to be slaughtered. . . ."

"Our problem," he continued, "is that we are each one of those rare persons who cannot help but think about the nature of life, its meaning, and our place in the universe. . . . People like you and me live in accord with more noble principles and ideas. Our very presence upsets the norm. And when we are truly in harmony with ourselves, we can achieve a measure of greatness. That is what gives us the capacity for endurance and self-assertion. . . ."

N pointed over the lip of the basket far to the north towards the flat plains of Moravia. "In less than two weeks outside the town of Austerlitz, I will face off against a large Austro-Russian army under the command of General Mikhail Kutuzov. Remember that name, 'Kutuzov.' Emperors Alexander I of Russia and Franz II of Austria will both personally be present with their respective entourages. From the safety of distant hills, they will each watch in despair as my *Grande Armée* crushes their forces separately. How will we do this? My troops, who are adept at espionage and deception, will secure our victory by first concealing their deployment. We will then take up a central position and separately attack each of those two armies at their hinge. By concentrating my forces against weak spots and then timing those attacks, it allows me to place the maximum number of troops at one front against my enemy and defeat it. After we fight one group with superior numbers, we'll pivot to face the other. My legions will inflict 25,000 casualties on a numerically superior enemy army while sustaining fewer than 7,000. Never forget, free men fight harder. Some historians will consider this Bonaparte's greatest victory. Afterwards, your Emperor Franz, realizing the futility of resistance, will sign the Treaty of Pressburg and leave the Coalition."

"I'm told both Emperors Franz and Alexander have lovely daughters. . . ." I said.

"Indeed, Marie of Austria and what's her name, the Russian, Princess Anna—Alexander's younger sister. . . . Look B, as Napoleon, I have fought sixty battles and I have learned nothing which I did not know at the beginning. Read Caesar—he too fought the first like the last."

"To his detriment Caesar crossed the Rubicon only to impale himself upon Brutus's knife and you, you suffered Moscow, Vittoria, and Waterloo. *Eh tu, Brute?*"

"A pity your impression of Napoleon Bonaparte is one of human frailty and excess. How little you truly know me and who I really am."

"You might be a master strategist or a ghostly magician filling my dream with your parlor tricks, but General Kutuzov, he certainly got the best of you at Moscow. What more do I need know?"

A cold shiver rippled through N's body and for just an instant, he appeared before me as I had first seen him at the onset of this dream—a general shivering in full winter garb: trench coat, cape, earmuffs, gloves, the tricolor hat of an officer, and those cavalry boots tipped with silver. A frozen tear lingered on his cheek. Moscow had proved that N, for all his godly pretense and inventive tricks, was merely mortal—a dead one at that.

"Come here," N reached over and tugged on my ear. "I want you to look through this window." N twisted aside revealing a two-foot-wide panel of glass in the side of the gondola. Needless to say it was no ordinary window, possessing as it did all the powers of a witch's crystal ball. N touched the glass and suddenly through this window we could see close up the entry way to the *Theater-an-der-Wien*. There was a line outside of patrons waiting to enter. Most were French officers though there were a few civilians, including some I recognized, such as the chemist, Harry Lyme, for whom my brother, Nikolaus, worked; and then there was the delightful pianist, my student, Dorothea von Ertmann and her husband, the Baron. The scent of her perfume, as intoxicating as champagne, always, always warmed my heart and more. . . .

"Would you like to see inside?" N asked.

"We can do that?"

"*Watch with eye and ear.*"

He touched the glass again and once more we were transported anew. This time we had a bird's eye view of the interior of the theater. The seats were indeed filling up. Off to one corner I spotted Fanny Giannatasio del Rio with her father, Cajetan, and her sister, Anna. The two girls, who in a decade would be the proprietresses of their father's boarding school, could not have been more than 14 or 15 years old. Below the stage in the orchestra pit, the musicians busied themselves tuning their instruments and checking their respective scores. In one of the seats up front, I saw Napoleon—a different Napoleon than the one beside me in the gondola. This little corporal with his steel-tipped boots sat beside Field Marshall General Bernadotte on one side and General Gerard Beynac, who would supervise the French occupation, on the other. I looked back at N as if to ask, how is this possible?

Once more his response echoed in my consciousness with the intonation of the gods. *"I am all that is and all that will be. I am the life in every creature and for this reason transcend every conception."*

"Of course," I said. Why did I even bother to ask? N seemed intent on convincing me he was all things—first the wind, next the life in every creature, instead of the harassed general he was, who even now hectors me from the grave.

Shifting back to a conversational tone, N added, "Look there." He pointed back to the window where I saw none other than my younger self preparing to conduct the overture. Before I could even frame a question about this, N answered. "*When we are free from all passion and desire, we join and become one with the universe. Thus transformed, the realm of possible stretches beyond the material to the infinite.*" Not at all comprehending a word of what he presented, I asked again for a simple explanation.

"Do you recall your conversation with young Ries about the potential music stored up in your *Guarneri* violin? Well, this is your story and what you are seeing is the manifestation of some of that potential in your life. Many of the key players in your future are now evolving inside this theater. What happens next is up to you."

It was then that I noticed the curtain to the Emperor's private box was moving back and forth as if someone was tugging on it from below. "What's going on there? Who's behind that curtain?" I asked, knowing that the Emperor and the rest of the royal family, including my friend and student, Archduke Rudolph, were in retreat to the east.

"Are you sure you want to know?"

"Didn't you just say the theater is like my violin? If this is my possible future, what choice do I have? Show me."

N echoed the words of Isis, "*No Mortal Man Has Ever Lifted My Veil,*" and then touched the glass anon. He was right; I was not prepared for what I saw. There, on the Emperor's own couch, was my brother Casper, fucking some young woman whose legs were splayed askew.

"Not just any woman," noted N. "That girl is Johanna Reiss, your future sister-in-law. And the seed your brother plants today will grow into your nephew, Karl."

"That bastard!" I screamed. "My brother with the Queen of the Night at the premier of my *Fidelio*? Damn him!"

"It's your opera. You wrote it," laughed N. "*L'Amour Conjugal*. Now you have it in spades."

"Fick das!" It had never occurred to me as we watched Casper and Johanna despoil the Emperor's couch through the magic of N's window that this was the origin of how the harpy trapped my brother into marriage.

"Do the math. Six months from now, in May, when Johanna can no longer hide this pregnancy from her parents and the local magistrates, Casper will be compelled to marry her."

"She's naught but a conniving whore!" I screamed again.

"Whatever . . . And on September 4th, nine months after the premier, your nephew Karl is born."

"How is this possible? How did this happen?"

N went on and described for me how when the royal family left Vienna, their servants took the chairs and couches from the Emperor's box. Johanna's father, an affluent furniture upholsterer, had been hastily commissioned to replace the seating in there. The nineteen-year-old Johanna, who oversaw the delivery, apparently bumped into Casper, whom I'd stupidly sent there on an errand. Lust encountered lust and the outcome would forever change my life. Unbelievable. *L'Amour Conjugal*! The little slut dropped her panties, lifted her skirts and spread herself out for my damn idiotic brother. At my premier! That horrible, conniving bitch! If only I had sent Ries to deliver those scores to the orchestra instead.

"Give it a rest, B. She's no more at fault than your brother. The definition of family is a cross to bear. You have your Casper and I have Jerome, my youngest brother. Bumblers both."

"I hate this. Johanna, Casper and Karl, they're going to make my life hell. Can't we change history? Can't we alter these events?"

"I know that you're tempted to treat your nephew Karl as if he's the 'Second Coming' of Margaretha, but these visions of ours, B, are just recollections of events that have come and gone. That which was, is unalterable. We can never unwind the past, but if good omens prevail we can change the future through our efforts in the present. To enter Elysium and experience the one day of joy you crave, you must complete just such a journey as you are on now.

"Is it really my fault that Karl will grow up and shoot himself? Am I responsible?"

"Are you responsible? I may know the future but only you can evaluate the valence of those conditions that weigh down your soul. And whether you succeed or not? Well *mon ami*, that is the one process over which only you have influence."

We look through the magic window again where I see my younger self poised to conduct the orchestra in the *Leonore* overture. It is the first of three different versions I would eventually compose for *Fidelio*—and, *ja*, Steffen is correct. Leonore—Eleonore—my Lorchen—is on my mind each and every time I scribble notes on staff paper. How could she not be? She and Wegeler are my best friends and I love her . . . always have . . . always will. . . .

However, just as this younger Beethoven raises his right arm and clenches his fist, the vision before us blurs and then shifts radically. Instead, what we see is my nephew Karl, now 20 years old, standing beside the ruins of Rauhenstein Castle outside Baden. In his right hand is a pistol, in his left, another. He aims both weapons at his head. His fingers caress the triggers.

A bolt of lightning abruptly splits the sky asunder. The magic window goes black, and though I witness N react to the crack of thunder and the torrential rains that follow, I hear nothing. *Ja*, still deaf.

CHAPTER 19

The Appassionata

Prince Lichnowsky's Estate at Gratz near Troppau, Moravia, Late September 1806

THE THUNDERSTORM was relentless and the drenching rain that accompanied it swirled around the coach. Between flashes of lightening, his Imperial Highness, the eighteen-year-old Archduke Rudolph, watched from the portico of Prince Lichnowsky's estate at Gratz as one of his servants steadied the six horses harnessed to his carriage. Up on the wagon's roof, a coachman, drenched to the bone, struggled to cover the trunks he had secured there with a tarpaulin—a task made near impossible by vicious gusts of wind. Their baggage was soaked, Rudolph's head ached, and his limbs felt as fragile and useless as moldy bread.

The Archduke wondered what else could go wrong on this journey that began with so much promise. If there was one deed Rudolph—the youngest brother of Emperor Franz—was determined to accomplish on this night regardless of his own health, it was going to be shepherding his teacher, Beethoven, away from Gratz before the composer's rage led to another violent encounter with the Prince, or worse yet, the French officers who had been Lichnowsky's dinner guests.

It had all started innocently enough two weeks earlier in Vienna, not long after the young Archduke had honored Beethoven's request by presiding over the baptism of his new born nephew, Karl. Rudolph, the coadjutor to the Archbishop of Olmutz, was ever desirous of doing favors for the one man in the Empire he considered his true master—Beethoven. Although B was not, by church standards, a religious man, his brother and sister-in-law attested that they were. Rudolph welcomed the opportunity to officiate at the ceremony before he and Beethoven set out on the journey to Gratz. Beethoven had been invited there to escape the lingering summer heat of the city by his long-time patron and their mutual friends, Prince Carl Lichnowsky and his wife, Christiane. The Archduke, who was an excellent musician, would use this journey deep into Moravia to not only be able to spend uninterrupted time with his teacher, but to also use those weeks to continue copying out the scores to Beethoven's recently completed pianoforte works. In the drive to improve his composition skills, Rudolph found it particularly useful to reproduce each and every note of Beethoven's scores himself by hand.

Life as a brother of the Emperor was both enviable and frustrating for Rudolph. Growing up at the Hofburg Palace, the young archduke lived a life of luxury and though he was witness to all that went on in court, he had no defined role. Rudolph, who was born in 1788, was the youngest of sixteen children. His father, Emperor Leopold II, died when Rudolph was but four. His brother, Franz II—some 20 years older—not only ascended to the throne but also became Rudolph's de facto parent and the one who oversaw his education. As a young child Rudolph undertook instruction in French, Latin, and Italian in addition to his native German. Later he also studied religion, history, court protocol, fencing, dancing, and, most agreeably of all, music. Franz ensured that Rudolph had no unsupervised time and was strictly disciplined.

Initially he was to be trained for a career in the military, but his health was simply not good enough. Weak and sickly as a child, Rudolph suffered from the disease that would impact many of his Habsburg relatives: epilepsy. Attacks of the "falling down disease" occurred every few weeks and left him bedridden, ill, and weak for days afterwards. Constantly in search of a cure, Rudolph spent much time at spas in Baden near Vienna or Teplitz and Karlsbad in Bohemia near Prague and Dresden.

The young archduke was genuinely devout, full of piety and true goodness of heart. With a career in the military no longer an option, Rudolph was directed instead by Franz to enter the church and as such was kept away from politics and statecraft—a judgment he found agreeable as it allowed him the freedom to pursue his greatest passion, music. By the age of 15, Archduke Rudolph's talents as a pianist had become well known in the same Viennese aristocratic circles Beethoven inhabited. He was a true amateur—a devoted lover of music and an avid collector of printed scores. He started and maintained a significant library that included works by most contemporary composers, including Bach, Handel, Mozart, and, of course, his favorite: Beethoven. Many of those scores he had hand copied himself in order to better comprehend their structure and flow.

Whenever Rudolph put pen to paper he felt as if transformed into a medieval monk of the highest spiritual order, one who was engaged in the sacred task of replicating God's work. Reproducing the musical expressions of these great composers, especially Beethoven's, was a holy writ that took him ever closer to his conception of God. And though it might be a bit heretical to consider a musical score as equivalent to the Old Testament, Rudolph justified the import of this labor of love through his belief that musical compositions of this caliber were the manifestations of God's divine wisdom expressed through the medium of humankind. As such Rudolph spent much effort glorifying God's work by embellishing the artwork and design on every page. His calligraphy was impeccable. Rudolph's only regret was that he could not compose his own works with this same singular depth of passion that distinguished the work of his musical hero above all others.

Regrets aside, it was his library that originally brought Rudolph into direct contact with Beethoven. When B sought to study the score of Handel's Messiah, Lichnowsky sent him off to see the Archduke's music library at his quarters in the Hofburg Palace. Rudolph was so delighted that the composer he most admired had come to him, of all people, that he not only lent Beethoven a copy of the score, he gave him the one that he had hand copied himself. Although the two men separated in age by some 18 years had little in common except their respective passions for music, they both instantly found a liking for the other. The Archduke's entire demeanor was so modest and unassuming that our B found it easy to be near him. And if it was music that first brought them together, it was paradoxically Rudolph's epilepsy that made them life-long friends. In the young royal, B saw a version of himself, a man cursed by the gods whose entire life would be defined not by his aristocratic birthright but by how well he surmounted his affliction on a daily basis.

During the three days of their journey from Vienna to Lichnowsky's castle near Troppau, Rudolph had hoped to talk music composition with his teacher. They did a little, but the always obstreperous Beethoven also shared with Rudolph an earful about his current troubles and aspirations. The composer was, first and foremost, furious with Napoleon and the French *Grande Armée,* whose troops still occupied much of the Habsburg's empire. Beethoven held them responsible for everything that had gone wrong of late. It began with the abrupt departure of his assistant, Ries, who was forced to return to the occupied Rhineland and face being drafted into Bonaparte's army lest his family be punished. Then there was Josephine von Brunsvik Deym exiling herself back to the relative safety of Martonvasar in Hungary; after that, the disastrous premier of *Fidelio* and lastly, the troubling union of Casper and Johanna. "*Camillus was the name of the Roman general who drove the Franks from Rome. I too would take that name if I could drive these French back to where they belong,*" concluded B.

By the time they reached Gratz, Beethoven had fortunately talked through his troubles and had shifted his energies back into composing. This pleased Rudolph enormously. Although he was generally empathetic to Beethoven's sufferings, there was little he could do to assist his friend on these matters other than being a patient listener. During their first few days at the castle, the Archduke and Beethoven routinely avoided mixing with the rest of guests, keeping adjacent suites in a remote wing of the castle where they were unlikely to either be disturbed or overheard by anyone else. Their days were spent in seemingly equal parts studying, composing, and hiking in the surrounding woodlands. Only after dinner would they join with the general company in concertizing.

Early mornings before breakfast were devoted to composing; Rudolph worked on the assignments given him while Beethoven refined his draft of an F-Minor piano sonata—the one that would be later on be known as the *"Appassionata."* Beethoven also continued Rudolph's lessons in composition, which covered writing out four-part harmonies, realizing figured bass melodies, and crafting contrapuntal pieces in accord with basic rules. B was particularly sensitive to Rudolph's unique compositional flair and did not impose his style on the young archduke. Instead Beethoven worked to correct Rudolph's efforts with a minimum of tweaks and notations, remarking once that, *"One must not hold one's self so divine as to be unwilling to make improvements in one's creations."* In turn, Rudolph developed work habits much like his teacher, right down to mimicking the idiosyncratic manner in which B wrote his bass clef.

After a morning meal and strong coffee, Beethoven would insist they go for a jaunt in the country. Rudolph asked B why these hikes were so important to him. In response Beethoven recited a poem of his own creation:

Almighty One
In the woods I am blessed;
Everyone is happy;
Every tree speaks through Thee.
O God!
What glory in the Woodlands?
On the Heights is Peace;
Peace to serve Him.

Although Archduke Rudolph's sheltered existence and frail health led him to feel somewhat awkward roaming about the hillsides with Beethoven, his teacher's deeply inspired love of the wilderness somehow made it all seem perfect; from hiking isolated trails and picking wild fruits to wading through knee-deep streams and stealing honey from a beehive. All the while during their walks B would stop and scribble out notes onto a pad of staff paper he would bring along. Rudolph realized that regardless of B's outward affect or activities, he was in fact always composing.

One particularly warm afternoon, while resting in the shade of an apple tree, he asked Beethoven about this. The composer replied, *"I carry my thoughts about me for a long time, often a very long time, before I write them down. Meanwhile my memory is so faithful that I am sure never to forget, not even in years, a theme that has once occurred to me. Your Imperial Highness asks me where I get my ideas. That I cannot tell you with certainty. They may come unsummoned, directly, indirectly. Sometimes it appears as if I could seize them with my hands right out of the open air; or I find them in the woods; or while walking; or during the silence of nights; or early in the morning incited by moods, which are translated by the poet into words, or by me into tones that sound and roar and storm about me until I have set them down in notes. I change many things, discard, and try again until I am satisfied. Then however, there begins in my head the development in every direction, and, in as much as I know exactly what I want, the fundamental idea never deserts me. It arises before me; it grows and I see and hear the picture in all its extent and dimensions stand before my mind like a cast, and there remains for me nothing but the labor of writing it down, which is quickly accomplished when I have the time, for I sometimes take up other work, but never to the confusion of one with the other."*

After their hikes—whose length was always unpredictable—B would make the time to review and correct Rudolph's assignments, noting that, *"Even your Imperial Highness must write every day. Just as drops of water wear away a stone in time, not by force but by continual action, it is only through tireless industry that compositions are achieved.*

One can truthfully say, 'No day without its line—null dies sine linea.'"

Whenever time permitted Rudolph would also continue to copy out Beethoven's *Fourth Piano Concerto,* which the composer had dedicated to him. Of all of B's composition, the *Fourth* was the one Rudolph found to be the most prayer-like and full of grace, beginning as it did with a poignant, almost pleading piano solo. When again playing student to Beethoven as teacher, Rudolph asked what motivated him to write such a spiritually inspiring work whose structure was so radically different from all those concertos that had preceded it. B answered simply, *"All things flow clear and pure out of God. There is no loftier mission than to approach the Divinity nearer than other people, and to disseminate the divine rays among mankind. Just as trees bend low under the weight of fruit, and clouds descend when they are filled with salutary rains, the benefactors of humanity should not be puffed up by their wealth. Though often darkly led to evil by passions, we return through penance and purification to the pure fountain—to God—and to our art. There it is and may it always be so."*

The Archduke firmly agreed not only with the validity of Beethoven's comments, he also bore witness to the impact his teacher's divine music had on listeners. Why even in the wake of *Fidelio,* Rudolph saw firsthand how this paean to freedom and conjugal love inspired many who worked on it or were involved with the production. For example, in the months after the initial and disastrous opening of the opera, Steffen von Breuning had joined with the Lichnowskys in helping B rewrite and edit the libretto. Somehow, by virtue of working on a story of *l'Amour Conjugal,* the Prince and his wife, Christiane, were inspired enough to find a degree of peace—however temporary—with each other. Rudolph—who knew well of Lichnowsky's frequent dalliances—had also never seen the Prince and Christiane happier than during their visit to Gratz. Every night after dinner, the Prince would gather all of his guests for musical soirees, which were often free-flowing improvisations of the highest order. Although Beethoven was the brightest star in this firmament, everyone took their turn. The Lichnowskys revealed uncommon skill and delight playing Mozart and Beethoven string sonatas. The joy they found through harmonizing together made them appear to Rudolph as if newlyweds. The *Fidelio* work even inspired Steffen to propose to and eventually marry Julie Vering, the daughter of *Herr Doktor* Vering—one of B's many physicians. The Archduke ascribed their engagement to the uplifting influence of *Fidelio* as well and it made him appreciate the sheer power of Beethoven's music ever more.

This sojourn into the country could not have been more pleasant and relaxing until the night Lichnowsky—anxious to curry favor with the local occupying French forces—invited their commander, General Gerard Beynac, and several of his senior staffers to dine at the castle. The treaty between the French and the Hapsburgs was always tenuous with little incidents here and there marring the truce. Although Rudolph's role as a churchman kept him away from the family business of politics, he understood not only the necessity of keeping the peace but of currying good favors with their occupiers. He was however concerned about Beethoven who had endlessly railed against Napoleon and the French during the earlier part of their journey. General Beynac was one of those "new" Frenchmen, a country peasant, whose father was a boatman on the Dordogne River. He rose up through the ranks on the strength of his bravery under fire and his native intelligence. His manner was brusque and direct, a complete contrast to the affected styles of the aristocracy he so despised. How would B fare if he was engaged in talk with Beynac who was seated beside him?

Fortunately, as Rudolph soon realized, conversation at dinner that night was exclusively in French, the language of aristocrats and diplomats. None of the officers understood German or its Austrian dialect. Consequently, the Archduke was not at all surprised when Beethoven avoided any discourse with the General—even when asked if he also played the "fiddle"—by falsely pretending he had little knowledge of their language. Perhaps, thought Rudolph, it was the Great Shepard's means of keeping his multitudinous flocks of sheep braying in harmony.

As was common practice, the Prince had arranged for yet another musical evening afterwards and he made a point near the conclusion of dinner of informing the French officers that the "great Beethoven" would perform as he had each and every prior evening. Unfortunately the Prince, being a prince and always accustomed to having his way, had failed to discuss this with the composer. When Beethoven realized what Lichnowsky had proposed, he abruptly stood up, threw down his wine glass—which shattered and stained the table cloth red—and declared aloud in German to everyone's astonishment, *"Ich werde knechtische Arbeiten für die Feinde meines Landes nicht durchführen!*—I will not perform menial labors for the enemies of my country!"

This utterly shocked Lichnowsky who fired back at him in German, "*Sie würden mich das ablehnen?*—You would refuse me this?"

"*Fick das! Ich bin nicht ein Hund!*—I am not a dog!" B shouted back at Lichnowsky.

"You . . . you . . . you refuse?" It was inconceivable to the Prince that, after supporting Beethoven as his essential patron—and friend—for over a decade, B would refuse this simple request.

"If I understood the art of war as well as I do that of music," declared Beethoven, "I would conquer this Napoleon and his French rabble!" With that, B stormed out of the room.

Lichnowsky was furious and as stunned as was most everyone else at the dinner table by Beethoven's reaction, everyone that is except Archduke Rudolph who had actually expected worse. Even General Beynac, though puzzled by the heated exchange, understood something was definitely amiss. The Prince was about to send one of his servants to B's quarters with instructions to bring the composer back when Rudolph, intending to calm the waters, interceded.

"Allow me instead."

The Archduke immediately left the chamber, intent upon reaching Beethoven and settling down his teacher before matters did in fact grow worse. Though Rudolph had never been allowed to be involved in matters of Habsburg diplomacy, he was sensitive enough to the vagaries of politics to know that, if left unresolved, such an insult could have repercussions far beyond the walls of Lichnowsky's castle. As he walked the long corridors of the estate, the Archduke gave thought to what he might say to Beethoven in order to calm him down, but no ideas emerged with any clarity—at least not any which had an iota of success. After all, General Beynac's mere presence at dinner had probably reignited all of Beethoven's barely suppressed rage at the French and Napoleon, an anger he knew B felt fully justified in nurturing and expressing. Lichnowsky's demand that B play music for the officers was just the match that lit the cannon's fuse.

Nearing their rooms, the Archduke heard the muted sounds of Beethoven improvising on the pianoforte. Turning the last corner, he observed that the door to B's room was closed. Checking the handle, he was not surprised to find it locked. He was about to knock but then thought the better of it. The only one who could calm Beethoven down was Beethoven. Rather than disturb his teacher, Rudolph imagined diplomacy was a more apt response. B's music was so profoundly beautiful and rich that Rudolph—caught up in listening to it—almost forgot the purpose of his mission and so, instead of interrupting Beethoven, he sat down on a bench, determined to not only wait out B's anger but to learn from it.

The one compositional skill that Beethoven could not teach Rudolph and the one Rudolph knew he struggled with to the highest degree was expressing passion—particularly the passion that accompanied heartfelt emotions. In that regard, he and Beethoven were complete opposites. During their three-day coach journey from Vienna, B had shared much of the darkness of his childhood with Rudolph, a childhood whose contrast with the Archduke's could not have been more diametrically polarized. As a Hapsburg prince and cleric, all drama had been bred and bleached out of him. And though Archduke Rudolph would never have surrendered his privileges for Beethoven's struggles, he was envious of his teacher's abilities to plumb the depths and range of human experience and then use that energy to construct his compositions.

And so when Beethoven segued from his free-form improvisations to the *Allegro* of the *F-minor Piano Sonata*, the Archduke let go his intentions to intervene, delighting instead in the sheer intensity of the *Appassionata*. No amount of copying manuscripts could teach him to capture a depth of emotions he did not ever experience but, oh, how he wished he could write like that. And short of composing as did his master, he resigned himself to simply enjoying the manifestation of God's work through the medium of his servant, Beethoven.

B was well into the final *presto* when an enraged Prince Lichnowsky, followed by an entourage of servants and guests, including the French officers, turned the last corner and arrived outside Beethoven's door. Hoping to signal the Prince to wait quietly, the young archduke Rudolph touched one finger to his lips and raised the other hand in a "stop" gesture, but Lichnowsky would have none of that, particularly in his own castle. With a wave of his own hand, the Prince signaled for one of his servants to smash down the door with an axe—which he did . . .

The music stopped as the door crashed open. Prince Lichnowsky strode into the room only to find that Beethoven had grabbed a wooden chair and was about to slam it down on the Prince's head. Heedless of the danger and without thinking, Rudolph jumped in between the combatants and the Archduke. Rudolph, using the full measure of his limited strength, shoved Beethoven away.

"Prince!" Beethoven shouted back at his patron, "What you are, you are by accident of birth. What I am, I am through my own efforts. There have been thousands of princes and there will be thousands more. There is only one Beethoven."

Lichnowsky—shocked at how suddenly everything had spun out of control—abruptly froze. His skin blanched white and it was this portrait of the Prince's face that was the last image Rudolph saw before the "falling down disease" turned his world black.

Passion has it consequences. . . . Rudolph's seizure left the exhausted young man unable to travel any farther that night than the cathedral residence in Troppau, a few leagues away from Gratz. Because of the intense rain storm, he nonetheless instructed his servants to deliver Beethoven all the way back to Vienna.

Upon his return home, Beethoven climbed the three flights to his apartment. The coachmen followed him up with B's trunk which was still drenched from the journey. The servants set it down in the middle of Beethoven's drawing room and left. Despite having several days on the road to calm down, B was still furious with Prince Lichnowsky as he pondered the awful truth—one he thought he had escaped through success and fame. To the aristocracy he was still and would always be just a servant, a music-maker. Someone less than equal—and vulnerable. Without Lichnowsky's annuity, he would be thrown back into financial chaos. Was Josephine's sister, Therese, right? How could he exist—much less marry a daughter of the aristocracy—on just the kreutzers that flowed in from the sale and performance of his works?

Even as water dripped off the lid of the trunk, Beethoven opened it up and pulled out what he had hoped was the final draft of his *Sonata in F-minor*. He would need to get a good sum for it from one of his publishers to keep going. Unfortunately the storm had worked its evil on him—the manuscript was thoroughly rain-spotted. What was it Archduke Rudolph had once said? *These are God's tears; shed because his children were fighting*. The involuntary laugh that burst out of B's chest was born of complete frustration.

Beethoven went over to the mantel by his fireplace where the alabaster clock and the bust of Prince Lichnowsky, that were gifts from his wife, Christiane, rested. He picked up the clock and was about to smash it on the floor when a bit of common sense prevailed. A clock was useful. He set it back down and picked up the bust instead. After raising it high above his head, he hurled it against the wall where it shattered into a thousand pieces. Good, he thought, let the housekeeper sweep up this *Scheisse* tomorrow.

Atop his writing desk he found a number of unopened letters, two of which piqued his interest. He opened the first, which was from Josephine Deym . . .

> *"Dear Beethoven, Absence from you all through these months has left an emptiness in my heart that neither time nor circumstances will erase. You have always had my soul. If such adoration can give you joy, then please receive it—from the core of my very being—for I have returned to Vienna.*
>
> *"For a long time I had indeed wished to have news of your health and I would have inquired about it long ago if modesty—and no small weight of trepidation—had not held me back.*
>
> *"Now tell me, how you are, what are you doing? Are you happy or sad? The deep interest that I take in all that concerns you, and that I shall take as long as I live, makes me desire to have news about these things. How is your health, your disposition, your way of life?*
>
> *"Or does my friend Beethoven—surely I may call you thus—believe that I have changed? What would this no doubt tell me other than that you, yourself, were no longer the same.*
>
> *"Votre ami chéri,*
> *"Your beloved friend*
> *"Josephine"*

"Beloved friend?" wondered B, what exactly did she mean or intend? Was there love there to be had or shared, or was this merely an expression of polite affection? *"You have always had my soul."* Did

she want him back? Or was she just offering up a gracious, '*Hello*'?

As he wrestled with these contradictory thoughts, he examined the second package. It was from Bonn, the address inscribed with a most familiar feminine handwriting—Leonore's! He tore open the wrapper. Inside he found a complete copy of Friedrich Schiller's poem, the *"Ode to Joy,"* written out in an astonishingly crisp, hand-crafted calligraphy that rivaled the Archduke's for grace and beauty. Accompanying the poem was a short note written no less formally and by the same hand on a single piece of paper cut out in the shape of butterfly wings:

> *In memory of Margaretha van Beethoven,*
> *To my Knight in Victory*
> *From this Daughter of Elysium;*
> *Hasten my brother on your way.*
> *Be embraced by love's heavenly sanctuary,*
> *What stern custom has divided, Let these gentle wings enfold, A kiss for you and all the world,*
> *Find joy in this beautiful spark of the gods,*
> *My wish for you, happiness and long life;*
> *But for myself in your consideration,*
> *I seek your favor, your friendship and you again.*
> *Until the sun of life sets,*
> *Your true friend,*
> *Lorchen*

CHAPTER 20

Recollections of Country Life

Outside the Ruins of Rauhenstein Castle, July 29, 1826, Karl van Beethoven Recalls a Day in the Country, July of 1808

On an overcast and humid Saturday, July 29, 1826, Karl van Beethoven, six weeks shy of his 20th birthday, stood on a hill a few miles outside Baden beside the ruins of Rauhenstein Castle. In his right hand was an ancient, pearl-handled pistol, in his left hand, its twin. Both barrels were aimed at his head. His fingers, damp with perspiration, caressed the triggers. Yes, Shakespeare had it right, *"the valiant never taste of death but once."*

He could think of no better place to terminate his life and end the suffocation he felt at his uncle's hands, than here, above the Helenenthal Valley and amidst the wilds of nature that his Uncle Louis loved so dearly. How often had his uncle pontificated about how his creative powers as a composer had *"drawn their richest nourishment here? Where ideas flowed to him in quantity? When you reach the old ruins, think that Beethoven often paused there; if you wander through the mysterious fir forests, know that Beethoven often poetized or, as said, composed there."* Let him compose this tragedy thought Karl as the sweat dripped off his hands and made the guns slide and slip in his grasp. Yes, *"cowards die many times, yet The valiant taste of death but once."*

Karl had ventured here numerous times with his uncle—or 'papa' as Beethoven had hungered for Karl to address him. Karl knew every inch of the terrain, from the meadow grasses of the valley floor and the stream filled with trout that meandered through it, to the oak forests and the castle ruins that dominated the rim of the slope. And it was here too that Karl had his first childhood memories of his uncle from a picnic eighteen years earlier in July of 1808 when he was just two years old. Though his actual recollections of that day in the country were vague and dim, he had heard the different and contradictory versions of stories about those events on numerous occasions from so many people in his family that it felt as complete a memory as was possible.

He wondered whether or not the day—and their lives—would have turned out differently if the Beethoven brothers had known that this was the last time the three of them were ever to be together. Instead of constant bickering and feuding, would they have found unity in the name of family? What came instead were years of endless tension, disputes, and downright cruelty. It all began when Uncle Johann—whom Beethoven insisted upon either calling "Nikolaus," or nothing at all—announced he was moving from Vienna to Linz, as he had purchased a pharmacy in that city. Uncle Johann and his boss, *Herr* Harold Lyme, had made a small fortune during the war years supplying medicines to combatants on all sides. Now a wealthy man—far, far better off than either of his two older brothers—it was his intention to leave *Herr* Lyme's shop and set up anew in Linz to grow his business ever more. Johann would celebrate his departure with a grand picnic in the country with his family and friends, one he would pay for in its entirety. He hired coaches to transport everyone from Vienna and paid a local grocer to supply an endless feast.

Karl's first recollection of that day was of his father, Casper van Beethoven, half asleep in the back of the coach with a fever and cough. Casper had been hacking away constantly so much so that for a time Karl believed his father's name was "*Halt-Husten*"—"Stop Coughing," for that is what his mother kept calling out to Papa. In spite of the warm weather, Casper would stay bundled up with blankets on a wooden sedan chair the entire day. Karl next recalled being lifted out of a carriage and enfolded into the arms of Aunt Julie, who smelled of jasmine perfume and whose touch was delicate, soft, and tender. Julie was Steffen von Breuning's new and very young wife—

who would die of influenza a year later—a tragedy, everyone would say. Julie embraced Karl, kissed him on the cheek, and then set him down in the meadow grass beside the carriage horses which didn't smell like perfume, they smelled like poop. Karl looked way, way up at one of the chestnut-colored draft horses that had pulled the wagons and petted its foreleg which was thick as a tree trunk. The horse shook its head and neighed at Karl, startling him. Karl bolted into the head-high blanket of wild flowers and grains that covered the meadow. The grasses in this pasture, golden-green with soft tassels, tickled his arms and neck as he ran through the endless waves. It made him giggle and laugh. Ahead he could hear the sound of a stream tumbling over rocks as it flowed through the valley. Behind he heard the voices of grown-ups and the sighing of the horses from the four carriages that had transported everyone to the valley from Vienna. He kept running farther and farther away and toward the sound of water. But the closer he got, the higher and thicker the meadow grasses became. Suddenly he realized he was all alone and lost. The weeds stretched far above the height of his head and blocked his view. Karl turned around from where he had come but was too short to see anything except a bright golden sun directly overhead that made him dizzy when he stared at it. He heard the "caw-caw" of a crow, then saw it dash across the open patch of sky. Karl stretched his arms out in imitation of the bird and started running again until he was flying through the weeds. Karl was caw-cawing like the crow when he tripped over a rock and tumbled to the ground. *Ouch!* His knee hurt. Karl was just about to break out in tears when out of nowhere giant hands flew around him and plucked him up into the air.

"There you are, you little rascal, you." It was Uncle who had snatched him up, Uncle Louis.

Karl had two uncles and sometimes three: Uncle Louis, Uncle Johann, and sometimes Uncle Steffen, who was sometimes an uncle and sometimes not. And he married Aunt Julie, who was also sometimes an aunt and sometimes not. He was never sure. But he loved

Uncle Louis most of all. Big as a bear and just as shaggy, Uncle Louis would roll around and play on the ground with him just like his pet dog, Caesar. But Caesar didn't come in the wagon. Caesar stayed in Vienna to guard their house—that was Caesar's job. Papa *Halt-Husten* stayed in the coach to rest—that was his job, Mama had said. And now Uncle Louis first lifted him way up so he could touch the sky with his fingers and then Uncle set him on his shoulders. From on high Karl could see over the grass. Uncle carried him toward the stream. Uncle Steffen walked with them carrying a bottle of wine, from which the uncles took turns imbibing, that was their job.

"Your brother could not have picked a more beautiful day for his farewell," commented Steffen about the weather, which was as ideal as a painting; warm and cozy with nary a cloud in the sky.

"And a good riddance it will be when Nikolaus finally leaves for Linz. Can you believe him wanting to spend all that money just for this? Give me a crust of bread, some hard cheese, and that bottle of Riesling. I can hike here anytime I want with freedom."

"Why so hard on him?" Steffen asked.

"Come on, Steffen, you know the only reason we are all here is so that Nikolaus can prove that he's more successful than either of his big brothers. If it weren't for me, Nikolaus would be a laborer in Bonn with barely enough for the rent. This feast is just his way of showing off. He has no respect for me —or Casper—or any of the endless kindnesses we've shown him over the years. "

"But how will it be for your family when he's gone?"

"Away from my sight and that much better not having to listen to him gloat about money. I've never trusted him or that war profiteer, Harry Lyme."

"Wasn't it Don Quixote who said, '*No matter how you came by money, you will not have started a new custom in the world.*'"

"That makes my brother no less of an idiot."

They had reached the brook. Uncle Louis took Karl's shoes and socks off and rolled up his trousers so he could splash around the edge of the stream and try to trap baby tadpoles and lizards with his hand—even if he couldn't actually catch any—but it was still fun and made him giggle.

"And what about Josephine? Why hasn't she joined us? You were going to invite her, yes?" Steffen asked as he and Beethoven both shed their shoes and socks.

"Josephine avoids me now as easily as these guppies dance around our hands." B took a long and deep swing of the Riesling.

"Still?"

"*Ja,* ever since her family returned from Hungary, the Brunsvik sisters have kept up the pressure on Josephine not to rekindle our relationship."

"What about the brother, Franz?"

"Franz? He says nothing. *Herr* Neutrality. Therese however is dead set against any permanent union between us. Yet the notes Josephine sometimes sends me speak otherwise. I envy you and Julie. It all seems so simple. Why not for me?"

But I thought you and Therese were good friends? Why does she advocate against you? Is it that she's *eine les . . . les . . . lesbische Fraulein?*" Steffen just couldn't say the word.

"Out with it, man. Don't be embarrassed. *Ja,* by most private accounts, Therese is a lesbian. She loves women. Say it, Steffen, she's a lesbian."

"She's a . . . a . . . les . . . lesbian."

"Lebian, lebian, lebian," prattled little Karl in imitation. "I caught a lebian." In his tiny hands was the limp body of a dead lizard.

"Therese may love women but she doesn't hate men—or me," said Beethoven, as he pulled a handkerchief from his pocket. "Drop it in here," he said to Karl, which the toddler did. "We'll show it to Papa later. Now go catch another." As Karl refocused his attention back to the stream, B resumed his discourse with Steffen. "I wish it was as simple as Therese hating me, but in sad truth, it's all about money and class—of which everyone tells me I have none. After Count Deym's death ruined Josephine financially, the sisters claim that there is no way she could survive living my life. Therese is probably right. And Josephine, she may dream and feel differently, but when it comes to arguing with her sisters, she has all the gravitas of a sparrow."

"My Julie said that to be so close to forbidden fruit is far too painful. She's convinced that Josephine does love you and that is precisely why she is staying away."

"But what of my pain? Her letters tease my appetite. She writes so sweetly that even a few lines arouse my hunger, but concurrently she commands me to preserve the distance between us. How often have I had to wrestle with myself in order not to breach that sort of prohibition. Truly, all my love's in vain."

"Have you shared this with her?"

"Better to share the wine," said Beethoven, upon reaching out for the bottle again. "Oh God, I beg that Heaven would grant me just one—just one undisturbed hour to spend with her. We would walk and talk without constraints and fix matters between us. . . . We used to be so happy. Where's that path now? Can my heart . . . can my soul be united with hers again? Twice I called on her—twice her servants refused me. How is it I am so fortunate as to never find her at home? She sent me this instead."

Beethoven pulled a letter from Josephine out of a pocket and recited it verbatim to Steffen, "*I did not intend to offend you, dear B! But since you took it as such, and I am well aware of the external laws of social convention that I—paying little attention—have violated, then it is for me to ask your forgiveness—which I ask all the more, since I cannot very well comprehend in these points how sensitivity can still find a place where true mutual esteem exists.*"

"What am I to make of *mutual esteem*?" he asked to Steffen. "Is that love, or not love?"

"You wrote her back?"

"Of course—and I would have delivered it myself if I did not suspect that her servants would bar the door for a third time. No, she no longer wants to be found by me—and I'm fed up with these refusals. I cannot go to her any more. If she does not want me, then she must be frank, *ja?*"

"You deserve as much. And in these circumstances you dare not say more."

Their conversation was interrupted by the screech of an eagle that swooped down and snagged a brown trout right out of the stream not ten paces away, startling Karl.

"Awk, awk," shrieked Karl, swinging his arms like wings.

Beethoven splashed through the water towards Karl and then lifted him up so that his belly lay across B's arms. "Flap your wings, little bird!" he said, "flap those wings. Let's catch that eagle."

"Watching you two together," said Steffen, "I have memories of when we were teenagers back in Bonn and you would play with Margaretha just like that. Karl even reminds me of her, especially around the eyes."

"Much as I adore Karl, he's not Margaretha," said B. "She was special—as much a prodigy as Mozart."

And then came the words—coarse and harsh that stuck like an undigested meal in Karl's gut for the next two decades. . . . Ones he would hear over and over again after the death of his own father, Casper, transformed him into Beethoven's ward.

"Karl . . . Karl will never be that good. No, he's just not good enough."

"Who could live up to such a standard? Is it not enough that we each be ourselves?" said Steffen.

"I cannot abide mediocrity," said B, just as they heard the voices of Johanna and Julie calling them to return up the hill to eat.

Beethoven boosted Karl back up on his shoulders. As the three of them climbed the slope toward the picnic, B shared with Steffen that he too was considering leaving Vienna.

"Where to? What for?" asked Steffen.

"I am tired of poverty and mean to improve my finances. Just this week I have been offered a position as the *Kapellmeister* by the new King of Westphalia."

"But Napoleon has placed his brother Jerome on the Westphalia throne. You would enter service to a Bonaparte? Our enemy?"

"What friends do I have here? Lichnowsky has forsaken me, and . . . No such offer has ever come from the Hapsburgs. And is not Westphalia close by Bonn? Oh, to be home again. How lovely to see my native country again and our great Father Rhine."

"I can't believe this—but certainly Wegeler and Leonore would be pleased by your return to our neighborhood."

"Say nothing to anyone on this account," said B. "The matter is not yet decided."

"Agreed, my friend, but do keep me closely informed," replied Steffen. "Leonore has written me of their intentions to visit us all in Vienna soon if peace holds—and you are very much in her thoughts."

"And she—they," said B, correcting himself, "are in mine."

When they reached the top of the hill they found that Nikolaus's servants had piled mountains of food on a long and narrow picnic table surrounded by rough-hewn benches. Nikolaus Johann sat at the head of the table next to his housekeeper, *Fraulein* Obermeyer, a not unattractive young woman who was *Herr* Lyme's sister-in-law. At the opposite end sat Karl's mother, Johanna. Beside her was Casper, still wrapped in blankets, still coughing. Scattered around the table were Nikolaus's friends and their children. Beethoven nudged Steffen with his elbow and growled under his breath, "What's this? See how my pseudo-brother claims the head of the table. Am I not still the elder of this family?" Beethoven set Karl back down on the ground and Karl ran straight off for the arms of his mother, Johanna.

"Lebian, Mama, I caught a lebian," Karl cried out as he pulled B's handkerchief out of his pocket to show his parents the lizard.

"Even Karl deserts me," Beethoven said to Steffen. "Like Horus of old he runs to Isis's breast."

"Let it go," replied Steffen in an equally soft whisper. "Come sit beside Julie and me."

Johanna took the handkerchief from Karl and promised him they would bury it after lunch. Karl, who was still not fully weaned, pulled at his mother's blouse. She gave him her breast. He nursed himself into contentment and then fell asleep quickly in her arms. He later learned that he missed a fabulous feast spiced only by Beethoven's sharp tongue as he sparred and sniped continuously throughout the meal, primarily with Nikolaus and on occasion with his mother, Johanna—but then again such fireworks were an everyday occurrence whenever the Beethoven clan was all together.

When Karl did finally awake, the sun was sinking in the west and the full moon was rising in the east. The sounds of *Romany* Gypsy music filled the valley, while all about him people were dancing around a huge bonfire. Seems during his nap a troupe of *Zigeuner*—gypsies—had moved their wagons onto the meadow for a feast of their own and had set up a *Zigeunerlager*, a Gypsy camp. Lured into each other's fest by the sounds of music, Nikolaus's party mixed happily with the *Romany*. When Karl looked for his parents, he found that his father, *Halt-Husten*, who in spite of the excitement slept still in his chair under a pile of blankets off to the side of the fire. His mother was dancing with a stranger, who had wild dark hair, gold-capped teeth, a white peasant shirt, and baggy red trousers. Uncle Louis and Uncle Steffen, who had each picked up a fiddle, were playing along with the *Roma* musicians. Karl ran to Uncle Louis and could smell the odor of wine prominently on his breath.

"Ah, my little Karl is awake! Come with me, I have a surprise for you," said Beethoven, who by this point in the day was very clearly drunk. He put down his fiddle and then, sweeping Karl back into his arms, he lifted him up onto his shoulders. They walked—wobbled might be more accurate—away from the fire and towards the heart of the *Zigeunerlager*. There they found a dozen or so Gypsy children sitting in front of a brightly painted wagon whose rear easily converted into a puppet theater. The program, a truncated version of *Julius Caesar*, held them all in rapt attention.

Though in later years Karl would come to know Shakespeare's play by heart, at this age he understood nothing. With the gift of hindsight though he could re-imagine the more famous lines mouthed by the sole puppeteer, a young *Romany* woman dressed entirely in black. She wore a lotus flower in her hair and had dense, dark curls that reached to her waist. Long-limbed and lean, Miss Lotus Flower had a blend of facial features and skin complexion that easily revealed her Gypsy heritage. The now drunken Beethoven was as transfixed by her presence there, if not more so, than all the children who were watching her. He kept muttering to himself throughout the performance, *"Avalokiteshvara, Aphrodite, Venus, Kwan Yin, Kannon, Mary, Isis; Avalokiteshvara, Aphrodite, Venus, Kwan Yin, Kannon, Mary; Isis, Avalokiteshvara. . . ."*

"Friends, Romans, countrymen," Miss Lotus Flower sings out, *"lend me your ears; we come to praise Caesar, not to bury him".*

The name *Caesar* confuses Karl, who remembers looking around for his pet dog every time she repeats that name.

"Yond Cassius has a lean and hungry look; He thinks too much: such men are dangerous," she continues.

Bouncing around from one stick figure to another, Miss Lotus Flower races through the play with more intensity than accuracy—not that any of the children, so caught up in the frenetic energy she creates, care or notice.

"Beware the Ides of March." From somewhere off in the night, a great horned owl hoots and screeches. *"The fault, dear Brutus, is not in our stars, but in ourselves."* The mournful cry of the owl is offset by a flock of nightingales nesting off in the trees where their chuckling sounds like laughter. *"Cowards die many times before their deaths; the valiant never taste of death but once." "Et tu, Brute!"* says Brutus, as the puppet flashes a knife at Caesar.

"Though art the noblest Roman of them all. As Caesar is valiant, I honor him; but, as he is ambitious, I slay him," says the Brutus puppet while attacking Caesar. Caesar falls and Brutus vanishes below the stage.

Miss Lotus Flower bangs and shakes a tambourine in imitation of a coming storm. A puff of smoke momentarily obscures the stage and when it clears a new puppet appears—it is a miniature twin of the puppeteer, complete with a lotus flower in its hair but with the addition of feathery wings.

"I am Isis," says the Little Miss Lotus Flower puppet, in an alteration of Shakespeare that only Beethoven could admire, *"I am the Daughter of Elysium and the fiery spark of the gods."*

The dying Caesar raises his right arm. His hand and fingers tremble as if reaching for the heavens.

Miss Lotus Flower continues, *"I am all that is and all that will be. I am the taste of pure water and the brilliance of the sun and moon. I am the sweet fragrance of the earth and the radiance of fire. I am the life in every creature and the hunger of all that is human."*

Miss Lotus Flower pulls Caesar up into her arms and embraces him in her wings, *"I am the courage and fear in their souls and the striving of every seeker. I am their sacred words and all vibrations of music in the air. I am that to which all owe their existence and I am the one who devours the world. I am Isis. My kiss for the world is tender as all tones and tunes in a time before creation. Caesar is dead. Long live Caesar."*

No sooner does Miss Lotus Flower utter her last line than the heavens above the Helenenthal Valley abruptly explode with a jagged bolt of electricity. As if out of nowhere, thunder and lightning command the night sky. Storm clouds race in, obscuring the moon and plunging the valley into an unexpected darkness. Windswept raindrops, thick as honey—first singly, then in clusters, and then ultimately in torrents. It pelts everyone and everything. Even the bonfires are extinguished by the onslaught.

People and animals run every which way. Lightning flashes illuminate the sky. Thunder rumbles. Karl once more feels himself swept up into his uncle's arms and sheltered by his coat. Everything is black and dark and wet but Uncle knows where to go. Together the two of them shelter in the cave-like ruins of the Rauhenstein Castle.

The storm does not subside until dawn, when Karl awakes with hunger in time to see the sun chase off the clouds. A flock of quail bob their heads as they pick up seeds driven to the ground by the previous night's rain. Uncle Louis is still asleep on the floor. Karl hears voices from nearby, a woman's voices, maybe his mother's voice. . . . He runs toward the sound, startling the flock of quail which bolt away in a fluster. Karl goes around a corner to another sheltered part of the ruins.

There she is . . . it is his mother . . . on the ground . . . eyes closed, sighing . . . moaning . . . Johanna's legs are splayed askew . . . her skirt up around her waist . . . Miss Lotus Flower's face and lips are nestled down between Johanna's thighs. . . . Johanna's fingers are entwined around the hair and head of the puppeteer. . . . Johanna's blouse is tossed aside. . . . The Gypsy man with the gold teeth, white shirt, and red pants sucks at her breast. . . . The white handkerchief with the dead lizard is beside them.

"Lebian!" cries out Karl, but before Karl can run to his mother, giant hands fly around him and pluck him up into the air and carry him away. . . .

That's the last recollection of that day in the country years before. Now, with guns in hand, he will end it all and erase that memory—and all others—forever. *Not good enough.*

The fault, dear Beethoven, is not in our stars, but in ourselves. Cry "Havoc," and let slip the dogs of war. Karl squeezes the triggers.

CHAPTER 21

O Freunde, nicht diese Töne!
Oh friends, not these tones!

BANG!!!

OUR *MONTGOLFIÈRE* explodes in flames. We plummet out of the heavens. Down we speed through the fog. Below us is the Temple of Isis. Our gondola strikes the ground in the middle of the oasis. Everything trembles. Our landing triggers a *terremoto,* an earthquake. Stone pillars shake, and buildings topple. A clock tower splits in half and collapses into ruins. Devastation is all about us.

N ever so calmly steps out of the basket and resumes his seat by the tea brazier, "Just a gas leak," he declares. "Accidents happen, even with these newer models."

"And that?" I ask, pointing to the ruins and wreckage that smolder in flames all around us.

"What you see . . . all this turmoil . . . it occurred centuries ago—not to worry." N snaps his fingers. A wind rises up and blows all of the ashes and dust off into the Nile. "So why is it you snatched Karl up and away from his mother's *ménage a trois?*"

"Why was I protecting him? You have to ask?"

"No. Of course I know the answer, but I thought it would be amusing to hear your response anyway, given that you fancy yourself quite the parent, don't you?"

N knows very well I was protecting Karl from the debauchery of his mother in the same way I formally used to shield Casper and Nikolaus from the rages of our father when he was stuffed with wine.

"I did raise my brothers. I was the man of our family and know a thing or two about children."

"And Margaretha? You protected her too, *oui*?"

"You are cruel. How mean-spirited can you be to bring that up again? You know she died in my arms. I did everything I could to help her, save her. . . ."

"Infants die, saints die, and even you will die shortly. Still, you carry this guilt about Margaretha. Why? Because you and Leonore were both hoping to get laid that day?"

He's right. For 20 years I've had this image of Margaretha's eyes closing for the last time. Such sadness on her face—and Leonore's—and mine. . . . How could I help but hold anything but morose thoughts?

"For God's sake, man, you were not even seventeen. And you still can't face your Lorchen like a man, much less have a relationship with a woman, any woman. I would tell you to 'Get a life,'" he adds, as he glances down at a shattered clock face lying in the ruins. "But your time is almost up. It's 4:58 pm."

"What am I to do with all these feelings then?"

"It's difficult to take the affairs of a lifetime, and arrange them at the river's edge, isn't it?"

"Only when you remind me of every error I've ever made, every failure I've ever experienced. Is that why I'm here? To have you shove my every weakness in my face?"

"Oh my friend," N sings out, "not these tones! Enough with being morose. Let us raise our voices in more pleasing and joyful sounds. Remember, fortune always leaves one gate open in a disaster to admit a remedy. Why else do you think Napoleon convinced his imbecile of a brother, Jerome, to offer you the *Kapellmeister* position in Westphalia?"

"You were behind that?" I am incredulous.

"Was it wrong for the Emperor Napoleon Bonaparte to ensure

that Europe's greatest composer, Ludwig van Beethoven, did not starve to death. In the end I am glad that Archduke Rudolph and your other friends, Kinsky and Lobkowitz, came through with their annuity instead. Trusting Jerome to do anything right cost Napoleon victory in Russia. When Jerome failed to attack and destroy Prince Bagration's army outside Minsk. . . . Well, you already know how that turned out." Once more N begins to shiver from that bitter winter which lingers in his consciousness. "Think now, had you taken the Kapellmeister slot in Westphalia, you would have been tossed out when the Bonaparte Empire collapsed. As is, your friend, Archduke Rudolph and his annuity fed you for a lifetime."

"But you said we cannot change the past, so what . . . ?" I ask.

"While it's true we could no more alter the past any more than we could raise up these ruins around us, fate has a way of knocking at our door—provided we answer. . . . Now let me tell you a story. Do you recall that American writer, Johann Gardner, the one you met on the eve of leaving Bonn when you were but twenty-one?"

"Ja."

"Do you know why *Monsieur* Gardner taught that every story begins when either a stranger comes to town or a man goes on a journey?"

"I'm sure you'll tell me. . . ."

"*Oui!* Stories begin that way because the existing equilibrium has been altered. In other words something new has been introduced. And you, *mon ami*, are on the road to Elysium. Your journey, your final journey is well underway but even so your equilibrium will be altered by the fates. . . . And when it comes knocking, remember what happens when you answer the door."

"I still don't understand."

"Of course you don't, which is why I am going to tell you that story I promised a moment ago. When, during the Ming Dynasty in China, Prince *Zhu Di* overthrew his nephew, *Zhu Yunwen*, and claimed the emperor's throne, *Zhu Yunwen* fled the capital, allegedly taking with him a rare black-and-white pearl, which symbolized the '*Mandate of Heaven.'* Without the pearl, Emperor *Zhu Di's* legitimacy as ruler would always be suspect. He needed the '*Mandate of Heaven.*' Fearful that the pearl would fall into the hands of his enemies, the Emperor called for a hero to step forward. The reward for success? Wealth beyond compare; the Emperor's daughter's hand in marriage, and the promise of Eternal Happiness. Despite many attempts, all of his retainers failed to recover the pearl. Finally *Ssu Ma Hao Hwa*, a warrior who had been the former guardian of the pearl under *Zhu Yunwen*, stepped forward. He declared that in recompense for allowing the pearl to be removed from his oversight in the first place he would rededicate his life to recovering it and thus restore the *Mandate of Heaven* to this Emperor. *Zhu Di* was elated. And so it was that *Ssu Ma Hao Hwa* traveled to the four corners of the known world in his search. The pearl, which was shaded black and white just as the *yin-yang* symbol, was said to reveal the secrets of the universe to whoever possessed it. *Ssu Ma Hao Hwa* went everywhere, looked everywhere, and in so doing, endured vast hardships and deprivations. He followed up on every clue, listened to every sage and seemingly traveled every road in the empire. In time he grew old and despaired of ever finding the pearl or the secrets it contained. Though diligent, caring, thoughtful, and concerned, *Ssu Ma Hao Hwa* finally had to acknowledge to himself that he had failed. He came to a temple devoted to the worship of the goddess, *Kwan Yin*, the one you know as Isis, and begged forgiveness. Now an old man, he traded his armor and sword for a new pair of sandals and a bamboo cane to support his weary back and arthritic legs. Thus, he set out on his return to the capital knowing he had to accept responsibility for his failure. While on his journey home, he ventured late one night past a hot spring. The cane began to glow enough to illuminate the darkness and so, hoping to soak his now ancient and aching bones in the warm water, he followed the light and hobbled toward the shoreline. There he shed his worn and filthy garments. It was then *Ssu Ma Hao Hwa* saw his reflection in the pool. His eyes had aged, his skin had toughened, his beard and long locks had gone white as the snow. As he pushed his hair back away from his face, he saw the pearl with the *yin-yang* symbol reflected in the water. It was there, on his forehead in the headband, that had once held his helmet in place."

"And it had been there the entire time?"

"Of course. . . . The real treasure was knowing that the secrets of the universe, that is, the road to the untold wealth of eternal happiness, had been there with him—within all of us—the entire time."

"And again, you are telling me this why?"

"So you will answer the damn door when fate comes knocking."

"By that you mean the day the Brentano women came to my apartment?"

"You asked for joy, right? One day of joy? Just as the goddess *Avalokiteshvara* shared with you your potential future compositions, so too I offer a spark that may ignite that prospect if and when you do finally reach Elysium."

I finally understood and knew exactly what he was talking about. . . .

A knock at the door. . . . It was the fifth of May, the year, 1810. I had fallen asleep in the middle of drafting a piano trio. It was a simple one in E-flat, especially designed for amateur violin and cello players who wanted to accompany a more talented pianist. I sought to create something with life and verve, yet basic enough where the string players would not have to struggle to keep up. For whatever reason, I tired of composing and put my head down on the pianoforte and, before I knew it, I was dreaming of Isis.

It seems I was married to that most mysterious child of the gods but we could not abide together for very long. We separated on a night filled with thunderstorms, each agreeing it was best. I walked off, bamboo cane in hand. Isis turned back and called to me as she spread her wings, "We'll meet again one day." So I slipped away from my home, heading off toward a distant land where darkness was considered a virtue. My path was obscured by fog. I went out into this wilderness, a composer absent form, until I was burned out from exhaustion, criticized, and derailed. All the while I was alone, my past lingered close on. I engaged my share of women, but Isis never left my thoughts. At last, in a little olive grove up on a hill I came upon an altar celebrating darkness and light. I begged for salvation and offered them up my innocence, only to be repaid with scorn. Just then I heard, "The goddess on the half-shell is yours." I turned around and found my Isis rising up from the sea. She wore a lotus flower in her hair and had a pearl bracelet around her neck. She strolled up to me and swept away my crown of thorns. "Yes," she said. "The Madonna will keep you secure." She lifted up a book of songs and sang to me. Crafted by an American poet from the twentieth century, every lyric she sang rang true. They glowed like burning embers, illuminating every chord as if they were etched by fire into my soul. Now I see Isis naked before me. Lightening flashing all around and snow falls on her hair. "Come here," she said. "I am yours. . . . I am your shelter from the storm." My dream ended abruptly when I was awakened by a tapping at the door, light enough to be a woman's touch. My housekeeper was away at the market and, given that I hated to be bothered by anyone while composing, I at first ignored the intrusion. Yet there was a voice in my head—perhaps it was Isis herself—insisting I break from my usual habits, rigid as they were, and open the door.

Standing there with her hand poised to strike the door post again was a dark-haired young beauty whose curvaceous body was barely constrained within a low-cut gown of crimson silk. She inhabited flesh as tempting as the female form could ever be. Around her neck she wore a strings of pearls, alternating black and white. How appropriate, I thought, it must be the *Mandate of Heaven* that brought this coquette to my door. At first glance this lovely creature, who introduced herself as Bettina Brentano, rivaled Isis in my male soul as a supreme champion of feminine beauty. Why, even as she turned and twisted about to present her chaperone, Bettina's *décolleté plongeant* trembled ever so with an allure infinitely distracting. *Ja,* I confess to being helpless in the face of such curves and softness. Her companion she introduced as her sister-in-law, *Frau* Antonie Birkenstock Brentano, a married woman of perhaps 30 whose reddish hair and face were half-hidden beneath a wide-brimmed *chapeau* festooned with flowers. However, I paid little mind to her, distracted as I was by Bettina's more obvious charms.

Inviting her . . . them . . . to enter, I inquired of Bettina as to the purpose of her visit. To this she replied with an invitation to a soiree later that week at the Birkenstock mansion, whose mistress was indeed her chaperone, *Frau* Brentano.

"And I bring you greetings from *Herr* Goethe whom I studied with in Weimar," Bettina added in a voice that was as lyrical and seductive as the lips that voiced them. Her very presence stirred in me a hunger to take this woman in my arms and kiss those lips, a desire I had not experienced since Josephine abandoned me and married an Estonian Baron, Christoph von Stackelberg. . . . And Bettina, with a posture designed I'm sure to arouse me even further, stood uncommonly close with her chest—lush and feminine as it was—pressed tightly against mine. Her hand—slight as a butterfly—brushed against my leg. "I believe Goethe finds great favor in your music, most particularly those scores and songs which you have based on his writings."

My dream of Isis must have mingled with the fantasies in the back of my head that culminated with a desire to bed this angel. Aware of the need however to constrain myself and gain a modicum of control, I instead breathed in and out as *Herr* Neefe had once taught me. *Mit unerschütterlicher Gelassenheit* I informed Bettina that Goethe's poems exerted a great power over me not only because of their contents but also because of their rhythms. "A musician is also a poet," I said. "I am stimulated to compose by this language. . . ." I prattled on about something while in truth the real stimulation I experienced was to undress her with my eyes. First her crimson silk gown melted off of her body and onto the floor. Her black hair, unpinned, tumbled down and framed those white shoulders with a dark contrast. One by one her corset and undergarments vanished, revealing breasts that were young and firm as Anjou pears. Her delicate pink nipples surrounded by youthful *areola* came erect under my gaze. My eyes traveled across the flat plains of her stomach to the delta between her legs, waxed, I imagined, in the Moroccan tradition. Her labia spread apart . . . her *mons veneris* exposed . . . her clitoris revealed. . . . All of which grew moist under my gaze of hunger. . . . I devoured the feast offered as if it were caviar until, in my imagined fiction, she collapsed into an orgasm of surrender.

"Then will you accept our invitation?" she asked, interrupting my revelry. Back on came those garments, much to my displeasure. "The crème de la crème of Vienna society will all be in attendance."

"Let's hope the crème has not spoiled by the time I arrive, for I seldom go any place where there is not a certain exchange of ideas and intellect. That's hard to do in Vienna. You must know I despise the arrogance of those aristocrats who do not intuitively feel that music is a higher revelation than all wisdom and philosophy. It's impossible for me to associate with such people."

Backpedaling, Bettina hastily acknowledged that she too despised the tyranny of Vienna's society life. She was, after all, a Brentano with Italian blood from Frankfurt where merchants, artists, and aristocrats mingled more freely. "I prefer to shed conventionalities and only obey natural impulses and the laws of human nature. She reached for my right hand. Bettina raised it to her lips and then—out of Frau Brentano's sight—she kissed each of my fingers with moistened lips and the tip of her tongue. Had we lacked for a chaperone, no doubts this vixen would have pulled me down into my own bed—or so I fantasized.

But why, I wondered, as I inquired, "Do you know my music?"

"Of course, does not everyone?" she said, but there was a subtle 'tell' in her voice that caused me not to believe this coquette for an instant. Too polished, too fawning, too insincere. . . .

"What have you heard?"

"A few sonatas, some songs, but my sister-in-law, Antonie," she said, again indicating *Frau* Brentano, "is even more familiar than I. She returns to Vienna every few years and even attended your concert at *Theater–an-der-Wien* the night you premiered your *Fifth* and *Sixth Symphonies.* And she plays too—we both do."

"Perhaps we've taken enough of *Herr* Beethoven's time," her companion spoke up from under her hat.

"Oh, not at all," I insisted. There was too much to enjoy here to chase off the Brentano women, and so I asked Antonie, "You heard my *Fifth* and *Sixth Symphonies*?"

"Yes. Despite the frigid weather and the length of the program, I stayed for the entire concert and missed nothing," said *Frau* Brentano, who finally looked up at me from under her hat. Her eyes—which were as blue as a robin's eggs—startled me with a depth that went straight to my very essence.

"And what was your judgment?" I asked. There were precious few moments in my life when I felt myself transported by the depth of a woman's eyes into a separate and more beautiful world; one where our inner-most souls would connect and, once met, would know each other in an instant. So it was when *Frau* Brentano locked vision with me. Instantaneously all my thoughts of Bettina—base and pleasing as they were—vanished. Instead, I felt a *déjà vu*. . . . It was as if I had rediscovered an ancient spiritual and emotional communion that had once united Antonie and me. . . . *Ja,* it was as if the clearest expression of Antonie's womanly strength, wisdom, beauty, and compassion that flowed directly from her soul into my mine. . . . And my own energies flowed back and were received by her in concert. Never before—or since—had I ever experienced such instantaneous communion. It was as if our own personal reflections about music, philosophy, or life would have brought us to the same conclusions, none of which needed to be verbalized. . . . *Nein,* ordinary people, especially the Viennese, never entered into such friendships, nor would they ever grasp that true affinity relies upon the union of like natures.

"When I listened that night to the performance of your *Fourth Piano Concerto*," she said as I traveled with her eyes back into what turned out to be our collective past, "I was returned to Prince Lichnowsky's palace and the premier of your *Opus One Trios.*"

"You were there?" I asked with some astonishment, for I could not ever remember having met this woman before.

"Magdalena Willman sang Dona Anna's aria from Mozart's *Don Giovanni*:

> *Shadows of midnight all around me were gathered;*
> *In my own quiet chamber*
> *Sitting alone,*
> *By misadventure and dreaming. . . ."*

"You were there, indeed." Though her voice was as graceful and polished as her very bearing, there was a hint of a profound sadness in *Frau* Brentano that went deeper than the lyrics.

"Yes, my father, Baron von Birkenstock—now deceased—brought me. And you, you were rather preoccupied with *Fraulein* Willman, if I recall with any measure of accuracy."

"Deceased as well, sadly. And my symphonies? Did they not make an impression?"

"You would value my opinion?" she asked with some surprise.

"Beyond all others," I said without knowing why those words tumbled out of my mouth. Who was this woman—this stranger—that I should immediately place weight upon her judgments—especially when I had spent a lifetime rejecting the criticism of everyone and anyone? But, it turns out, Toni—for that is the name she preferred to be known by—was well positioned to become my favorite—and only—accepted sounding board and critic.

About the *C-minor Symphony*, she made a few comments that, though far from what a pedant or musician might consider profound, demonstrated an insight into what my intent was as a composer: *"In its very structure you once more reveal yourself as a master of the art of developing entire movements from small, seemingly inconsequential motives. . . . You also utilized the concept of rhythm as a narrative element in its own right and in so doing, you were able to make it an essential component in the creation of that drama. . . . Your first theme reveals a brutal rhythmic power. . . . It is simple yet angry music, full of tense and deeply tragic emotions. . . . The Fifth is clearly a vehicle for a drama in which light and hope ultimately triumph over the forces of darkness and despair. . . ."*

She spoke with a confidence and surety that impressed and, though she claimed no special knowledge of music or my works in particular, she nonetheless embodied wisdom in spades—the rarest of commodities, especially in Vienna.

Toni then went on to contrast the *C-minor* with the *Pastoral Symphony in F* and here, too, she understood my purposes: *"For all the angst of the Fifth, you crafted its mirror image in the Sixth, which extolls a love of nature and the tranquil beauty therein. Your varied repetitions of country life, portrayed by those simple, rustic themes and the dances you incorporate throughout, elevate our notions of program music to a level never before achieved. But more importantly, there exists a profound balance—a cosmic balance, a universal balance—between the two symphonies. One is light, one dark—yet even in the heart of each lies the other—just like this,"* she said. It was only then that I realized that *Fraulein* Antonio Birkenstock Brentano, daughter of Baron von Birkenstock, sister-in-law to Bettina Brentano, wife of the merchant *Herr* Brentano, and the mother of four children, had a pendant around her neck that held a single, over-sized pearl, shaded black and white. In the middle of the black was a small white mark, and in the middle of the white was a corresponding black spot. It was a three-dimensional representation of the same symbol N had once drawn for me in the sand.

"Is that what the Chinese call the *yin-yang*?" I asked.

"My father, Baron von Birkenstock, was a great collector of artifacts, especially those from the Orient, most of which I am now preparing for a series of auctions. You must come. I am returned here to Vienna for only so long as it takes to close out his estate. This pearl—which once belong to the Ming Emperor, *Zhu Yunwen*—was one of my favorites from childhood. It even has its own name," Toni added, "the *Mandate of Heaven.*"

This day was rapidly becoming ever more intriguing and I connived what I could to make these fine ladies stay the afternoon. . . .

"You had them play the *E-flat Trio* with you, *oui*—Bettina at violin and Toni on the cello?"

"Bettina tried to impress but I could not take my eyes off of Toni. She hugged that cello as I wished she'd embrace my soul."

"Shades of Liliana and the unfortunate *Monsieur* Ries, but more about her later."

"Before taking up the cello, Toni removed her *beau chapeau* and unpinned her hair. When those fiery locks tumbled out and down to her shoulders, I gasped. Now there was a redhead I'd gladly elope with."

"Not Bettina? As has been suggested by innumerable writers in the future?" N makes a quick gesture over his shoulder towards his endless library where those volumes that mention Bettina glow red.

"*Mein Gott, nein.* . . . Bettina was naught but a temptress—a superb one at that—who aroused me sexually, but so what if she was seductive? Charming? Articulate? She was all that, but compared to her sister-in-law, Bettina was nothing but a petulant child. Toni, now there was a woman of substance, a woman to love, to share a life. . . . One might say I was tempted by Bettina's body, but was brought to my senses by Toni's brilliance and the workings of her brain."

"A married woman. Did you forget?"

"A mere trifle."

"With four children."

"More trifles. This new hope—I had to let it nourish my soul. Hope has been a neighbor all my life and nourishes half the world. . . . Without hope, what would become of me?"

"And your '*ménage a trois,*' how did that work out that afternoon?"

"By '*ménage,*' you mean the trio the three of us played?

"*Oui*, the *Piano Trio*. In the future we call such malapropos a 'Freudian slip.'"

"Why? Because you assumed I was going to sleep with both of them simultaneously?"

"You are learning. Even the gods in Elysium have amorous fantasies—especially after Napoleon had to surrender Josephine and took on Princess Marie Louise as his bride. The poor girl was as timid as a flea and tight as an old shoe. She bore Bonaparte an heir like a dutiful cow but love, passion? Your illusions of a naked Bettina hold more intrigue."

"The truth is, N, I forgot Bettina was even there," I say even as I begin to wonder why N has started to refer to himself in the *third person*. "The moment we began the opus," I continue, "Toni locked eyes on me and I her. Shakespeare was right, vision turned 'round is indeed the portal to our souls. Toni and I communicated more essence in that quarter hour than I had with any other woman in my life save perhaps Leonore or Josephine. . . . And those two were in my past. Toni could be my future—and I, hers. Our bond, shaped inexplicably and without words, was mutual."

"And her husband?"

"Ah, my heart was gladdened to learn that her husband—the true source of the sadness I detected in her—was still managing the family residence and business in Frankfort, five hundred miles away. And hope, *ja*, hope—or at least the prospect of hope—had indeed become my neighbor."

The soiree at the home of the deceased Baron von Birkenstock was as many I had attended in Vienna—overflowing with poseurs vying to see and be seen along with a coterie of musicians hoping to hear and be heard. I had no sooner entered than I saw Toni gliding towards me. She wore her ubiquitous pearl and was dressed in a gown of white linen with golden trim tailored in the style of an Egyptian princess. She verily floated above it all like Cleopatra on her barge until our eyes met and renewed their acquaintance. Why that moment, that single moment of visual connection, triggered such contentment in my soul, I could not then understand but would grow in time to luxuriate in. Taking my hand—hers felt so soft and compelling—Toni pulled me aside, away from the din of that maddening crowd. "I feared you would not come," she said, and I dared not tell her that, more than anything, I feared not being in her presence.

Her sister-in-law, Bettina, was only too happy to play hostess to the myriad of royals that filled the grand music salon. Toni used the opportunity and freedom created therein to lead me around the Birkenstock home—and I followed all too willingly.

The mansion, whose walls in room after room were covered with paintings from all the known masters, also displayed many thousands of engravings, as many drawings, along with hundreds of antique urns, marble vases, and Etruscan lamps. Successive chambers and salons held glass display cases overstuffed with the coins of all nations, collections of minerals, sea-insects, telescopes, countless maps, architectural plans of ancient kingdoms and lost cities, the mummified remains of hands and feet, precious historic documents under glass, and even an antique bamboo walking stick reputed to have magical powers.

In another grand salon, one she nicknamed "the Temple of Isis," we explored collections from not only that ancient kingdom but Persia, India, China, and beyond. The walls were lined with books and artifacts of all descriptions, including numerous statues of that great goddess, Isis, herself. Some were cast in the ancient Egyptian style; others owed more to Venus and Greco-Roman interpretations. All were fully naked celebrations, testaments to the beauty of the female spirit. Several particularly archaic pieces from those Nile kingdoms revealed the young god, Horus, nursing at the goddess's breast. Over the next two years I would come to know this vast collection with an intimacy far beyond my imagination. Would that I could know its guardian mistress as well. . . .

At a small table in front of a stone replica of an Egyptian temple sat the two oldest of her four children, Georg, who was 9, and Maximiliane, 8 years old. They were so engaged in a game of chess that they barely acknowledged our presence, even when Toni insisted they pause to introduce themselves to *Herr* Beethoven. In due time I would come to know all four of them well, including the two youngest, both girls, Josefa, then six, and Fanny, who was only four—the same age as my nephew, Karl.

"Imagine a life," she said, "where it's always warm and secure. This is where I played as a child and these are my libraries."

Toni went on to explain how Baron von Birkenstock, married her off to the father of her children—a merchant and banker 20 years her senior—when she was still but a child herself. News of that engagement came to her at the premier of my *Opus One Trios* and nearly broke her spirit—And the organist at her wedding at St. Stephens was none other than my own brother, Casper. It's little wonder I felt connected to her; our lives were entangled long before we had actually met. Toni loved her children and was grateful for their presence in her life, but her husband, *Herr* Brentano, whom she described as a "good man," nonetheless remained a stranger even after all these years. She despaired of life in Frankfurt, a commercial center lacking any culture or refinement, and survived her life there only on the condition she was allowed to escape and return home to Vienna every two years to visit her father. And now that the Baron had died the preceding autumn, she faced an awful prospect. Once the sale of the estate and all its holdings was complete, she would no longer have reason to ever return to Vienna or reside therein. That terrified her and would soon trigger a depression so severe that she would take ill and remain bed-ridden for months on end.

I had seen that before, depression that is, with Josephine, but there the comparison ended. Josephine was akin to a leaf blown in the wind that despaired her fate and fell victim to circumstances. Toni was a strong, vibrant, compassionate woman of superior intellect who knew what she liked and what she needed but had been sold abroad and imprisoned like a slave into a life she did not want. She fought daily to find an escape. Despair would be one potential answer, love and affection, another. But not that day, the day of the soiree. She soon confided that those brief minutes spent together performing my *Piano Trio* were among the happiest moments she'd experienced in Vienna since her father's death. In return I found myself promising to play with her and for her whenever she desired—a prospect that by contrast brought nothing but lightness and the prospect of joy—*ja*, N's promised moment back into my poor existence.

In the "Temple of Isis" room she opened up wardrobe after wardrobe to show off the Baron's collection of Chinese silks and Japanese kimonos. There was one especially beautiful red silk kimono that I would later purchase and send off to Leonore in Bonn as a tenth anniversary wedding gift, continuing our childhood pledge to keep each other warm and held close within the confines of our respective hearts. Little did I suspect then that the intrigues triggered by that seemingly innocent present to Leonore would command my future in a most unexpected fashion.

The Birkenstock library also fascinated me, filled as it was with myriad volumes of recently translated scriptures from across the great span of Asia. As often as I would return to the Birkenstock mansion to play for Toni, she would reciprocate by reading to me selections from those great works. Understand that, though I was self-taught in most areas, I made continual efforts to grasp "the measure and wisdom of each age and culture," a practice that Toni enjoyed facilitating.

From the *Bhagavad Gita* she introduced me to the Hindoo conception of God, one identical to my own notions of a loving father, our Creator, in that starry canopy above us all; "*Brahma; his spirit is enwrapped in himself. He, the Mighty One, is present in every part of space. His omniscience includes our spirit and our conception of Him. It is independent of everything and yet it contains all others and is therefore the greatest. 'O God, thou are the true, eternal, blessed, immutable light of all times and spaces. Thy wisdom embraces thousands upon thousands of laws and yet thou dost always act freely and for thy honor. To thee be praised with adoration. Thou alone art the blessed one, the Bhagavan. Thou art the essence of all laws, the image of all wisdom, present throughout the universe, thou upholdest all things. Sun, ether, Brahma.'*"

And when I asked Toni about the profusion of Hindoo Gods

and Goddess and the attendant worshipers and cults that revolved around them, she answered: "*The many are all simply manifestations of the one and what does it matter if we pray to Jesus, Isis, Shiva, the relics of a Catholic saint, a cross of wood, or Napoleon at the crossroads of our times. Are they all not equally representations of the One? What differences does it matter what we call them or what language we use, when in fact each one separately merely leads us to understand the unity of all?*"

"Amen to that," I said.

From yet another work of the poet Schiller, *The Mission of Moses,* she read to me about an Egyptian priestess who recognized the same single highest cause of all things, a primeval force, a natural force, the essence of all essences. I felt so in accord with those thoughts that I would later have those words copied out and placed under glass on my desk. *"I am that which is; I am all what is; what was what will be; He is only and solely of himself and to this only one, all things owe their existence. No mortal man has ever lifted my veil."*

Ja, I would come to know well Toni Brentano and her children over the next many months, though not in the biblical sense. Much as my longings and desires chaffed against base instincts, we remained platonic lovers. . . . But first a quick footnote. . . . Toni and I were hardly ever alone. One day it would be Maximiliane with us, another day Josefa or Fanny. *Ja,* her children or her servants or her sister-in-law were our inevitable chaperones, eliminating as it were any opportunities for affections of a more physical nature. And this was a good fortune, compelling our bond to be not one of sex but of spirit, intellect, and soul.

Still, there were two moments whose polarities defined the boundaries of our affection. The first—which I still treasure—occurred most innocently during the soiree. While ushering me from one room to the next, Toni put her arm around my waist. Without thinking, I reflexively did the same, yet when my hand landed on the curve of her hip, it felt inexplicable . . . as if resting my hand there was the most proper and natural gesture in the world to do . . . it was as if we'd been coupled together as such for lifetimes . . . and as if we belonged forever united into the future. . . . Toni looked back at me—our vision connecting anon—her hand tightened its grip around me, and I knew we both felt the same perfection. "Blame it," she whispered, "on *the Mandate of Heaven.*"

The second incident transpired several months later on the first anniversary of her father's death. Toni asked me to join her and Maximiliane at the city cemetery where they would place flowers on the Baron's grave. That day Toni was quieter and more distracted during our walk than I had expected. Tears filled her eyes. Perhaps it was the old emotions surfacing again. I pulled her close and kissed her check where a drop had fallen. Recalling a poem to a beloved I was to set to music, I sang those lyrics in a whisper as tenderly as I could while holding her gaze in mine:

The tears of your silent eyes,
With their love-filled splendor,
Oh, that I might gather them from your cheek
Before the earth drinks them in.

Still her sadness hung across her *mien* like a veil too stubborn to move away, until at last she confided the news that threatened to crush her vitality. Toni spoke to me as if pronouncing a judge's harshest sentence of some criminal: "*Herr* Brentano," she said as more tears flowed from those blue, blue eyes, "disheartened by the long absence from his children and wife, is forthwith moving his business to Vienna until such time as his family can return to Frankfort."

CHAPTER 22

Twenty-Two Variations and Improvisations; 1810–1812:

Für Elise
For Elise

As HE STARTED up the three flights of stairs to Beethoven's apartment, Prince Carl Lichnowsky acknowledged to himself that he was known for many bad and licentious things—especially to the women in his life—but being a fool was not one of them. Though for the sake of propriety and personal pride, he had ended his stipend to B after the incident at Gratz, he did not end the friendship—nor did Beethoven. The Prince considered B the brilliant son he never had, the star musician Christiane could never birth. But B had been right: *There are thousands of princes, but only one Beethoven.* And given that the Prince's protégé had been composing and performing such divine music since they had first met at Mozart's apartment, Lichnowsky was not about to throw all that away over one single incident. The Prince knew that even the fiercest storm eventually wears itself out, allowing the heavens to spread a blanket of calm over the world. . . . And so it was with Beethoven. . . .

And by all appearances General Beynac was more entertained by B's antics that evening than he would have ever been listening to the master's piano-playing. As if proof of that claim were needed, the General, in fact, did fall asleep and snore loudly later that evening when the Prince and Count Oppersdorf were performing a cello sonata together—this, much to the embarrassment of the junior French officers who had accompanied Beynac to the castle and had to carry him home. Add to that Beethoven's growing reputation as a mad and eccentric genius and Lichnowsky welcomed the realization that there was nothing to fear. There was little B could do that, in the end, would shock anybody. Shock is what they expected.

Almost twenty-five years had spun by since "*Herr Louis*" had stunned Mozart with his improvisations and variations. And B had only gotten better. . . . Lichnowsky remembered that night with sweetness as he approached the landing to the second floor, and it made him wonder what had happened to that ageless wonder, his masseuse *Fraulein* Lokitzvarah, she of the perpetual lotus flower. *Fraulein* Lokitzvarah had first appeared as if by magic at Teplitz and then just as serendipitously disappeared. Of all the women who had entered his life, she was not only the one he savored and missed the most, but also the one he found to have always been the wisest and most spiritually balanced and centered. *"It is the very nature of existence that causes all humans suffering and pain,"* she had once told him. *"No one escapes, no one, not you, not Mozart, not the Emperor. The secret to life is learning how to manage that pain."*

B reputedly encountered her again at a cabin outside Heiligenstadt but the composer's description of that day sounded more like a *Traum* than an experience of flesh and blood. And what flesh. . . . B claimed that *Fraulein* Ava Lokitzvarah body's seemed to meld into his and they became but one creature. Together they played the pianoforte and what B ultimately heard was the expression of his own essential self. She had revealed to him his musical soul and the music inherent in his very being as well as all of his *potential future compositions* if he chose life over death. *"Play the future."* She had insisted. *"Turn off your mind, relax, and flow downstream. This is not dying."* Indeed, the Prince believed that B's near-death experience over his progressive hearing loss and his reputed encounter with *Fraulein* Lokitzvarah at Heiligenstadt may have been the very catalyst that pushed Beethoven into the most productive composing jag of his life. In those eight years past, B created such an astonishing number and range of works—from his best symphonies and piano concertos to incomparable string quartets, piano sonatas, songs, and oratorios—that only Mozart, prodigy that he was, would have been capable of maintaining such a pace with quality assured.

Reaching the top of the stairs, Lichnowsky heard Beethoven noodling away on his piano and recognized the piece. B was working through variations on a gentle bagatelle called *Für Elise* or *Für Therese,* which Lichnowsky—having known B for all these years—personally thought of as *Für Elysium.* The Prince suspected this little valentine was more about the paradise B felt in the arms of a lover than any particular woman. Which actual woman might have inspired the piece, Lichnowsky didn't know and didn't care. . . . Although there were rumors about Vienna that B was now seeing a young woman, Therese Malfatti, whose father was a doctor who had treated the composer's increasing deafness, Lichnowsky didn't hold much credence in those stories. He suspected that B was seeing someone either "*High-Born*" or married or both and was therefore deliberately masking her true identity so as not to trigger a scandal or a repeat of the familial conflict that had occurred over his affair with Josephine von Brunsvik Deym. That little disaster ended when Deym ran off and married a baron from Estonia named Stackelberg.

Although the Prince had come many times to B's flat to hear him work through new material, there was something ineffable and sweet about these tones that made Lichnowsky stop himself from banging on the door. Rather than disturb his protégé, the Prince resolved to just listen and dream. . . .

He sat down on the steps outside B's door and this is what he heard. . . .

Für Franz Gerhard Wegeler, My Good Old Friend:
Spring, 1810

"Although I have given you no written proofs of this, you, my friend, are still ever most vividly in my thoughts. There has even been for a long time among my manuscripts one which is intended for you and which you will certainly receive this summer. For some time I have had to give up my rather quiet and peaceful way of life and have been inspired to move in society.

"The cause of this? If you have guessed a woman, a new love, you would be close to the mark. I sleep little, to be sure, but I prefer being awakened thusly to all slumber. Who can escape a tempest of this sort raging about him? Oh, this life is indeed beautiful, but for me, well, I pray that you will not refuse a friend's request when I ask you to obtain for me my certificate of baptism which I may need for that which our friend, Ferdinand Ries, calls my 'Marriage Project.' If you would be willing to make the journey from Koblenz to Bonn, charge all expenses to me. Meanwhile take note of the fact that I had an older brother born before me who was also called Ludwig but with the additional name of 'Maria,' and who died after six days. The sooner you send me the certificate of baptism, the greater will be my gratitude.

"Think of me with some goodwill, however little I may deserve it.

"Embrace and kiss your beloved wife, Leonore, and your children on behalf of your friend,

"Beethoven . . ."

Für Bernadotte:
Late November, 1810

Forced to ponder his own progressive hearing loss whenever he plays the piano—and when doesn't he?—Beethoven once again curses the gods, though with less vehemence than in the past. He is, after all, getting used to being crippled. Some men are born lucky, others less so. B considers Field Marshall General Jean Baptiste Bernadotte who sits beside him and Lichnowsky in the Prince's salon as one of those rare individuals for whom the heavens always shine. Bernadotte, the son of lowly tailor from the city of *Pau* in the southwest corner of France, has risen up through the ranks of the revolutionary army from a mere private to that of Marshall of the Empire, a man second in command to only Napoleon himself. And now? And now Bernadotte, the former ambassador, is traveling incognito from Paris through the capitals of Europe to Stockholm to become the adopted heir to Charles XIII of Sweden. Bernadotte and his bride, Napoleon's old lover Désirée Clary, are now destined to become the King and Queen of that northern empire. . . . A tailor's son. . . . *Vive la Révolution!* Talk about a self-made man. . . .

B looks up from the piano and asks Bernadotte and Lichnowsky, "If I were to go to Paris, would I be obliged to salute your Emperor Bonaparte?"

Lichnowsky is incredulous. "You would consider going to Paris? To France?"

"I've gone back and forth in my mind about this Napoleon. Earlier I could not have tolerated him. Today I think completely otherwise."

"Now you reconsider?" Lichnowsky shakes his head in amazement.

"Napoleon Bonaparte holds you—or at least your music—in greater esteem than he does me," replies Bernadotte.

"I'm told the *Paris Conservatoire* plays Mozart's concertos better than any orchestra on the continent."

"Then you must go, if only for a fortnight or two," says Bernadotte. "My apartment is at your disposal."

"But isn't it also true that the Parisians consider me an 'unlicked bear' better suited to the steppes of Russia?" B asks.

"What does that matter to you?" replies Bernadotte. "It is evident you do not know the French. Paris is not Moscow in the winter. It's the home of liberty and of freedom from social conventions.

Distinguished men are accepted exactly as they are pleased to show themselves, and should one be a trifle eccentric, especially a stranger, that only contributes to his success. You would do well in Paris—far better than Emperor Bonaparte would if he tries to take on Moscow."

Adagio Für Toni:
February 1811

It begins with a Yuletide chill that rapidly morphs into a cold. Toni withdraws from family life and takes to bed. From there the congestion migrates into her lungs. That god awful coughing comes next, after which her doctor diagnoses influenza. Every gesture, every movement causes her pain and exhaustion. Her four-poster bed becomes her new home and medicinal rubs her only perfume. She stares out her window at her frosted-over rose garden and thinks about death and what it would be like to escape the despair of this world. And even when the symptoms of her illness clear, she is plagued by the grandest fatigue, one so great she can barely find the strength to face each day. She rarely ever leaves her four-poster or the sanctuary of her feather quilts.

But Toni is wise enough to realize her decline is more the result of a deep and dreary sadness than any physical ailments. Her husband's recent arrival from Frankfort is little cause for celebration and throughout her illness he visits her hardly at all . . . and if he does, the less said about that carnal intrigue, the better. . . . They remain strangers even after all of these years—he's head of the household, she's well-bred breeding stock. When *Herr* Brentano isn't working on his accounts, he's either off traveling on business or bending an elbow with other merchants in a local pub. She feels guilty for hating him. She is not a hateful person, but theirs is a match ill-conceived and without affection. She is poorly suited to the role of dutiful and silent spouse. The boundaries imposed that define her life grow smaller and feel ever more akin to a prison. She finds lying in darkness preferable to the future that waits. Wracked by headaches, depression, and fatigue, she remains indisposed, unfit to see anybody. And if *Herr* Brentano insists upon her return to Frankfurt when the estate auctions are over. . . . she knows not what to do. . . .

And so it is with some surprise one dark and overcast afternoon, when the sun struggles to break through, that she hears the most heavenly piano music verily wafting towards her from the antechamber. It's the *adagio* of Beethoven's *Fifth Piano Concerto*. . . . Is she dreaming? Toni imagines she's listening to a choir of angels celebrating a world of light and love, somewhere. It has to be; it is Beethoven playing for her. She sits up in bed, not conceiving that there can be such power in music, music so transcendent that it could even uplift the spirits of the damned in hell.

As Beethoven segues into a *Danza Tedesca,* the depths of emotions in his soul speak to her through these improvisations, filled as they are with such compassion and grace . . . . She hears in them the manifestation of his tenderheartedness. How can anyone listen to his piano compositions and not find their sufferings alleviated? Toni sobs uncontrollably, and for the moment her grief finds both expression and transitory relief. B plays on with a half-dozen or more improvisation until her tears exhaust themselves. Then, at last, he comes into her room and wipes dry her cheeks. Has love come, she wonders? Are my days of loneliness gone? *Have I at last found a dream to call my own?*

Fidelio Redux:
Early March 1811

"Is it true?" asks Beethoven.

"Is what true?" replies Steffen. He and B have been meeting for dinner for weeks on end now, redrafting the score of *Fidelio*. Steffen knows the libretto has to be shorter, tighter, for the underlying drama to work. Tonight they are at the Black Raven Tavern eating grilled lake trout, the night before it was salmon at the Café Emporium. B is fond of fish and prefers to dine whenever he hears one pub or another has a fresh haul.

"*Fidelio.* Is it true that a wife, any wife, would risk herself as our heroine does to save her husband? Do you believe it's so?"

"I do," says Steffen. "But it would take an exceptional woman."

"How is it then that fate has me fall flat at the feet of women whose feminine spirits favor infidelity and fickleness over courage—fearless courage?"

"To be in love, to truly love, to surrender oneself to another, that is the most courageous act of all."

"Would your Julie have shown such bravery? Would she have sacrificed all for you?"

"Yes, Julie would and I for her. And if I could have saved her from dying by taking on the pneumonia myself. . . ." He doesn't need to finish. B easily understands by the pained look in Steffen's eyes. In the two years since Julie has perished, the wound in Steffen's heart has still not healed.

"And your sister, our beloved Lorchen, would she do that for Wegeler?"

Steffen looks his friend straight in the eye and speaks without hesitation, "For you, yes."

"For me?" B gasps as if choking on a fish bone instead of hearing an answer most unexpected.

"Yes, for you," repeats Steffen. "For you."

A Piano Concerto for the Emperor in E flat:
March 20, 1811

The diplomatic pouch from Vienna arrives just as the Emperor Napoleon Bonaparte hears the 101-gun salute that signals the birth of his son. Inside the pouch, along with the usual array of documents from that black sheep Bernadotte warning of tension with Czar Alexander along the Russian-Polish border, is a first edition of a new Beethoven *Piano Concerto,* his fifth, which Napoleon orders delivered to the director of the *Paris Conservatoire.*

When at last one of Marie Louise's nursemaids brings the boy swaddled in blankets to him, Napoleon's eyes fill with tears of relief. Finally he has an heir—a son, Napoleon II, plump and healthy—whom he believes will bring together the people of Europe and serve as a living testament to France's alliance with her former foe, the Hapsburgs of Austria. Napoleon is certain that with an Austrian mother and a French father, the blood in his son's veins is emblematic of a newly unified continent and the continuity of the Empire. As Napoleon contemplates his next moves on the chessboard that is Europe, he wishes his son could have also carried the blood of a Russian princess as well, then all Bonaparte's problems would be forsworn.

Cradling his son tightly to his chest, Napoleon returns to Marie Louise's chamber but finds the young mother sound asleep. After kissing her forehead, he continues on to the grand salon where a chamber ensemble from the *Paris Conservatoire* awaits. As soon as Napoleon enters with the boy, the orchestra strikes the first chords of Beethoven's *Fifth Piano Concerto.*

"Listen well, my son. This is for you . . ." says the Emperor. "The path of genius is a meteor that lights up our century and changes the face of the world. Remember that while glory is fleeting, and obscurity lasts forever, true greatness never fades."

Fantasy for Pianoforte, Opus 77 dedicated to Franz Brunsvik: June 18, 1811

"A thousand thanks my friend for your readiness to travel with me. Let me inform you that on my doctor's orders I have to spend two full months at Teplitz. Hence I could travel with you by August. My doctor is quite

annoyed with me for putting off my departure for so long, although he himself knows that the company of a cheerful friend would do me good. Have you got a carriage? Now do let me have a reply with lightning speed, for as soon as I know whether you still want to travel with me, I must write about rooms for both of us. Accommodations there are said to be very quickly filling up. I am awaiting your decision in this matter. All good wishes, my friend, to you and your sisters Charlotte and Therese—and to the Baroness Josephine von Brunsvik Deym von Stackelberg if she has not altogether banished me from her memory and will receive even so much as a warm greeting from . . . Your sincere friend, Beethoven"

A Trio for Archduke Rudolph:
July, 1811

Toni still cannot believe she's sitting in her nightgown and robe in her rose garden playing the cello with Archduke Rudolph at the piano and Beethoven on the violin. Though her hair is still wet from her morning bath, here she is, sight-reading. It's a recently completed draft of a *Piano Trio in B-flat major* that Beethoven has dedicated to the Archduke. She's barely adequate playing the cello but B has been irrepressible and insistent this morning. Beethoven and the Archduke had shown up with B's *Guarneri* violin and cello and the *Trio* score at her estate less than an hour ago and B insisted she pull herself together and play. On went the robe, up went her hair, and down went the pot of coffee her servant brought. They just barged in . . . really . . . the Archduke! Without notice or warning.

She feels a disorganized wreck but she welcomes the relief. It is one of the few antidotes to the dread that never leaves. She wakes with it each morning; she falls asleep to it each night. A life of suffocation with a man she doesn't love and who doesn't love her. How can this go on? Each day is a torture waiting for the next disappointment, the next touch of a cold hand, the next disagreement. Much as she adores her father—or at least the memory of her father—she rues the day he accepted this marriage arrangement.

The *Trio* is magnificent, grand with a touch of nobility that shakes the slumber from her sleepy head. As she bows the antique cello, she feels the vibrations—the warm-honey-rich vibrations of the *Andante cantabile* flow from the strings, through the wood, and thence directly to her thighs. She caresses the instrument between her legs and remembers. . . .

Each day after waking and before the dread clamps itself around her chest and keeps her from breathing, she touches herself down there to relieve the tension. It's a lesson learned as a cloistered school girl and mastered as a wife left alone in the dark. Some nights—most nights actually—she falls asleep that way and some mornings—this being one—she soaks in a steaming hot tub and, as the warm water melts her body, she uses her index finger to find that relief yet again. The window in her bathing room also looks out to her rose garden. Through the seasons she watches those blood-red buds emerge. Now in summer come the hummingbirds and the bees. Dodging the thorns, they drink in the nectar and spread its scent everywhere. . . . The rose petals expand and express themselves as great beauties only to freeze, she knows, hard and brittle in winter. Lying in her tub looking down at the flower of her womanhood, hidden amidst its own ruby-haired delta, she feels as if she is one of those roses—one that needs tenderness, affection, and a man's caresses before she too turns to frost.

She is there, lying in the tub, blushing in the afterglow, when her servant knocks at the door—*Beethoven and the Archduke are here!* She hastily dries herself and throws back on her nightgown and robe . . . and her pearl. *Beethoven is here! And Archduke Rudolph?*

B is effusive. Insists they must play. Must they? Yes they must. But first he wants to show the Archduke the collections that are up for sale, which they do, but it seems like a gallop and she can scarcely keep pace. Archduke Rudolph picks this and that to buy as does Beethoven and before she knows it, they're back amongst the roses.

The *Trio* is much too difficult for her. She's a guitarist, a pianist, but not much of a cello player. And he wants her to sight read. How can she?

"Trust me," he says. "There's lots of plucking, lots of pizzicato—just like your guitar. Watch my eyes. Follow me. But above all, don't think. Just play. Play with audacity."

She stops her mind from doubting and bows the cello as she never has before, feeling every note, every vibration as they travel right down to the marrow of her soul. . . .

And then it comes to her . . . like Romeo and Juliet . . . she loves this man. . . . The forbidden love of a married woman. . . . And he?

And he stands before her, holding in his arms, the violin, the female soprano voice . . . the cello squeezed between her thighs, the masculine tenor voice. . . . How perfect. . . . She makes the man sing, he makes the woman cry out. In the middle of dark is light, in the middle of light is dark, and together they are a swirling harmony in motion, the *Yin-Yang*, the *Tao*, the path, the way . . . the *Mandate of Heaven*. And between them at the piano—their altar to God—is Archduke Rudolph, a man of cloth . . . . Marry me, marry me. . . .

Can she? Could she? Would she break the Brentano bond of marriage? Destroy convention? Risk her children? Challenge faith, God, and her church? Is she strong enough? Can she? Will she? We'll see. . . . Indeed.

Sirens of Teplitz:
September 17, 1811, Night of the Autumn Equinox Masked Ball

Naked except for the costume facemask of an Eagle, Therese von Brunsvik leaves the arms of a blond-haired Lynx with lovely breasts and swims towards the far side of the baths. There, through the dense mist, she sees a Grizzly Bear roar with laughter. It's Beethoven, *naturlich*. Drunk—and obviously so—as are the four naked creatures arrayed around him in the pool: a Tigress, an Angel; a Wolverine and a Black Swan. At this late hour the baths are lit only by candles. Bottles of Champagne are everywhere. Steam rising off the waters and thick clouds of sweet incense obscure visibility even farther. And music? If one can consider it that—it's an odd mix of Gypsy rhythms interwoven with a *tabla* drummer and a *sitar* player that her Lynx's husband invited back after a recent voyage to India—odd but exotic and adding to an otherworldly feel.

Most consider the northern Bohemian spa town of Teplitz a "Little Paris," but for one night a year, the night of the Autumn Equinox Masked Ball, the Kaiserbad—the most luxurious of all the baths—becomes *Carnevale* in *Venezia,* replete with a gourmet's menu of alcohol and eroticism. Teplitz, the oldest and perhaps the most fashionable of the spa towns in the region, draws upon an elite aristocratic crowd from across both the northern German states and the southern Austrian Empire. They come from as far away as Berlin, Vienna, and Budapest to not only savor the thermal waters reputed to cure most every aliment but to also enjoy the relaxed summer social life that revolves around the parks, cafes, music halls, and *amour* among the shadows.

As a most secret *lesbische Fraulein* in a world where such practices—at least publically—are considered abhorrent, Therese excels at the art of discretion. Out of a necessity to protect herself, she routinely observes people—studying their attitudes, their strengths, and their foibles—before ever engaging with them. Beethoven is the one exception. He saw through her right from the very start when they first met more than a decade earlier. With the issue of physical sex between them pushed aside, they had become dear friends and confidents—after all, they share three, maybe four loves in common: wine, women, song, and her sister, Josephine. And Louis is fun. They laugh together; share ribald jokes and stories together; even 'girl-watch' together. Their ease and comfort with each other so impresses the gossip-hungry Viennese that they are often yet mistakenly considered lovers. That Therese is the dedicatee for his *Piano Sonata in F-sharp major* reinforces that error. For her part, Therese welcomes the camouflage and the social deception that follows. And for B? Well, she imagines that being cheerful around a female friend unavailable for courting—

ever—is rather relaxing and pleasurable, especially when he is not otherwise involved with anyone else.

Tonight is no different. Although Beethoven had initially travelled to Teplitz with Therese's brother, Franz von Brunsvik, some six weeks earlier, Franz had by early September returned to the family estate in Hungary. That left Therese and Louis to shepherd each other around. The masked ball marks the informal end of the season. After this, visitors to the spa town will gather themselves and their families up for their journeys home to an infinite range of distant locations across all of central Europe.

What attracts Therese most to masked ball is that on this one night, the Venetian notion of *Carnevale* returns to its "carnal" roots—discreetly of course but erotic and exciting nonetheless. As this is Louis's first excursion to Teplitz he has no idea what is actually planned. And when she insists that B attend the ball in costume, he at first balks, repeating his oft-stated line that he doesn't dance. Only when Therese shares with him that the ball is merely a warm-up for the "after party" held *sans* costume at the Kaiserbad, does he consent to attend. Beethoven, *naturlich,* comes as a Russian Bear with a fearsome, shaggy mask.

After a summer of pampering in the spa, Therese recognizes some of the masked women in the baths by their voice, others by the shape and size of their breasts, and still others—a more select group—by the sweet petals of their lotus garden. Therese understands that among all of these ladies who live most of the year in states of repressed sexuality, Teplitz is a bubbling caldron of licentiousness. These wives and *amorati* of aristocrats are often 20 to 30 years younger than their male partners. . . . Married off to older men in their decline, these child brides are just coming into their own sexual prime. And that libidinous energy is often thwarted, stymied, and buried under the rules of societal convention and motherhood. And some, like her Lynx, the Duchess Martina von Nordhoff, are fellow lesbians who have to suffer marital service while fighting off their own inner nature. But after two, three, or even four months of gentle relaxation in nature, where bodies at the spa are soaked, massaged, oiled, and generally well-tended, those carnal hungers re-emerge and are sated late at night in out-of-the-way places. . . . And the bath party after the Autumn Equinox Masked Ball is their final opportunity to quench the fires down below. After midnight the only acceptable attire at the Kaiserbad is the aforementioned mask, a wine flask, and the skin of our birth.

As Therese nears the group of women surrounding Beethoven, she hears the Wolverine singing a comic tune—a little bit tipsy and off key—and recognizes her as Amalie Sebald, an earthy singer from Berlin, who's a temptation to men and women alike. . . .

I was alone with Chloe,
And wanted to kiss her;
But she said
That she would scream—
It would be a futile attempt.

While Amalie sings, the blond Angel uses her long fingers to play along as if the surface of the water is her imagined piano. The Angel is lean and tall with slender legs and skin so pale that Therese can detect the veins in her otherwise perfectly proportioned breasts. It has to be Dorothea von Ertmann, B's former keyboard student and one of the finest interpreters of his piano works.

The Wolverine continues . . .

Yet I dared, and kissed her
Despite her resistance.
And did she not scream?
Oh yes, she did;
But not until long afterward.

Everyone roars with laughter at the last line and then the Black Swan speaks up. A dark, thatched delta gives her away as the poet,

Rahel Levin, who befitting her status as the often outcast Jewess, choses the identity of that mythic bird.

"I have one," she says. . . .
If it's your desire,
To sail through my Lady's Ring of Fire,
Candy is considered dandy,
But liquor is infinitely quicker"

There's more laughter. Beethoven, who always presents a noble and elevated sensitivity towards women, whether in friendship or love, addresses Rahel. His face is animated with a charm and child-like innocence that women adore, "I don't know if I will ever make it to Berlin, but do tell your friend Varnhagen that I would welcome hearing more about your ideas for an opera." This pleases Rahel, who bows her head appreciatively.

The Tigress next takes her turn. This lustful creature has sharp, pointed breasts and a pubic triad waxed bare in the Moroccan tradition. Therese recognizes her as Bettina Brentano, only recently married to the writer, Achim von Arnim. Our Tigress floats onto her back and spreads her legs in front of Beethoven. She declaims aloud, "To our Bacchus who ferments glorious wine with his music; music that intoxicates and renders us spiritually drunk. Liquor may be quicker but be assured, my candy never fails."

"And if you, my dear, were not so newly married," says B, "I would be flattered to dine at your table. But truly, when I open my eyes, what lies before me is contrary to my religion."

Beethoven turns away from her to greet Therese. Bettina, feeling slighted by his sarcastic wit, backstrokes her way across the pool to where the poet Goethe, a Great Horned Owl, all too willingly sweeps her into his talons. Together they disappear in the mists. Therese is happy to see this Tigress vanish, imagining neither Bettina nor Goethe will be seen again until dawn's cold, harsh light of propriety returns to Teplitz. One down, three to go.

Therese, having supported her sister Josephine while she stumbled through yet another tragic marriage, has come to realize that money and class mean nothing without happiness. With that thought foremost in mind, she makes her move. Therese swims past the Angel, the Wolverine, and the Black Swan. And then, as if claiming her prize, she gently glides onto Beethoven's lap and puts one arm over his shoulder. This maneuver lifts her torso out of the water and, as she does so, she takes one of B's hands and places it firmly on her breast in clear view of her fellow creatures.

And although B remains surrounded by the temptations of these beautifully endowed and naked females, Therese notices that he seems indifferent to them—even his fondling of her breast seems absent-minded and mechanical. When he was younger, Beethoven would have been all over these women—and they him. Now, even as the three remaining naked ladies drink, laugh, and chat Beethoven up, he remains reserved despite his otherwise good humor. Therese wonders, why? After the Angel stumbles through a tart limerick of her own, B smiles so kindly in response that one believes not only in him, but in the benevolence of all humankind. True, B's temperament is easily excitable. Therese has often seen his outbursts arise and depart quickly. Nonetheless they're frequently followed by his own admission of an error, particularly when his bursts of anger, mistrust, and withdrawal derive from his "*dreadful deafness.*" She knows it would take a woman with unique qualities of mind and heart to make him happy—one who understands his flights of genius, who can take on the additional burdens of everyday affairs, and who can shield him against the assaults of the outside world in a feminine way. And none of these three creatures are it. It would take a true angel, such as his *Fidelio's* fictitious heroine Leonore. . . . Or her sister, Josephine.

"*Cet homme est le mien.* This man is mine," she finally says to the other women.

"Ah, true love has found me at last," says the Grizzly Bear as he toys with her nipple.

Beethoven's gesture of intimacy followed by Therese's amorous sigh—gently faked, *naturlich*—inspires the other three to swim away.

He then addresses Therese. "You chased off my harem. How cruel is that?"

"You looked bored," she says as she removes his hand.

"*Ja*, my thoughts are elsewhere. I'm anxious to return to Vienna and rejoin the most beautiful woman in the world."

"Yes, me too. But watching you now, I felt guilty."

"Tell me all. Let this Russian Bear be your Father Confessor."

"I was wrong about you and my sister. You two. . . . You were joyful together. And I apologize for every word I said that may have pushed you apart."

"A wise man once told me we cannot change the past. What's done is done. If Josephine had truly loved me, she would have ignored your pleadings as much as I did."

"She suffers terribly under Stackelberg and I do not believe their union will long endure." Therese looks past the mask and deep into Beethoven's eyes, "Perhaps there is a future?"

Ein Duett für Geliebte:
A Duet for Lovers:
November, 1811

Herr Brentano and the children are all away—though separately—until tomorrow. Toni studies her makeup and eye-shadow until certain all is correct. She fusses with her dress, her jewelry, and especially her undergarments. She splashes perfume on her neck, around her cleavage, and lifts her skirts to dab some down there in anticipation of Beethoven's visit. They have still yet to be alone together, though she believes today might be that day. The rooms are cleaned, her blood red roses adorn credenzas and tables everywhere, and her bed is freshly made. All that's left is to tune her guitar.

B has been in great spirits since his return from Teplitz despite the fact that two months of treatments did little to impact his hearing. Though she missed B all throughout the summer, his absence did her good—without his constant affection, she confronted her own despair and decided to stop blaming circumstances, her father's death, and *Herr* Brentano for her troubles. To stay mired in depression gives far too much power to others, who have neither asked for nor wanted it. If she is a prisoner of fate, then her prison cell, she realizes, is one she has constructed herself. The key to open the door and release Antonio von Birkenstock Brentano from jail lies within her own heart. Hardship touches us all; it is what we make of it that counts. Toni feels B's true affection and though she knows not where her hunger for him will lead, she nonetheless feels reborn. The future is hers to own and she will make of it what she will.

When B finally arrives, it is with an apology. His nephew, the now 5-year-old Karl, has come with him.

"Johanna, Karl's mother, my sister-in-law, was just arrested this morning. My poor brother Casper left Karl with me while he tries to get his damned Queen of the Night released from jail."

She sees the pain in his eyes as they reconnect with each other. "What happened? What did she do?" Toni asks, well aware that whatever illusions she has for the day have vanished. "Are you all right? Can I help?"

"It seems our brazen little thief bought a necklace worth 20,000 florins on consignment and then reported it as stolen. There's going to be a criminal hearing before the Vienna Magisterial Court and there's every chance she'll go to prison. My brother is devastated."

A Concerto for Solo Violin and Orchestra in D Major: Smorgonie, Lithuania, December 25, 1811

The specter of war wearies all those who live along the ever shifting boundaries between the armies of Russia and the opposing forces of the Emperor Napoleon Bonaparte. Although the chill of winter works to quiet tension, the *luthier* Reuven Silke fears the spring thaw when armies will once again trample across the landscape. Brutality, death, and destruction are sure to follow.

And so it is on the occasion of his wedding to Liliana Donishefski, Reuven presents his bride with the finest instrument he has ever assembled: *La Immortale Adorato*. Reuven, whose violins and cellos are compared to those crafted a century earlier by Stradivarius and Guarneri, shaped his masterpiece from ancient spruce and maple he considers sacred—the remnants of an ark that had once held the Torah in Smorgonie's fifteenth-century synagogue. That temple was burnt to the ground by Czar Alexander's marauding Cossacks. His father, Jacopo, the village rabbi, raced into the flames to save the ark, only to die from a heart attack afterwards. Reuven wonders, *why is it that every time an army practices for war, they practice on the Jews?*

When Reuven crafted his master-work, the burn patterns on the flame-licked wood created a distinctive swirling pattern of light and dark on the body of the violin akin to the shadows on the moon. The unique qualities of that sacred wood give the *Adorato*—as the violin is known to history—a warmth and depth of tone rare among the stringed instruments. And due to the limited supply of that wood, the *Adorato* is ever so much smaller than a standard violin—a trait that gives it exceptional range on the high end of the scale.

Reuven's masterwork allows Liliana to fulfill her one and only wish for that day. At the reception for the congregation afterwards she joins with the village's other musicians to perform Beethoven's *Violin Concerto in D major*. This composition she considers the single most godlike and heavenly violin concerto ever composed. And does she ever play. . . . Liliana's vibrant yet delicate touch transforms the piece into a prayer to God for the safety and sanctuary of her husband, her family, the new temple, and her people standing as they are on the crossroads of history and tragedy.

The Queen of the Night Condemned:
December 30, 1811

With her lawyer, *Herr* Gudet, at her side, Johanna stands before the Chief Judge Solomon of the Vienna Magisterial Court as they await sentencing. Casper sits directly behind them. Farther away, in the back of the courtroom, Beethoven waits with little Karl sitting on his lap. Judge Solomon, a kindly looking man, peers out at the court through spectacles. Having heard all of the evidence against her, he speaks softly.

"Johanna van Beethoven, we have no choice but to hereby sentence you to one year's penal servitude."

Johanna's head drops and she begins to cry. Casper gasps. "Oh God, no."

Herr Gudet immediately announces his intention to file an appeal and requests a stay of sentencing.

Solomon points to Karl in the back of the room. "Madam, is that your son on *Herr* Beethoven's lap?"

Too ashamed to speak, Johanna nods affirmatively.

Solomon turns back to her lawyer. "*Herr* Gudet, your motion on behalf of *Frau* Beethoven is accepted. We shall delay imposition of the sentence until such time as *Frau* Beethoven's appeal is adjudicated."

"We thank the Court for this kindness, your honor," replies *Herr* Gudet.

"But I warn you, Madam, you best behave yourself during this time or I will double the sentence. Are we understood?"

Für Leonore:
Koblenz, February 1812

Wegeler pries open a wooden packing case that has just arrived from Vienna as Leonore unfolds the note that has come with it:

"To my most tender beloveds on the occasion of your tenth wedding anniversary, from your most loving friend, Beethoven."

Carefully unwrapping each object, Wegeler finds an assortment of antique scientific instruments from all over the world for him. For Leonore there is a red silk kimono tied in a bundle with purple ribbon. Leonore immediately throws it on over her gown and while Wegeler fusses with the lenses of a Persian microscope, she most discreetly hugs the silk close to her body. Stroking herself through the soft fabric, she dreams of Louis and the Garden of Venus. . . .

Der Kuss:
The Kiss:
March 2, 1812

The newly published score of *An Die Geliebte*—composed by *"Ludwig van Beethoven"* and dedicated to the *"Baroness Antonie von Birkenstock Brentano"*—lies beside Toni on the ground of her rose garden—her picnic blanket lavished with their petals—their scent an opiate that warms her soul.

Alone at last; his touch—his sweet, gentle touch—sets her thighs trembling. Resistance is futile; she melts. Her eyes close in surrender. She spreads her lips. The tip of his tongue caresses her. Ravished in the garden; she stifles the passion of Venus that begs to cry out.

And did she not scream?
Oh yes, she does;
But not until long, long afterward.

And he too. . . . Together. . . . In secret harmony. . . .

Für Casper:
April 1812

"*Halt-Husten,* Papa—Stop Coughing," says a 6-year-old Karl to his bedridden father, Casper, but to little avail. The stress of Johanna's court case and appeal weakens a resistance low enough already. This time around the consumption has worked its way into Casper's lungs. Beethoven, who stands nearby, has fear in his eyes—he has seen this before, his mother, Margaretha. . . .

Casper sips on an elixir prepared and sent to him from Linz by their chemist younger brother, Nikolaus Johann. The elixir softens his cough as he hacks his way through his brief speech to his brother, Louis. "How can I trust Johanna? Should I die, who else can I trust to love Karl and see to his welfare?"

"You are going to be fine—Doctor Malfatti is certain. But if you insist, sign the declaration. I will be there for this son of ours. Is there any duty more sacred than to raise and educate our Karl?"

With much difficulty Casper scribbles his signature on a declaration prepared by their lawyer, *Herr* Gudet: "*Since I am convinced of the openhearted disposition of my brother Ludwig van Beethoven, I desire after my death, he undertake the guardianship of my surviving minor son, Karl Beethoven. I therefore request the honorable court to appoint my said brother to this guardianship upon my death, and beg my dear brother to undertake this office and, like a father, to assist my child with word and deed in all circumstances.*"

Variations on a Russian Dance:
April 1812

The French Emperor Napoleon Bonaparte fumes as he reads the dispatch from Moscow: Jean Baptiste Bernadotte—the son of that tailor from *Pau* and now next in line to the throne of Sweden—has sealed an alliance with his enemy, Czar Alexander I of Russia. Together the two insist that the French turn control of the Duchy of Warsaw and the surrounding Polish lands back over to Moscow or risk war. . . .

Leonore, Redux:
Early June 1812

Beethoven dines with Steffen at the Emporium.

"On doctor's orders, I am headed to Teplitz at the end of the month."

"You'll travel through Prague?" asks Steffen.

"Of course. Why do you ask?"

"I've heard from Wegeler. The French are compelling doctors from the Rhineland to travel to Dresden to provide support if war breaks out. If he's drafted for duty, Leonore may travel with him as far as Prague."

"Leonore in Prague?"

"Yes, Prague."

The Grande Armée:
Mid-June 1812

War it will be. . . . Destination: Moscow. Goal: the submission of Alexander I. Napoleon's *Grande Armée* – now at some 600,000 troops—the largest force ever assembled on the continent, marches across Europe. Pausing briefly in Dresden where he holds court, Napoleon sends a dispatch to all of his commanders:

> *"War is the Way of deception.*
> *Therefore, when planning an attack, feign inactivity.*
> *When near, appear as if you are far away.*
> *When far away, create the illusion that you are near.*
> *If the enemy is efficient, prepare for him.*
> *If he is strong, evade him.*

If he is angry, agitate him.
If he is arrogant, behave timidly so as to encourage his arrogance.
If he is rested, cause him to exert himself.
Advance when he does not expect you.
Attack him when he is unprepared."

In Teplitz, neutral ground only a few miles to the south, his young bride, the Empress Marie Louise, his infant son Napoleon II, and their retinue take up residence for the season. There they are reunited with her parents, the royal family of Austria: the Emperor Franz and Empress Maria Ludovika and their court, all of whom have traveled from Vienna, through Prague to Teplitz.

Für Maximiliane, Piano Trio in E-flat, WoO 39:
June 15, 1812

B stares into Toni's blue-green eyes and begs that she allow him to dedicate the *Piano Trio in E-flat* to her. "My angel, my all, is not our love as firm as heaven's vault?"

She refuses. Even though it is the very same piece they played together at their first meeting, Toni insists two dedications in succession are sure to arouse *Herr* Brentano's suspicions. "However much we pretend," she says, "we cannot alter the fact that you are not yet wholly mine, and I am not wholly yours."

Yes, Brentano will eventually learn of their plot, but not yet. She will make the break on her terms, not her husband's. "Have courage, my love," she says. "Our love will endure, but only through sacrifice."

Much as Beethoven wants the *Trio* to be for Toni, he pencils out a dedication to her daughter, Maximiliane, instead.

Toni consoles B, "I am resolved to live apart only until that day when I can throw myself into your arms and say that we are truly at home together." As far as *Herr* Brentano is concerned, the auctions are over, the estate sold, and when they leave Vienna at the end of the month for Frankfort, with a stop in the spas of Bohemia for the summer, it will be forever. Forever. . . . Toni embraces B and wonders just what that will truly mean. . . . Forever, with this man? Her man?

The Travels Plans of Baroness Josephine von Brunsvik Deym von Stackelberg
June 23, 1812

Therese does not interrupt Beethoven, who is scrutinizing the orchestra's rehearsal of his *Third Symphony* at the *Theater-an-der-Wien,* until the final movement ends. Watching him carefully, she grasps that B's hearing has deteriorated to the point where he can no longer use his ears to determine if the musicians are playing the right notes; that he relies instead on observing the movement of everyone's hands.

"What is it?" he asks her.

She waives a letter in front of him and speaks clearly so he can follow her. "It's is from our Josephine. She's left Stackelberg. She knows from our brother, Franz, that you are off to Teplitz again and asks, "*Will you inform our dear, dear Beethoven—if he will still acknowledge my existence—that I will be passing through Prague on the second and third of July and beg leave to meet with him, if only for an hour.*"

"Josephine in Prague?" he asks.

"Yes, Prague," she says.

The Eroica
June 24, 1812

At the same hour Beethoven in Vienna raises his baton to conduct the symphony once named "Bonaparte," Napoleon orders his troops to cross the Neiman River at Kovno, Lithuania. The *Grande Armée* has swollen to such a size that it will take a full week for all his troops to make the crossing. From there they will commence their invasion of Russia.

But even before the concert in Vienna ends, an advance party of French cavalry transporting a large wooden cask reaches the village of Smorgoni and seeks out the most trusted man there, the rabbi's son, the *luthier,* Reuven Silke. He meets them in the basement of the new synagogue, where the cask is wrestled into place by strong arms and hidden behind a false wall Reuven creates.

Coda at Midnight; the Black Horse Inn:
Prague, the night of July 2nd & 3rd, 1812

A summer thunderstorm rages outside Prague's Black Horse Inn where Beethoven dines with the writer, Karl August Varnhagen, and his fiancée, Rahel Levin. The couple is anxious to develop a *Macbeth* inspired opera with him. It's about Napoleon on the danger of unchecked hubris, greed, and power. Varnhagen has selected a unique approach to this drama by positing it from Josephine Beauharnais's point of view, a tactic Rahel advocates with immense passion. B is intrigued, though every time he looks at Rahel all he can see is last summer's Black Swan. These thoughts though only remind him of how much he misses Toni.

Succumbing to his wine and drowsy from too many days on the road, Beethoven begs leave to head up to bed. *Ja,* Rahel is an exotic beauty indeed—a brilliant and lyrical poet—and he struggles to recall why it is they had not engaged each other further the previous season when they were both mutually unattached—not that she holds any interest for him now. But he would have then, perhaps, if not for Toni. It would have been so easy to sweep her up as Goethe did with Bettina and spend the night tumbling about in each other's arms.

After promising Varnhagen and Rahel that they'll meet again the next night to continue their conversation, he departs from his dinner companions. With a candlestick in hand, up the stairs he goes to his room on the fourth floor.

He sets the candle down, then pours himself a shot of schnapps—which he gulps down. He pours another glass, then sits by the window to watch the electrical storm. It's after midnight and those bold flashes of lightening that illuminate the Prague Castle on the hillside across the river are the only lights in an otherwise dark city. His hearing is so diminished that the bursts of thunder come across as dull rumbles. Down by the river the rest of the city is hidden under a deep layer of fog. Lost in thoughts of his own *Seventh Symphony,* B sits and sips his liqueur ever so slowly. Although his ability to hear the sounds of the world around him is steadily diminishing, his acuity for notes and chords inside his head grows ever stronger. Every beat of the *Allegretto* rings crystal clear. Working through them, he loses track of time. It is only after he hears a nearby church chime 1:00 a.m., does he become aware of a knocking on his door. At this hour?

Leaving his perch by the window he goes over to the entryway and opens the door. Standing there before him in a hooded cloak is a woman. Only slowly by the flickering of a lantern is he able to recognize her and see the tears rolling down her cheeks.

"My angel!" he takes her into his arms. "Why this deep sorrow? Whatever it is, my beloved, I am here with you."

She buries her head against his shoulder and sobs openly. "Kiss me. Kiss me as if it were the last time."

CHAPTER 23

The Apothecary of Linz and the Vivid and Continuous Nightmare

November 9, 1812

NIKOLAUS JOHANN BEETHOVEN loved his brother dearly, but there were occasions when he thought Louis would be served better living in an asylum—and this was one of those times. And although Johann—as he preferred to be called in honor of their father—was the youngest of the Beethoven brothers, he found it remarkable that of the three, their mutual acquaintances considered him the mature and stable one in this family. Poor Casper had been ill on and off for years—and despite all the medications and elixirs Johann had sent him, he knew their middle brother was most likely doomed to a short life, one as painfully brief as their parents. And Louis? What wasn't wrong with Louis? A lost-in-the-clouds artist who couldn't even shave or sharpen a pencil without shredding himself? More importantly, Louis couldn't balance his own meager accounts without constantly going into debt, or even converse and disagree according to accepted social norms without turning into a screaming, raging lunatic? A lunatic who threw punches when debates didn't go his way—as the recent scar on Johann's cheek would attest to.

Matters could not have gotten worse since Louis—heartsick and despairing again—had unexpectedly shown up in Linz a month ago and Johann did not know what to do. As he wrestled with the options available to him, he feared the consequences of each possible path, knowing as he did the repercussions would affect the brothers for a lifetime. Aware of this, he sought counsel from Casper through a letter he would draft and send along with a package of medicines to ease his brother's chronic coughing.

However before he was able to do that, he had one last order to complete for the older, white-haired man who stood before him, a seeming veteran of Napoleon's invasion of Russia who suffered frostbite and fatigue. As soon as that task of blending several different elixirs together was complete, he handed the vial to the veteran and watched him shuffle out of the apothecary. Johann returned to his desk, pulled out paper and quill, and began to write.

"My Dearest Brother Casper!

"Yesterday I returned from the Cathedral of Linz and found your letter of last month had arrived. It gave me much joy that your health is indeed improving. It was a farther blessing to learn that your unfortunate wife, Johanna, has escaped the wrath of the courts and will not have to spend an hour longer under arrest. All good wishes to her, to you and my dear nephew, Karl. I would have replied sooner but have not been able to do so until now. The cause of this has been the visit of our brother Louis, who unexpectedly came to Linz from Teplitz—surprise that it was—a month ago in a most frightful state—one that even my chemist's supply of cures could not repair. We must do something but what I do not know.

"You would have cried to have seen him then: ragged, disheveled, agitated at every turn. Still, I embraced him and welcomed him into my home. My housekeeper, Therese Obermeyer, whom you met on the occasion of my farewell picnic at the ruins of Rauhenstein, arranged a comfortable room for Louis upstairs with a stunning view of the Danube—one so sweet and pleasing that locals have nicknamed our shop and residence the "Water Apothecary." Fraulein Obermeyer offered him every manner of kindness and courtesy. Even her daughter, 5-year-old Amalie, took it upon herself to wait on Louis hand and foot. Still during one of his hysterical hallucinations Louis even ordered Amalie to sing for him, all the while insisting that she was a 30-year-old singer from Berlin that he met at the baths. Imagine our venerable brother, weeping at every turn about the

death of love and this innocent child consoling him. Upon his arrival here I imagined him needing a full week to recuperate, and now, though it's been a full month, he is still raging daily as would a madman.

"Much as I love Louis, I cannot possibly remain quiet any longer about his mental state. Although you and I are the younger brothers to Louis, I have often felt as if we are the ones responsible for managing our older brother's business and his often outrageous behavior. When Louis and I first conversed I was truly moved by the account of his pitiful affair with a woman—one whom I believe to be married and with children already. He would not name her or offer up any of the true facts relating to this abortive romance other than repeatedly ranting that the Goddess Isis has abandoned him. Such madness. How often have we heard his plentiful praise of some young beauty that he has been charmed to have made the acquaintance of and perhaps share some form of intercourse with—and to a one, each woman he professes to love, loves him as a musician and appreciates his art—but no more?

"He seems so distraught by the collapse of his latest romantic affair that he works again only with the greatest difficulty. I tried to distract him through music, going so far as to introduce him to my friends, including the Kapellmeister of our local cathedral, Herr Gloggl, who organized several wonderful soirees that normally would have charmed and delighted Louis.

"Though it has always been my fervent wish that all of his compositions are presented and published with great success, I am beginning to imagine that no longer happening. His wellspring of creativity appears drained and his ability to continue as a composer may be in doubt. His hearing has deteriorated ever more so and I fear the longer he dwells on this sad state of affairs, the longer he will remain unproductive. And as we both know, an unproductive and increasingly deaf composer no longer accumulates praise, just debts—debts I am loathe to continually make good on.

"Any success will come all the harder to him and therefore we may experience some new tragedy, such as being obliged to help Louis find the financial means by which he may be able to support himself in the future.

That said, I fear he may require hospice in some asylum if we cannot alter his course of action.

"He repeatedly restates his desire to have some sort of domestic relations with a woman—but one sufficient to the task of living with our mad, sad, crazy brother has not yet appeared on this earth. I fear at the moment it is impossible for fate to favor him in this manner, especially since this month he is preoccupied with a larger and more pressing work, namely interfering with my life.

"And as you will no doubt hear from Louis himself upon his return, it was decidedly not fraternal affection that brought him here to Linz—his absolute and sole desire was to ensure a separation between me and Fraulein Obermeyer. It was never my intention to marry my housekeeper, yet Louis has gotten it into his head that Herr Lyme's sister-in-law—or my little strumpet, as he repeatedly called her—was never going to be deserving of the name Beethoven. Though I confess brother to brother that Fraulein Obermeyer does have a bastard daughter and a bit of a history with men, I take great comfort in having this gentle woman share my bed. It is—or was—a most private arrangement that suited us both all too well. . . . And marriage or any form of a more permanent arrangement, well, that was never ever contemplated. Is it therefore my obligation, to allow Louis to reproach me for taking comfort in the embraces of a willing young woman? Would he not do the same? It is a thousand pities that our beloved and talented brother wastes his time so prodigiously while interfering in matters of the heart that are not his own. Yet our Louis, distraught over the collapse of his latest romantic disaster, did just that. He took it upon himself to prevent that which was never going to happen.

"During his sojourn here, Louis has so completely exceeded the boundaries of acceptable social intercourse, including numerous activities which have been the cause of great embarrassment for me in my own village. He even went to our Bishop and the mayor of our good city to insist they have Fraulein Obermeyer removed from my home. Of course, they practically laughed our mad brother out of their presence, but can you imagine the shame Therese and Amalie experienced? Not to mention my constant humiliation at having to right everything before my own townsmen?

"I suffered enough from Louis's condescension when I lived in Vienna. I hated those fawning aristocrats that surrounded him. Pompous, arrogant—even the von Breunings, who consider themselves more brother to Louis than you or I. If they disliked me, I scorned them equally for their pretensions of superiority through the arts. I have worked hard and suffered much deprivation to reach a modicum of comfort and respect here in Linz. Until Louis let loose with his invectives, I was seen as wealthy, well-respected, and considered a successful participant in our little community.

"When I refused to throw Fraulein Obermeyer out of my house, our distraught brother eventually went so far as to get an order from the local Magistrate's court to have my Therese removed to Vienna as a woman of low moral character if I did not have her discharged from my household by 10 November. That was it. We fought and fought bitterly. Though I can easily hold my own against Louis, he sported a new ring encrusted with jewels which caught me on the cheek and sent blood spewing everywhere as facial wounds often do. Now I am obligated to grow my beard to cover up the scar. After our fight Louis went through his usual cycle of sorrow, anger, remorse, and apology—but I realized I could no longer trust this madman.

"His miserly actions have hastened the very end he wished to preclude. Yes, having returned yesterday from my own visitation with the Bishop of Linz, I am now married to Therese Obermeyer and instantly father to her bastard child Amalie. Like your Karl, she is a sweet girl whose natural father I know not, nor I further confess does my new bride—she who will now and forever be known as a Beethoven.

"I would wish instead that Louis had the wherewithal to draft yet another new symphony instead of composing a concerto of chaos around my life. Let it be in his next libretto that he plays out his delusions and fantasies. Still were it not for his reprehensible behavior, Therese and I would gladly have him remain with us. Given his anger and resentment all hope for fraternity is lost—so this is impossible. And the longer we hesitate and suffer his abuse, the harder it has been for me to call him 'brother.'

"I am frustrated and finished with him. He shall return to Vienna on that same mail coach that carries this package to you. I fear he will only get worse upon his return. Perhaps doctors there can do much more for

him. Who will he blame for it? Me, of course for he has not the good common sense to manage his own miserable existence and so entreats us to respect his invasion of our affairs. Better for him and for all of us if he were to perform his oratorio of blame and shame on friends and lovers of his own account and not mine. I therefore implore you to make a firm resolution and not to let Louis disabuse you of the truth of our circumstances and family history as he has done with our beloved father. I am weary of the lies he tells of our childhood. And be aware that you—or more likely your wife Johanna—will become the renewed target of his wrath.

"I believe the mail coach from Linz to Vienna should be at your home by week's end along with the medicines I have prepared for you. This new elixir should ease your cough more effectively as it contains a blend of morus bark, fritillary bulb, anemarrhena, ophiopogon root, and a tincture of scutellaria. Use it as often as necessary. Would I have the time, know, dear brother, I would have delivered these supplies to you in person. Now that I have a new bride and daughter, it will be a long time yet until I can visit with you in Vienna.

"Your faithful and loving brother, Johann"

As soon as Johann signed the letter, he inserted it into the package for Casper. Leaving his study, he encountered his new wife in the foyer, whom he embraced warmly.

"Well my dear *Frau* Beethoven, have you seen my brother? Is he still upstairs?" Therese smiled at being called '*Frau Beethoven*,' and kissed Johann on the cheek.

"He walked into town with Amalie an hour ago to await the coach."

"With Amalie? And without his bags?"

"We placed them in your wagon before they left. Let him depart in peace. . . . Amalie's presence damps down your brother's temper. And amen to that."

Johann shook his head in frustration then went outside his shop where his cabriolet waited, already packed with Louis's luggage. Taking his buggy whip in hand, Johann drove the five minutes into town to the stage depot.

Adjacent to the depot was a pub and from inside he could clearly hear his brother at the piano playing, appropriately enough, his *Sonata in E-flat major*. After instructing the mail coach driver to transfer Louis's bags, he walked into the pub. As he did so, he passed the old veteran whose order he had just prepared sitting at a table near the door.

"He plays well," said the veteran to Johann.

"Annoyingly so," replied Johann.

Little Amalie sat beside Louis as he pounded out notes. . . . Johann watched as after every few measures Louis would insist that Amalie repeat what he had just done. But she could not. In fact she had absolutely no idea what to do, never having touched a pianoforte before. Louis grew ever more frustrated with Amalie. He even called her "Margaretha," as he grabbed her fingers and forced them to the piano keys. "Like this, Margaretha, you can do this," he insisted as he banged the keys again.

Amalie looked up at Louis with total confusion before twisting around toward Johann. She had tears in her eyes, and that did it for Johann. He quickly took Amalie by the hand and pulled her away from the piano.

"Come, Amalie. We're going home now. Say *auf Wiedersehen* to Uncle Louis," said Johann.

Amalie wiped her tears on her coat sleeve, then waved goodbye.

Johann glared at his brother, "You're a coward and a weakling. Some woman has hurt you, and you, you take revenge on the rest of the world. You want us to feel sorry for you, don't you? Well my brother, I don't. With so much at stake all you can think of is your own feelings. The coach is ready. You best get going, because right now, I hate you."

The old veteran situated himself in the mail coach just ahead of Beethoven, who sat opposite him. They were the only passengers onboard for the journey towards Vienna. The older man's face was weather-beaten, his hair long, grey, and scraggly, his clothes worn and patched, but there was something in his man's twinkling blue eyes that Beethoven must have recognized.

"I know you, don't I?" asked Beethoven.

"It's been my pleasure to know lots of people," replied the man. He stretched out his gnarled hand to B. "Johann Gardner. And you are?"

"Beethoven, Ludwig van Beethoven."

"Ah, the composer. And what was that you were playing?"

"*Das Lebewohl,* a sonata in E-flat major."

"*'The Farewell,'* how appropriate. And the girl, your niece?"

Beethoven snapped off a response, "One never choses one's in-laws."

"Indeed," said Gardner. The veteran was unsure of what to make of this wild-eyed composer who still seemed unusually agitated by the earlier exchange Gardner had witnessed with the Chemist of Linz.

"Bonn, it was Bonn," Beethoven abruptly declared as if he'd just been awarded a prize. "The autumn of 1792, *Frau* Koch's tavern. You're that American writer and teacher. '*The vivid and continuous dream,*' that was you, wasn't it?"

"Excellent memory, *Herr* Beethoven." As a lifelong writer and instructor, the veteran had trained himself to be a keen observer of human nature and he knew that opening a conversation with affirmative compliments often serves to soothe and salve a wounded soul such as the one who sat opposite him. "And you, you've made quite a name for yourself. I've heard your music played from London to Moscow, though never better than in a tiny village outside Vilnius," replied Gardner.

"Are you traveling all the way to Vienna?" B asked as the coach began to roll out of Linz.

"Baden first." Gardner flexed his fingers in front of B. Half stiff and discolored with the aftereffects of frostbite, they ached constantly. "Rest and recovery, before all else. My last six months were in Russia. . . . With Napoleon. . . . A vivid and continuous nightmare, if you will."

"Napoleon troubles my sleep as well. Every time he invades Vienna he makes my life hell."

"Then you've met the man and taken his measure?"

"Only his cannonade when he bombarded Vienna in 1809. For twenty-four straight hours I was compelled to spend every moment huddled in the basement with pillows over my ears to protect them. But your misadventures with that miscreant are certainly more current, *ja*?"

"Yes," said Gardner. With that, the veteran, who had a natural gift for storytelling, let his tale unfold for Beethoven. He recounted how for most of the past 20 years he supported himself by writing and teaching. His manuscripts, mostly novels with an historical bent, he sent back to a publisher in New York, where they sold briskly. That income plus the extra coin he earned teaching had allowed him to live comfortably while traveling all about the continent. About a year ago, while in Berlin, he heard of a position in Vilnius for an English teacher and translator. Fluent in a half dozen languages already and anxious to improve his command of Eastern European tongues, he set out overland on horseback for Lithuania. Approaching from the south, on Christmas Day he found himself at the village of Smorgonie, a few day's travel from Vilnius. As it was growing cold and dark he sought out a room, the only one being in a small boarding house adjacent to the local Jewish synagogue. The proprietress, a slim, dark-haired woman of perhaps 30 named Sima Krane, noted that they had no meals prepared that evening but if *Herr* Gardner so desired, he could join the neighboring congregation next door for her cousin's wedding. The entire community was there as were a number of musicians from Vilnius. She assured Gardner that he would not only be welcomed warmly as one greets the Prophet Elijah on Passover; he would be well fed and entertained.

"I arrived there just in time to hear this village orchestra perform one of your works," he said to Beethoven as the coach bounced along the road.

"Dreadfully done I'm sure," said Beethoven. Gardner watched the still over-emotional Beethoven cringing, no doubt at the thought of one of his compositions being performed by peasants.

"Quite the contrary. The performance was exquisite—and perhaps life changing. It was to my admittedly untrained ears the finest performance of compositional music I had ever experienced in the entirety of my 47 years on this earth. Later I learned it was your *Violin Concerto in D major*. I found in your music the analog to my compositions and teachings and swore to learn more about them. I've even considered doing a novel about a musician such as yourself but structured as if it were a piano concerto—and here you are!"

"*Ja*, fate has graciously knocked on our door," said Beethoven, whose manner, though sincere, still rang ever so slightly manic—and even a bit pompous. "Whom else can one consult concerning that great goddess of art except another practitioner? Indeed, *Herr* Gardner, we shall travel together with the muses as our companions. May they bless our journey."

"*Prosit*," said Gardner, as he toasted Beethoven with the elixir that Johann had prepared. "May the goddess enfold us in her wings and transport us to Elysium!"

"*Prosit*," echoed Beethoven.

"I must share with you, *Herr* Beethoven, that the violinist that night, a young woman, the bride actually, was as brilliant as this secular Hebrew wedding ceremony was unorthodox. I'm no expert in music, but her performance was that of a true virtuoso. Every note she played on this exceptional violin she wielded, from the high end of the register to the most mellow low ones, echoed directly into my soul. She brought joy and tears to my heart as no one ever had before. Her name was Liliana. . . . Liliana Dona-something. . . ."

"Donishefski? Was it Liliana Donishefski?" Beethoven's eyes lit up.

"Indeed. You know of her?" The serendipity of them both encountering the same young women surprised Gardner.

"Truly. She studied here in Vienna some years back when she was just a teenager. My poor assistant, Ries, had a crush on her but could never . . . Never mind. . . . Liliana played an excellent cello, but I was soon to discover she was even more gifted on the violin. In fact while waiting for Ries to show up one day, Liliana saw a draft lying about of my *Violin Sonata in A major,* the one known as the "*Kreutzer,*" and asked if she could run through it with me. Though not expecting much, I played pianoforte while she read the score over my shoulder. Mind you, the *A major* demands on a violinist are extraordinary. It calls for true virtuosity. No mere amateur could ever master this work, not then or since. Still, after going through it once, I was so impressed with her playing that afterwards I leapt up from the keyboard to salute her with these words, *'Fantastic! Once more, my dear girl.'* By now Ries had entered my apartment and he watched in astonishment as we played it once again for him—only this time Liliana did it without even looking at the score. In that first reading she had committed the entirety to memory . . . and that's a feat no musician does except perhaps a Mozart. Her command of the third movement finale was a tour de force. . . . To this day she's the only violinist who can play it as crisp and at as fast a tempo as I intended. So tell me, her husband? Whom did she marry? Another musician who appreciates her genius, I hope."

"Perhaps even better. You know of the *luthier,* Reuven Silke?

"Only through his instruments. Liliana had one of his cellos with her when she was in Vienna. She married this Reuven?"

"Yes, and his wedding gift was a violin he crafted especially for her: *La Immortale Adorato.* As you can probably imagine, when Liliana played her solo it was so sweet, so touching, but with a power and gusto that astonished. . . . Members of the congregation openly wept and I counted myself among them. Yes, my friend, it was one moment of perfection to be savored in our lives—lives that are all too often filled with tragedy. It was that rare most perfect day of joy, a day this conjugal pair celebrated with their community and beloveds. They even concluded the evening with a grand chorus, everyone singing the *Finale* from your opera *Fidelio*. I envied them," said Gardner, who unexpectedly broke into song with a powerful yet sensitive voice. . . .

"Oh Lord!—What a moment this!
Oh unspeakable happiness!
Just, oh Lord, your judgment is, You try us, you desert us not."

Beethoven covered his face with his hands and shook his head back and forth and moaned, "Oh my God, to have that, to experience that, oh to have been there. Not 'there' there, you understand, not in Lithuania, but to be anyway, anytime, with a beloved woman, oh to have experienced that one perfect moment of joy. I envy you, *Herr* Gardner, much as you envied Liliana and Reuven."

"Yes, but such joy was only a prelude to my nightmare. Joy is always ephemeral, *Herr* Beethoven; it flees as a mouse before a cat, or the cat before a wolf, and my odyssey has been no different."

"We have each had our share of darkness, *Herr* Gardner, but do kindly continue with yours. And please, address me as 'Louis,' as my friends do, for I feel this journey shall bind us as true brothers." Beethoven thrust his hand out towards Gardner once again.

Gardner accepted Beethoven's handshake, though this too felt agitated. The cost of genius, the veteran thought as he recommenced his narrative. He shared how the next morning he traveled on to Vilnius in the company of the musicians who had played along in support of Liliana. They made for good travel companions and in no time he found himself inside the gates of the city Jews in the region called the New Jerusalem. There he was again welcomed warmly.

"A new Jerusalem!" exclaimed Beethoven. "I have experienced visions of the old Jerusalem in my dreams. A new Jerusalem. . . . Though I have never seen these provinces, I should like to go there some day. But tell me the truth. . . . When Liliana was in Vienna, she spoke of how she trembled before her first performance in Vilnius's Grand Synagogue when she was but 10 or 12 years old. She claims it seats five thousand. Is it truly that spacious?"

"Indeed. Do you understand the precarious position of the Hebrews in our Christian lands? When the Grand Synagogue was constructed some 200 years ago, it was built of stone and on a massive scale, for it was also intended to serve as a stronghold within which the Jews could take refuge in times of danger—no rare occurrence there given the numerous *pogroms* launched by their neighbors, all of whom proved hostile. Though they were a plurality in the city, with four of every ten inhabitants being a Hebrew, power alternately resided with either of their three antagonists: the Poles, the Lithuanians, or their Russian overlords—and they in turn fought with one another for supremacy. Though the four groups have co-existed for hundreds of years, there is no measure of affection amongst them. The Jews were most often oppressed by whichever of their Christian neighbors was on top. And as church ecclesiastical regulations specified that a synagogue could not be built higher than a church, the Hebrews, in order to obey the law and yet create the desired interior height, dug a foundation deep enough for the synagogue's floor level to be well below that of the street. Outside, the synagogue looked to be about three stories tall, but inside it soared to over five. Even Napoleon, who stood on the threshold of this synagogue on the eve of his Russian invasion, gazed at the interior and was speechless with admiration for their ingenuity."

Gardner recollected that his new employers were secular Jews who had established a college of science and literature not long after Napoleon had granted equal rights of citizenship to the Hebrews and ordered the gates of the ghetto torn down. At first everything was wonderful. Vilnius was beautiful, his lodgings cozy and comfortable, and his students eager, smart, and enthusiastic. He even had an occasional lover, a charming young woman who owned a local bakery up on a small hill overlooking the city, appropriately called 'The Bread Loaf.'

On the surface every aspect of his new life seemed perfect but he could never shake a feeling that something was amiss and deeply troubling. Every time he went out, he saw joy on people's faces but behind them, he noticed—or rather, felt—an aura of shadows and darkness, of *Nacht und Nebel,* night and fog. There was this invisible sense of foreboding that clung to the city. And in the evening when he fell into bed he experienced nightmares. Not just once but almost every night. Each evening after he crawled under his feather quilt and blew out the candles that lit his room, he slept only fitfully and was disturbed with endless dark torments. He heard women screaming, babies crying, men shouting. He saw the flashing of knives and bayonets, the sparking of guns, bombs exploding, body parts rotting in the streets. A dog running through an alley, a human arm in its teeth. Blood everywhere.

Even on the nights he spent with his lover, the nightmares kept coming. He dreamed he saw her frail body stripped naked and thrown live into a crematorium. On another night inside those now dreaded visions he watched a mother hide in a basement from green-uniformed soldiers with rifles. She cupped her hands over the mouth of her baby so its screams of hunger would not alert her pursuers. She escaped their dreaded round up only to discover that, in so doing, she had smothered and killed her own child.

"There are doctors in Vienna," said B, "who specialize in the interpretation of such dreams. After your stay in Baden, perhaps you should consult with one."

"And I'm a writer who reuses such experiences to plot the pages of my books just as you turn the beatings of your heart into the pleadings of a pianoforte sonata." Gardner insisted that he had no explanation for these forebodings other than the invisible hate that existed beneath the calm of the city. He would awake each morning in terror, while outside his apartment, the day would dawn sunny and beautiful. Children played in the streets, young wives went about their shopping in the market, and his students enthusiastically read in translation the great books he shared with them, Voltaire, Cervantes, and Machiavelli. He changed apartments twice, altered his diet, eschewed spices, even stopped drinking hard spirits—but the nightmares did not stop and his unease at being in this new Jerusalem grew ever more potent.

When the French arrived in June preparing for their invasion of Russia, they needed translators and, anxious to escape the foreboding he felt, Gardner volunteered to join them on what he thought would be a quick victory against Czar Alexander I. His first assignment brought him coincidently right back to Smorgonie on the opening day of the invasion in the company of a cavalry patrol. His task was to arrange with Reuven Silke for the secret caching of a cask, a barrel some eight feet tall, in the basement of the new synagogue.

"What was in the barrel? Corsican wine for the Bonapartes?" asked Beethoven. "And if so, why leave it with the Jews?"

"Napoleon's proclamations about rights and religious freedom found favor among the Hebrews. Reuven, who held the congregation together after his father's death until they could engage a new rabbi, was only too happy to secret the barrel away—And there it would stay hidden until the French either returned or sent for it. I was never told the contents, but given the weight and noise the cask made when moved, it wasn't wine—though you should know that our Napoleon never travels anywhere without cases of Malbec from the Dordogne in his supply wagon. Maybe it's just the novelist in me but I've long suspected that the barrel was filled with bags of gold and silver *francs*. . . ."

"And after that brief adventure in Smorgonie," Gardner continued, "by virtue of my age, life experience, and wisdom, I was assigned to stay with Bonaparte and his command staff. As such I not only had an insider's view of the General and his strategies, which at first felt brilliant and confident, I was provided with a daily ration of that Malbec. An excellent red."

Gardner went on to explain to Beethoven how Czar Alexander out-Napoleoned Napoleon. If Bonaparte had declared that war was the path of deception, then it was the French Emperor who in his own arrogance failed to realize he was the one being deceived. The more confident the French grew as they chased the Russians across the steppes, the more Alexander refused to meet the French in open combat. The Czar feigned timidity and weakness and thus the Russians steadily retreated into the heartland, constantly evading the strengths of the *Grande Armée*. As the Russian army fell back, their Cossacks horsemen were given the task of burning villages, towns, and crops so that the French, who were dependent on living off the land, would be unable to supplement their vulnerable supply lines that stretched hundreds of miles back to the west. This scorched-earth tactic greatly surprised and disturbed the French. Even Napoleon, a student of Machiavelli and republican populist that he was, found the willingness of the Russians to destroy their own territory and harm their own people difficult to comprehend.

"Not for me," interrupted Beethoven with even more agitation in his voice. "I know much about this Alexander and his tactics through my dear friend, Count Razumovsky, the Russian Ambassador to the Hapsburgs. The brutality of the Russian, even in our era of Enlightenment, is something even Razumovsky detested. Ten years ago I dedicated my violin *Sonata in A major Opus 30 Number One,* to this young Czar and he has yet to honor the bill. Your sad account makes me ever more heartened I made the right choice when I cut the fourth movement of that sonata and moved it to the '*Kreutzer'* as the *Finale Presto* after hearing Liliana play it at my apartment."

"Yes, the behavior of the Russians forced the French to squander troops defending a supply system that was incapable of feeding such a massive army in the field. And as the old adage goes," said Gardner to Beethoven, "an army travels on its belly. Hunger and privation compelled French soldiers to leave their camps at night to forage for food. These men were frequently confronted by parties of Cossacks, who captured or killed them. The *Grand Armée* became less grand with every mile of Bonaparte's invasion. . . .

"Nonetheless, through a series of forced marches Napoleon pushed his army rapidly through the western steppes in an attempt to compel the Russians to fight. We traveled surprisingly fast for such an unwieldy body of men. Bonaparte's soldiers won a number of minor engagements that enlivened the spirits of his troops but in truth meant nothing strategically and in fact only added to the forces of attrition diminishing his army. Although the Czar's forces under General Kutuzov continued to retreat, they would nonetheless send their mounted Cossacks to harass the long column of French soldiers at our most vulnerable points—our supply wagons—in lightening raids. These attacks, which caused considerable damage, quickly worked to undermine morale. Sadly, we lost most of the feed for our horses not to mention Bonaparte's Malbec to those vodka-drinking swine. . . .

"In August, after two months of this war of attrition, Napoleon finally caught up to the Russians at Smolensk, the city where Bonaparte had planned to winter his troops. And though we thought we had our foes cornered, the Russian's once more slipped away from the engagement while leaving the city to burn. The destruction of Smolensk troubled Napoleon. He was forced to change plans. Thus, we pursued the Russians deeper into their country and ever closer to the capital at Moscow."

"After yet another month the French encircled General Kutuzov at Borodino with 130,000 troops," said Gardner. "But Kutuzov held the high ground in well-defended positions. It was already autumn and the grasses that were turning brown were soon to be stained red in what proved to be the single bloodiest battle of this campaign. The *Grande Armée* did capture the Russian positions, but in victory our Napoleon lost 30,000 troops—men who now lay dead or dying upon that battlefield. He considered chasing and then crushing the retreating Russians who lost twice that number but feared risking his only reserves so far from home. That day I watched Napoleon vacillate—a truly rare event for a general normally so decisive. In the end he decided not to send in his own Imperial Guards who might have won the day and perhaps the war. Was he right? I don't know. Kutuzov escaped with the remnants of his army, battered as it was, and as the cliché goes, the Russians lived to fight yet another day. . . ."

"If you had seen one day of war, *Herr* Beethoven, you would pray to God that you would never witness another. Just before night fell a chill wind blew in from the north accompanied by snow flurries. There is no way to describe the carnage. Afterwards I walked the battlefield with Napoleon and General Beynac. They both sought to offer hope to the wounded—most of whom would later freeze to death where they lay that night. At one captured artillery position, we came upon a Russian soldier dying and unconscious. His dog, a full grown wolfhound, would not leave his side. Howling with grief the animal lay by its master and refused to move until Beynac put a bullet through its head. Napoleon turned to me and said, '*This has been the most terrible of all our battles. Though my Grand Armée showed itself to be worthy of victory, the Russians have proved themselves invincible.*' Whether it was the icy winds or fear or just the realization that in triumph he had lost all chance of winning the war, I saw Napoleon tremble uncontrollably from head to toe, so much so that when he tried to draw out his sword and use it as a cane to stabilize himself, the blade dropped from his hand and he fell to his knees."

"You witnessed that? On his knees, Napoleon quaking in fear?"

"Yes. . . . Shaken to the core. . . . An admission of his own mortality. . . . Even General Beynac, that gruff old warrior, was stunned to see the Emperor thusly and insisted that none of us say a word about it to anyone. A week later we reached the gates of Moscow, but in another twist of events that Bonaparte found puzzling, there was no delegation to meet us in surrender. The Russians had evacuated and ordered the entire city burnt to the ground. This denied us, the occupying forces, sufficient food and shelter to remain long in their capital. Napoleon's prescience proved sadly correct: Victory on the battlefield did not bring him victory in this war. The loss of Moscow meant little to the Czar, who refused to sue for peace. Alexander knew—as we all did—that with winter fast approaching, our position would grow worse with each passing day. Napoleon again vacillated. Alexander's strategies truly confounded Bonaparte, who was torn between staying in Moscow throughout the winter or retreating back to the safety of Lithuania and the Duchy of Warsaw. After several weeks of indecision Napoleon ordered us back out on the road to Vilnius, now some five hundred wintery miles away. . . .

"Not long after departing Moscow the weather turned against us. Snow fell in enormous flakes all through the day and night. When marching we lost sight not only of the sky, but of the men and wagons in front of us. Then came the cold, so bitter and hard. Though swathed in fur and heavy coats, we had no protection for our faces. Our lips became cracked, our noses frost-bitten, our eyes blinded by the glare. We were constantly harassed by Cossacks, and though the road was miserable, it did not pay to wander off. For those French soldiers who did stray, Russian peasants were there to welcome them with black bread, vodka, and a warm bed. The troops that went to sleep drunk never woke up. Those hospitable peasants would slit the throats of the French and feed their bodies to their pigs and dogs. I myself saw sixty dead and dying naked men lying in a row against a fallen tree trunk as the local peasants bashed their brains out with clubs and axes. For many of us the struggle to eat and get shelter became the only thing that mattered. There was no fodder for the horses that pulled our wagons. Many a steed died from eating snow. During the day, the temperature was so cold that men could cut strips of half-frozen flesh from living horses without the beasts noticing. Men ate that meat raw to sustain themselves. Others drank the coagulated blood of the dead or dying horses. At dusk the troops would disembowel the horses that had died and then crawl inside the carcasses to keep warm. To sleep without protection was instant death. Many were the frozen corpses I tripped over merely trying to make my way forward. To think these bodies were once our cheerful companions and protectors. And sadly, as soon as anyone died, either of wounds or frostbite, his fellows would strip him of his boots and clothes, take the food from his knapsack, and then leave the naked body unburied for the wolves. The unrelenting cold drove all pity from our hearts."

"How is it then that you are here? And what of Bonaparte?"

"My last sighting of Napoleon was during a surprise attack on our supply lines by a small group of Cossacks who raced in on horseback. Though the enemy did not realize it at the time, they almost captured the Emperor and we, his aides and staff. Only a quick counterattack by his personal guards saved us all that day. It was then I knew I had to escape or die trying—to stay was surely tantamount to death. Taking the stallion of a dead Cossack, I fled south away from the battle lines and made my way to warmth and safety."

"Such horror. . . . Does Napoleon yet live?" asked Beethoven. "If he perishes, I have already written his requiem."

"I know not, but even if he does, all of his fair-weather allies will desert him and change sides. The revolution is over, the Empire is lost. As I traveled farther west, I heard rumors that in Paris a former general, Claude-Francois de Malet, had staged a coup with troops from the National Guard. Even if Napoleon lives, all Europe salivates at the prospect of turning out the Bonapartes."

"No doubt we will see yet another war rape this continent. And you, *Herr* Gardner, what will you do next? Will you write again?"

Gardner pulled a bound volume out of his luggage. "What is a novel, but a collection of lies we tell to reveal greater truths? I will heal in Baden first and if fortune shines on me I will purge this vivid and continuous nightmare from my soul before ever putting pen to paper."

"You will no doubt find the spas of Baden akin to the sacred Temple of Isis," said Beethoven with a renewed touch of mania in his voice, "it's a sanctuary for rebirth, a place where the Goddess's purified fire shall swallow up all of your troubles. Perhaps you will find the arms of Isis more welcoming of you than they have been to me. I have seen the death of love herself. However, praise be, you shall awake anew as would a phoenix. . . ."

"Have you read the poet Schiller?" Gardner asked. His question triggered another fevered response from Beethoven.

"His *'Ode to Joy'* is among my favorites—one I hope to someday set to music. Schiller's poetry excites me not only because of its content but also because of its rhythms. Such language begs me to compose. It's task enough to score the work of any great poet and reveal their spiritual depth through the agency of harmony and voice, but for a writer as immortal as Schiller, well, he deserves no less than my best."

"I have faith that whenever you do take on the 'Ode,' *Herr* Louis, it will be done brilliantly. Napoleon loved Schiller as well and when we camped at night on that frightful retreat, the Emperor lent me his copy for solace. I would read a few lines, then look up at the night sky and wonder aloud if above that starry canopy, a loving father did indeed dwell? Or would this tragedy put an end to my existence, alone and in tears? Or would some measure of good fortune assure that I survive long enough to share life's jubilation with my true friends? Or with a noble wife? "

Beethoven reached across the space between them and embraced Gardner as one would a brother and then asked with all seriousness, "Throughout your travails, did you ever sense the power and wisdom of our Creator?"

"Wisdom?" Gardner laughed heartily at Beethoven's naivety as he handed him the book he had pulled from his luggage. "*Herr* Louis, it doesn't take much to see that in this crazy world, the problems of a few little people don't amount to a hill of beans—even for our Lord. Do you understand that? I mean truly, truly understand that?"

Beethoven opened the book as if looking for answers and then showed surprise when he realized the pages were blank.

"It's a *Tagebuch,* a diary," said Gardner. "My gift to you. Having witnessed that little scene between you and your brother back in Linz, God knows you'll have more need for it than I. And from everything you've told me about your recent disappointments, I don't imagine you're going to be being very productive these next few years. If I should ever write a novel about you, I am going to need to capture those inner thoughts you will fail to express through music."

CHAPTER 24

Beethoven's Tagebuch, A First Entry or The Piano Sonata in C minor, Opus 111

YOU MUST not be a human being, not for yourself but only for others: for you there is no longer any happiness except within your art. Oh God! Give me the strength to conquer myself; nothing at all must fetter me to life. With her everything has gone to ruin.

Submission, deepest submission to your fate, for only by this sacrifice can such disappointment serve. Oh what hard struggle! You shall still find everything that your most cherished wish can grant, yet you must bend your will to it. Maintain an absolutely steady attitude. Do everything that still has to be done to arrange what is necessary for the long journey.

CHAPTER 25

La Immortale Adorato

The Village of Smorgonie on the Night of December 3rd & 4th, 1812

LILIANA DONISHEFSKI-SILKE never expected to spend her 27th birthday pregnant with twins and waiting to be dragged in front of one of Napoleon Bonaparte's firing squads while conjuring up memories of Beethoven and the healing power of his music. These past few months since her wedding to Reuven had gone from the best of times to the worst—times when no cruelty, no barbarism, no depravity was left impossible and evil held sway over her land. Once before, when she was a teenager in Vienna, Beethoven had unexpectedly emerged as her champion and protector from the likes of Prince Lichnowsky and Bridgetower, and she prayed that he—or at least his music—would save her again. And she vowed to herself that if she survived beyond sunrise, she would find a way to lead what was left of her family out of this hell.

Through a window in the basement she could see outside to the square in front of the synagogue where the former contents of Reuven's workshop had been turned into a bonfire. Polish Light Cavalry troops who had fought alongside the French against the Russians warmed themselves around the embers of some of the most exquisite string instruments the world would never hear again. Liliana watched as a quartet of Reuven's creations—two violins, a cello, and a viola—ones he had just completed on order for the French Counsel General in Vilnius—were added to the bonfire. The instruments composing this quartet were all made from the same imported woods and painstakingly decorated as a matched set. Designed to honor the French Republic and the Revolution, they were each designated in turn as *Liberté, Égalité, Fraternité,* and *Justice*. The Poles even burnt Reuven's wooden tools, shelving, and supplies—not that any of it would matter to Reuven anymore. Her husband was dead, murdered along with dozens of other Jews by marauding Lithuanians at Ponary woods less than a month ago.

None of God's chaos in the shadow of this new Jerusalem, the Promised Land, made sense to her anymore. How was it that she now sat prisoner along with other women of her village in the basement of the very synagogue they had all helped rebuild by hand after it was burnt down by the Cossacks when all they had wanted to do was mourn their dead. Guarding the doors outside was that ragtag squad of Polish horsemen. The Poles—half starved and nearly frozen—had arrived first in Smorgonie to secure the town for the arrival of the retreating Napoleon and his command staff. The villagers initially welcomed the return of these French allies but instead of treating the Hebrews as friends, the anti-Semitic Poles ignored the orders of their officers and rampaged through the town, looting, raping, and killing anyone who stood in their way.

Yes, chaos and more chaos. It had been that way for weeks now. Once word of the disastrous French retreat from Moscow had spread, all order in the provinces of Lithuania and Poland broke down. Ancient hatreds and rivalries reemerged. Ethnic Russians fought with ethnic Poles who fought with ethnic Lithuanians and all of them attacked the Jews. The Hebrew's crime? The old standby of anti-Semites: blood libel. The Poles accused the Jews of murdering Christian children to use their blood in satanic rituals. That such claims were old lies told to inflame hatred made no difference to these illiterate and uneducated soldiers.

It had been well after midnight when Liliana had heard the crackle of gunfire outside yet again. She had wondered who had been silenced now and when would it be her turn to die? Soon thereafter Napoleon himself had entered the basement with Generals Murat and Beynac, all three of whom looked haggard and frostbit. Bonaparte was a small man with a thick, overgrown beard. Bundled up from the relentless cold, he little resembled the portraits Liliana had seen of the great and powerful emperor.

"Lève-toi!" Beynac had ordered. "Stand up."

Liliana had hastily translated the French into Yiddish for the other women, "He wants us to get up." Barely able to stand herself, Liliana's mind was whirling. Her limbs had gone weak, her mouth dry, her body shook, and her hair felt as if standing on end. How could any good come from this? All signs had bode evil. Her willpower was paralyzed by utter confusion. What stratagem would overcome this sorrow and pain that sapped her of all strength?

Napoleon had pointed to *La Immortale Adorato* which rested on a table beside the synagogue's pianoforte. *"Qui joue du violon,"* he had asked. "Who plays the violin?" His voice was firm, powerful, and absolute.

At first no one had spoken, no one that is until Napoleon fixed Liliana in his gaze, and she finally recovered her tongue and replied with equal resolution.

"I do," she had said, remembering what Beethoven had once said to her when she trembled before a solo concert. *"Despair and weakness in a time of crisis are mean and unworthy of you."* B had been kind and gentle with her back in Vienna, offering up the mental tools to guide her interpretation of any score. *"Do not yield to such weakness."* B had treated her as an equal talent, albeit one with less experience, but a peer nonetheless. He insisted she face the world with *unerschütterlicher Gelassenheit*—a skill she would now rely on if she was ever to save her life and those of her friends held in captivity around her. Liliana needed every bit of that strength and reassurance as she stared back into Napoleon's blue-grey eyes.

"Then play," Napoleon had insisted.

His request had startled Liliana. What cruelty was this? To fiddle on their way to the firing squad? To play for their lives? Or was this their opportunity? She didn't know. In truth Liliana was so numbed by the events of the past month as to be beyond caring. *"Fear is our only true foe,"* Beethoven had once said to her with heroic theatrical gestures so grand they were almost comical. He had melded his favorite quotes from Homer and the Hindus into a goulash of heroic spiritual wisdom that somehow worked and she had loved him for it, "*When tragedy arises"* he would tell her, *"the wise grieve neither failure nor success. If you have fallen, if your hour has come, embrace the moment and find inspiration. Arise with a brave heart; and ere you perish strike some valiant deed whose echo men shall hear for all time. That will vanquish your enemy."* Yes, she would play for the Emperor Napoleon, but what? Liliana's mind raced through her repertoire, scanning for a piece both sublime and majestic, one that would not only explode upon Bonaparte with divine power, but would also strike a blow of defiance. Nothing less than a tour de force would do. . . . And then in a flash it had come to her. . . .

Liliana turned to her cousin, Sima Krane, who stood beside her and whispered, "*Kreutzer, Finale Presto.*" The third movement of Beethoven's *Opus 47* was B's most brilliant splash of virtuosity. Driven by tarantella dance rhythms and with a whirlwind finale, *Opus 47* was the most dazzling violin section Beethoven had ever composed, one where he had driven the genre to unheard-of limits.

Without hesitation, Sima slid onto the bench of the pianoforte. Liliana moved to tune the *Adorato.* Although she and Sima had played together since childhood and knew each other's style intimately, this performance—perhaps their last—would be one for the ages, one which Liliana was determined that—victorious or not—would resonate for all time. . . .

As she adjusted the tuning pegs, she noticed just below them a Hebrew inscription scratched into the wood that she had never seen before. They were in Reuven's handwriting and now represented his last words to her: "*Even when our power over men and gods or the wealth of an empire seems lost and empty, know this: There has never been a time when you and I have not lived and loved nor will there ever be a time when truth fails us on the path of eternal liberation. Beyond the sacred altar of our affection lies a font of gold. In the hours of darkness, draw strength, transport, and freedom from it"*.

She missed Reuven. Caressing his gift to her, the *Immortale Adorato,* in her arms for perhaps the last time, Liliana lifted her bow and prepared to strike the first note. With the whole world crumbling, how was it that they had picked this time to fall in love? Liliana never imaged Reuven would perish so young, perish before their twins were born, perish before they saw tomorrow. Aware she had scant minutes to perhaps save their lives and those of her yet unborn children—yes, the future—Liliana locked eyes with Napoleon and ever so slightly nodded her head *mit unerschütterlicher Gelassenheit.* Liliana signaled her cousin, *"Un, deux, trois. . . ."*

On the count of three, Sima nailed the opening chord which Liliana followed with eight and one half minutes of white-hot violin playing. Knowing nothing less than her best would suffice, her mind raced back to Beethoven's words. *"Art, the persecuted one, always finds an asylum. Did not Daedalus, shut up in the labyrinth, invent the wings which carried him out into the open air?"* I shall find them too, these wings, she thought as she played.

Liliana felt Reuven's strength and warm embrace fill her soul with every note emanating from the *Immortale Adorato.* This gave her a power beyond human capacity, a power belonging to the gods, the likes of which stunned Napoleon who had never encountered anyone who played as dynamically as her before. It was as Beethoven had said when he taught her to not only read the notes of a piece but to uncover their soul and spirit. *"Life is short, art eternal, and by performing one's own craft, one worships the Creator who dwells in every creature. Such worship brings us to fulfillment. By devotion to one's own particular talent, everyone can attain perfection."*

And it was perfection that she needed now, the *"Kreutzer"* being the musical equivalent of a high-speed clash between two master swordsmen dueling back and forth with rapiers. First one took the lead, then the other attacked, then the first came back again and again and again. Liliana bowed the strings ever faster, until they felt as if they'd burst into flames. But she knew the *Adorato* would hold—

there was no finer violin ever—a magical gift from her beloved. And sadly, there would be no more. Through the basement window behind Napoleon she could still see the conflagration outside as it thoroughly consumed *Liberté, Égalité, Fraternité,* and *Justice.*

As she wondered where those four mercies were now, B's decade-old lessons flowed through her consciousness with every note of the "*Kreutzer.*" "*Even a little step toward spiritual awareness will protect you from the greatest fears. It is the war within,*" he had said, "*The struggle for self-mastery that every human must wage if we are to emerge from life victorious. On this path of discovery effort never goes to waste and there is no failure. Go on,*" he would insist, "*do not practice art alone but penetrate to her heart; she deserves it, for only thusly can she raise us to the godhead and life eternal.*"

Life and death. At least her Reuven had died a happy man, secure in his ignorance of the nightmares that followed. Yes, ignorance was bliss. Reuven had been the first to be killed by a single shot that came from out of nowhere and only his ghost would know anything of the brutality that came in the wake of the French retreat. Reuven had left Smorgonie by wagon five weeks ago, heading for Vilnius. He was to use some of the money the French paid to hide their cask to hire a new rabbi for Smorgonie.

Reuven had travelled through Vilnius to meet the French Counsel General and then southwest of the city to the woodland town of Ponary to meet the young *Yeshiva* graduate, Rabbi Elijah Novasolek, and return with him to Smorgonie. As they left Ponary, Reuven shared with the novice rabbi much about Smorgonie and the congregation. He was in the midst of telling Elijah how happy he was that Liliana was expecting twins in February, when a single gunshot passed through Reuven's heart. He died instantly. The rabbi was not so lucky. Along with two dozen of his fellow villagers, Novasolek was among the first group of Jews rounded up and driven at gun point into the forest by their former Lithuanian neighbors and friends. The novice rabbi was stripped of his clothes, tied to a tree, shaved from head to toe, and castrated by the village barber. He was then compelled to bear witness as the rest of the male prisoners were ordered to dig a massive pit that would serve as their grave. When the digging was done, the men were all stripped of their possessions and clothes, lined up at the lip of the pit, and shot by the very Lithuanian merchants, farmers, and shopkeepers they had patronized for decades. A group of women and young girls taken from the village next were even less fortunate. They too were robbed, stripped, and then raped repeatedly until the Lithuanians—young men, old men, teenagers, killers all—were fully satiated. Those women that resisted were gutted like pigs on a spit. Afterwards the now naked and traumatized women were thrown live into the pits. Babies and little children were likewise tossed wailing and screaming into that hellhole. These unfortunates cried and begged for mercy until one by one they were shot and silenced by their neighbors as if they were animals jammed into a slaughterhouse. A second wave of captives was brought in to shovel dirt on top of the first victims; and after the second waves was disposed of, a third wave was similarly brought in. The killing continued all day and all night until the village of Ponary was empty of Jews. When the orgy of abuse and murder ended, the Lithuanians dumped firewood and cooking oil onto the remains and set them all ablaze. The acrid smoke comprised of burning human flesh could be seen and smelt all the way back to Vilnius. It was a scent Rabbi Elijah Novasolek never forgot, for only Elijah was left alive, like the Biblical prophet to speak of the unspeakable horrors he had witnessed.

And now? And now Reuven's quartet was little more than a tragic footnote to that ungodly history, the last legacy of a *luthier* who loved his work, who loved his wife, who loved his unborn children, who loved his people, and whose bloodied body was burnt and buried along with innumerable kinsman in that horrid but as yet unmarked pit in the forest.

As Liliana and her cousin rocketed through the last bars of *Opus 47*, the door to the basement blew open and a gust of wind-driven snow showered over Napoleon. Like a dog trembling through a nightmare, the Emperor began to shake uncontrollably. Fate be damned, she thought, *Love alone liberates us from your chains.* Liliana would not let go of Napoleon's blue-grey eyes. *Vive la revolution!* With her last ounce of strength, she would force him to see what she saw: a savagery, a brutality that mocked their grandest dreams; *Liberté, Égalité, Fraternité, Justice*? Where were they now?

CHAPTER 26

Song for a Distant Beloved or a Pregnant Pause on the Path to Elysium

THE FIRES guarding the entrance to Isis's temple burn evermore fierce, and I am left to wonder if I will ever be capable of passing through those flames to enter her sanctuary and be reborn in Elysium? Or is it my muse's intention to use her ring of fire to block my entrance and thus abandon me for all eternity? Is she so capricious and uncaring? Like Prometheus of old, have I dared too close to revelations reserved for the gods alone?

"Are we not the children of our own works?" observes N. He sits at our sanctuary beside Isis's temple dressed in the rainbow hued robes of a Hindoo sage that are as bright and colorful as his army of butterflies. His clothes contrast sharply against the storm clouds above us that darken the sky with what must be the anger of the gods. A chill wind swirls dust devils around our desert oasis. My hands and feet feel drained of warmth. It is as if the vitality of my flesh now surrenders bit by bit to that dark and creeping shadow we call death.

"What have I done in this life that I should thus be barred from entry? Surely Isis, my sweet goddess of compassion will help me, guide me, and grant me this, my final wish. . . . One day, one day of pure joy for her poor Beethoven."

"Only your soul can answer that but to find the truth you must be brave enough to confront your every weakness and flaw and we're still just getting started. Remember, B, between the extremes of greed and fear lies courage."

"Courage? Why must we always prove our courage to the Gods?" I ask. The heavens above us continue to grow ever ominous, triggering irregular flashes of lightning. The scent of an impending snow storm lingers in the air. "And what about Liliana, didn't she prove hers before Napoleon? Does she yet live? Did she survive the winter of 1812? And her unborn twins, what of them?"

N turns the question back around, "What would you have done, B? Feed and shelter Napoleon's soldiers? Or let the lives of a few women stall his troops while the hungry wolves of the Russian army nip at their heels? Wasn't it the Emperor's duty to preserve order with what was left of the *Grande Armée*?"

"The problems of the world are not my department. I've no desire to tangle in politics, nor would I ever deign to serve as an emperor, a general, or a master of war. I'm a musician. Our lives are tragic enough without the provocation of the military. Better to sing songs in praise of love and our common humanity. May the daughters of Elysium let me compose a piece that brings people together, not apart, one that casts off and discards such hatreds."

"As I suspected, B, you're a rank sentimentalist. You know how you sound? *'Not interested in politics.'* Like a man who's trying to convince himself of something he doesn't believe in his heart. Each of us has a destiny, for good or for evil. . . . And occasionally, a little of each. . . . Fortunately for you, for me, and for the world, one day your efforts shall be recognized. Your "*Ode to Joy*" will become the anthem of a Europe united in ways that Napoleon never could achieve. And know too that from his perch in Elysium, Bonaparte will take pride in your success."

"Thank you," I say in all humility, for isn't that a dream fulfilled? Peace? Unity? Yet how ironic that I have become so deaf in these later years that despite several triumphal performances in Vienna, I have never even heard a single note of my *Ninth Symphony*. Where's the joy in that?

N answers my thoughts. "As all knowing as I am, B, even I was amazed that you pulled that one off. You write what is perhaps the single greatest composition in the entire history of Western music without being able to hear a single note. Not bad. Well, as my friend Quixote says, '*There's a cure for everything except death,*' isn't there? Still there is much to learn before the clock strikes five. Now, B, please observe carefully if you truly desire your questions about Liliana and her family answered."

N pours his cup of soma onto the sand and then mumbles a prayer which I take to be either Hindoo or Buddhist, "*Om mani padme aum.*" The moist grains at our feet begin to twitch and shiver as if a snake shedding its skin.

"What are you doing?" I ask.

"It is foolish, B, to think that things in life will last forever in one state. On the contrary, everything goes in cycles, just as time revolves on a continuous wheel. Now watch!"

N points to the quivering sand, then snaps his fingers. A bolt of lightning rips across the sky. What had been the dust of the desert suddenly transforms itself into a violin. . . . Liliana's *Adorato* by the looks of it. The violin's distinctive pattern of swirling dark and light wood resembles nothing less than Toni's pearl, the *Mandate of Heaven*. . . . N cradles the *Adorato* in his arms. He caresses her strings as one would a lover. . . . "Oh my friend, I adore these tones," he notes, "but let us raise our voices into more pleasing and joyful sounds!"

N grabs my bamboo walking stick, the one that had been a gift from Fanny Giannatasio Del Rio, and sprinkles soma on it. He snaps his fingers anon. Another lightning bolt strikes my walking stick, causing my cane to levitate up into the air. There it spins around like the blade of a windmill ever faster until it abrupt stops mid-air, its transformation into a violin bow complete. N snatches it out of the air and begins to play.

Even though N bows furiously, I hear nothing. *Ja,* still deaf. N realizes this and snaps his fingers a third time and the subsequent flash across the sky is the charm. Suddenly a musical score appears before me in the form of dancing butterflies. . . . Thousands of little blue butterflies bursting with energy. . . .

I watch them dart about and somehow, inside my head, I can sense every note. Mind you, it's not sound and I am not hearing anything through my ears, yet my consciousness is fully awakened to every vibration. *Ja,* N is at it again—somehow he uses the *Adorato* to play a fully orchestrated score of the opening movement of my *Seventh Symphony*. . . . Not just the strings, but the entire score. . . . Drums, horns, flutes tympani . . . all coming from this one violin. Magical indeed.

N plays with such gusto that I am driven to stand up and dance. Me, dancing! Twice in the same dream. My boots, the ones with the silver tips, can do naught but move. Rhythm is everything and I surrender to it until I reach exhaustion. N plays with such fury that when he blasts into the last measures of the first movement, the strings of the *Adorato* turn white hot and begin to smoke. Flames spark everywhere, the violin, the bow, even the butterflies shoot out bursts of fire. After the last chords, the *Adorato* explodes into flames. It then disappears from our sight in a conflagration of smoke and fire. The bow falls and clatters to my feet. My walking stick, as if released from the entrapments of a magic spell, resumes its original shape.

"What fun," declares N. "Napoleon hasn't enjoyed himself this much since he overthrew the Bishop of Rome."

I pick up my cane and notice four Chinese characters inscribed on the underside of the handle that I had never seen before.

Ever watchful, N studies me as I look at the inscription. "*Ssu Ma Hao Hwa,*" he translates. "It was his cane."

"What are you talking about?" I ask. "This was given to me as a gift by Fanny Giannatasio Del Rio after I had my nephew Karl boarded at her father's school."

"Ah, Fanny . . . Fanny Giannatasio Del Rio. . . . We'll hear more, much more from her later." N snaps his fingers again and a book suddenly appeared in his hands. "What a lovely young woman she is. I have Fanny's diary here. It's a fascinating read that you must hear before you depart for wherever. . . . But tell me B, were you even aware that our Fanny had been infatuated with you for some time—years before you brought Karl to her school?"

"Was not a teenaged Fanny, along with her sister and father, at *Fidelio*? Didn't we see them through your magic window?"

"Did it ever occur to you that Fanny could grow up and become the one for you? It's all the more the tragedy B, that you, so absorbed in the admiration of your own genius, have little appreciation for the faithful and unobtrusive assistance offered you by Fanny and the Giannatasios. "

"It was not genius or narcissism that distracted me in those days but grief and trouble. My brother had just died and I was thrust into the role of father to Karl and courtroom foe to his mother, Johanna. If not for the intercession of the Archduke Rudolph and others with the magistrates, I might have lost my boy forever."

"Indeed, B, you lost Karl long before he ever thought of raising a gun to his own head. Such endless conflicts you engender—all the more reason I am going to read to you from Fanny's diary. It was after the performance of your *Seventh Symphony* during the Congress of Vienna that she truly fell in love from afar and commenced to write thusly, *'December 3rd, 1814; On Tuesday, Beethoven's masterpieces enchanted everyone. His spark of divine fire inspires me with admiration.'*"

"What of it? There are a thousand young women in Vienna who could have written the same pronouncement."

"*Oui, mon ami,* but only one woman in Vienna had the foresight and, shall we say, divine inspiration, to purchase the very walking stick our hero, *Ssu Ma Hao Hwa,* had once possessed on his journey to find the *Mandate of Heaven.* She bought it at one of the auctions your beloved Toni Brentano held of her father, Baron von Birkenstock's collections. Fanny did all that, though at the time she knew not why. Even her diary is absent on that subject. But let us just conclude that Higher Powers were at work and play here."

"And you know this how?" I ask.

"Have you forgotten, my dear B, that I am that Higher Power?"

"Then please, tell me, *Herr Omniscient One,* why did Bonaparte tremble and fall at Borodino . . . and at Smorgonie?"

"Why did Napoleon reveal his humanity? You have to ask? B, when mortals leave this world and go into the ground, you must know a prince's path is as narrow as a peasant's."

N takes another sip of soma, then looks directly at me and into my eyes. He then nods as I do when facing a hostile audience. Abruptly and without any warning N begins to grow in size and shape until he once more transforms into his avatar, Shiva, the Hindoo God of Destruction. Now twice my height, this Shiva towers over me and waves his ball of fire back and forth. "*You can seek our Creator above this starry canopy,*" this god chants with a voice as leathery as a Nile crocodile, *"but know well Isis dwells within us all and we dwell within her. To gain entrance to Elysium, even those as grand as Napoleon, must stumble and pale before the Great One. How will you prostrate yourself?"*

Shiva reaches into the ball of fire and one by one pulls out the four instruments of Reuven's quartet that were dedicated to the spirit of the Revolution: *Liberté, Égalité, Fraternité,* and *Justice.* Shiva stares at me with the same piercing, blue-grey eyes as Napoleon. All unto himself, this incarnation of the gods uses his multiplicity of arms to launch into the *Molto Adagio* of one of my last string quartets, *Opus 132 in A minor.* He does not speak but the essence of his consciousness flows through my brain once more, *"I am their sacred words and all vibrations of music in the air."*

Naturlich Shiva's quartet plays the Molto Adagio as solemnly as a hymn to any deity. When the movement ends, Shiva morphs back into his former incarnation as N. I am left to wonder: In this endless dream that N insists is not a dream, have I just witnessed N masquerading as Shiva or has it been Shiva masquerading as N all along? And if Shiva is just another incarnation of the One, the true path, the Tao, from which the multitude spring, what then? Is such a confused and disputed reality the true nature of my existence?

Before I have a chance to contemplate this thought further, N—once more dressed in his winter uniform—calls to me again, "And *Monsieur* Gardner, I understand you played for him after he deserted the Emperor Bonaparte?"

"I confess that after he recalled the nightmares of his midnight in Moscow we were both so despairing that we agreed to banish our sorrows at the next rest stop with pints of brown ale. Fortune shined on us when the first pub we found had a pianoforte, an ancient creature well out of tune, but neither one of us minded."

"When you least expect it, out jumps a rabbit. You couldn't hear and he couldn't care. The *Alla Danza Tedesca* from *Opus 130*—you played that, didn't you?"

"*Ja*, more than any other composition I found that the *Alla Danza Tedesca* brightens my heart as much as your *Taschenlampe* illuminated that cave you brought me to in *Pech Merle*. It's such a sweet delectable composition that it's hard to be anything but upbeat and joyful while either listening or playing." As I finish speaking, my cane begins to glow again as it had at the beginning of this endless dream—only this time its light sparkles off the falling snow. "Why is that?" I ask N. "Why does it glow?"

"Do you recall what Schiller wrote? '*Joy, beautiful spark of the gods, Daughter of Elysium, We enter fire imbibed, Heavenly, thy sanctuary.*' Shiva, Isis, Kwan Yin—they are not some external being, human or superhuman, but the spark of divinity that lies at the core of the human heart. Think of your cane as a sort of an emotional barometer—a *Taschenlampe*—that illuminates the path."

"What path?"

N yanks me by the ear. "What path? *Gesu*, B, the one you are on; the eternal path of illumination, of wisdom, of acceptance, of love. That path."

"No heart has ever beaten so intensely or so eagerly, yet in vain for love, as mine has and still . . ."

N cuts me off. "No complaints. Fortune is a drunken and capricious woman and worse still, blind. She doesn't see what she is doing nor does she know whom she is casting down or raising up. The trick is to know that and not care."

"Seek perfection, accept failure?"

"Exactly! But tell me, *Monsieur* Gardner, he found respite in your music as I do?"

"So much so that when we returned to the coach, we agreed to alternate. On those occasions when we stopped for rest, we'd find another pub with a piano and I'd play for him. And whenever we were on the road, he would recite from memory the gist of his various novels and short stories, most of which were delightfully comic."

Gardner, being of Welsh extraction, had as much a gift for storytelling as the Italians have for opera. His tales were rich with misbegotten characters. He started with his first book, *The Moonlight Dialogues,* a farce about feuding brothers and sisters, and then segued to *Niccolo's City,* another satirical effort set amongst the eccentric and all too inbred aristocratic families of Machiavelli's Florence.

"Mind you," I add, "As much as we laughed together, beneath the veneer of his comedies were insights to the human condition that were as brilliant as anything Cervantes created in *Don Quixote.*

"Laughter always eases digestion of the toughest truths," comments N. The snowfall is now so dense, even N is now half-buried by it. "On the retreat from Moscow, *Herr* Gardner would read each night to the French officers huddled around a campfire. The tale Napoleon loved the most," notes N, once again referring to Bonaparte in the third person, "was the old English tale of *Beowulf* from the monster's perspective—*Grendel,* he called it. Hearing the deeds of dragons and long-deceased heroes kept the Emperor entertained through many a chilling night when the world order as he conceived it appeared to be vanishing beneath a layer of white."

"Gardner started to recite that tome as well from memory. He was perhaps two-thirds of the way through his *Grendel* just when our coach arrived in Baden. I insisted on hearing the end and wouldn't separate from him until he finished. We found our way to Lichnowsky's villa and were joined by the Prince but Gardner refused to go any farther until he heard me play something new, something that expressed the truths inside my soul. He would accept nothing less. Drawing upon the deep pool of music I had played once upon a time with *Fraulein* Lokitzvarah, I let the chords emerge from my inner consciousness and out came the essential themes that one day I would meld into my *Hammerclavier Sonata*. . . ."

"By the time I completed my performance for Lichnowsky and Herr Gardner, I was overwhelmed with exhaustion. Every emotion, every bit of turmoil that had been coursing through my blood since the day I had left my Immortal Beloved in Prague had been drained from my flesh. Gardner applauded me and cheered, insisting that '*Music should strike fire from a man and by Jove, you've done that.*' Later, only when he finished his recitation of '*Grendel*,' did I fully appreciate its theme."

"What? That we are each our own dragon," remarks N as he purses his lips and blows out a stream of pure fire that ignites the teapot and turns it to smoldering ash. "And that inside our soul is the heart of darkness we each fear the most?"

My hands are as clammy and white as my *Grossvater's* before he slides across the great divide. I warm them over the burning remnants, yet feel nothing. "*Ja*, Gardner's works were akin to multilayered cakes that revealed their core only slowly through deep and patient contemplation. All in all," I tell N, "the journey from Linz in *Herr* Gardner's company proved to be the most delightful and transformative trip I had ever taken—aside from this one. By the time I returned home to Vienna in the company of Prince Lichnowsky, I felt revitalized and with enough energy to compose yet again. Sadly though, the Prince fell ill and died not long afterwards. And *Herr* Gardner, after healing in Baden, he returned to his beloved upstate New York."

"That only proves the maxim that great hearts should be patient in misfortune as well as joyful in prosperity," N adds. "After all, grief is made for humans not animals, but if we feel despair too deeply we become beasts ourselves. We must use our opportunities when we find them as in life, there's no road so smooth that hasn't an obstruction or a pothole, including the path of self-realization that you are on."

"I know the fate of nations after the collapse of the French Empire, but what of Liliana? You still haven't told me what happened. Does she yet live?"

"She does, as do her twin sons, Avraham and Moses. And the Polish Lancers? The sound of gunshots Liliana heard that night was the last echo of French justice. Napoleon had the miscreants put to death by his firing squads before ever insisting that she play."

"May the devil take Bonaparte for tormenting her so. . . ."

"How else could he have gotten Liliana to find the strength to rise up and exorcise the torment in her soul?"

"Really?" I ask, "You delight in taking us all on these torturous roads, don't you? Alright, I get it. And so what about the cask of gold coins Reuven had hidden?"

"*Monsieur* Gardner told you of his suspicions, didn't he? A smart man, that Gardner. Indeed, the barrel did hold Napoleon's cash reserves—the very coin required to pay his troops. But with nine out of every ten soldiers of the *Grande Armée* dead, deserted, or mutilated on the battlefield, that urgency was very much diminished. Understand: those were desperate times for Bonaparte. Though the wars were far from over, Napoleon already knew his fate would be to die in exile. It was in Smorgonie that he received a dispatch from Paris about Malet's attempted coup. After meeting with the remnants of his general staff in Smorgonie, Napoleon determined that he needed to race back to Paris as rapidly as possible. Kutuzov and the Russians were so close behind, each army could smell the other's campfires. Rather than risk having the payroll fall into enemy hands, the Emperor left it hidden. Napoleon turned command of his less than *Grande Armée* over to his closest confidant, General Murat. On the night of December 5th, he had the best horses still available hitched to a sled. Two weeks later he arrived in Paris."

"And the gold remained hidden in the synagogue's basement?"

"*Oui,* but only for three generations—ninety-nine years to be exact. . . . The story of its eventual 'repatriation' is a tale worthy of *Monsieur* Gardner's retelling and one central to the very existence of this opus."

"How so?"

"Without distracting from our greater purpose here, B, just know this, to finish this odyssey we must dash deep into the future. Of Liliana's two sons, Avraham Silke moved north and settled in Daugava in Latvia for two generations before most of his grandchildren migrated to America where they would eventually reconnect with the other branches of their family. Her other son, Moses, stayed in Smorgonie, and retained his mother's last name, Donishefski. Moses's grandson, named Reuven the Younger in honor of their martyred great-grandfather, became a luthier and it was while repairing the *Immortale Adorato* in 1911 that he discovers the elder Reuven's inscription under the tuning pegs. Do you recollect it?"

Although I had never seen or heard the inscription I am able to recite it for N as if it arose from my own share of a collective human consciousness, "*Even when our power over men and gods or the wealth of an empire seems lost and empty, know this: There has never been a time when you and I have not lived and loved. . . .*"

"Your memory isn't bad for a man about to exhale his final breath," chuckles N. "But the secret the younger Reuven discovered was in the last line, '*Beyond the sacred altar of our affection lies a font of gold. In the hours of darkness, draw strength, transport and freedom from it*'. That same year, 1911, a Jewish painter from Warsaw, Jan Rosen, arrived in Smorgonie to paint a recreation of the day Napoleon fled the village for Paris. The painting was to be part of a centennial exhibition of the Russian invasion. Rosen had also heard rumors of Napoleon and hidden treasures. Both he and the younger Reuven suspected that his ancestor had left the clue to its location in plain sight. Suffice to say Reuven the Younger located the false wall behind the synagogue's altar. Removing it, he uncovered the lost payroll of the *Grande Armée,* and as conditions for the Jews had grown only worse in the century since Bonaparte's invasion of Russia, Reuven took his great-grandfather's advice and wisely used the gold to pay for his family's escape to America. There Liliana and Reuven's descendants reside today—merchants, musicians, lawyers, artists, and, most germane to you, *mon ami*, writers who live to tell tales."

"Like Gardner?"

"*Oui*, like Gardner."

"And the *Immortale Adorato*, what happened to it?"

"The earthly fate of the *Immortale Adorato* waxed and waned and waxed again—much as the ideals of the Revolution did in Europe and the world. Here today, gone tomorrow, and then back anon. It is the only one of Reuven's instruments that has survived the tragedy of years. With luck you'll revisit the Revolution and the *Adorato* again. After Moscow, Napoleon and his empire were but shadows of their former selves. And though Bonaparte passes into Elysium six years before you, sadly, the Revolution he carried in his heart ended at Borodino."

"Not Waterloo?"

"An afterthought. Despite the joy people felt at the end of twenty years of war and five million dead, the aristocracy came back into power. The prince and princesses at the Congress of Vienna that so welcomed your music—and made you rich—turned back the tides of change. When the crowned heads of Europe recovered their thrones, new state boundaries were fixed and repression of the rights of man became the currency of the day under that fox, our dear friend Austrian Prime Minister Prince Klemens Metternich. Still," N noted as he etched a *Yin-Yang* symbol in the snow with his boot, "fortune changes faster than a mill wheel, B. He who was on top yesterday, is on the ground tomorrow. The days of monarchy and suppression will eventually end provided your fellow humans stay vigilant. And speaking of vigilant, did you know that despite all precautions, she's pregnant?"

"Who? Who's pregnant? Fanny Giannatasio Del Rio?"

"Your Lady Abbess? Of course not. You've got to be kidding. Think again," chides N as he slips back into song—the 'Blues' once more, I suspect:

"And when I die, and when I'm gone, There'll be one child born In this world to carry on, to carry on."

"Then who? Tell me, who?" I prod N with my cane—which glows bright red—even as I wonder if this news is at all relevant to me. "Who's pregnant?"

"*La Immortale Adorato.* Your Immortal Beloved."

CHAPTER 27

From Beethoven's Tagebuch; a Convalescent's Holy Song of Thanksgiving in the Lydian Mode

*M*UST I BE DENIED *and forego that role of father by her and stay alone as such? This terrible circumstance does not suppress my longing for domesticity, but now certainly hinders its realization. Speech is like silver but to be silent at the right moment, I am told, is pure gold. I must learn quietude and say naught to her. Nonetheless such affection deserves never to be dismissed or forgotten. I shall be as good as possible toward her.*

Oh God, look down upon this unhappy B. How different my life has become from that which I often pictured for myself. Do not let it continue like this any longer. Even if the clouds were to rain rivers of life, never will the willow tree bear dates. Without tears fathers cannot instill virtue in their children. And many are the tears I have shed but to what avail?

The best way not to think of these woes is to keep busy. There is much to be done on earth. Do it soon! No time passes more quickly or rolls by faster than when my mind is occupied or when I spend it with my Muse.

Though I have need of separation from my past, the past has created this present. If her absence from my life be the death of love, let me not sink into the dust unresisting and inglorious. How then shall I accomplish great deeds of which future generations shall hear? Art demands sacrifice. This I owe to myself, to humankind, and to the Mighty One, from which all things flow clear and pure.

CHAPTER 28

A Turkish Marche Militaire in which N, Adopting the Piccolo Voice of the Lady Abbess, Reads Aloud From the Diary of Fanny Giannatasio Del Rio

January 25, 1816

WHAT I HAVE *often vainly wished for, that Beethoven should come to our house, has at length happened. Yesterday he brought his little nephew Karl to reside at our boarding school. I cannot describe the delight I feel at being thus brought into communion with a man who I honor so much as an artist and esteem so highly as a man. It seems like a dream that my wishes are at last realized. How delightful I should be if we could really enter into friendly relationships with Beethoven whose music has banished so many dark clouds from my soul. My hope is to make a few hours of this great man's life pleasant for him.*

March 1st

Beethoven informs us that the Magistrates have appointed him as the sole guardian of his nephew over the mother—beast that she must be. He promises to visit often. One would almost think Beethoven had divined how much I wished for just that. In this hope life has become an enjoy-

ment to me and now I feel a deep interest in the prospects of the days to come. I am unable to believe that my veneration for his genius will be lessened by a nearer acquaintance with the man. If I find him half as genial and kind-hearted as he has been represented to be, my esteem for him must only increase.

May 12th

It is impossible for me to think of anything but agreeable emotions resulting from our acquaintance with Beethoven which renders him only more worthy. His appearance and the modesty of his disposition pleases us extremely. He passed the whole evening with mother and me, and during that time proved to us that he is moved by such rare high moral principles, and is such a noble estimable man, that my enthusiasm for him is in every way increased. The sorrow which that unhappy connection with Karl's mother entails, preys upon his spirits. It afflicts me too, for he is a man who ought to be happy. He has won my heart. May he attach himself to us and by my warm sympathy and interest, find peace and serenity.

July 27th

I fear greatly that when I come to know this noble excellent man more intimately, my feelings for him will deepen into something warmer than friendship and then I shall have many unhappy hours before me. But I will endure anything, provided only I have it in my power to make his life brighter.

October 23rd

Beethoven was with us again yesterday evening. While mamma was out of the room I spoke with him on the subject of his compositions and music and was enabled to observe his character at the same time. Beethoven allowed us to see in him the goodness of heart which is his special characteristic. He left a very pleasant impression on my memory, making me wish to enjoy many more an evening like it with him. How delighted I shall be if he continues to enjoy our circle of companionship.

December 2nd

My sister, Nanni's, advice not to fall in love with Beethoven pains and troubles me beyond measure. Even he has declared that a life devoted to loving, even if it entails a few sorrowful hours, is better, far better than to let one's warm heart vegetate in an empty deathlike monotony. Such a genius! And yet such a noble heart like his is exactly according to my longings. He must become dear, very dear, to me. He can and may become that. Shall I think about a closer union which common sense tells me is impossible? How can I be so vain as to believe or imagine that the power of captivating such a soul as his is reserved for me? His gift to us, the score of his "Battle of Vittoria" symphony, gave me great pleasure, all the more so as it is a proof that he thinks of us. And of me?

March 7, 1817

Beethoven has no idea of how fond we are of him—I in particular. He has been very dear to me lately. His conversations are so imbued with true deep feelings. His appearance, his face, pleases me: his manners too are original and all he says has weight. Yesterday evening I was carried into a state of ecstasy by the music he played for us—themes he said for a new symphony. Under its charming influence I was able to forget the trouble both Karl and his mother are causing him over the guardianship. The poor man takes it so much to heart that he will, I fear, become ill over the court battles she has caused. I hope he will continue to come often and attach himself truly to us.

June 17th

Once again Beethoven was with us the whole evening. He brought a clutch of violets which he had spent the entire afternoon gathering. I had feared he might grow weary of visiting but we treated him so warmly that he even consented to take supper with us. We intensely enjoyed listening to his rich, original remarks and puns. I spoke with him about his walks, the baths in Teplitz, and Karl's mother, whom he refers to as the "Queen of the Night," a reflection certainly on her immoral behaviors. He did not leave until nearly midnight. This gave me great pleasure. I would willingly surrender all sleep for this to happen often.

August 13th

Can I conceal from myself that which makes me long to weep continually? Yes, it must be confessed: Beethoven interests me to the selfish point of desiring him, nay, longing that I and I alone may please him. I am deeply ashamed to make this confession. Beethoven too insists he has a heart capable of untold powers of loving. But with whom? Does he understand these exquisite feelings of mine? Must they be hidden away out of sight and suppressed? Until I have attained this mastery over myself, and so gained peace, I will try to think less of my future on this subject. I shall wait with childlike patience and in the meantime continue to live as a true and faithful daughter, sister, and friend. In this manner I shall live on until I can overcome the longings of my heart. A little hope thus brightens my existence and so I will dream on!

October 11th

I saw Beethoven again for the first time in the month since he fell ill—laid low by the suffering we feared hanging over him. He spoke of Karl's father, his brother Casper, who had passed away, and said, "It is a sad man who does not know how to die." He remarked that his own life was no longer of any worth. Though Karl gives him much grief, he only wished to live for the boy's sake and protect him from that most unfit and horrible mother.

December 3rd

After playing 'Margaretha's Theme' on the piano for us, Beethoven said many bright and kind things. He has a wonderful bantering, teasing manner in which he displays as much ingenuity and originality as he does in his music. Though I do not like his calling me the 'Lady Abbess' when I am busy with housekeeping, his few words help dispel the sadness I felt that night as it was this time of year when my own betrothed passed away.

February 28, 1818

During the days I was ill and suffering earlier this winter, Beethoven came to see me twice and I intensely enjoyed his visits—though the difficulty I had in speaking with him, owing to my weakness, sadly increased my fever and brought about a fit of depression that lingered for weeks. Still, I would willingly suffer this over and over again to have the pleasure of hearing such a highly gifted, interesting, and frank-minded man talk. He is far above ordinary mortals and truly too sensitive in soul to mix with the world. His devotion to and admiration for truth and goodness have lost none of their intensity through his ongoing difficulties with both Karl and the Queen of the Night. Perhaps I am expecting too much from him?

May 23rd

Father thinks Beethoven will not live long, for he is far too sensitive and feels things too acutely in his delicate state of health to bear up against his troubles much longer. It is scarcely possible for another human being on the face of the earth to so earnestly desire the happiness of this noble man as I do. And yet I fear that my wish and desires will never be satisfied.

October 20th

Yesterday Beethoven arrived quite upset over Karl running away to be with his mother. Tears were running down his cheek when he told us of how the police were summoned to return the boy to his care. The rumors concerning this bad woman have so upset me I am fit for nothing today. That such a generous man with a pure childlike soul should be so unhappy in life is a great grief to me.

February 13, 1819

I cannot put it aside or crush out of existence the intense joy I felt upon hearing the news that Beethoven will spend a few days with us next summer at Teplitz. Is there a world of hidden meaning in those few words? Teplitz! Well, and what then? Though I ought to check my growing and all absorbing interest in this noble being, it is beyond me now. Might I even hope for that which I dare not!

May 9th

Karl has been nothing but ungrateful for all Beethoven has sacrificed for him and his welfare. I pity Beethoven with all my heart as the guardianship of this nephew of his will cause him naught but a great deal of sorrow. How I wish he could be free of these outside worries so that his creative powers could be restored and progress. His music, the wonderful powers of his creative genius, always stir me to the innermost depths of my soul.

August 3rd

Nanni remarked that Beethoven would always be more devoted to his art than to any wife. I know a girl who, if beloved by him, would truly make his life happy.

September 14th

We arrived last night in Teplitz for the end of the summer season masked ball festival and prepared our costumes. Beethoven arranged for our accommodations to be adjacent to his. I slept restlessly, aware he is so near to me as I lay alone in my bed.

September 17th

Yesterday I passed such an intensely provocative evening with Beethoven at the Kaiserbad that it will require several days to elapse before I regain possession of my usual quiet state of mind. I am quite undone . . . And my poor sister, mortified.

November 10th

After an absence of several weeks, Nanni and I visited Beethoven at his apartment in Vienna. My sister could not resist the temptation to peek inside his Tagebuch. This great interest we take in Beethoven caused us to indulge our curiosity to an extent that proved painful. I could not sleep afterwards, for in those pages Nanni found proof that he still loves another!

What more do I want, silly girl that I am? I ought to be satisfied that he cares for me as much as he does. I have no right to expect more, though I find it difficult to cast away my thoughts and emotions. What I feel is the need of loving and being loved, the right of being sympathized with, and my soul infused in another soul. That this wish should arise from knowing a man like Beethoven seems a natural thing to me and because this wish is there, I do not feel I am so unworthy of him. In time the very force of my feelings for Beethoven must be felt by him.

December 16th

On the occasion of his birthday, I presented Beethoven with an antique walking stick from China that had once belonged to the Baron von Birkenstock. It pleased him greatly and when he arose and hugged me, I could imagine no greater joy than to be held in his arms. I prayed he would never let me go.

Yet, when at dinner father asked Beethoven if there was no hope of finding him a wife who could attend to all of those numberless offices his sad handicaps require with a patience and devotion impossible to expect from anyone else, his answer crushed me.

I listened with the most intense and painful discomfort while Beethoven confessed to what I had long since feared in my heart; that love was in vain! He acknowledged that five years ago he made the acquaintance of a lady, whom to marry would have been the highest happiness life could have afforded him. It was not to be, though.

It was quite impossible and in fact was a chimera. Still, his feelings toward her remain the same now as then. His last words, words which pained and hurt me beyond calculation, were these: "I cannot excise her from my thoughts and dreams. She is and will always remain my Immortal Beloved."

CHAPTER 29

A Last Symphony of Lightning and Thunder

"STOP," I scream at N, who at last puts down Fanny's diary. "Must I suffer such humiliation and torment all over again?"

"On your knees," N orders, and I comply by kneeling in the deep snow already covering the oasis. "Confess."

"Of course I knew about Fanny's infatuation. And, *ja*, I was attracted to her, but . . ."

N cuts me off again and goes into a reverie of his own about Fanny, "And why not? What's not to like? She was so, so cute with a lovely figure, full of those sweet curves you adore . . . and those greenish-blue eyes . . . sometimes dreamy, sometimes animated and sincere. Can't you picture her chestnut brown hair cascading across your pillow at night and then again in the morning? True, she's a bit melancholy and shy by nature but she adored you, B. Fanny wrote comic poems and loved music. Who else does that? In her you had a talented singer who embraced opera and was particularly enthralled with your *Fidelio*. True, being around you made her nervous as a rabbit. It's sad this poor, love-starved creature would feel so embarrassed that she would run away rather than let you see her face blush red. She so desperately wanted you and yet, B, you stayed away?"

"I had to. I had no choice." I go on to explain to N that I held back and avoided sliding into romance—as easy as that would have been—precisely because in the wake of the aborted affair with my Immortal Beloved, I had come face to face with a tragic truth that nearly broke me; I was incapable of handling an everyday genuine relationship with any woman. Domesticity would never be mine. As *Fraulein* Lokitzvarah had once cautioned, only my art shall be my true betrothed.

"The death of love," notes N, reading my thoughts. My legs grow ever more numb and cold. Is it from the snow, I wonder, or death ever encroaching?

I muster the energy to tell N that, in regards the feminine gender, I had two choices to console me in my final years: sex or friendship. There were of course those sweet desserts—'*Later day Magdalenas*' N calls them—women I could take to bed where neither one of us had any expectations of a tomorrow. And there were those—such as my *lesbische* companion, Therese von Brunsvik, whose hearts glowed as warm as my bamboo cane with a friendship that never wavered.

As attractive and willing as Fanny was to me, and as much as I treasured her company and that of her family, I knew her heart would thrive only through a sincere domesticity I could not provide. Only friendship would be ours. This became ever more apparent at Teplitz when Fanny and her sister accompanied me to the masked ball but fled afterwards, overwhelmed by the bacchanalia at the *Kaiserbad*. Conquest for its own sake no longer held sway over me as it did when I was young and seen as an Adonis able to bed any princess seeking an expression of repressed desires. To have slept with a woman such as Fanny without true affection would have been to slay her with my sword. That I could not do.

"Quit the sanctimonious crap," insists N, as he hands me a mirror. "By turning the Giannatasios into a surrogate family for you and Karl, you used and abused Fanny more brutally than if you had actually raped her—perhaps even more so. Look at yourself, you had no business pretending to be a father to Karl or anyone else—certainly not at that stage of your life. You were an incompetent bachelor going deaf with no notion of how to raise a child."

"It was my brother's dying wish. I had to."

"Bullshit."

I look at my face in the mirror but only see the butt end of a bison—a defecating one at that.

"You betrayed Casper's last wishes. Your brother never wanted you to be sole guardian regardless of what the courts ruled. Think about what you did. You're growing progressively deaf, yet you take a boy who had just lost his father and then you deny him any contact with his mother. After that you turn him into a lonely and resentful orphan by abandoning him at a boarding school. Such abuse. In a life filled with missteps, B, this was your biggest and perhaps cruelest."

"But I had to protect Karl from that witch of a mother. . . ."

"More bullshit!" declares N. The stench of feces lingers in my nostrils. The snow falling from the heavens turns the oasis as dark as a stormy March night. Random flashes of lightning draw ever closer while growing in intensity. Though I cannot hear their accompanying thunder, I feel the vibrations rattle my bones.

"Johanna van Beethoven was an honorable and deserving mother. *Queen of the Night?* Hah! Whatever faults she may have exhibited during her life pale in comparison to your own excesses. Such cruelty masquerading as love. . . ."

"That is what Steffen von Breuning said to me once."

"And it nearly destroyed your friendship. Steffen was right. You were blind to the truth and had not your other politically connected friends such as Archduke Rudolph and his brother, the Emperor, lined up behind you to manipulate the courts, you would have never been granted custody of your nephew. It was your finger on the trigger that nearly murdered Karl. Stay on your knees and thank whatever gods you please that he was only wounded that day in Rauhenstein. Fortunately, you raised Karl so incompetently that he didn't even know how to pack and load his gunpowder."

"I did raise my brothers and Margaretha. I knew what—"

He cuts me off yet again. "*Merde, Fick Das.* On Judgment Day, this is the greatest sin you will be forced to account for, the destruction of your brother's family."

"There is a *Judgment Day*?" I ask, as a tremor—chill as a Moscow winter—ripples through my flesh.

"Remember what your grandfather once said, '*Not knowing life, why worry about death*?'"

I nod but still feel as bitterly cold in the marrow of my soul as I am sure Napoleon did in Russia. The wind picks up and swirls snow all about him. I can scarcely see N though he sits just a few feet away.

"There's no such thing as Judgment Day—it's just a myth—but I thought I would test you and it worked. You are terrified, aren't you?"

N is right. I failed. In my own fear and delusions I screwed up big time and ruined all those I loved around me in the name of art and ego. I failed. I failed.

I bow my head and beg Isis to help guide me. Is all hope of redemption vanished? I am a disgrace, worthy of being shoved off life's stage without mercy or compassion? Or is there yet a path I can travel to find redemption and escape this fate?

Immediately upon hearing my pleas, N once more pivots our conversation back to my first true infatuation, Leonore, whom I had not seen since leaving Bonn all those many years, nay, decades, ago. "Your Lorchen, your Leonore, the unacknowledged inspiration for *Fidelio*, never made it to Prague but she did still write to you on your deathbed, didn't she? N recites her letter from memory as if it had been addressed to him: '*Franz and I have the sincerest hope that you will soon recover completely and visit us, thus granting me fulfillment of one of my greatest wishes—to see you again after an absence of too many years. We shall remind each other of the hundred happy and sad occasions of our youth and tell stories of Lucchesi and Mozart; of the Elector and Waldstein; of Babette Koch and Jeanette d'Honrath and your beloved Margaretha. My children, now 20 and 23 years of age, know you so intimately from these tales, that you would be a beloved uncle to them. Know, my dear friend, that when I rise each day in the chill of the morning that I warm my heart by wearing the red kimono you gifted and when I stretch my fingers upon the keys of my pianoforte it is in time to your music. If love heals, then let that be my prescription.'"*

Indeed the correspondence from Leonore and Wegeler did arrive just weeks before this endless dream—my final journey—commenced. Though I very much wished to write back, I was, in the weeks before my passing, too weak to even hold a pen. Thankfully Steffen's son, Gerhard, would come by my apartment at the *Schwarzspanierhaus* almost daily to read and entertain me. I dictated to Gerhard my last letter to my friends, which was a final leave-taking. *"Forgive me. Much to the detriment of friends and family whose kindness I do not deserve, in the grand mathematics of life I have sacrificed the best part of my years to the heavenly Muses. Though I feel as if I have hardly composed more than a few notes, I will leave behind me what the Eternal Spirit has infused into my soul and bid me complete before I depart this world and attempt to reach the Elysian Fields. Of my heart and all its omissions, I will say nothing more; it is and remains empty in the absence of you, the dear companions of my soul, and this void is harder to bear than one would think. Sometimes my most cogent attempts at reasoning fail and feelings overflow. I cannot overcome tears by force of reason or litigious defense. The best course I am told is to make up my mind that I can do nothing, alter nothing, and that, someday, perhaps, eternal forgiveness will arrive on the wings of a goddess and things will be better and we shall rejoice in one another's company again."*

"*Gesu*, B, you're beginning to get it. Perhaps there is hope for you yet. 'Tis a pity you never had such closure with your Josephine von Brunsvik Deym von Stackelberg. And then there's the issue of her daughter, Minona, who some will claim as yours, purportedly conceived in Prague on a night as dark and stormy as this."

"How could she be mine?" I ask. The Baroness von Stackelberg never made it to Prague either, and though her sisters and brother remained friends until my end, poor unhappy Josephine died alone, somewhere back east in Livonia in the spring of 1821—coincidently within a month of Bonaparte's exit from this life while in exile on St. Helena in the south Atlantic. Napoleon's departure for the halls of Elysium made all the newspapers, my Josephine's did not. I only heard that sad report from Therese when she returned to Vienna and together we lifted glasses of Tokay in memory of the woman we both loved. I again ask N about Minona and why they think she's mine.

"In the future," says N, "the world is all too often populated by those of small minds who find conspiracies under ever rock. It's discouraging to think how many people are dismayed by honesty yet dwell in and find virtue in deceit."

"And this girl, Minona, her bloodline is the object of those lies? Is she my daughter?"

"No, but given your misbegotten romantic history and the fact that many view you as crazy and eccentric, it's simple for those suffering from microcephaly to insist that one plus one is three—thus she must be your progeny."

"If it amuses the world to talk and write about me in that manner, let them go on. All that concerns me now is knowing whether or not I am capable of passing through the sacred fires of Isis's temple."

"What have you learned?"

"I have failed those I loved and there is no forgiveness for the wrongs I inflicted upon them."

"Especially Karl."

"*Ja*, especially Karl, Johanna, and my brothers. . . ."

"And every woman you ever cherished."

"*Ja*, and there is no way to go back and repair those failings."

As I finish speaking, all hell breaks loose weather-wise . . . the winds whip a blizzard of snow around us with great ferocity. Dozens of random lightning flashes rule the dark sky. I lose sight not only of the heavens, but of nearly everything else around our oasis. N, however, is in his element. He reaches into the pocket of his military overcoat and pulls out his earmuffs.

"You're ready," he tells me, much to my surprise. "Let's do this." He starts to hand me his earmuffs but suddenly stops and pulls back. "One last question before you go. The letter, the one Steffen and Gerhard found in your desk . . . did you even send it to her? And why keep a copy?"

"That's two questions, not one," I reply. "And if you are as omniscient as you claim to be, you already know the answers."

"Say it again, B. For old time's sake. Say it, B. Say you wrote it for every woman you've ever loved and lost and I'll believe you. Answer and pass through Isis's gate unmolested."

"Under that cynical shell of yours, N, I suspect that at heart you're the sentimental one. You want me to kiss and tell? No, I'm not going to answer. Some secrets are best left for the future to unfold."

"Okay, fair enough," agrees N. He hands me his earmuffs and insists I put them on. I do. They're an odd pair, attached as they are to black strings that connect to a wallet-sized black box of glass and metal. "Though you cannot change the past and you may never be forgiven for your failures, B, there is one way you can make amends before you leave this world."

"There is? Tell me, please tell me and I will do whatever it is you ask."

"Do you remember my question from the start of your journey on this path?" he asks. "What is the sound of a kiss in a time before Creation?"

"Of course," I say. "The answer is right here." I reach into my coat and pull out the score of my *Ninth Symphony*. I hand it to N. Though my fingers are numb, I touch them to my lips and blow out a kiss, "*Diesen Kuss der Ganzen Welt.*"

"*Precisamente!* Though you have stumbled through your years like a broken-down goat, B, know this: Sometimes a kiss is more than a kiss. Your music has the power to enrich the world far beyond the measure of your weaknesses. Has never there been a time when the world has not lived and loved?"

N points to the flames guarding the entrance to Isis's Temple, which are now the only lights in the overwhelming blizzard of darkness, fog, and snow. "After you cross over," he tells me, as I struggle to stand up on legs that are no longer mine, "press the glass right here."

"What is this? Another magic window?"

"Don't ask, just do." N reaches out to me and shakes my hand in friendship. I gaze into his eyes and I see my own face reflected back at me. It is as if N and I are one and the same creature.

"We are," he notes, reading my mind once again. "You are your own dragon. Now go."

"Will I see you again?"

"Me? Of course, Louis. This is the start of a beautiful friendship."

A bolt of lightning—one more powerful than all the previous ones combined—strikes Isis's gateway and sets the oasis trembling.

I step into the fire. It hurts at first as the flames consume every sadness, every failing, every one of my life's missteps and errors, but I remain focused. Having now been compelled by N to grasp fully an awareness of my all too human failings as a man, I call out to Isis and beg forgiveness anon. Though I hear no answer, I feel the beating of my heart as it vibrates inside my chest as Shiva's drum once shook this oasis. Those vibrations grow ever more powerful. They spread throughout my body, forcing all suffering out of my flesh and into the fire. By feeding my troubles to these eternal flames, I am soon able to conquer the pain. Is that not what *Fraulein* Lokitzvarah once taught? Isn't the secret of life to manage the pain that inhabits us all?

Finally, on legs that feel weak as a newborn calf, I stumble towards the other side. Then, just as Lot's wife once did, I turn back around to look for N. Though it takes a moment to focus my eyes, he is gone. Through the curtain of fire, smoke, and fog I see instead the Emperor Napoleon Bonaparte in full dress regalia strolling along the *River Seine* hand in hand with his beloved Josephine Beauharnais, Empress of France. He hands her a red, red rose and whispers in her ear, *"France, Armée, tête d'Armée, Joséphine,"* before the two of them vanish from my sight and into history. . . .

And suddenly I realize, I can hear. I can hear.

CHAPTER 30

The Last Notes: A Letter from Steffen von Breuning of Vienna to Antonie von Birkenstock Brentano in Frankfort, March 30, 1827

"I HESITATE to bring you sorrow through the tragic news concerning our friend Beethoven. I did not write sooner partly because I did not want to make you sad and also because I hoped that providence and the human art of physicians might have restored the health of our hero. But the Book of Fate rules differently. Ludwig van Beethoven entered the land of peace on the 26th of March in the evening at 5 o'clock. The weather itself was dreadful; at the time of his death there was a terrible thunderstorm, with lightning and thunder and a heavy snowfall, almost as if the elements were rebelling against the death of this great mind. The sufferings of Beethoven in the course of his last year were really more terrible, and made his death desirable. My son, Gerhard, and I saw him often, but his shattered appearance—a consequence of his pain—his complete deafness, always made me sad. Now he travels toward Elysium where he will be at peace. All those who saw him during the last period of his life and loved him were relieved to see him freed from the torture of such an existence. . . . Yesterday we buried him, as you can see from the attached announcement. I have also enclosed two items he wished you to have—the score of his String Quartet in B-flat major, Opus 130, and his favorite walking stick—once the possession of your father. I will keep you informed should I learn more details with regard B because I know what a great interest you, honored lady, take in his Fate."

CODA

Willkommen zu Elysium
Welcome to Elysium

FOG RULES THE DAY . . . it is as dark and foggy on the far side of the entrance to Isis's Temple as that cave of our ancestors in *Pech Merle*. The first sound I hear is the pipsqueak voice of Margaretha, "*Willkommen zu Elysium*."

How beautiful is that? I can't see her, the mist is too dense, but I feel her tiny hand in mine.

"Play it," she says, "play it again, Louis. Play my song."

I start to hum.

"No," she insists. "Touch the glass. Turn on the music."

I fumble around in my coat pockets until I find the black glass box connected to my earmuffs. I press as N had instructed and instantly we are rewarded with sound, not just any sound but that of my *Ninth Symphony* played to perfection.

Can you imagine my joy, the sheer pleasure of sound once again? I feel reborn.

I certainly feel better than I have for months. The pain in my chest is gone. My stomach—once bloated with fluid and disease—is flat and youthful. The aches of age in my shoulders and hips have vanished as well. My skin, without pockmarks or scars, feels smooth to the touch. A young man's complexion. Even the scars from those bed bug bites that had tormented me nightly and made sleep inconceivable have vanished. . . . And I can hear! Everything!

As I pause to gather my bearings the mist seems to pulse and dance in time to the *Ninth* as if it too is a living, breathing, animated creature. How wonderful is that? I look down for Margaretha but instead see in my hand a small bamboo baton—the child of my walking stick. It's glowing.

"Where are you?" I ask.

"I'm here," Margaretha says, though I cannot see her. "I will always be here with you. Now use the baton."

As I lift it up, the glowing warmth of the baton begins to melt away the fog around me just enough that I can see a chamber orchestra and a choir behind it. Seemingly every lover I've ever known—the daughters of Elysium—are all there singing my *'Ode to Joy':* Josephine, Magdalena, Giulietta, Babette, and so on. Each of these lovelies is dressed of course in little more than mist and dew—and all wear a single lotus flower in their hair. Magdalena, yes, Magdalena Willman winks at me as her lips mouth the words, *"Willkomen."*

Magdalena then steps aside and behind her I see another woman, a woman in a hooded clock. This other woman pulls the cowl back and reveals her face. It is my Immortal Beloved.

"Kiss me," Toni says, "kiss me as if it were the first time." And we do.

We throw ourselves into each other's arms. As our lips and tongues meet, I weave my fingers through the locks of her thick, red hair and know that I am home, truly home, our souls wrapped in the land of spirits. Fate has heard us. We can exist together totally; no longer condemned to wander far away. Oh God, to be united with the one I so love and become the happiest of men. . . . No one else shall ever possess my heart.

The wisdom of her soul speaks to me. True love, she declares, transcends all space and time. Only those bonds nurtured and growing inside our hearts have weight to measure upon the scales of our existence. Such emotions, such truths, have sustained her for all the days of her life, even though the pull of years and circumstance kept our bodies apart while we lived. Such boundaries, she declares, no longer exist. We are the gods and they are us.

I feel a tug on my coat and look down. It is Toni's youngest son, Karl Josef, supporting his rickety legs with a bamboo cane, one stained and hardened with the sweat and toil of every Chinaman, Hindoo, and Turk that had cut, shaped, and transported it from the forest of Asia to the markets of Vienna and beyond.

"Is this my son?" I ask. "I want to know him."

"Our lives as lived are exactly what they need to be in order for us to be who we are; to suffer and thrive; to create and produce according to the command of our muses. You were a father to a 'Karl'—does it matter which one?"

Nothing is perfect in life. . . .

"Nor in death," Toni says, as she takes my hand between hers and lifts it up to her lips. She kisses my ring, the one that now holds the pearl she gifted me, the *Mandate of Heaven*. Toni then leads me on a rose-strewn path back to my room in the *Schwarzspanierhaus*. "It's time," she says. "Go to her."

"What?" I'm confused. The air rushing past my lungs is filled with a sweet, smoky scent reminiscent of a swaying incense censor at a Saint Stephens requiem mass—or is it just a woman's perfume? Devilishly pungent. Hunger. I feel hunger, a man's hunger for a woman. Even here. A prisoner of flesh to the very end.

"Go to her," Toni repeats. She stops at the doorway and ushers me forward, alone, and then disappears. I am alone . . . alone?

Steam rises from the waters. Only in the logic of this dream that N always insisted was not a dream do I see waiting for me in the bath at the Garden of Venus, my Leonore. Yes, my Leonore.

Surrendering to God and nature, Leonore verily glides onto my lap and we share our first and only kiss. My one day of happiness has arrived. . . .

We lie down together as my choir of lovelies continues to sing out the lyrics of the *"Ode to Joy."*

Through the dense fog I sense all of my old friends and family crowding around me. They join in our jubilation, sharing kisses and wine and together we exult as knights in victory.

"Plaudite, amici, Comoedia finite est."

There's a flash of lightening followed by the loudest crack of thunder I've ever heard. *Ja*, dead, but no longer deaf. Everything around me goes white. I clench my right fist. The last thing I feel as I raise my arm and punch through the fog is Leonore's enfolding embrace come around me at last.

I float upward as gently as I once did inside N's *Montgolfière*. As I rise ever higher up through the clouds I see and hear visions of the "Ode to Joy," played by orchestras and choirs all over the world. First Vienna, then Prague and Frankfort. Over Berlin I see sledgehammers smashing down a graffitied wall as all around people sing in triumph. I drift ever higher and see the outlines of Europe shrink away. From concert halls across the globe I continue to hear the *Ode*. In cities as far away as New York and Osaka I see stadiums filled with thousands of people raising their voices in triumph. Approaching the heavens, the envious moon winks at me. Looking back at the earth, I see naught but a dusky pearl floating in space.

I embrace the world and send her my last kiss.

My angel, my all, I have just learned my coach leaves immediately; therefore I must close at once so that you may receive this epistle without delay. . . .

Love me today, yesterday, tomorrow. Ever yours . . . Ever mine . . . Ever ours. . . .

EPILOGUE

Die Geburt von Beethoven
The Birth of Beethoven

OUTSIDE B's rooms at the *Schwarzspanierhaus*, a fresh measure of snow from a late-season thunderstorm muffles the chimes of St. Stephens Cathedral as they ring out the hours for the old city.

Eins, Zwei, Drei, Vier . . . Funf Uhr. Five O'clock.

Our Beethoven rests contentedly, as he has for the previous two nights, his body and soul bound by a transition whose greatest virtue is that it is irreversible and will, joyfully, be his last. Though his chest muscles and his lungs push like heroes in favor of the approaching blackness, his breathing is paced so peacefully that his final breaths are like choral whispers spreading a blanket of calm over the distant rumblings of the heavens.

Muss es sein? Ja, es muss sein. Beethoven is returning home. From on high, this Goddess celebrates his entrance to Elysium by hurling a spear of lightening at Vienna. My sweet bolt of thunder sparkles outside the frost-covered windows of his apartment with a harmony so warm and inviting that it lures my beloved back into consciousness.

B's eyes open like a newborn, at first glassy, then focused. He gazes upward—only we gods know what wonders he sees. He raises his right hand and clasps his fingers around mine. His arm trembles as he stretches toward the heavens. *"Oh what joy,"* he cries, *"in the open air; freely to breathe again! Up here alone is life!"*

Tears of joy flood his eyes as I pull him up into my arms and enfolded him in my wings.

I am Isis and this has been my story.

I am the Daughter of Elysium and the fiery spark of the gods. I am the Way and all that is and all that will be. I am the taste of pure water and the brilliance of the sun and moon. I am the sweet fragrance of the earth and the radiance of fire. I am the life in every creature and the hunger of all that is human. I am the courage and fear in their souls and the striving of every seeker. I am their sacred words and all vibrations of music in the air. I am that to which all owe their existence and I am the one who devours the world and restores it anon.

I am Isis and my kiss for the world is tender as all tones and tunes in a time before creation.

Beethoven is dead. Long live Beethoven.

The End Das Ende Fini

"What is a novel, but a collection of lies we tell to reveal greater truths."
—Johann Gardner

For those who want to know more about Beethoven, his music, his life, and times, listed below are many of the books and recordings the author consulted during the writing of *Beethoven in Love; Opus 139*.

Books on Beethoven

An Unrequited Love: An Episode in the Life of Beethoven, from the Diary of a Young Lady, Fanny Giannatasio Del Rio, Ludwig Nohl, Translated by Annie Wood, Richard Bentley & Son, 1876

Beethoven, Joseph Kerman & Alan Tyson, The New Grove Series, W.W. Norton & Company, 1983

Beethoven, Second, Revised Edition, Maynard Solomon, Schirmer Trade Books, 2001

"Beethoven, A True Fleshly Father?" Susan Lund, *The Beethoven Journal*, 3-1, 1988

Beethoven and the Catholic Brentanos: The Story Behind Beethoven's Missa Solemnis, Susan Lund, BookSurge, 2007

Beethoven and the Archduke Rudolph, Donald W. MacArdle, in Beethoven Jahrbuch, Beethovenhaus, Bonn, 1962

Beethoven and the Spiritual Path, David Tame, The Theosophical Publishing House, 1994

Beethoven, Biography of a Genius, George R. Marek, Funk & Wagnalls, 1969

Beethoven Essays, Maynard Solomon, Harvard University Press, 1988

Beethoven—His Spiritual Development, J. W. N. Sullivan, Alfred A. Knopf, 1936

Beethoven Im Zeitgenossischen Bildness, Theodor Frimmel, Verlag Karl Konig, Wien, 1925

Beethoven: Impressions by His Contemporaries, Edited by Oscar Sonneck, G Schirmer, Inc., 1954

Beethoven, Letters, Journals and Conversations, Edited & Translated by Michael Hamburger, Thames & Hudson, 1984

Beethoven Remembered: The Biographical Notes of Franz Wegeler and Ferdinand Ries, Franz Wegeler, Ferdinand Ries, Notes by Dr. A. C. Kalisher, Translated by Frederick Bauman & Tim Clark, Great Ocean Publishers, 1987

Beethoven, The Man, The Artist, as Revealed in His Own Words, Ludwig van Beethoven, Edited by Friedrich Kerst and Henry Edward Krehbiel, Hard Press, 2010

Beethoven: The Music and the Life, Lewis Lockwood, W.W. Norton & Company, 2003

Beethoven's Hair, Russell Martin, Broadway Books, Random House, 2000

Beethoven's Letters with Explanatory Notes by Dr. A.C. Kalischer, Ludwig van Beethoven, Translated by J.S. Shedlock, J.M. Dent & Sons, 1926

Beethoven's Only Beloved: Josephine, John E. Klapproth, CreateSpace, 2012

Diagnosing Genius, The Life & Death of Beethoven, Francois Martin Mai, McGill-Queen's University Press, 2007

Die "Unsterbliche Geliebte" Beethovens; Giulietta Guicciardi Oder Therese Brunswick, Alfred Christlieb Kalischer, Verlag von Richard Bertling, 1891

Late Beethoven: Music, Thought, Imagination, Maynard Solomon, University of California Press, 2004

Letters to Beethoven and Other Correspondence, Volumes 1-3, Translated & Edited by Theodore Albrecht, University of Nebraska Press in Association with the American Beethoven Society and the Ira F. Brilliant Center for Beethoven Studies, San Jose State University, 1996

Memories of Beethoven: From the House of the Black-Robed Spaniards, Gerhard von Breuning, Edited by Maynard Solomon, Translated from the German by Henry Mins and Maynard Solomon, Cambridge University Press, Canto Edition,

Thayer's Life of Beethoven, Volumes 1 &2, Revised & Edited by Elliot Forbes, Princeton University Press, 1967

The Beethoven Compendium: A Guide to Beethoven's Life and Music, Edited by Barry Cooper, Thames & Hudson, 1996

The Letters of Beethoven, Volumes 1-3, Edited & Translated by Emily Anderson, W.W. Norton & Company, 1985

Related Readings

A Source Book in Chinese Philosophy, Translated and Compiled by Wing-Tsit Chan, Princeton University Press, 1963

Archduke Rudolf, Beethoven's Patron, Pupil and Friend; His Life and Music, Susan Kagan, Pendragon Press, 1988

Don Giovanni, Libretto by Lorenzo Da Ponte, Music by Wolfgang Amadeus Mozart, 1787

Friedrich Schiller, Charles E. Passage, Frederick Ungar Publishing Co., 1975

Ghetto in Flames, Dr. Yitzhak Arad, Holocaust Library, 1982

Mozart, A Life, Maynard Solomon, Harper Perennial, 1996

Mozart's Letters, Mozart's Life, Wolfgang Amadeus Mozart, Edited and Translated by Robert Spaethling,

Napoleon, Vincent Cronin, HarperCollins, 1971

Schubert's Vienna, Edited by Raymond Erickson, Yale University Press, 1997

Tao Te Ching, Lao Tzu, Translated by Gia-Fu Feng and Jane English, Alfred A. Knopf, 1972

The Bhagavad Gita, Translated by Eknath Easwaran, Nilgiri Press, Second Edition 2011

The I Ching or Book of Changes, Wilhelm/Baynes Edition, Princeton University Press, Third Edition, 1967

The Life of Friedrich Schiller: Comprehending an Examination of His Works, Charles Follen, George Dearborn & Co., 1837

The Life of Napoleon Buonaparte, Emperor of the French, Sir Walter Scott, Longman, Rees, Brown & Green, 1827

The Tibetan Book of the Dead: First Complete Translation, Translated by Gyurme Dorje, Penguin Books, 2005

Turandot: The Chinese Sphinx, Friedrich Schiller, 1801

Water Music: Making Music in the Spas of Europe and North America, Ian Bradley, Oxford University Press, 2010

The Music of Beethoven

"Beethoven: the Cello Sonatas," Lynn Harrell and Vladimir Ashkenazy, 2 CD set, Decca Records, 1987

"Beethoven: the Complete Piano Sonatas," Claude Frank, Music & Arts, 2002

"Beethoven: the Complete Sonatas for Piano & Cello," Yo-Yo Ma and Emanuel Ax, CBS Masterworks, 1987

"Beethoven: the Complete String Quartets," Alexander String Quartet, 3 CD set, Foghorn Classics, 1999

"Beethoven: Diabelli Variations," Rudolf Serkin, Sony Music, 2002

"Beethoven: the Five Piano Concertos," Alfred Brendel with James Levine and the Chicago Symphony Orchestra, Phillips, 1983

"Beethoven: Grosse Sonata fur das Hammerklavier, Opus 106," Stephan Moller performing on a ca. 1830 Bosendorfer fortepiano, The American Beethoven Society, San Jose State University, 2014

"Beethoven: Moonlight Sonata," Maurizio Pollini, Deutsche Grammophon, 1992

"Beethoven: Missa Solemnis," John Eliot Gardiner with the Monteverdi Choir and the English Baroque Singers, Archiv Produktion, 1990

"Beethoven, the Nine Symphonies," Franz Bruggen and the Orchestra of the Eighteenth Century, Phillips Records, 1994

"Beethoven: Piano Concerto No. 5, Emperor," Rudolf Serkin with Leonard Bernstein and the New York Philharmonic, CBS Records, 1962

"Beethoven: Piano Concerto No. 5, Emperor," Van Cliburn and the Chicago Symphony under Fritz Reiner, RCA Victor, 1994

"Beethoven: Piano Trios," 2 CD set, Vladimir Ashkenazy, Itzhak Perlman, Lynn Harrell, EMI Records, 1986

"Beethoven, the Ten Violin Sonatas," Corey Cerovsek and Paavali Jumppanen, Claves Records, 2006

"Beethoven: Triple Concerto and the Choral Fantasy," Itzhak Perlman, Yo-Yo Ma, Daniel Barenboim with the Berliner Philharmoniker, EMI Classics, 1995

"Beethoven: Triple Concerto and the Piano Concerto in D major, Opus 61a," Don-Suk Kang, Maria Kliegel, Jeno Jando with the Nicolaus Esterhazy Sinfonia, Naxos, 1997

"Beethoven: Variations & Vignettes for Piano," Alfred Brendel, Vox Music Group, 1992

"Beethoven: Violin Concerto and 2 Romances," Thomas Zehetmair and the Orchestra of the Eighteenth Century, Frans Bruggen, Philips Classics, 1998